CW01622630

# False Tidings

## A Fool's Errand

*A mind all logic is like a knife all blade. It makes the hand bleed that uses it.*
*Rabindranath Tagore*

Book 1 of The Fool's Journey series by Stephen J Grant

# Foreword

The story takes place in a rough representation of medieval Europe and is intended as a somewhat historical fantasy told with a dash of humour here and there. Occasionally, I've taken something from a later period, just because it suited me. Every place name used represents an actual location either with minor spelling modifications, or a reference to the Roman or Etruscan or even Italian name of the place. Thus, Anglonia is England, Italica is Italy and Gallia is France. Rome has become Trusca and London, Ludnam. Some readers have found this useful in visualising the world I have described. Many of the weirdest things described here have a basis in fact, and the nerds among you may want to look at the chapter notes that appear at the end of the book to understand what I invented vs. what has some historical basis. Feel free to email me with corrections and I will aim to incorporate them should a new edition ever be forthcoming.

Please note this novel was produced without any assistance from AI and that no character represented here should be taken to represent a living, or recently deceased person. No witches were harmed during the creation of this book.

Please be sure to sign p to my newsletter at http://www.stevegrantauthor.com for updates on all things foolish.

# A note on language

I'm British, born and raised, and therefore write in a very British style. You will find a smattering of basic British slang, a sprinkling of regional dialect, and the occasional dollop of words I made up. If any of the sentences are hard, I recommend the following. Empty the contents of the book into an oven proof dish, add sliced turnip, then place in the middle of a preheated oven at medium heat for two hours, or until the words go squishy. Then garnish with nettles and enjoy!

# Dedication

*For the four most important women in my life who made me who I am, Faith, Anita, Jacqueline and Skye*

# Contents

# Prologue

She almost ran right into it, which was odd since none of the other candidates had reported finding a rockfall, and neither had the wily mistress of apprentices who had set this, the final challenge. At stake here was a precious place with the elite bodyguard to the Low Queen, a position of huge prestige. It would therefore be best if Laddà took the cautious approach. She should finish the task, and report back what she'd found. But, she was well ahead of schedule, and, well, she could be cautious when she was dead.

She let her echo sense pass over the boulders and debris, looking for the cause, and to decide if there might be further falls. And found… an opening. It was a bit of a squeeze, but her curiosity drew her on and moments later, she found herself in a long, sloping passageway. This was clearly anything but natural. The smooth surfaces of floor, walls, and ceiling meant it *had* to have been carved, but who by was impossible to say. How long had *this* been here? She had to explore it. But in which direction should she go? Her instincts told her downwards. She set off.

Minutes later she picked up the sound of fast flowing water. Aware of the dangers of flooding so far below ground, she froze, held her breath, and focused. An underground river was running some distance away, but the sound was neither growing nor receding, and there was nothing to suggest danger. Laddà continued.

A hundred paces on, the shaft sloped steeper downwards and took a sharp turn to the right. There ahead coursed an impressive torrent as it bore into the rock, too deep and too fast to wade through. No matter, she jumped to the roof of the cave, and scampered across, her wrists suctioning to the smooth surface. Touching down on the opposite side, she balanced, ready for anything. She sensed no threat.

Another twenty paces, and the shaft curved around to the left, opening up into a vast cavern. Bigger than the great hall of the citadel, the roof loomed far above her, while below, the floor fell away into a void, its depths unfathomable. What was that glint ahead in the far reaches? Sunlight? This deep below ground? Laddà shuffled forward to get a better look. There had to be a fissure, a fault line in the rock that led all the way to the surface. Her echoes confirmed a crack, and in a recess, a smooth, reflecting object, half the size of her fist. Could it be? It seemed so improbable. If this were what she barely dared to hope, there'd be other clues, symbols or designs carved into the floor or wall. There, what was that? She swept the flat of her palm over the wall, and found an outline. Intrigued, she pulled a taper from the pouch at her hip and struck it against a rock. It sparked into life, and she stood back to appreciate the pattern in the dim, flickering light. It was a spiral arrangement of seven distinct loops rendered in the colours of the rainbow. And, at its core, an ancient sacred form. Bisgattù, the two headed cat.

She'd discovered the cavern of the long yearned for Crystal of Life! She was about to be famous. She would sit at Queen Nannua's right hand. Folk would celebrate her forever in their songs and recount her in their tales. Her excitement mounted.

The flame fizzled out.

Something was moving ahead, something that made a low rumble like distant thunder. Whatever it was had an intense and almost rat-like musk and seemed to be getting closer. She turned around and retraced her steps. The sound grew, no longer a rumble, but a rasping, grating noise such as that made a large animal. By now she was running, ducking, and twisting past obstacles and around corners. She tore over the river, then tripped, barely avoiding a fall. She had to get out and tell the elders. Almost there now. Diving past the rockfall, she staggered breathless out into the passageway. And listened.

Silence. She was safe.

Picking her way back towards the surface, she brought to mind the legends that foretold of how no Janasà could take the Crystal of Life without bringing the deadliest of curses down upon them all. Instead, the Anointed One would come from afar, one of those disgusting human males, a tall man, pale of skin, blond of hair, and weak of heart. Nausea welled inside her. This *man* creature would solve the challenge of the two headed Bisgattù and bring forth the crystal. And good luck to him, because, with the crystal delivered, they would tear him to pieces, making of him a fitting sacrifice to the gods of the earth.[1] The prospect of it made her glow inside.

# ✦ One ✦

The castle loomed out of the thin mist as the lone oarsman strained against the current, the only sounds being those of the rower grunting in exertion and the splosh of the oars as they sliced into and out of the brittle water. From William's position in the boat's prow, the sheer scale of the slab grey edifice perched upon a high crag above the town of Ebury meant it looked to be menacing the tiny haphazard dwellings below. The castle's most striking feature, a single, slender, ice-kissed tower, poked out of the gloom, soaring above uneven lines of severe granite blocks. Many said it most resembled a gnarled middle digit extending out of a clenched upturned fist, an exhortation for any approaching army to return whence it came. To William, at that early hour, it was a finger that beckoned him toward his future, a future for which his learning, he at least wanted to believe, had amply prepared him.

Thoughts of recent events tempered his mood of light optimism: the sadness of his father's sudden passing, his consequent ejection from the monastery, and more than anything else, a sense of concern for Verity, the girl he'd left behind.

He instinctively reached to stroke his patchy beard, its presence still unfamiliar, before a voice at his shoulder pulled him back into the moment.

"What're *you* here for then, my lovely?" asked his only travelling companion, a round, rosy-cheeked, middle-aged woman cloaked from head to toe in heavy wool.

"I'm sorry?" said William, turning to face her.

"You seems a mite nervous to me. Don't worry, can't be all that bad. I'm Aileen Spey, housekeeper to the Earl. And you are?"

"I'm… I'm William, William Grey."

"Is that so?" She looked him up and down. "You're a nice enough looking boy, William Grey. Tall. Is that blond hair you've hidden under that cap? And I bet all the girls love your dimples, but I'd perhaps lose the beard; it looks like a lost rabbit." She chuckled at her own joke.

"Um…"

"Don't worry, I'm not going to bite you." She smiled. "Where do you hail from, then?"

"Coxwell. Do you know it?"

"Isn't there a monastery there? You don't look like no monk."

"I'm an apprentice messenger. I was told to report to Anthony Ackroyd. Do you know him?"

She chuckled again. "The famous Ant? Course I knows him. I works for him. He's the Earl's steward, his right-hand man. Runs the castle for him and a lot more besides."

"Ant? Why such a strange name?"

She smiled. "Oh, it's just what they calls him, love. You'll soon see why."

The boat followed a bend in the river, where a cottage stood in a clump of trees, and he caught a waft of wood-smoke and damp leaves. Near the opposite bank, the ripples generated by the boat rustled the tall rushes, a lone grey heron wading between them. Before he could take in anything more, the boat bumped a narrow jetty below the overhang of the castle, and a man approached to tie it off.

"Hail, friend," said the boatman to the figure, handing over the end of a rope. "Bit fresh this morrow." He blew into his hands for warmth and stamped his feet on the bottom of the boat.

"Aye, 'tis that. Proper chilblain weather." The jetty-man turned to address William's fellow passenger and continued, "Good morrow, Mistress Spey, welcome back. Give me your hand."

She stood, and the jetty-man helped her step off the boat.

William's gaze switched from this exchange to the dark mass of the castle above. "How on earth do we get up there?" he asked to anyone that would listen.

"Follow me, my lovely," called Aileen.

She walked the short distance to the end of the walkway and grabbed at something hanging there. William followed. "What? Up this?" He pointed at a narrow ladder.

"Unless you can fly, young William. Come on."

Behind them, the resumed sploshing of oars told him the boat had already left. No chance of going back then.

Aileen gave her bag to the jetty-man, who tied the handle to a cord and hoisted it out of view. Then she lifted her skirt above her plump, grey stockinged ankles and ascended, her feet disappearing nimbly above.

The man nodded upwards. "Now you, young Master… What's your name?"

"William. Will to my friends." William looked at the ladder. "Um, how high is it?"

"Only a couple of hundred feet, Mr Will, to my friends. You'll be up there before you know it."

William baulked. Surely, they didn't expect… "Stop dithering man we don't have all day. Give me your bag and get on with it. The sooner you start…"

"Right. Thanks. Mind, it's heavy."

"Sun and Moons, you're not kidding," said the man, for a moment unbalanced. "What's in this thing?"

"Books. Mostly. And a few clothes."

William turned to the ladder and got started. He soon wished he'd worn something more sensible as his mittened hands struggled to cling on and his boots slipped on the wet rungs. The first part went well enough, but then the ladder bowed under his weight and twisted back on itself. "Mubble fubbles," he cursed, as his bag whizzed by close to his head. Shame they couldn't have hoisted him up as well.

A hundred and eighty-seven rungs later, he stepped a little breathless onto a narrow wooden platform not much wider than a cart. At one end, a bridge arched out over the river, its far reaches indistinct in what remained of the mist. Of course, there had to be other ways to reach the castle for carts and marching armies and so forth, although he supposed it inaccessible from the water. And at the near end, the platform curved out of view, hugging the rock wall. William unhooked his bag from the pulley and shuffled along close to the rock-face, keen to stay well clear of the drop on the other side[2].

He followed the deck around and stood facing an imposing iron clad gate a dozen paces wide. A "psst" coming from the wicket gate off to the side drew his attention. Aileen stood there beckoning him. "Come on William Grey, it's this way, my lovely."

Stepping through the wicket, a stocky, helmeted man blocked their way. "State your names and business," he said.

"You know full well who I am, young man," said his companion.

"It's the rules, Mistress Spey. Ant's orders."

"You've just given my name, dolt. Really!"

The man shrugged in embarrassment. "Fair enough. And you?" he asked William.

"William. William Grey. Apprentice messenger?"

"You asking me or telling me?"

He paused for the briefest of moments, thrust out his chin, and answered. "I'm to meet Anthony Ackroyd."

The man looked William over and shook his head. "Well now. Can't see you lasting here long. Yes, Master Ackroyd warned us to expect you." Addressing someone out of sight, he called, "Two coming through."

"Righto. This way," came the answer.

Another guard opened a second door and gestured for them to pass into a courtyard beyond. They continued up a flight of steps, through a second gatehouse and then out into a bailey or open area, at one end of which stood the squat keep of the castle. Above this, the castle's tower reached through the mist, forcing William to crane his neck to take it all in.

The guard nodded. "Impressive close up, eh? The Earl's father had it built thirty years hence."

"Did he keep atop it a fair princess awaiting rescue by her prince?"

"No, just 'is pigeons. Proper shat everywhere, they did. Come on, the great hall's through 'ere. I'll let Master Ackroyd know you've arrived."

In William's mind, the great hall was where he'd find a huge fire roaring in the grate, minstrels playing in the gallery, and the Earl himself presiding over the important business of the county. Instead, he stood shivering and alone while he waited for Anthony Ackroyd to appear. He took in the austerity of the plain vaulted ceiling, the absence of artwork, the unadorned whitewash on the walls, and a layer of frosting covering the high narrow slits that passed for windows. "Good morrow, William," said a voice, approaching from behind.

He turned to view the new arrival, a wiry balding man, a full head shorter than himself. "Master Ackroyd?" he asked.

"The very same. I hope you had a pleasant journey. From Coxwell, is that right? I knew your father. How is he, may I enquire?"

"Ah, well, he died last week. He'd not been himself for a long time. How did you know each other?"

"We both enrolled to become priests. It seems like a lifetime ago. Yes, yes. We were good friends, Harold and I. Sorry for your loss." He looked wistful for a moment. "Come this way. We have a room above ready for you. Well, not so much a room, more of a closet, but at least you don't have to share with anyone. Just the one bag?"

"Yes, for now. When will I carry my first message?"

Ant shook his head and frowned. "I'm afraid it'll be some time before the Earl trusts you with anything important. In this castle, everyone starts at the bottom."

Moons and Stars. Seriously? That wasn't what he'd wanted to hear. "But I was hoping to prove myself, by the spring, if not sooner."

Ackroyd raised an eyebrow. "By the spring indeed? That's a show of admirable ambition, but not, alas, how it works here. There are five other messengers on the staff, all senior to yourself. You must understand, the role of an apprentice starts with spells in each of the main tasks of the castle. There are the kitchens, the stables, the armoury, the porters… Oh, don't look so glum. You'll get your chance soon enough."

He led William through a great door at the rear of the hall, past a row of enormous portraits of grand, austere looking men in military costume, and stags' heads hanging on walls. "I'll keep you away from His Grace for now. He is, how can I put it, a robust man? He says what he thinks, doesn't suffer fools, and so forth. An acquired taste, some might say."

As Ackroyd scurried ahead, it struck William how right Aileen had been; the man bore an uncanny resemblance to an actual ant. From his brown complexion, his head sweeping from side to side as he scanned the room, from the tufts of dark hair peeking up like antennae over his ears on an otherwise naked crown, and from the wiry limbs that jutted out from his body as he navigated his habitat, stopping every so often as though to sniff the air for anything out of place that might require his intervention.

After climbing several flights of steps, Ackroyd opened a door halfway along a corridor and motioned for William to enter. It really was no more than a closet, barely allowing for one man to fit into the space alongside the straw mattress.

"Where can I put my books?" asked William.

"What?"

"You know. Books. With words."

"Yes, yes, I know what a *book* is, thank you very much. Continue like that and I'll have you flogged, regardless of how well I knew your father. Hmm. Under the sleeping roll for now?"

"I only brought twenty with me. The rest should follow next week, but I'm not so sure where I can put them."

"We could add a new wing to the castle to house your collection; would that be to your liking? And pregnant sows might float over our heads." He wafted a slender hand around in the air to convey the idea. "Enough of this. I haven't got all day, you know."

Back down the stairs, Ant led William to a small room off the great hall. "This is where you can usually find me," he said.

A spot riddled page approached with a bundle of clothes. "Ah, thank you, good lad." He dismissed the page with a nod. "Now, here's your apprentice messenger uniform. My much beloved wife designed it. Hmm, yes, sorry about that, she can be very insistent. Anyway, make sure you put it on right; I'm a stickler for detail, you know." He shuffled some papers on his desk, then stopped and turned to face William. "Well, why are you still standing there? Am I to dress you myself, boy? Shoo. Get changed, then report to Mistress Spey[3]."

William spun on his heel and hurried away. He couldn't afford to get off on the wrong foot with this Ant fellow.

~~~

William located the stairway again, climbing one slow step at a time, his mind on a mathematical proof he'd been reading two days earlier, and failed to alight the correct landing. The doors all looked much the same; plain oak, no varnish, bare iron handles. Finding the third door on the right, he pulled it open and poked his head into the room. And stopped in his tracks. This room was an altogether larger sleeping space than his own, but just as sparse in its furnishings, its shutters spread open to the elements. An athletically built man posed side-on before an enormous mirror, one hand balanced on his hip while, with the other, he used a light sword to trace patterns in the air, as though scratching a message onto parchment. He seemed not to have noticed William at all, his concentration intent on the arch of his back. William froze, uncertain how to react to the man's state. Naked?

His gaze drew of its own accord toward the man's generous mid-section.

"What's wrong boy? Stop gawping," said the man, his gaze still holding his reflection. "Haven't you seen a shriving beard splitter before?"

"A what?"

"*What?* What do you mean, *what*? A cranny cudgel, a fulgent fiddle, a shriving stick. Who are you? The new stool boy?" His voice rang clear, confident and, well, loud. Before William could summon a response, he continued, "Doesn't matter. There's a full pan there. Get rid of it, good man. You can leave it outside when you're done."

Unsure of whether to speak, William chose to remain silent and instead did as asked. The words of his father came to mind. *If you've nothing useful to say, spare the air the inconvenience of bearing your voice.* He carried the bowl of steaming excreta out of the room at arm's length, as the heavy door closed shut behind him. He took it along to the hole in the wall[4], then left the emptied vessel next to the doorway, relieved not to need to disturb the man
~~~

again. Who was he? Would the Earl himself behave in such an un-lordly manner?

Safely returned to his room, it took all of a minute to empty his bag and arrange his few possessions, after which he set to changing into his uniform. He had to leave the door part open to allow some light in, but even then, it was a struggle to make sense of the stiff garments. Which bit was supposed to go where? He tried one way, then another. Nothing made sense. A light cough announced the presence of someone behind.

"Let me help you with that, my lovely," came the soft burr of Aileen.

"Mistress Spey?" he asked, reddening, while clutching his tunic across his groin.

"No need to be shy with me," she said. "I seen it all before, I can tell you. Look, you puts your legs through here. Right, now the arms. Now let's get these things fastened, and… there. Very good."

She stood back to check him over. "You'll do. Now come this way. Ant says I'm to show you around then get you started polishing the silverware in the cellars."

The castle was rather smaller inside than he'd expected. They quickly took in the kitchens, armoury, cellars, and service areas. Outside, they passed the stable block, the guards' quarters, and the various storerooms. Inside again, Aileen pointed out the castle's temple and the door to the library. At the mention of a library, William's interest piqued. "Before you get any ideas young man, there are rare books in there so it's strictly off limits to castle staff. Not that any of the others would know what to do with a book, save for perhaps to stand on it to reach a high shelf." She chuckled to herself.

With the tour over, she took him down into the cellars and showed him the brass and silverware. "Here's some rye bread to keep you going. The staff are all dining together this evening. Just listen for the gong."

"But mistress."

"Yes?"

"Is it true I won't carry a message for a long while?"

"Yes indeed. His Lordship has to know you're reliable enough, but don't worry, Trusca wasn't built in a day, my lovely."

There was nothing for it but to get working. He got started rubbing and buffing at the items from a heap of tarnished metal. Soon a fair pile of shining salvers and goblets stood aside from the rest. Comfortable in his own company, the time passed quickly enough and before he knew it, a gong sounded above. This had to be the summons for the castle to eat. He placed the rag carefully next to the polish, took a moment to admire his work, and scurried out toward the stairs, now uncomfortably aware of a full bladder that insisted on being emptied. Passing the entrance to the great hall, he wandered out into the main bailey and a guard directed him to a privy. His business concluded, he hurried back. At the library, he couldn't help but notice the door stood ajar. Surely there could be no harm in taking a peep? The sight that greeted him filled him with wonder. Long aisles of bookshelves stretched out to the far wall crammed from floor to ceiling with more volumes than William could have imagined existed. So many words. What marvels would they convey, what worlds could they take him to? What depths of learning might be locked within the dense lines of text? The familiar tingling he'd experienced right from the first moment he'd set foot in a library ran down his spine. He couldn't resist the urge to step closer. Checking behind him for anyone watching, he stepped in. He'd only be a moment.

Inside, the sour, stale aroma of old parchment filled his nostrils, transporting him to another place and time. Images filled his fancy of diligent scribes down the long centuries, scratching away in candle-lit attics to copy and preserve precious documents. Reaching out to the first shelf, he pulled down a thick volume and felt its reassuring heft. he ran his finger along the smooth binding, marvelling at the delicate golden-embossed lettering. Euclidio's *Elements of Geometry* said the title. A wondrous collection of writings indeed, including proofs for the spherical nature of the earth[5]. He placed it under his arm and reached for another. Roughly translated, the title of this one read *A Treatise on the Ills of Women* by Aelius Galenus, the Truscan name for the great surgeon and medic, Galennio. He opened it and perused the first few pages, impressed by the elaborate script and exquisite illustrations of anatomical dissections. He'd never seen anything so captivating. Entranced in the moment, he didn't notice someone approaching from behind until a booming voice thundered out the words, "Boy, do I know you? State your name and your business here."

He spun around to find himself facing the same gentleman he'd met earlier. Except this time, he was dressed in a colourful, but elegant tunic and britches with a heavy gold chain across his chest. This could be no one other than Lord Sir John Fitzpatrick Scratchface himself, flanked by Ackroyd and a pair of pages.

"S-sorry, if it pleases you, Your Grace, I am William of C-Coxwell[6], and I am a new messenger in your employ." His face reddened under the concentrated intensity of His Grace's glare.

The earl frowned, his piercing blue eyes fixed menacingly on William's. "C-Coxwell, what devil of a place is that to come from? And wasn't it you that took my night pan this morning?"

Ackroyd scuttled forward, head wobbling, doing his best to repair the situation. "Your Grace, I'm so sorry," he said, as he took the two books from William's hands and placed them back on the shelves. "This is the new apprentice I engaged. Do you remember us discussing how we needed to replace Jackson?"

"Jackson? Jackson? Oh *him*. The one that ran off with that comely scullery maid, if I recall. Swine got to her first, and good for him."

Scratchface turned to address William. "Well, William of C-Coxwell, answer the question. Speak, man."

William brought his stutter under control. "Coxwell is indeed my birthplace, and, yes, it was I that wandered into your rooms by mistake, for which I am most dreadfully sorry. I am at your service," he said, adding with a flourish, "Your Grace!" He bowed almost to the floor in what he hoped to be the proper manner. A page behind Earl Scratchface smirked.

"Well, I'll be jiggered," said the Earl, frowning. "What on earth are you doing down there? Now, Anthony, have this boy report to my chambers on the morrow. He can bring my breakfast."

His chief steward took a moment to recover from the surprise. "You understand your Grace that he is as yet untested?"

"Then I will test him!" shouted the Earl, already heading for the door. "Now to eat! Fetch forth the pheasant I killed this morning and a plate of beef fat. I have the hunger of a bear today!"

"Get out!" hissed Ackroyd, glaring at William as the Earl disappeared from view. "I'll deal with you later."

~~~

Wandering disconsolately from the library, William couldn't help but think back to the events that led to his arrival at Ebury. Two days earlier, he had been summoned to see the new Abbott. The winter solstice had not long slipped away as all things must, and outside there were still signs of a recent snowfall scattered about in the surrounding fields. Inside, there was ice on the shutters and the ale had frozen solid.

*"Ah, William. Please be seated."*

*"Thank you, Lord Abbott. How can I be of assistance?" He sat straight with his fingers wrapped in his smock, looking at his feet and wondering when the feeling might return to his toes.*

*"Let me get to the point. The Lord High Priest of Anglonia has decreed that all monasteries are to cease secular learning and to focus solely on the Glorification of Lord Sola and His Moons."*

*William looked up with concern. "Yes, Lord Abbott? But are the Sun and Moons not symbols of something profound rather than actual deities?"*

*"Heresy! I could have you arrested and tortured that you repent."*

*William swallowed. He wanted to debate the subject. It was absurd. An offence against reason. However, he thought better of pursuing it. "H-Heresy…?"*

*"Oh, don't look so worried. I will leave it to Lord Sola to judge you when the time comes, although you should be more careful to whom you voice such thoughts." The old man sighed and put his reading spectacles aside. "How many summers are you now, William?"*

*"Twenty-six, Lord Abbott."*

*"And my predecessor allowed you to follow the path of the scholar within our order? How extraordinary."*
~~~

*"He was like a father to me. He and the others raised me. And I've always worked for my food and board. I can tend a garden, and I'm told I am a capable scribe."*

*"This may be true, but we have other gardeners and other scribes. And I'll trouble you to address me correctly. All this has to stop. We are a religious order, not a philosophical talking house."*

*William sagged and put his head in his hands. "You can't mean it. Please tell me there's another way, Lord Abbott."*

*"I cannot. Here is your novice habit. Take it and come to the temple where you will take your vows before the body of the monks." He held a piece of folded sackcloth out to William and motioned with a nod to leave with it.*

*"Or else, Lord Abbott?"*

*"Or else? I should have thought that was obvious. Leave here. And any book in the library that does not glorify Lord Sola must be burned. Can I entrust you with that task?"*

*William jumped up. "Never!"*

*"Sit! I can no longer allow this place to be used as a hotbed of ... faithlessness. I'm sorry about the loss of your father, I truly am, but I cannot understand what got into my predecessor to support the child of one so fallen as him. There will be no such misplaced charity while I am Abbott here."*

*William sat again in silence. What did this mean? He'd always known he'd have to leave one day, but he'd hoped it would be to take Verity as a wife and live in his own house. He wasn't ready.*

*"Please Lord Abbott. Can I have more time? I need to think. I need to plan. Where will I go? What will I do? Please reconsider."*

*"Will you take your vows?"*

*"I cannot, Lord Abbott. My conscience will not allow it."*

*"I suspected you would refuse. Well, in that case, my hands are tied. I am not unreasonable. I anticipated this outcome and have secured a suitable apprenticeship messenger position for you at Ebury under an old acquaintance. You will depart at dawn on the morrow and take the riverboat to the castle, where Master Anthony Ackroyd will await you."*

*"But..., My whole life. I've known nothing else."*

*"You are dismissed," said the Abbott. He'd already picked up a bundle of papers.*

*William bowed and backed out of the room. Leaving his home was bad enough, but what of Verity? He hurried down to find the librarian. He couldn't allow a single one of the precious books to be destroyed. He'd have to take them with him.*

~~~

For dinner, the castle's full complement of staff ate together, arranged by role and by order of seniority. At the top end were the falconers, followed by the fletchers, the blacksmiths and then his own group, the messengers. At the furthest reach, the solitary man sitting well away from everyone else had to be a gong farmer[7]. Of the messenger class, only one other sat with William that evening, an older, wiry grump who ignored him. Fine, it was the man's loss. His own concerns crowded in. After less than a day, he'd already upset Ackroyd by disobeying a direct instruction to stay clear of the library and, most likely, got on the wrong side of the Earl, a formidable gentleman, if ever there was one. What would this Ant do with him later, and what could Earl Scratchface want with him the following morning?

A little along the bench sat a group of what turned out to be stable lads, presided over by a slight, narrow-faced boy with a smooth, almost girlish complexion and an unkempt mop of mouse coloured hair. At least five years younger than William, he introduced himself as Ridkin. This Ridkin, clearly the joker of the bunch, made frequent quips about other servants, sending his companions into stitches. "Are you that William?" he asked in the thickest Ludnam accent William had ever heard. William noticed how the younger man fidgeted with his hands when speaking. "The bloke what sleeps with books?" he continued, while pretending to hug and kiss something book sized to appreciative giggles from his mates. "How come you're slumming it with us?"

"Um, I'm afraid I don't understand."

"Oh don't he talk all la-di-da? *I'm afraid I don't understand,*" he said, mimicking William's accent, then belched, causing fresh peals of laughter. "You need to watch your back, posh boy, or something might 'appen to
~~~

you, sudden like." He mimed the act of a fist smacking into the side of his head.

William took this as a genuine threat and decided he wasn't so sure he liked his new home. It especially annoyed him that this lout had criticised his reading. "What have you got against books, anyway?" he asked.

"Dunno. They're great as kindling, I s'pose." He snorted. "Give me one good thing that's ever come from gawping at a book?"

"Well, if you want to know. There's everything you need for a considered life in the old writings. Philosophy? Science? Rhetoric? Logic? That's four things right there."

"Look, pal." Ridkin made a stabbing action toward him with his finger. "I grew up in the *school of life*. No fancy words ever put food on the table. The only philosophy Ridkin Fairchild needs is these." He held up his fists as his friends barked their laughing approval.

As the meal ended, Ridkin leant into William. "Just wait till I gets you alone, soft boy."

~~~

After the meal, Aileen assigned him to help with clearing away the tables and carrying the leftovers of the supper to the kitchens to be readied for sending out to the poor of the town. That finished, he traipsed up the narrow stairs leading to his attic, miserably preoccupied with the day's events. Before he could reach the top, a group of younger servants crossed by him on their way down and deep in excited conversation. One stopped to introduce himself and his friends. He looked no more than sixteen years old and made William feel oddly old. "Hi, are you William? I'm Jack. Why don't you come with us for the evening? It's better than moping around here."

"I'm sorry? Why? Where are you going?"

"Oh - just for a jar of the best ale in town and some banter. Come on, you'll be back before you know it."

It sounded preferable to ruminating on things alone and, well, it might even be fun. The three of them took William through the cramped streets
~~~

of Ebury to an unremarkable, grubby tavern in the heart of an area they called *The Scrambles*. The sound of merriment came from within the taverns and alehouses, and partially dressed women stood in doorways offering themselves for business despite the chill air. He did his best not to catch their eyes, not wanting the embarrassment of having to excuse himself from their bountiful offers, and mindful of the pox[8] that had become common throughout the kingdom. A small waif-like child with a hair-lip ran across the narrow street to a tired-looking woman in rags, mucus running down its chin. The woman lashed out with the back of her hand and kicked at the child who tripped and broke into tears.

William moved to intervene.

"Will, what are you doing?" asked the boy, Jack.

"We have to help her," he said as he bent to pick the girl up.

A man shouted behind him. "Leave the lass alone, what are you, some manner of pervert?"

The man, tall and wiry with pox ridden skin, loomed over William, cudgel in hand.

William's companions dragged him away protesting. "Leave me be, I have to save her."

Jack raised his palms in placation. "It's alright mister, he's new around here. We'll be out of your way in a jiffy."

They turned a corner. "What were you thinking?" asked another of the lads. "You can't save every urchin in the realm. Sometimes you have to let things be. Look, here's the alehouse."

As they approached the door of the establishment, The Kings Arms, he spotted a notice nailed up with a rough likeness of the King himself drawn in and some script crammed in tightly below. Fascinated, he stopped to read, all thought of the little girl for now banished from his mind.

"You can understand that?" asked Jack.

"Yes. Give me a moment."

"What's it say, then?"

"It says atop *Great Tidings*. And below, it's talking about the King's achievements in the five years since he came to the throne. He's increased oat production in the kingdom twenty-fold, and brought fecundity to couples the length of the land. And here it says about the number of street robberies, saying there are far fewer now, thanks to His Majesty's tough stance on law and order."

As the others, no longer interested, filed through the low doorway, he stood in awe. These were astonishing achievements, and the realm was indeed most fortunate to have such a wise, caring ruler. He wandered in to join his companions. "Amazing," he said.

"You don't believe all that guff, do you?" asked Jack. "Here, landlord, our friend here thinks the latest tidings are amazing."

"You mean he can read that? Doesn't he realise it's just some of that *propaganda* that people keep going on about?"

"What does proper gander mean?" asked William. "Something to do with geese?"

"No, it's nonsense, stuff made up to make the King seem grander, cleverer. Not Great Tidings. False Tidings. They want to tell us what to think." The barman placed the first jar on the bench and started pouring the second. "You should pay it no heed."

"They wouldn't dare speak lies of the King," said William, scandalised. "If it's written like that, with his likeness and all, then it must be true."

The four men facing him stood in silence. Before he'd left the monastery, Brother Anselm had told him, *Things out there are not the same as in here. You'll have to think on your feet if you want to get along*. Perhaps this was what he'd meant; clearly not everyone in Anglonia held the monarch in high regard.

Aware that he'd said the wrong thing, he stared into his ale. "Just kidding," he mumbled.

The group burst into fits of laughter. "Brilliant. You nearly had me there," said Jack. "Tell me, what do you think of Boulderpants?"

"Bold who?"

"Boulderpants. That's what half the women of the county call the Earl, on account of…"

"I'm sure he gets the idea," another lad interrupted.

Jack wasn't to be stopped. He leaned towards William, his elbow on the low bench. "They say he only has to walk into a room and every woman wants to drop her kirtle." Despite being seated, he did a passable mime of a woman lowering a garment.

"Her what?"

"He's winding us up again," said one of the boys. "That's funny, but don't overdo it."

William made a mental note to ask Aileen what a kirtle was. Just then, their ales arrived, and they all toasted the King before drawing deep draughts. Thirty seconds later, the other three had finished their drinks. "Come on, Will, drink up. It's your round."

William shrugged and emptied his beaker. "Four more ales, landlord," he said, reaching for a few coins from his purse.

The tavern door opened and in strode the group of stable lads he'd sat near to earlier in the evening, including the ringleader, Ridkin. When the boy saw William, he adopted a certain swagger, making it a point to knock William's shoulder with his own as he made his way through. Thereafter, he could be seen muttering to his friends while directing an uncomfortable stare in William's direction.

However, a couple of hours later, the alcohol had softened William's nerves, and he took the obvious animosity directed his way with the appropriate pinch of salt. Having had their fill, his companions pulled on their coats and dragged William out into the night, where the chill at least sobered him up enough to attempt walking. Two streets on, it filtered into his addled mind that he hadn't peed since leaving the castle. He cut into an alleyway, stood at the side of a ditch and did what all young men do at some point, which is to find a wall and see how far they can go up it. Vapour rose into the frigid air from the collected pool before him. Mission over, he fiddled to reorder his parts and turned to follow his friends, but… they'd vanished. He lost his footing and tipped sideways into the trench, falling through a thin layer of ice into foul smelling waste. He'd have stayed there a while to collect himself, but the stench threatened to overpower him, so he crawled up onto the cobbles, only to feel a large boot connect with his chin, followed by blows to the chest, back, and legs. Someone pushed him down with a knee and relieved him of his purse before bestowing a last kick in the head and running off.

Blood trickled down William's cheek. He rolled over. The twin moons and stars shone bright in all their glory, before commencing a slow, graceful loop around the sky. Everything faded out of focus. Bile rose in his stomach and he retched up its contents over his cloak in great gasping spasms. Mubble fubbles[9]. No way could he return in this state. He sat against a wall and tried to think. His career as a messenger appeared to be over already. He shivered, his wet mantle offering no protection against the biting temperature. He cried out, "Help. Help me," hoping someone in the darkened house behind him would hear, or maybe a passer-by. "Help me."

He had to move. Yes, that would be the best thing. He shuffled up against the wall and hitched his bottom against it until he reached a sitting position. Now for the difficult bit. He pressed his palms into the ground and pushed back with his feet, using his shoulders as leverage, ignoring the searing pain in his right knee. If he could just get upright, he'd stagger out of the alley and attract help. He twisted into a crouch, and attempted to rise, but his leg buckled, and he tipped forward, watching fascinated as the cobbles rushed up toward his head. Impact. His body coiled up in shock, the universe spiralled above him and...

# Two

William awoke as pale daylight brushed across his lidded vision. His forehead hurt. He tried to lift his arms, but they felt heavy and remote. A cough welled up and provoked a pain in his chest to wake the Moons and Stars. Someone had kicked him there. How much earlier? An hour? A lifetime? He closed his eyes to await the welcoming embrace of the Stars that were supposed to ferry the dead across the sky. He was keen to get on with being dead. There were a lot of questions he wanted answering.

A gentle snoring somewhere behind jogged him from his reverie. Surely nobody snored in the afterlife? He raised his head and experienced a shooting pain down the back of his scalp, into his neck and across his chest. "Ow," he moaned. "Where am I?"

The snoring stopped. "Well, aren't you a fine one, my lovely? They brought you to His Lordship's temple," answered a voice that sounded a lot like the soft burr of Aileen Spey. "Try not to move. You've had a nasty bump to the head."

Feeling seeped into his limbs. His right knee ached. "Why am I here? How did…? Am I dead?" he croaked.

"Shh. Not dead. They put you in here last night so they'd not disturb the rest of the castle, and so as I could keep an eye on you, my dear. The stable lads brought you in, drunk as a lord and swearing at the Stars. And such language as a lady never heard! Ridkin said three of them struggled to get you home."

"Ridkin, you said? The stableboy, Ridkin?"

"Aye, him, and it's lucky he stumbled across you down some ginnel[10], else you'd really be dead by now. Frozen, most like."

"My chest. Did someone stab me there?"

"No. Maybe a rib's broken. Your knee has swollen up like a gourd, and the scar on your face looks worse than it is."

He reached to his face and found a cut on his left cheek. It stung to the touch.

"Don't worry, we've cleaned it up. Other than that, you're in one piece."

"Oh, my Stars, everything hurts."

"Here, drink this," she said, helping him to sit up.

She held a cup of water to his lips. "Ant says he'll explain to His Grace that you're in no state to serve him this morrow."

"No. I want to do it. If it hurts, I deserve it. Oh, my days." He sagged back down, holding his forehead.

"I'll go see if anyone's in the kitchens yet."

Aileen bustled away. When she returned, he asked her, "Why do you care so much, Mistress Aileen?"

"By rights, I don't know." She sighed, looking off into the near distance. "Perhaps because you remind me of my own boy, stolen from me while still a babe in arms. He'd have been about your age by now I reckon, that's if he survived."

"I'm sorry Mistress. I don't deserve it, I'm sure."

"Tsk, think nothing of it. Are you really sure about this morning?"

"I have to be. I want to."

"Well, if you're set on it. Here's your uniform. The cook's just fetching his Grace's breakfast things. Come on, let's make you presentable."

He was grateful for her help in getting the britches on, and the tight tunic strangely supported his hurting chest as it fastened. He stood and stretched, at once regretting it. Everything hurt like the furies.

A cook entered, holding out a tray. "Take this up to His Grace, and mind not to drop it. I'll send a kitchen lad up soon with the rest of it."

He limped slowly to the stairs and up the first two flights, to where he now knew His Grace resided, determined not to further attract ireful attention by stumbling and dropping the load. He knocked and a commanding *Come!* issued from within.

~~~

John Scratchface was known to be his own man. Direct, combative and yet fair, he was respected among those in his employ, and came from a long line of similar men, well used to the command and obedience of others. With his high cheekbones, neat goatee, moustache, diverse collection of military scars, and full musculature, he was easy to admire, or even desire. His blonde hair flowed to his shoulders in a way that might be described as noble, and the overall effect was of a man who had few doubts and fewer regrets. This time it didn't shock William to discover him in a state of undress, balanced on his toes with sword in hand. Neither did the frigid air cause him any concern. No, what surprised him was the presence of an equally naked, generously proportioned woman posing before the mirror. He'd never seen one undressed before and his mouth fell open in surprise. She had actual breasts, and not the type that hung from the chest of the plump Brother Anselm back in Coxwell. And far from being a lustily raging monster, as he'd been assured would be the case by Brother Bool, the downy area between her legs seemed quite homely and welcoming. He dragged his eyes away from their feast to look directly at His Grace.

"Don't mind Lady Charlotte," said Scratchface, as the woman approached and took the tray before William could tip forward in senseless shock. She placed their breakfast on a bench and walked into an adjoining room before returning, this time thankfully wearing a robe.

The Earl pointed his weapon at a basket near the door. "Take that down to the launderer and when you return, I have something I wish you to do for me." Then he appeared to notice William's face. "I say, splendid gouge you have there," he said, with an approving look. "I hope you gave the other man as good as you got."

William took the dirty linens out, wondering what on earth could be required of him next. Would they also expect him also to disrobe then take part in some perverse activity? He returned from the laundry to discover, with relief, both parties now dressed and seated, tucking into their breakfast.
~~~

"Right," said Scratchface, swallowing down a mouthful of bread and meat. "If you look on the dresser there, you will find that book you picked up in the library yesterday. I am curious to know if you can understand it." He laid down his napkin, stood, and reached for his sword, giving it a few swishes. It *sounded* sharp.

"You wish me to read it aloud?" asked William.

"What else would you do with it, clod? Eat it? Read it, then explain its meaning. If you cannot, I'll cut your balls off and throw you from the bridge." Scratchface placed a hand on his hip and took a crouching guard.

William stood for a moment in complete shock before collecting himself enough to walk over to the book and pick it up. "Any particular section?" he asked, his hands shaking.

"I want to learn what Gallenio thought of the wandering womb[11]. Find me those passages and read them."

For the first time since casting off from the safe shores of the monastery, he glimpsed the possibility of finding firm ground on which to anchor himself. He silently thanked the old monks for having drilled him so relentlessly on his ancient Truscan grammar, then leafed through the pages in search of the right place to start. He spotted the heading easily enough. Chapter three.

If he'd expected things to proceed calmly from here on, he was to be very much disappointed. As he began reading, Scratchface lunged forward with his sword, stopping just short of William's gut. He went through a series of accelerating moves, thrusting and parrying at an increasingly discombobulated William.

"Be very careful, boy. If you move by so much as a hair's breadth, you are likely to lose an ear." And to emphasise the point, the whoosh of the weapon passed close by his head.

Despite the strangeness of the situation, what he read fascinated him; "It says a woman's womb is the root of many serious ailments suffered by the fairer sex, who indeed are rendered fairer by the capricious moods of their reproductive organs."

A tilt from his Grace tickled William's side before a following sweep swished through the top of his hair. William continued, determined not to flinch.

"It seems that a womb not involved in the act of sustaining a foetus will thrash around inexhaustibly in the body, causing injuries to other organs and even reaching up through the gut to cause strangulation. Gallenio recommends vigorous massage of the organ by a wise maid as a means to alleviate the condition. What does that even *mean*?"

The Earl grunted with the effort of stepping away and then pirouetted to make another leaping thrust at William's groin that, had he been impassioned, might have circumcised him. William, incredulous as regards the description, continued to read the original text while explaining its meaning by way of simile and allusion, trying not to gesticulate for emphasis. The Earl stopped his sequence and looked at him, eyebrows raised.

"Why can't you just say what it means, man?" he shouted. "It's a medical book, not some bawdy alehouse tale. Continue and don't mumble."

So, he continued to the end and gave a direct translation, wincing at some of the words he now had to utter. The Lady Charlotte appeared quite unconcerned by it all, continuing to munch on slivers of meat and to slurp from a jug of wine.

As William finished, he held his breath while waiting for the Earl's next move. However, after a short, but worrying pause, the man clapped in appreciation. "Extraordinary. The writings are complete balderdash, but I'm amazed that an apprentice messenger, a faceless nobody in my employ, should be able to read and translate them. I think we must put your talents to better use. Let me speak with Ackroyd. We can find you productive work in my library, between other tasks, of course. And you never wavered a jot."

Mixed emotions swirled into William's mind. On the one hand, working in a great library such as that of the castle was a dream assignment almost unheard of to the likes of him. On the other, he doubted a librarian would earn coin enough to take a wife.

"Thank you, Your Grace. May I think about it?"

"Don't push your luck, boy! Hmph. You may think on it as I throw you a hundred feet into the river, or else you can do as I command. Now get out of my sight."

William bowed low to the Earl, then to The Lady Charlotte, who yawned while studying her fingernails. He headed away for the stairs, hoping Verity would wait long enough for him to become wealthy. It might take a while.

~~~

As William wended his way away from the Earl's chambers toward the kitchens in search of something to balance his still queasy stomach, a page handed him a letter. His heart leapt a notch; it had to be from his darling Verity. He tore the seal and opened it, stopping in mid-step to take in its contents. It read:

*Dearest William, I hope you reached Ebury Castle safely, and have settled into your role. I am missing you already and cannot wait until you return. Kathleen from the buttery is helping me write this letter*[12]*. I try, William I really do, but those squiggles on the page get all jumbled up and I am quite befuddled.*

*Today Mr Peewee caught a mouse and brought it into the house. It was horrid! And the rooms have been so cold. Mother is giving me more and more of the chores and beats me if I dawdle. By evening time, I declare I'm quite worn out with it.*

*So much for life here in Coxwell. Please write and tell me how things are now that you are settled at the castle. Now I must write of another, more serious matter.*

*Sir Bereforth called to visit father today and to inform him that Edmond Rowbotham, the miller's eldest son, has offered the sum of ten poundes to free me from my indenture*[13] *and to marry him. Oh, William, Edmond is horrid. Sir Bereforth says he liked your father and will so grant you the period of six months to find the indenture release money, after which time, he will accept Edmond's proposal. I beg you to use all means possible to raise the sum yourself and return to free me.*

*I also have news that the wheelwright, Richard Armitage, has an apprenticeship available. Could you return and take this up? Perhaps Richard would even lend you the money?*

*I am, I do so very much hope, your darling Verity.*
~~~

He froze stock still, his anger rising. Just six months to prove himself or lose Verity forever! And that an oaf of a man such as Edmond might marry his lovely girl and take her to his bed, well, that horrified him. How on earth was he to compete with someone who would inherit the mill? Not as a simple minder of books, that was for sure.

He found a lit candle and burned the letter, not needing to read it again: he'd always been able to memorise the contents of a page, as if captured by a skilled painter.

What should he do? Return to Coxwell or stay in Ebury and complete the task he'd begun? Certainly, he could go home, his tail between his legs, and become an apprentice wheelwright, but why would Armitage lend him ten poundes? Besides, the man was a boor and despised all learning.

Perhaps he'd just have to run away to the big city, Ludnam, and seek his fortune there. A ridiculous notion. Having no useful skills and with no family connections, there was little possibility of finding and completing an apprenticeship in six *years*, never mind six months. He'd starve on the streets if he didn't first fall prey to the thieves and murderers, he assumed infested the capital. He needed an opportunity to be entrusted with an important task and then the good luck to succeed at that. It looked so hopeless.

~~~

"So you're back, my lovely. How was His Grace?" asked Aileen, concern written across her face.

"Um. He just wanted me to read to him. I think he likes me."

"Really? How extraordinary! I was sure you'd be leaving us."

"Where do you want me now, Mistress Spey?"

"Well, now. Cook is short of a couple of porters so you can lend a hand there. Off you go."

William made his way through the door and across the courtyard toward the kitchens[14], happy that the warmth of the ovens at least would offer respite from the frigidity of the castle. There he found the head cook in a
~~~

state of calm chaos, directing a small army of kitchen staff with a myriad of boiling pans all around him.

"You, quick, grab this kettle and pour the water away. I need these herring boiled for a pie."

"Over here?"

"Yes, that's it."

For the rest of the morning, he ran in all directions, lifting and stirring and, he had to admit it, rather enjoying himself, despite the two burns he received while working with the ovens. Wigglesday was a fish day, one on which the priesthood ordained it a sin to prepare or consume meat. The instructions were simple enough to follow though, and all went well until, late morning, disaster struck. The fish cook gave him an enormous platter of freshly poached trout to take to the back oven to warm. He struggled with its awkward size, his thin messenger boots slipping over the wet flags as he entered the room. His damaged knee buckled. He slipped and dropped the entire tray onto the floor.

"Mubble fubbles," he muttered, looking around to see if anyone had noticed his mistake. As heavy footsteps approached, he hurriedly scooped everything back up and wiped his hands on his apron in time for the cook to give him his next task, stirring a vast vat of eel soup. It was astonishing how the whole service came together, ready for the servers to arrive and carry the complicated courses out and over to the main hall.

"Can we eat now?" William asked one of the kitchen hands, thankfully recovering from his hangover and with a hunger to wake the Stars.

"Not likely. We need to start on the evening meal."

Four hours later, he dragged himself out of the kitchens and trudged toward his room, too exhausted to speak to anyone along the way. However, before he'd even reached the stairs, Ackroyd called him over, clicking his mandibles.

"Ah William," he said, "I have an urgent letter for the King here that His Grace needs taking to Ludnam."

"But I'm only an apprentice. How come you trust me to do this now?"

"Well, here's the thing. All the other messengers had the trout for lunch, along with half the castle, and they are all consumed with vomiting as we speak. I tried to suggest to His Grace that we send an experienced page, but it seems he likes you and insisted you bear it. You are to leave for the palace at first light in the morning."

"But, but... how? I wanted a chance to prove myself, but… Ludnam? And why me?"

"Don't worry. I have a solution. There's someone here that knows Ludnam well. He'll get you there and back in one piece." He took William by the elbow and led him to the stable block, which they entered, passing to the rear. "Allow me to introduce you to master Ridkin Fairchild."

~~~

William stayed up late in the Great Hall, taking advantage of the candlelight to read. Tonight, he needed the comfort of his thoughts. His mind drifted away to his early life at the monastery...

*He was five years old and sitting on a chair several sizes too large for him, his soft thighs poking out below his thin tunic and splaying over the rough wooden seat. He reached up to touch an equally vast desk, seeking some sense of security that didn't arrive.*

*"Call me Brother Bool," said the monk standing over him, bouncing on his toes, his hands clasped behind his back. "The Abbott says I am to teach you algebra and logic. Do you know what these things are?"*

*William shook his head. Bool brought a wooden stave down across his knuckles. He yelped and pulled away.*

*"You will address me by my name and using complete sentences. Now put your hands on the bench. What is algebra? Hands!"*

*He placed them back. They throbbed with pain. "Please sir, I don't know."*

*The rod thwacked down again, but this time he was ready for it. He whimpered and didn't withdraw.*

*"Brother Bool! That's my name. Say it!"*

*"Brother Bool, if it pleases you."*
~~~

*"Better. Algebra is an ancient method of reasoning from the east. However, for now, we will turn our attention to logic. In these classes, a thing is true or false. What is it?"*

*"True or false. Brother Bool."*

*"Correct. Let us begin..."*

In truth, none of the brothers had been cruel to him. He loved many of them. Despite their inexperience with children, they were more fathers to him than his own remaining parent, who'd never recovered from being forced to leave his position as Abbott Strange's predecessor. None of the adults had been able, or at least willing, to explain the circumstances of it all, but he'd pieced things together over the years from snippets of overheard conversation. His father had apparently disgraced himself by getting his mother, a girl not from the immediate locality, pregnant[15]. The first the brothers had known of it, however, was when William's father, the Abbott at the time, had turned up from a pilgrimage unexpectedly carrying a baby boy, naming him William and declaring he would raise him as his own. There'd been a scandal, of course, and his father had fallen into a state of permanent melancholy, leaving the monks to raise his son. From there on, the man had spiralled down and become a cold and empty husk, incapable of showing the least warmth or support, while of William's mother, nothing was known.

William regretted not knowing his father better, not making more effort to, but as the Stoics wrote, there's no point in lamenting what is already done. It seemed good advice.

# Three

Feydor the Fool knew his flame red hair and emerald-green eyes to be striking in the extreme, which suited him fine. His pale, hairless, almost feminine skin looked good for a man of thirty-seven years, save for a scar on the chin where his little brother Jasper had tried out his first sword. He took care to tie and adjust his waist cord over a freshly pressed red and green tunic. Hmm, he'd put on a bit of weight again. Not that his girth really bothered him. After all, a certain rotundity was almost expected in his line of work.

Satisfied, he shrugged on his cloak, causing the bells on his immaculate cox-comb hat to jangle, and scurried across the palace gardens in the early morning Ludnam sunshine, heading for a side gate. The twin moons, Luna and Runa, were already showing faint crescents low in the sky.

He needed to get a wiggle on if he wanted to avoid another of his mother's epic moaning rants, but on reaching the palace gate, a long, dreary line of people stood waiting to be frisked down by the guards. "Boglets," he muttered under his breath.

One of the men on duty was new and still as keen as the proverbial condiment. He was taking an inordinate amount of time to check every man or woman who passed. At best now, he'd be late. At worst, arrested for smuggling out the gold candleholder hidden under his cloak. He almost doubled back to deposit the trinket in his chambers for another occasion, but he'd already missed his chance: another of the guards, the ignoramus Pollock, spotted Feydor and made straight for him.

"Oi it's you. The fat faced bastard of a jester. What did you call me last week?"

"I believe I said you were a vacuous ninny with prunes for brains." He smiled broadly. "I'm sorry. I am a simple man who can but speak the truth."

Pollock narrowed his eyes. "Right, smartarse. Let's see what you're hiding under that cloak." He shoved Feydor hard against a wall, but the jester in him couldn't help but respond with the widest of grins and, with a finger, jangled a bell on his hat.

Pollock glared. Then he brought his knee up hard between Feydor's legs. Feydor pushed the man back, smirked, then blew him a kiss. "Pathetic. A castrato such as myself is as untroubled by balls as you are by a father." He pirouetted away, just ducking under the man's heavy fist.

"Go on, beshrew thee, hedge-born disgusting half-man," shouted Pollock.

Feydor skipped on his toes through the gate. "I am indeed half a man, but I'll vouchsafe 'tis better than your half a wit. Good morrow sirs."

He enjoyed balancing on the edge of disaster, but that had been close. Not that he'd doubted the outcome for a second. Pollock and the others might look for a way to retaliate, but the men that patrolled the grounds and gates of the palace weren't noted for their intelligence, and Feydor would always find a way to get around them.

He judged himself ahead of schedule, so he ducked into a nearby tavern, pressing the candlestick into the hand of a man there, receiving a substantial bag of coins in return.

"Trav asks, can you get any figurines next time? His old dear of a mother would love to have one of them Grecan ones in her parlour."

"Tricky. Tell Mr Travis I'll see what I can do," he replied as he left, exiting toward and out through the Alder Gate.

He stopped off on the corner of Long Reach and Kingsway to speak to his favourite beggar, Blind Harry. "It's going to be cold again tonight, Harrold. Here's two groats. Find yourself some shelter and something to eat."

"May Lord Sola bless you Feydor," replied Harry.

Harry could in fact see perfectly well, but Feydor indulged him all the same, along with an extensive network of others like him, as well as dropouts, miscreants, and other ne'er-do-wells, the sorry street detritus of this part of Ludnam. Strictly, he insisted to himself, to buy their eyes and ears in case they might prove useful in the future. But money, sadly, did not rain down from the Stars, so he stole royal knick-knacks to pay for it all. He thought of it as an equitable redistribution of wealth and a stab in the eye for his avaricious, vain, preposterous, whining, supercilious, and pompous ass of a patron, King Inglebert.

His route skirted Martin's Fields, a welcome oasis of green in the greater desert of malodorous filth that sloshed and squelched over his boots along with the half-melted snow. The disorganised overhanging buildings blocked out the light, much like the top branches of a forest. A forest, however, tended not to stink badly enough to strip whitewash from a wall. He hurried on.

His destination was the Castle and Ball tavern, not very affectionately known to the locals as the Turret and Testicle. As he arrived, he met Rod, Ludnam's most depressive landlord. Rod had his elbows planted on the serving bench while he frowned at a pamphlet, The Daily Tidings, his mouth forming the words. "Goat… gives… birth… to … pig. Hmph typical. Why can't I have a goat like that?"

"You don't even keep goats."

Rod scowled. "I could if I wanted. What's it to you, anyway?"

"Nothing. Nothing at all. Full of the joys of the season, are we Rodnye?"

"Avaunt, Feydor, and good luck with your mother. She's got a foul canker about her today."

"When has she not?" asked Feydor.

"After she's had a man up there," he replied, smirking, as he crudely mimed a sexual act involving his rear end. Feydor winced at the thought of his mother's carnal appetite and quickly made for the stairs that led to her rooms.

~~~

Feydor detested with every fibre of his being the power his witch mother held over him. However, he hadn't as yet worked out how to break
~~~

away from it. Which wasn't to say he couldn't manipulate her when the need arose. It was all about knowing how to play on her vaulting vanity and how far he could go in arguing with her.

Her living space comprised a single low room about thirty paces long by half that wide, a significant chamber for a single person. At one end was a curtained sleeping area and at the other, shelves and cupboards were piled high with a higgledy-piggledy clutter of what Feydor could only think of as junk. In the room's centre, a raised wooden dais sitting atop a stone slab was where she did a lot of her magic, and against one wall, stood a hearth spattered with animal fat and candle wax, harbouring an iron stand on which she had a pile of unwashed pots and a spit. For light, three sets of ill-matching shutters were all thrown open to the elements.

"Ah, look, it's that pathetic tallow catch[16], Feydor. Perhaps I should just burn you as oil for my lamp." She sat reading a thick volume on which were depicted magical designs, while she fiddled distractedly with her amulet.

"Good morrow mother dear. Having a horrible day, I hope?"

"Don't mother dear me, stool for brains," she said, her gaze still locked on her book. "I'll roast your heart while it yet beats in your chest."

He smiled to himself. "At least I'd be suffused with warmth for a few seconds."

Today, as usual, Feydor discovered Imelda sitting at her burnt oak desk, while bright sunlight streamed through the shutters, picking out sooty motes of dust that mingled and churned with the vapour of her breath. He pulled his thick cloak tighter and blew warmth into his mittens, but his mother displayed no such discomfort. A few bats fluttered around in the chamber. As one approached too close, she plucked it from the air and bit into it.

She twisted towards him, her black pinhead eyes boring into his. "What dull tidings bring thou from the royal court? Something that might warm the heart cockles of a poor woman, I hope?"

Feydor, unimpressed, ignored the blood trickling down her chin. Poor woman? Who did she think she was kidding? "Only the usual tittle-tattle. I spied Thomas Crumbwell dallying with the Queen's niece. That could come in handy if I need to blackmail him. Otherwise, things are normal, humdrum, tickety-boo."

Her mouth curled into a sneer. "Crumbwell? Even you can do better than the King's First Minister. Give me a baron or an earl I can sink my talons into. Oh, I deserve so much better than you."

Feydor stared at her pitiless expression. "Just where are you going to find someone more capable, more serving, more patient than *me,* mother? Someone prepared to put up with *you*?"

"Hogwash! It's down to me that you are where you are. Men are all such useless creatures."

"So, my achievements have nothing to do with my own efforts? Is that what you think?"

"Pah." She waved her hand as though batting away a tiresome moth. "Enough of your prattle. Luckily for us, I at least have something to share that could be big. Enormous."

By *for us* she meant *for her,* of course, it was only ever about her. She stood and reached for a book from a shelf above her desk. He took a moment to regard his mother in her pomp. Although she was beyond sixty years of age, she passed herself off as one half that. As for her attire, mutton dressed as lamb. Why couldn't she clothe herself like any normal foul witch and just let her cloak hang about her body like an old sack? Not his mother, no. Her attempt at sophisticated allure came off as both creepy and pathetic. Witch Provocateur, she called her style. It was a shame about the egg stain on her front. She drew a deep draught from her rune encrusted pipe and belched out a cloud of thick blue, herby smoke, masking, praise the Stars, her characteristic odour of stale sweat, cabbage and lye.

"I'll read you a page from this book, the Grimorio Minore. Are you sitting comfortably? It says, *The crystalle Nurragù, the first of the keyes three, the stonne of liffe shalt be founde aneath the city of Nourrù and protected by the guardian cat Bisgattù. Touch ye not the crystalle, lest a great pestilence be wrought upon the children of the earth. Fathers shall erupt in boiles, mothers shall eat their babies.* I'll skip this section. It goes on like that for another couple of pages. Here's the interesting part: *Yet shall a tall mortal man, pale of skin, blond of hair and weak of heart, travel from far lands, answer a riddle, touch the crystalle, and breathe.*"

He pondered this before saying, "And what, pray, does this crystal of life do?"

"Oh, a few small things. It confers immortality, the power of healing, the usual."

"Nothing much then. Anyway, so what? It's a myth, surely."

"Perhaps. However, I've heard the ugly Queen Nannua and her nation of gnome-like Janasà think they have discovered it buried deep under Nourrù."

"And you believe it?"

"I trust my source."

"What source? Where's this Nourrù, anyway?"

"That's *my* business, and it's the home of the Janasà in Sardonica. I want it and my adoring son is going to get it for me, regardless of what he believes. And besides, I can't risk anyone else getting their hands on it. My bitch witch cousin Mary, for instance, would use it to finish me, and you too, most likely."

"If you want this crystal that badly, you've only to go there yourself and take it. You're more powerful than a bunch of grinning half-goblins."

"Did you not listen to what I said? *A mortal man, pale of skin, blond of hair, weak of heart* etcetera. And besides, I have too many things here to attend to. Here's what I want you to do. Put your best thinking hat on and return on the morrow. We'll come up with a plan together."

"The King always hunts on a Wigglesday, so I suppose I can set off over here once dawn arrives. Just don't imagine I'm going to Sardonica for you. You know I don't travel well."

She sighed. "Now, to show how much I still care about you, open that basket over there and see what's within."

A present? He hoped not, seeing as the last thing she'd given him was a live scorpion on his fifth birthday. Feydor stepped over to a plain wicker container four hands tall. As he opened it, something covered in black hair screeched as it leapt out and attached itself to his head. "Hell's britches! What manner of devilry are you inflicting on me now?"

Imelda, for the first time in their encounter, smiled, but with a disturbing impression of benevolence.

"This is Filthy Mote[17], your new monkey. Every jester should have one. He'll go everywhere with you and even help you distract the King when he gets more difficult."

Feydor tried to push the animal's head from his, and it paid him back with a deep bite to the thumb. "Arghh Boglets! Avaunt!"

"I've put a charm on him, so he'll never leave your side. Nor you his."

"What!?"

Filthy hissed, bared his fangs, and spat in Feydor's eye. By Sol's teeth, he despised it already, but he loathed her even more.

"Now go back to whatever you do over in that palace and return on the morrow with a plan to get me that crystal."

He sighed. "Yes, mother."

She turned to her desk and reached again for her book, while he stuffed the squirming simian into its basket and gathered his cloak about him. As he stepped through the door, she added, "Oh, he eats nuts, by the way."

~~~

The stairs down from his mother's rooms creaked under Feydor's significant bulk. Still shivering, he shrugged his hood on and stepped outside, setting off into the city's permanent gloom rendered all the more impenetrable by the late afternoon mist. He wished the basket under his arm contained anything but a rabid pet. That his mother should have given him a monkey came as no surprise. After all, as a jester himself, his father had always kept one. That the creature should be such a spiteful demonic hairball, however, and that it should so despise Feydor himself, was a cruel touch, typical of her. He thought of his father, Alfred, former jester to the Earl of Stratfield. His fondest memories were of the times he'd spent balanced on the man's knee, listening to the stories of the most famous, even notorious jesters.

First came Reginald, the flatulent master jester to King Herbert I, who, for a simultaneous song, jump, and a fart each winter solstice, would receive land and gold. They would often lament Trebuchet, the Gallian female humpback jester, renowned for her acid wit and excoriating insults, so much
~~~

so that her royal patron, the Empress Narcissa, had had her executed for straying just a little too far beyond the bounds of acceptable parody.

Lost in his reverie, he avoided by a rat's whisker getting flattened by a runaway cartload of turnips. "Watch where you're going, carrot head!" shouted the driver. He held back from firing a curse at the guy. What would be the point of it?

His favourite story was of the Moorish Pantesco, who, for his wisdom, had become a gentleman courtier and confidante to the King of Portão. All of these performers made exemplary role models, but if he could be half as wise, patient and outright hilarious a jester as his own dear departed father, well, he'd be one of the great fools[18].

What would the man say to him today? He'd be proud of his son, that much was certain, but he'd have told him to take fewer risks, be steadier and less impatient, less angry. *Anger wastes energy and fosters rash deeds*, were the exact words he'd often told him, along with *two wrongs don't make a right* and *don't break wind too close to an open fire*. He should heed such counsel now. *Ah, father.*

His mother was a very different jug of eels. She'd never shown him the tiniest morsel of warmth or kindness. Her mention of her witching rival cousin Mary brought into the centre of his mind a cold, brutal fact that Mary had revealed to him the previous year. Something he'd always suspected: that his own mother had authored his castration. Of course. Who else? He'd known at once it had to be true. It made sense. She'd wanted that his focus never waver from the task she'd given him: to rise in the noble houses of the land until he could reach the giddy heights of being the jester to the King of Anglonia himself. She'd even had his younger siblings sent away to an aunt in the west country so she could focus all of her attention on just him. Imagine it! Since then, every day of every year, his hatred for his mother had become a kernel around which to build a bitter stone, like the blackest of pearls accumulating layer by layer inside the bitterest of oysters. But to avenge himself, he had to be patient and to give no hint that he harboured anything other than devotion to her. He could do patience.

As for Mary, he'd not seen the conniving hag for many a moon. She had, apparently, just shacked up with some exiled Albian prince, although he couldn't remember which one, given how the Albians were always exiling or imprisoning their royalty. That said, it sounded too fascinating not to follow up on, if for no other reason than to goad her. He made a mental note to surprise her with a meeting.

Entering the palace, he took the passage leading to the north wing where the principal groom, Sir Morris, had allocated him his quarters. The main room had a high ceiling painted with frolicking nymphs and angry serpents, and wall mounted tapestries covered in naked horned warriors, each adorned with an improbable set of genitalia[19]. What kind of artist spent all day painting these exquisite, detailed phalluses? The overall decorative effect had, he understood, the aim of promoting fecundity among its occupants. He presumed Sir Morris to either possess a sharp sense of irony or else to be a castrato hating zealot, a common enough prejudice of the time. For although no man he knew of had ever volunteered to have his low hanging fruit removed, a castrato still faced constant lies and discrimination for their talents and proclivities. People claimed they could invoke miscarriages, give rise to rickets, collapse wombs, cause three-headed babies to be born, provoke premature disgorgement, and even spark wild outbreaks of folk dancing.

He cast his heavy winter cloak aside and deposited his new pet in a corner, still in its basket. As an afterthought, he draped his cloak over the container, then he set to tidying the already pristine room before settling down with a cup of mead to read some poetry. He'd worked through the first few lines when a polite knocking interrupted him. "Mr Foolson, the King commands your presence for court this afternoon. Shall I inform Sir Thomas you will be there?"

"Boglets, may his manhood wither away with the pox," he muttered to himself.

"What was that Fool?"

"Nothing. Yes, yes, of course. I will arrive anon."

It would be a routine affair of desperate boredom punctuated by brief opportunities to amuse, but at least he could make the time pass more quickly by thinking of how he might break out from his mother's control.

He sighed and made for the door, forgetting for a moment having left Filthy the monkey in his basket, but a tug at his throat reminded him he was now bound to the infernal creature. Boglets, he'd have to bring the pet with him.

~~~

Feydor had a lot of time whilst in the company of His Grace to explore ways in which to describe his royal patron, King Inglebert, who had to be one of the dullest monarchs to ever occupy the throne, making him, rather than Feydor, the real fool at court. He took crass banality to towering new heights, daily challenging Feydor to come up with ever more creative adjectives to apply. Gormless, addle-pated, bone-headed, useless, insipid, tepid, vapid, turgid, vacuous, bromidic, drab, the descriptions gushed out from his mind like pus from a boil. His shining vanity, his hollow, narcissistic pomposity, his goose saddling uselessness, and his inability to grasp and hold on to the simplest of concepts strained Feydor's credulity. The suppurating wart on the end of his nose possessed a sharper intellect than the man himself. The crowned monarch reeked of rank mediocrity, seeming to drive all sentient thought out of any room he walked into, causing it to tear off in search of a sharp blade with which to slash its own throat. Feydor had blown farts more erudite, his ears had eructated gobs of earwax more sapient, and his nose dripped snot stains more scholarly than the ruler of Anglonia.

All this should have made him easy to please and influence, but it did rather the opposite, instead rendering him capricious, imperious, and demanding. This King, a show don't tell kind of ruler, preferred it when Feydor fell on his arse, or collided with door frames, or stood bent double farting a tune. All beyond hilarious, but the constant humiliation made Feydor seethe with anger and resentment. And then the Queen. The tall, haughty Luthenian beauty, who never wasted a chance of treating Feydor
~~~

like an inconvenient stain on the rich carpet. He had yet to see her smile, to demonstrate the least sign of any authentic emotion, making her, in his mind, a sad, dreary waste of the very air she breathed. An empty skull in which a pea might rattle away for hours before encountering resistance.

Feydor arrived at the outer privy chamber where most court proceedings took place, and entered without fanfare, being the most recognisable member of the royal entourage. With him came two grooms dressed in brown smocks, carrying between them a heavy item covered in sackcloth. The grooms placed their cargo just below the regal dais and bowed to the King before leaving. Feydor stepped over and, with an elaborate flourish, pulled away the sacking to reveal a throne that bore a remarkable resemblance to that of King Inglebert. Except that its proportions were, at best, child-sized. He made a great show of straightening his tunic in imitation of his patron and sat with the same slouching repose and bored aspect of the man himself. Even Filthy reclined on his lap and yawned. All went quiet.

Putting on Inglebert's reedy voice, Feydor commanded, "What are you all standing around for? Continue!"

The crowded room held its breath.

"Your Grace," said the odious Lord High Priest, Ignatius Stackpole, "shall I have the Fool removed and disciplined?"

Instead of replying, Inglebert clapped and encouraged the other courtiers to do the same. "Bravo Feydor," he said. Addressing the court at large, he said, "See how the Fool brings me back down to earth? Excellent."

Feydor couldn't help but notice that the King's expressions did not align with his speech. Did he detect a note of irritation? Perhaps he'd gone too far this time. His father had always said there was a fine line between pleasing and offending. As for Stackpole, his power and influence over the King grew by the week, and he might yet turn into a dangerous adversary. He had no major reason to fret, having more wit than the lot of them together, but it paid to be careful.

Inglebert continued. "Now where were we? Ah yes, my groom of the stool[20] was about to provide his latest observations on the royal effluent? Sir Compton?"

"My liege, I, and the First Medic have examined the movements with the greatest attention and confirm that, while the consistency is good, the proportions are troubling. We recommend eating more turnip."

"Sun and moons, not turnips again. Stackpole, what say you?"

The priest cleared his throat and intoned, "We see no particular portents in the royal fruit, save perhaps this coming year will bring forth a fine barley harvest."

"What the blazes are you talking about? But speaking of harvests, where is my minister for sustenance?"

"You dismissed him last month, Your Grace."

"Well… fetch me the new one, at once."

"You didn't appoint anyone yet, Your Grace. I suggested to Your Grace the incomparable Sir Bates."

"The Master of the Hand? No, no, quite inappropriate. He is too good at what he does. No matter, I'm sure the peasants will always muddle through. Now who here can explain to me the state of the royal forests? Will I have stags enough to hunt down this coming season?"

The King began conversing with several officials while Feydor feigned boredom. His head rocked back, he settled into his thronelet, and snored lightly. He shook a leg theatrically in the air and jangled his bauble. The King ignored him.

"So, what else do I need to know? First Minister, tell me, have we refilled our coffers with taxes yet?"

Before the official could respond, Feydor sat up and interrupted. "My liege, it is said in the streets that your fiscal policies are harming the realm. Your taxes on employment and trade mean the rich no longer wish to pay their skilled workers, which has resulted in a collapse in confidence in our ability to pay our debts, trade is collapsing, and now the usurers are charging triple or even quadruple the interest payments because of the uncertainty. The serfs and villains are in danger of starvation. Some are calling it *Inglenomics*. Among other nations, we are becoming a most frightful embarrassment."

There. Somebody needed to say it.

"Intolerable! Your Grace…" interrupted Stackpole, but Inglebert silenced him with a wave of a hand, then templed his fingers, appearing this time to waver as to how to react to this latest outrage. Feydor held his breath. Seconds passed. "Really Fool?" said Inglebert, at last, waving a hand dismissively. "You come out with the most tiresome of nonsense. You have such a poor grasp of politics. What say you, First Minister? Is my Fool an actual fool?"

First Minister Thomas Crumbwell answered before Feydor could take further liberties. "Well, in his prattling, he may have touched on a germ of truth."

"Meaning?" said Inglebert, glaring at his First Minister.

"Meaning it appears, your Grace, people are reluctant to spend and therefore we are, contrary to expectation, collecting far less tax revenue than before."

"Moons and Stars! Fewer taxes, you say? This is serious. Crumbwell, round up the culprits and hang them anon."

"And the taxes, Your Grace? Should I restore them to their previous levels?"

"What? Oh, I see. Very well," said the King, slumping deep into his throne. "I blame you for this, though, Crumbwell. You have ill-advised me."

Crumbwell had, in fact, argued at length against the changes, but it was he, the low born fool who had helped ensure common sense prevailed. Not that he cared much for the state of the realm and its people; in his book, it was every man for himself.

An official entered and whispered something in Crumbwell's ear.

The First Minister intoned, "Your Grace, I have fortuitous tidings. The new Gallian ambassador has arrived and seeks an audience. Should I admit him to your presence?"

"Really? Now? Oh, very well, I suppose we must show civility to such tedious guests. Permit him to enter so I may at least canvass his opinions on important matters of state."

The official exited, returning soon after with a small but lively man, dressed in the manner of the latest Gallian fashion, right down to his silk doublet, crimson cape, and the yard long points on his shoes[21], a regular court dandy.

"Your Grace, may I present Monsieur Antoine De Longuedongue?"

The ambassador entered and made an extravagant bow. A condescending smile playing across his lips. "Your Grace!"

"Monsieur er.."

"De Longuedongue, your Grace."

"What? Longer d… d… Oh, never mind. Welcome to my court. Perhaps you can assist me with a vexing matter?"

"I am at your service, your Grace."

"Excellent. Now, tell me, of what import do you consider the size of my stool?"

~~~

"Here he is. My fat kidney'd pillock of a son, late as usual. By the Stars, I should never have let you near my paps at your birth."

It was afternoon and Feydor had arrived again at his mother's lair. As far as he was aware, his mother had handed him to a wet nurse at birth and never, in fact, succoured him.

"I love you, too, mother," he said, as he released his diabolical pet out into the open room. "I bring interesting tidings, but if you'd rather just moan at me, go ahead."

She glared at him. Her look made Filthy scamper behind a low bench.

"Speak then, dullard," she said. "It'd better be good."

"I'm working to get close to the Queen through her ladies-in-waiting. I've already learned much."

"Really? Such as?"

He hated how her silence could worm things out of him, how she could be such a force to be reckoned with, even when not appearing to do anything. However, on this occasion, he'd planned it this way.

"For one thing, Queen Ruthenia is using leather shields to thwart her husband's desires for an heir."

"The mind boggles."
~~~

"But that's not why I'm here. Would you like to discuss the crystal?" he asked.

"Ah yes, the crystal. How do you propose to deliver it to me?"

Feydor collected his thoughts and began. "It's obvious that if neither you nor I can travel to Sardonica, then we must send someone else. Someone audacious and resourceful enough to improvise and seize the right moment to act."

"Oh, Sun and Moons, is that your idea, winknot? Did I raise you for this? How the Stars will anyone gain the trust of the Janasà, get into the citadel, and then perform such a theft?"

Another pause. "Ah, but there would be someone else there to create a distraction. Was it not my father who called misdirection the most powerful tool in such a situation?"

"Don't bring that useless simpleton into it. What misdirection? Go on." She sounded anything but convinced.

Feydor paused just long enough to show his disapproval of her opinion of his father.

"Oh dear, did I offend little Feydor's memory of his daddy? Never mind, poor baby." She mimed suckling an infant, and Feydor had to breathe deeply to keep control. Losing his temper now could spoil everything.

"We can make the Janasà think we want something else, something trivial or ridiculous, and while they are laughing their pathetic little faces off, we can grab the jewel."

"That could work. What did you have in mind?"

Her naked ambition had taken over her whole demeanour. Now she was rapt.

"Water."

"Water? What are you blathering on about?"

He smiled. "Not just any water. I spoke last week with a diplomat from Italica who told me about an aphrodisiac spring under the mountains of the Janasà. Such water might help Queen Ruthenia get with child."

"But you just told me…"

He smirked. "Aye, but the King doesn't know about the Queen's trickery."

"Go on. Explain more."

"So here is the misdirection I have in mind. I believe I can have the King send someone to trade for some of this water."

"You mean an envoy?" she asked.

He nodded. "Something like that, but a gullible one who will hold the sincere belief that he is doing important work for the King. One might even describe it to him as a quest."

"And while negotiations are ongoing for this water, an accomplice can steal the crystal? But what can the envoy offer in return?"

He shrugged. "Gold. A treaty? Who cares? He doesn't need to succeed."

"Why on earth not?"

"Suppose that travelling with the envoy we sent a thief capable of waiting till the Janasà were looking the other way, and then of stealing the crystal from under their noses. Would that make sense?"

"It might. It seems complicated. How would this all work?"

"This is where I need you, mother. Locate for me a thief. I can find someone in the palace gullible enough to run the trading errand. Then we just have to put the two of them together and set them on their way."

"The choice of thief is easy."

"How so?"

"Jasper."

He feigned surprise. "Which Jasper? Oh, you mean my dearest brother, Jasper?"

"Of course, *that* Jasper. Dearest brother, you call him? Ha, that's funny. He's perfect for the role, though. Can't you see that?"

"And that unfortunate business in Catatonia?"

"He assures me burning down half the city was an accident."

Feydor's sainted siblings could do no wrong in her eyes, but as his father had taught him, don't brood on unfairness, use it.

"Where is Jasper right now?" he asked, knowing full well where his brother was at that moment wreaking mayhem.

"He is in Italica."

"Why's he there?" he asked, determined to drag it out of her.

"He's with your sister on a minor matter of revenge. Nothing for you to concern yourself with."

"Ah, of course." His sister Morwena was the youngest of Imelda's three children and a fierce swordsman. However, Imelda had high hopes of the girl settling down to a quiet life of dark witchcraft, not that his sister had showed the slightest interest in any of that. Still, Imelda continued to hope.

Now that voices had calmed, Filthy crept over and jumped into her lap. She scratched his tummy, causing him to roll over, squirming.

Feydor saw this as the moment to go back over the plan. "So, in summary: we send a tepid and inconsequential envoy to the island of Sardonica on a bogus trade mission on behalf of Inglebert, but with him we can have Jasper, and if it pleases her, Morwena. They will join the party as guides and protectors. They know the country and its ways, and both speak some of the lingo, I would hope. But when they arrive in Sardonica, they will steal the jewel."

She scratched behind the monkey's ears and the creature squealed its appreciation. "See how he just wants some attention? He's such a darling!" Without looking up, she continued, "Very well. I'll get the message to Jasper once we have more flesh on the bone. Will it not be difficult to make the King do as you ask?"

"Don't worry yourself on that score, I have been amusing his Majesty these last few weeks by having him send grave men on risible quests. Last week, I had the eminently gullible Sir Eccles sent to Albia for a jar of elbow grease. The King was laughing all day about that one. He will be more than happy to do this."

"Very well, I will trust you, but do not fail me. Now leave."

Feydor crossed through the empty tavern and out into the street with his mind racing. Identifying a victim to carry out their plan was just one more intrigue to add to his list of spinning platters. He couldn't wait to put it into action.

# Four

They set off as dawn broke free of its shackles, and Lord Sola showed the first sliver of his golden disk. The long night of the twin moons had left behind a hard frost that had painted the rooftops a gleaming white like the sails on a tall ship, while below, it had frozen the filthy puddles on the street an unwelcoming black, like pools of pitch. William rode on Milly, a gentle old mare who, according to Ridkin, *wouldn't know how to throw him off.* Ridkin led on his favourite, Max, a dark stallion, with *a bit of life in him.* They picked their way through the narrow maze of streets and alleys of Ebury, making for the main south gate. William twisted to glance back at the castle's finger-like tower now glinting in the sharp early sunlight. What fascinating secrets did it hold? What tales could it tell? He'd get a good look inside it when he returned and find out. It had to be used for *something,* right?

Once out of the city, they rode in silence through the undulating landscape for the entire morning, with neither man showing much inclination for conversation. They passed forests of scotch pine and fields marked off into farmable strips with tied men hacking away at the frozen soil. William's mind drifted to thoughts of Verity, determined to make the most of this opportunity and prove himself to the Earl. Failure wasn't an option, and besides, how hard could it be? "I can do this," he muttered to himself.

"Got anything to say, messenger boy?" asked Ridkin.

"No, no, just talking to myself."

"Pillock," mumbled the younger man.

Without thinking, William reached to his beard. He thought it gave him better definition to his chin, but there were gaps on his cheeks that he wished would fill in more. Perhaps a goatee would work better? Moons and Stars. Why was he bothered about such things? Did it matter? And then he remembered the cut on his cheek and shifted his hand across to trace its outline. A short gouge with raised ridges. It wasn't *as* bad as he'd feared, and the honey poultice Aileen had applied seemed to have helped. As for his chest, it complained at each jolt of Milly's gait. He could ignore it, although he'd sneezed once, and that had been spectacular. Not to be repeated.

As the morning wore on, he burned with the need to ask his companion what made him so sour. Since leaving Ebury, Ridkin had oozed angry resentment from his every pore, keeping his horse on the other side of the track from William's and avoiding eye contact. A clear message. What was the problem here? William could hold back no more. "I'm sorry, can we start again, please? I'm William."

"Your sort don't talk to my sort," came the sullen reply.

"How do you know what my sort is?"

"It's like this, see. You talks all posh. You wears good clothes, your hands are soft, you can read. My sort, my sort, are none of those things."

"Tell me of your sort, then."

"You want the truth? Ludnam street vermin is the name what they gives us. We grew up with eleven of us kids in two rooms and me mam a widow. Ever seen anything like that? Thought not. Ran away up north to escape the gangs when I was eight. Anthony found me shivering, and half dead in the alley. He took me in, gave me work in the stables. He's the only reason I agreed to help you." He calmed a little from his tirade. "Once we're done with this journey, that's it. I never want to speak to you again."

"Fine with me." William meant it.

As the lazy winter sun got as high as it could be bothered, they stopped to eat the rye bread and sliced meat Ridkin had taken from the kitchens, then got back into their saddles and pressed on. Ridkin never ceased looking every which-way, like he expected trouble. So William asked him, "Are there many dangers out here?"

"I always assume the worst. I got jumped once, and I ain't letting it happen again." He paused for a moment. "You read books alright, but you haven't learned to read the road yet. Look around. Tell me what you see."

"A few trees, a clear sky. I'm not sure what you mean."

"Well, look at it this way. If you was a dodgy sort fixing to rob a pair like us, where would you hide?"

"There's a dip in the land on the left there. And a clump of trees to the right. What would you do anyway if someone jumped out?"

"You missed the low stone wall just behind us. You want to know what to do? Where I come from, you don't wait for introductions. Get your strike in first, and if there's a load of them, run for it. Why do you think I chose to ride Max here?" He gave the flank of his mount an appreciative pat. "Don't hang around to be no victim. Simple, right?"

"Not really. I can't fight and I can barely stay on a horse. What do I do?"

Ridkin sniggered. "Become a monk? You ain't no messenger."

William smiled at the irony. "I almost did. Become a monk. Wasn't for me though."

"Wouldn't work for me, neither. No way. That's no life."

Just then, they met travellers coming from the south and had to find a way between them without falling into the deep holes in the rutted road.

"What's your plan once I gets shot of you, posh boy?" asked Ridkin.

"Truth is, I don't have much of a plan. Work my way up in the castle and earn enough to marry my true love, I suppose."

Ridkin scoffed. "You? In love? Hah. Where did you find a girl sappy enough to want you?"

He felt stung. "There's nothing sappy about her. She's a decent girl and we plan to be together. And she has a name. Verity Bull."

Ridkin looked sceptical, one eyebrow raised. "I just hope she's a patient sort. Tell me. Those books you have with you. What's really in 'em? Anything useful?"

"Um, not really, nothing practical. Just now I'm reading a new book from Iberica. It's a story like no other, called Don Creosote[22]. It tells of a knight errant who rides his horse, Rocinante, and with his squire, Sanchez, in search of glory, righting wrongs, and rescuing damsels in distress."

For the first time, Ridkin wore half a smile. "Is that how you see us? A knight and his squire? Not too many damsels around here. And none what would want rescuing by the likes of you."

"I grant you I'm hardly knight material. I lack the years of training and the required high birth. You'd make a good squire, though."

"And the other book?"

"It's a philosophical treatise about the divine right of kings to rule."

William caught Ridkin's blank stare. "A treat what? Divine right? My arse." He scratched his rump for emphasis. "Anyway, are you all religious like? Praying and chanting and stuff."

"Not really. I wanted to believe in The Great Lord Sola and His Moons, Luna and Runa." Ridkin rolled his eyes, but William continued. "And how the Stars are spirits who carry the dead across the sky. And I tried to become a monk, I really did, but once I read the Grecan writers, that was it. I saw it all as superstition and as a way for the wealthy to control the poor."

"Well, here we are. At last, we agree on something."

"But I do believe a decent man doesn't lie."

Ridkin's voice rose half an octave. "Oh my very aunt, what did you just say?"

"I was taught, *Every time you tell a lie, a sparrow falls down from the sky.* I know they don't actually fall down, but you have to believe in something. By your face I can see you don't agree. What do you believe?"

"What do I believe? I believe the only thing what Sola and his Moons ever done for my kind is punish us with terrible harvests and grind us into the dirt. And don't get me started on the King of the land. He's the biggest leech of the lot of them. Mind, don't you go reporting me to the priesthood, or I'll cut you open." He mimed a knife slashing across his throat. "What I can't believe right now is how I've been saddled as nursemaid to a useless lickspittle. Right, we've ridden far enough for today. There's a village ahead that I know has a decent inn."

Reaching the inn, Ridkin disappeared inside to ask for rooms. He emerged, saying. "We have beds and a meal. Come on, let's get the horses settled."

William waited for some time outside the stables while Ridkin talked with the stable lads. He picked up the flow of easy banter between them and the chorus of laughter when Ridkin said something crude. He envied the young man's ability to make people feel comfortable. Shame he was so selective.

The rudimentary accommodation comprised a single dormitory over the main drinking area that both men and women had to share. For sure, bed bugs would come out of the rafters in the night, and that the following morning he'd be itching like the furies. But it would improve on the alternative of sleeping in the icy cold outside. Just.

A low buzz of people talking and eating filled the fire lit, smoky area downstairs, and they got chatting over their meal and warm ale with two men on their way north from Ludnam. William was keen to know if there was any news of where they were going, but before the conversation could get started, another man reached across, took-William's mug of ale, downed half and spat in the rest, placing it back on the table.

"Got a problem?" the man asked.

"No, no, I'm sorry, not at all." William avoided eye contact, afraid of provoking further trouble.

"What you sorry for, boy? You've a mug ugly enough to wake the Stars an' all. Let's take this outside and see how sorry you are."

He raised his hands. "No, no, it's alright, no offence intended."

"Offence taken!" and the man reached over to grab William's shirt at the neck.

William froze. Nobody had ever done anything like this to him. Why on earth would they? He offered a quick silent chant to Sola and prepared to be beaten. However, out of nowhere, Ridkin leaned across, loosened the man's grip and head-butted him full in the face. The man fell back, shouting in dialect, before the landlord and another man grabbed him, dragged him to the door, and threw him out into the night. "I've told you Fred, not to come in 'ere making trouble," shouted the landlord. "You're barred, be gone with you." He slammed the heavy door.

William sat, shocked, before saying, "Thank you! I owe you a great favour. Again."

"Don't thank me, thank Ant. I promised I'd see you safe. If it was down to me, I'd have let the man have his fun. He guessed you'd be a weakling, and I'd say he thought about right. Just goes to show, me and you are, well, from different places. But listen, I reckon that cove will be hanging around out there at dawn ready to have another pop at you, and he might well have some mates with him this time. I say we get going well before first light, just to be safe."

The following night, they found a smarter inn, but taking no chances, they tried to sit well away from the other guests. William, however, thought the different conversations fascinating and shifted closer to better listen.

A man sat arguing with his companion about the great contagion that had struck the continent of Yorpia twenty years earlier. "You know that disease everyone bangs on about, what is it, the Scarlet Lurgy? Well, I have it on good authority that it's all fake. False Tidings. Well, I'm not falling for it."

"Why would anyone invent that? I had a dose myself, and it's proper nasty, I can tell you," said his companion, who carried the pockmarks on his face to prove it.

"Nah, that was just the common pox. You mark my words, the whole thing's made up by the fancy lawyers and merchants to keep decent folk like us in our place."

William expressed wide eyed wonder. "Is that so?" he asked. "I never would have imagined it."

After ten more minutes of this, Ridkin interrupted. "Listen sirs, I've heard there's an outbreak of the Scarlet Lurgy not half a league north of here. Why, we passed it ourselves only yesterday. People are saying they've red lumps on their bodies and such like. But I'm sure you won't be put off heading that way. 'Specially seeing as how it's all made up, right?"

"Um, well, perhaps we'll head westward from here, and give it a miss. You know, to be on the safe side?"

Ridkin turned his back on them and pulled William away. "You really are wet behind the ears. It'll be a minor miracle if you make it back to Ebury. Not that I care that much either way."

~~~

Two mornings later, they browed a hill and spotted, for the first time, the city of Ludnam spread out before them, part shrouded in mist such that only the higher white stone guard towers of the legendary walls poked through here and there like a baby's teeth breaking out of their gums.

At the city gates, even at that early hour, a long line of stationary carts had built up.

"I suppose we have to join the end of the line and wait our turn," said William.

"Nah, not likely. This is my manor, and I knows a shortcut. Follow me."

Ridkin led them around what had appeared at a distance to be lakes, but as they approached them, turned out to stink like the furies. "Tanning pits," he pronounced[23].

"That stinks. Isn't there a better way?"

"It's just a smell. Can't really hurt you."

"I've read a man may be overcome by the vapours of such a place."

"You reads too much. You can join the line of carts, if you want. I'll be waiting for you inside by the Moor Gate with a glass of ale." Ridkin set off ahead, showing scant concern for what William did.

"But… if you're sure it's safe…"

After a few minutes, William noted, "It doesn't seem so bad now."

"The stench goes with the wind, and right now it's blowing away from us and toward the main road."

"Ah, you knew that would happen, didn't you?"

"Yep."

They arrived at a narrow door out of sight from the roadway, and Ridkin jumped down and knocked.

"Who's there?" called a voice from above. "Tickle off and use the main gate like everyone else. This is the King's Gate. Sling yer 'ooks."

"Open up," shouted Ridkin. "We carry a message for the King."

"We'll see about that. Wait there."

Half a minute later, a latch drew back, and a hand reached out. "Show me."
~~~

William climbed off his horse and pulled the letter from his satchel, showing the ornate seal to the guard.

"It's genuine," he confirmed, but appeared dubious. "You still ought to use the other gate, but I 'ad a good night with the missus, and since it's Wigglesday, enter, friend."

Ridkin signed an ironic salute and sauntered through the narrow gap, horse trailing, as if he owned the place, followed by William, who at once felt grit in his eyes and a demon stabbing at his throat.

"Ludnam smoke. You gets used to it."

"Why would anyone want to get used to it?" asked William, coughing hard, as he stepped into what appeared to be a puddle before sinking half up his shin in sludge.

"Don't step in the puddles," said Ridkin, sniggering. "You gets used to avoiding them."

They turned a corner and the first thing to strike William was a man's flailing arm striking him in the face as he ran full pelt with another man in pursuit, his other arm clutching a protesting chicken. The two of them crashed into carts, horses, and women with baskets, causing their wares to spill onto the muck covered road before disappearing along an alley. A cart load of pig's heads wended its way across a crossroads. A boy child grabbed one off the back and ran off with it, and the carter shouted a stream of curses at him. Everywhere William looked, people crowded, shouting, singing, dancing even. Dogs barked, a goat bleated, a child screamed. It overwhelmed the senses, but Ridkin appeared in his element.

"Right, first things first. Let's find an alehouse and get a jug of real Ludnam ale."

Spotting one, Ridkin crossed the street, dodging around a loud argument between two middle-aged women. He walked up to a short, hooded man with a huge belly standing by the low doorway. They began a conversation of which William understood barely a word. "Give the bloke a groat," he told William, as he handed the reins to their horses over. "He'll make sure we get them back. This place is full of thieves, and I should know, I used to be one of 'em."

William stooped to enter the tavern, its floor covered in stinking rushes and sawdust. Red-faced drinkers packed the place out even at this early hour as they laughed and shouted, rendering conversation difficult. Not that you could see many of them, given how the smoke was even denser in here than in the street. What exposed wood was visible was stained and riddled with woodworm. Ridkin ordered two glasses of ale that arrived in filthy beakers. William's stuck to the bench and there was a scum on the surface of the liquid. He sniffed at it.

"Cheers," said Ridkin, smiling. He downed his beaker in one draft and put it back on the bench before burping. "Another, landlord."

William took a sip out of what looked to be the least disgusting edge of his beaker, and spat it out. "That's no ale like I've ever tasted. What is it, river water? Let me guess. You get used to it."

"You're getting the idea," replied Ridkin, already halfway through the next one.

"So, this is it?" said William. "The biggest, grandest city in the land. The world, even. The streets are paved with gold, so I've heard. Can't say I've noticed much of that."

"Biggest and the most dangerous. But not a lot of gold except in the pockets of a few. Right, we can't stay in these backstreets for long." As he took another draught with one hand, he waved the other to the right. "It's that way to pick up Long Ditch and King Street. We'll soon be there. Tell you what. How about I drop you at the palace and leave you to get home to Ebury on your own?"

He waited with a stern frown on his face before bursting into laughter. "Just kidding. I promised Ant, I'd see you safe and I'll do it. Right, if you're not going to drink that, give it here." He sank the rest of William's ale and turned to exit.

Emerging onto the street, Ridkin took the reins of the horses and busied himself checking the animals over. Under his breath, he said, "Don't look, but we're being watched."

William couldn't stop himself. His head shot up to view the other side of the street.

Ridkin grabbed his arm. "I said don't look! For the love of the Stars, do you ever listen?"

"Sorry. Who is it?"

"There's two of them working together. They've been tracking us since we entered the city. Dead dodgy, like. Well, it takes more than two to follow *me* unnoticed, although there'll be more of them soon enough. My bet is they're part of Walter Travis's gang. Trav they calls him. I didn't expect they'd clock me. I've changed a bit like, but seems they did."

"And who is this Trav?"

"He's the one what reckons I owes him. I should've taken us around the city and entered from the south, but I didn't fink Trav operated this far north. It'll be the quality of these horses that stood out, like. I must be going soft in the 'ead to take the risk of coming this way with you. Look, it's me they want. If I draw them away, chances are they'll let you be. You take the horses south. Go up Long Ditch and King's Street and Bob's yer uncle. How's that sound?"

"I don't have any uncles. Not a chance, though. I'm not leaving you. It's not who I am."

"What you are is a pillock."

"Fine. If you say so. You know I'd get lost."

"Yeah, right enough. Or worse."

They both stood in silence, thinking.

"Ever heard the Grecan story of Tentacles," started William, "who lent his horse in return for his freedom?"

"Grecan? Are you having a laugh? How the Shining Stars does that help us, anyway? Who would we trade with?"

"I didn't mean literally. You tell me the horses mark us out? So we just leave them here."

"I'm not leaving these animals here. They'd be killed and made into pies by the end of the day."

"Right, I expected you to say that. Then how about we give them to this fine gentleman here? What are they worth?"

"Fifty groats a piece, I'd say. I'm not giving them away, and that's a fact."

"Hear me out. We hand them over and offer the guy double what they're worth if he can get them to the palace by the end of today. I assume we could dodge those men on foot?"

"Maybe. These two coves look heavy, a bit slow, like. They'd be a nightmare in a fight, but in a chase? We'd have a chance. Won't that leave us short of coin for the return trip?"

"It will, but we'll figure that out later. Right, you'd better talk with the man. I can't understand a word he says."

Ridkin's conversation with the minder involved lots of pointing and gesticulating, but he returned with good news. "He'll send his son with the horses. We're to walk them around the back to the stables and from there we can scarper."

Five minutes later, they were on foot, heading into the tight alleyways that ran behind and between the streets. After another ten minutes, Ridkin stopped at a corner to look for anyone tracking them. "They're still with us," he announced, although William saw nothing.

The younger man appeared to weigh up his options for a moment, then said, "We climb. Please tell me you can climb." He shimmied up onto a large barrel and held his hand to pull William behind. Then he stepped onto a low roof and headed up and over the other side. "What we need is to find a roof that's a bit dodgy, so those two lubberworts fall through."

William froze. "Mubble fubbles, I can't" he said, but then heard the wheezing of a man as he climbed the barrel behind him. A head poked up. "Come 'ere Rondine, Trav'll be gentle, he promises."

"Yeah, right. Like I'm going to fall for that. Will, you have to come now. Right now." He vaulted over an alley onto the next roof.

The first pursuer had his knee on the low roof, and the second had scaled the barrel. William shifted like he'd never done in his life. "I'm coming, I'm coming" he shouted, a wild rush of fire in his veins. He jumped over the alleyway and the waiting Ridkin caught him.

"Come on," he shouted. "We need to get higher."

At the end of the second roof, a vertical wall brought them to a halt. Ridkin peered around the corner. "There's an open shutter here," he said. "I reckon we can swing on that."

"Are you sure it's safe?"

"No idea. Are you coming or not?"

Ridkin jumped and grabbed the top of the shutter, swinging in a graceful arc before jumping onto the next roof. "I'll swing it back to you, then you do what I did."

"Seriously? Oh my Stars." He jumped but lost his hold with his weaker left hand. "Mubble fubbles." He dangled with feet flailing in mid-air, before swinging his left arm and finding purchase with the tips of his fingers. The shutter creaked as it swung away, and Ridkin caught his elbow as he dropped onto the tiles of the next house.

A convenient ladder allowed them to climb up onto another much higher roof. Looking behind, Will saw one of the men using a stick to pull across the shutter and perform the same manoeuvre as he and Ridkin. He hoped it would break off its hinges with the weight of the man, but it held. The second, larger man wasn't so successful. With a rending of timber, the shutter came away from the frame and dropped into a courtyard along with the flailing man. The screams, the snarling noise of angry hounds and the ripping clothes suggested he hadn't fared well there. Ridkin tried to prise the ladder from the wall on which it leant, but the fixings refused to budge. He grunted, then ran up the roof to its apex. A curse came from close behind, something angry that William couldn't understand.

They stepped off the other end of the roof, and Ridkin hopped across onto the opposite building. The way everyone built higher storeys closer together over the street had its uses. Unfortunately, it favoured the chasing man just as much, and he was soon again on their tails.

"Over there," said Ridkin. "There's a much older roof that might just cave in when big-mouth gets onto it."

"It could cave for us as well."

"Got a better plan?" asked Ridkin, not waiting for a reply. He clambered over toward the older building, a warehouse of some sort with yawning gaps where the old thatch had come away. Only one rafter looked to be solid, so Ridkin took that in a light scamper, while William crawled behind him. The ancient timber complained, emitting percussive creaks and cracks. Plumes of rotten dust floated free, but the beam held. They leapt across onto the next building, just as, behind them, a louder crack was followed by the full splitting of the old timbers as the chaser swore and vanished screaming into the dark space below. A moment later, came a dull thud, a gasp, and then… silence.

William stopped, heaving for breath, his hands on his knees. "Wait, give me a moment."

"Let's get out of here. There's an open window." Ridkin shuffled toward where he'd pointed.

William stood to follow, but a loose tile slid away from under him, and he lost his footing, slithering down behind it. The slate dropped and then he reached the edge and lost a leg over the side. Then an arm. He clung on as best he could, but felt himself slipping. "Sun, Moons, Stars, and my old auntie."

A hand grabbed the scruff of his neck as William's other leg slipped out of sight. "I got you. Stop struggling, you're making me lose grip. That's better. Right, here we go, get one foot on, now the other." Moments later, William laid flat out on the roof, panting wildly, too winded to speak.

Ridkin hauled him to his feet and over to a part open shutter, which they climbed through, disturbing an old man in bed as they ran out. "Good morrow, kind sir," William called as he exited the room behind Ridkin, then they took the stairs.

They descended into a candle shop and, ignoring the indignant shouts of the woman there, Ridkin stood at the door and scanned the street beyond. "It's clear," he said.

The narrow track gave onto a much broader, busier one, full of horses, carriages, and carts. "Long Ditch," said Ridkin. "That idea with the horses was a good 'un, as it happens. You're not as dumb as you look. Not quite, anyway. Let's get out of here and find the palace."

"Who's this Rondine?" asked William, recalling the name the men had called Ridkin.

"What? Oh that. It's just a nickname. It's nothing. Come on, it's this way."

They reached the palace gates early in the afternoon and William handed Ridkin the groats he'd need should their horses turn up. After showing the guards the Earl's letter with its grand looking seal, the men directed them in different directions; William towards the main service entrance with instructions to find the First Minister's office, and Ridkin to a low-fenced area just inside the palace grounds. It seemed William would need to go ahead alone.

"Be sure to ask for clear directions at every turn. You're bound to get lost otherwise, and I can't come to rescue your pathetic arse in there," said Ridkin, who looked little convinced that William could manage it. "The place is ginormous."

He asked the first people he met, a pair of women in maids' uniform, and received directions in an accent he could barely make out. As Ridkin had feared, he got lost. Almost nobody had the time of day for a confused stranger, and when he got help, well, each person contradicted the last. Trying to retrace his steps, he made further mistakes, passing bustling kitchens, laundries, the armoury, a library, and a courtyard full of soldiers at rest. Everyone rushed about looking busy, or important, or both. Everywhere looked the same. He tracked along dim corridors, climbed up, then down narrow stairways, and at last stood before a small door through which he would have to crouch to pass. He debated for a full minute whether to open it, but felt desperate to deliver the letter and get out, so decided that if he were to enter somewhere he should not, he would at least be confident in doing it. So, summoning up that confidence, he opened the door and walked through it. Moments later, four men pointed knives at his throat. They had the cold, calculating faces of born killers, and appeared less than content to see him.

"And who, pray, are you?" shouted an indignant and entitled sounding voice. Looking up, William had time to observe that the speech had some relationship to a bald, bearded, and regal looking figure sitting on an ornate chair. His profile looked familiar. Could it be...?

"Mubble fubbles," he whispered, before someone grabbed, hooded, and bundled him away.

# Five

As William's eyes adjusted to the light, he took in a low, windowless space with clean, whitewashed stone walls. What faint flickering illumination there was came from recessed torches that lined one of the longer walls and the red glow of a brazier. Opposite, was a row of frescoes depicted people being subjected to the full gamut of torments, and on the far wall, polished tools hung on neat rows of hooks, reflecting the torchlight in what, in a different setting, might have been pleasing. If you liked that kind of thing. Chained to a bench with a headache to wake the Stars, William, in his current state of rising terror and confusion, did not.

"Is this a traitor I see before me?" asked a rasping voice from just behind him. "Do you know what King Inglebert does with traitors?" The man's huge face loomed close to William's, his breath bringing an unwelcome stink of onions and turnips. "He has them boiled alive in a kettle. That's what he does. We like kettles, oh yes, and not just for making nettle tea! Now tell me, boy, who sent you?"

William tried to mouth some words, but his dry throat had constricted and refused to generate sound. He struggled to draw breath. His reward for not speaking was a heavy slap to the face.

"This will get very uncomfortable for you if you don't start talking," said the voice.

"Where… am… I?" was all William could manage, and for that, he received another stinging blow. He found himself shaking.

"You are in the Tower of Ludnam, my man, and in deep trouble. Few men ever walk out of this room with a full set of parts still attached, so get ready for a long night. My advice, for what it's worth, is to be stoic. That's how a guest last week explained it to me. Carpe diem, seize the day, he said, just as I seized his liver. I get all sorts in here, and like to think I provide a good, personalised service. Anyway, how about the two of us getting nice and comfy before this fire over here? We can soon warm up and have a friendly chat. I'm known as a caring, sensitive torturer. You do realise this is what we are doing here, I hope?"

"No." said William.

"A man of few words, then? Hmm. By the way, do you like what I've done with this room? The clean lines, the use of muted colours, the sense of space?"

"It's shit."

"Oh dear, and I thought we were going to get along. Never mind. Now, I am obliged to say that I will be asking you for feedback on completion of our, how shall I describe it, service today? Can I report that you are happy to help?"

"Get stood on! And let me out of here. I've done nothing. Didn't you find the letter I was carrying?"

Whack. William received another slap.

"In here, you speak when asked. And it's me what asks the questions, oh yes."

The voice belonged to a giant of a man, pierced and hairless with the red cross of Anglonia tattooed across his crown. Below his tattoo covered neck, he wore a plain woollen jerkin and an immaculate leather apron. On the backs of his fingers, he had the words MUMY and DADY traced in black ink.

"Oh, I'm sorry, it's me that's being rude. I haven't introduced myself yet. Everyone in the trade calls me Ballache for reasons that will become apparent. Feel free to call me Arthur if that makes you more comfortable."

The man, known as Ballache, beckoned an assistant and together they dragged William's table over to the brazier. He continued talking in the same amiable manner, as if he were an innkeeper showing a valued guest to his room for the night. "You know, everyone thinks my job is easy. Don't get me wrong. I love what I do, and I'm a real people person, but I always imagined working in a fine tavern serving quality imported wines, or something to do with travel. Well, it's not easy, I can assure you. I have to listen to people moaning at me all day. Between the poor buggers they bring me and the officials what tell me what I need to find out, all I hear is moan, moan, moan. I mean, we all need a bit of recognition from time to time. Don't you agree?"

As he prepared the tools of his trade, the knives, pokers, saws, and pliers, he sang a pleasing ditty that William recognised as a nonsense rhyme from his childhood.

"Here comes the King with his arse on fire…"

The man took William through his array of implements, explaining the finer points of each. He held one up. "Look at this one. See the beauty of its crafting, the articulation, the lines. A sign of a master blacksmith, I'd say. It's for crushing the larger teeth at the back of your mouth. We shall start there, oh yes, and these others here are for breaking open the little ones at the front, one by one. They hurt the most, so I am told. Now, why don't you tell your friend Arthur the truth? Who sent you to kill the King?"

"Nobody!" His breath rasped in his throat. "I am on an errand for Lord John Scratchface…" he stopped to breathe. "…of Ebury with a letter for his Majesty. But, well…, I just took a few false turns. I get confused with left and right. Check the letter…" He gulped another breath. "Please. It's simple. You can see that, can't you?"

"See it? I only see a lying, conniving, dirty bastard of an assassin before me. Nobody told me about no letter. Scratchface is behind all this, then. Lovely jubbly, that is a surprise. His Majesty will be so happy with me for uncovering this plot against him. And my family will be so proud. Now tell me, who else is involved? How was you plotting to do the deed? Tell me, or the agony starts right now."

He'd made a simple mistake, and now he faced punishment with torture? He fought to control his rising panic and a surprising vision came to him: of his father shaking that old grey head of his in a sad and gentle reproach, sitting on his battered three-legged stool. At least the old man had passed and would never know the shame of him being held in the Tower.

"Well?"

"But I'm no assassin," he shouted. "Why aren't you listening?"

Ballache sighed. "Oh dear. Let me explain how things work here. I ask a question and you give me a truthful answer. It's easy. Shall we try again?"

"I'm telling the truth. What more can I say?"

"Ah, but it's not the truth what's written on this slate."

"What *is* written on there?"

"I'm not allowed to tell you *that*. More than my job's worth."

"What? That makes no sense. Isn't there only one truth? Anything else is, well, untruth." He took a deep breath. "Wasn't it Aristopheles who said, *What is false says of that which is that it is not, or of that which is not that it is; and what is true says of that which is that it is, or of that which is not that it is not.*"

"Priest on a donkey! What does it even mean?"

"It means the truth is independent of what we say about it."

"But I say 'tis not."

"It is!"

"And yet, I appear to be the one holding the implements."

"This is how I see it," said William, getting into flow. "If I tell you the objective truth, I get tortured and then boiled alive as an assassin. If I give you your version of the truth, do I still get tortured?"

"No. I mean yes. Maybe just a bit, you know, for appearances."

"A pox on appearances!"

"No need to be like that. Let's try again. How did you plan to kill King Inglebert?"

Before the torturer could get any further, or William could panic any more, the door to the room opened with a loud crash and a flame haired court jester entered, with two soldiers behind him. "Stop!" the man yelled, in a voice like that of a woman. Could this get any weirder?

"What a fantastic idea," said Ballache. "The delicious irony of me inserting a hot blade under his fingernails while someone provides entertainment? Perfect! Let's get this show started…"

"You will do nothing of the sort!" commanded the intruder, perhaps forgetting that wearing stockings and pointy shoes with bells looked less than commanding. "The man speaks the truth. He is just a messenger, and besides, the King has another use for him."

Ballache folded his arms and blocked the jester's way. "Oh, yes? And what would *that* be?"

The jester wandered over to the far wall and took down an assortment of knives and other sharp, pointy implements. He juggled them, his gaze elsewhere. "I don't see how that's your concern. Guards. Take this man back to the King."

He tossed the various items he was juggling over his shoulder, and they thudded into the nearest closed door in a neat, heart-shaped pattern.

As the soldiers released and dragged William out of the chamber, Ballache shook his head with not a little disappointment etched on his face. "But we were just getting to know one another."

~~~

Leaving his charge propped up by the soldiers outside, Feydor entered the King's chambers and discovered him completing his easement[24]. Time hadn't been kind to the obese, red-bearded, near-bald king. Gravity even less so. He bowed. "Your Grace."

A gentle cough from the other end of the room gave away the presence of the oily Ignatius Stackpole, religious leader of the Kingdom and, by royal appointment, official pain in the arse. Feydor despised the man almost as much as his own mother. Boglets, he'd been hoping to get King Inglebert alone. Feydor nodded a polite greeting toward the priest and received only an icy stare in return.

"Sire, I have something to put to you, something that may cure your dark mood."

"Sun and Moons, Fool, what the Stars are you doing here?" said the priest, his mouth drawn into a sneer. "His Grace didn't send for you."

The King looked exhausted. Feydor smiled to himself; they'd either been performing an immoral act or else the King had a new medical ailment.

"I'm so sorry, my gracious liege. Should I rejourn later?"

"What the blazes does that mean? You are here now, so may as well speak while I dress. This had better be worthwhile, though. I have no wish
~~~

to hear your fripperies this morrow, much less your opinions. Now help me with my tunic, both of you."

Feydor and Stackpole helped the King dress while Feydor continued.

"Very well. Sire, I have a most diverting partition to propose, something that will curdle your Grace's fancy." Feydor shook his bauble, jangling the bells for effect, as he examined his royal patron and tried to gauge his mood. The King stared ahead, his face a mask of misery. The way the wart on his bulbous nose was becoming inflamed and oozing pus might have had something to do with it.

"Have the surgeon brought to my presence. I would consult him about my face."

"As you wish, my liege."

As the King slowly eased himself onto a chair, Feydor bowed, went to the door, and relayed the order to the privy member there. He returned and then paused for thought. How to proceed? Might he play on the King's bottomless vanity? Or he could he entice him with a promise of better amorous relations? Yes, that sounded most likely to work, ruled as he was, by the shrivelled thing between his legs. And yes, the Fool had seen it.

Queen Ruthenia, dressed in the latest of elaborate gowns direct from Italica, entered with Jane[25], her own jester, and sat next to her husband. Jane, in turn, sat at her feet and made hen-like clucking noises while she scratched at her arms, causing Feydor to experience a rare twinge of sympathy for the simple woman, who got treated as little more than a pet. Filthy scampered over to her and curled in her lap, much to Jane's delight.

Feydor bowed to the Queen and remained low until she inclined her head to show he could continue. "My Queen, may I say how radiantly you illuminate our day once again? Your colour today is vermillion, is it not?"

Queen Ruthenia made the slightest of nods in recognition of the due fawning he'd given her.

Addressing King Inglebert, "If it pleases Your Grace, I have heard tidings of a hot spring in the mountains of Sardonica, the water of which possesses many unusual properties. It is said that it can make you twice the man, if you understand my meaning?"

Before the King could respond, the weaselly Stackpole interrupted. "Your Grace, if I may speak, surely the Fool's tidings are false. How dare he bring this pathetic attempt at seeking favour?"

Feydor, anticipating something of the sort, persisted, warming to the challenge. He had the ace card up his tunic sleeve. "For women, besides its ability to prevent inconvenient headaches, this water is also a powerful aphrodisiac. I understand that it even promotes fertility." He made the faintest of complicit nods in the direction of the Queen, which, if she were to take offence at this, could make things tricky. The King glanced toward her, his eyebrows raised in hope. In return, she smiled in such a way as to say, *In your sad regal dreams, my dear husband.*

"Your Grace, I must protest. This is patent nonsense," said Stackpole.

"Shut up Ignatius," said Inglebert.

Stackpole shot Feydor a glance of ice. The King wasn't to be diverted. Feydor had hit the right chord and now just needed to focus attention on the details. He gave himself a metaphorical pat on the back.

The King's first minister entered, and Inglebert motioned for him to approach. "Lord Crumbwell, the fool has an idea that interests us. I expect you to help with the details of how we can bring it about. Fool, explain."

Feydor outlined his plan while First Minister Thomas Crumbwell listened. "Well, your Grace, may I suggest that a military operation would be ill advised, since the army is already engaged with the Albian hordes, and our last attempt to use mercenaries ended in a diplomatic disaster with the Scandi. No, if I may make a humble suggestion, as your mere servant, your best chance of obtaining a supply of this water is perhaps the simplest: to send someone to trade for it. If I understand it correctly, the spring of which the Fool speaks is in the stronghold of Queen Nannua of Sardonica. Is that not so, Fool?"

"Indeed, Sir Lord Crumb-Crumb! You are well informed as ever," said Feydor, bowing and shaking his bauble again, but happy to let someone else run with the nonsense and lead the King in the right direction.

"In that case, we need a high-ranking functionary, or at least a senior messenger, to go to Sardonica and bear the request, perhaps in the form of a trade mission."

Feydor grabbed his chance. "Your Grace, might I make one more humble suggestion?"

Crumbwell raised an eyebrow, but the King signalled for him to proceed.

"I have the perfect man to send on such a quest, and he is waiting outside this very chamber. May I summon him to your presence?" The King made the lightest of nods, which Feydor took as assent, stepping to open the door once more and gesturing for the soldiers holding William to bring in their prisoner. They led William through and made him lie prostrate before the King.

"What? This is the man who tried to kill me! Take him and boil him alive now! Fool, you will pay for this!"

"Well, sire," said Crumbwell on cue. "We checked the letter he was carrying, and it is authentic. He is a messenger from Lord Scratchface, who, it seems, got lost in the passages of the palace. Of course, if it is your Grace's pleasure that I have him boiled, I will take care of it this instant."

"A messenger, is that so?" He made a long kingly pause, appearing to weigh up the options with all the studied wisdom that he could affect, which wasn't a lot. "I suppose we might allow him to live. Shall we send him alone on this quest or should we make this an official delegation?"

"Sire, delegations can be rather expensive to organise, so I suggest instead sending him with an introductory letter. A simple invitation to accept special trading status, or some such, should suffice. Perhaps we could also give him more gravitas by knighting him." Feydor stared hard for the slightest sign of irony in the minister's expression, but saw nothing.

"Excellent idea, Crumbwell. Hand me my ceremonial sword."

"Here it is, your Grace."

"Well, boy, are you going to lie there all day, or will you step forward to serve your king?"

William appeared to not realise he was being addressed and had to be dragged in clear disbelief into the correct kneeling position, ready to receive his inexplicable knighthood.

"What is your name and from where do you hail?"

"Mubble fubbles. Um… no, sorry, William, sire… from Coxwell near Axeford."

"Cock Swell, fantastic! I dub thee a knight, arise sir William of Cock Swell!"

"I'm sorry. Might I choose a different place to be named after, sire?"

"Hmm, well now. If you care to look, you will find, held very close to your neck, a heavy sword. Do you wish to speculate on how keen is its blade?"

"No no, sorry Your Grace, of course, you are wonderful and most wise. I am at your command."

"Very well then, leave on the morrow for - where was it now? Yes, Sardonica, and don't return without a flask of this water and an agreement for further supplies. Fool, now sing me a merry galliard." And he clapped his hands twice.

As Feydor took his lute and started singing, Thomas Crumbwell led a shocked William away.

~~~

Thomas Crumbwell was a tall, sallow man of around fifty summers with a hook nose and a noticeable stoop. William had heard of him; everyone in the Kingdom had heard of the quiet, determined, and dangerous common born lawyer who the King trusted with his most complex affairs. His power and influence approached that of even the priesthood. He led an awestruck William away to another wing of the palace and invited him to sit outside a large chamber filled with men scribing. A scriptorium. The sound of thirty quills scratching at parchment was like music to William, and he twisted his neck to peer into the room. It might have sounded like a chorus of hoarse frogs to anyone else.

"Ahem," said Crumbwell. "Wait here while I have the necessary documents drawn up."

"Your Grace. Am I to understand that I am commanded by King Inglebert to perform some important quest on his behalf?"

"Yes. What of it?" the man's manner was brisk and to the point.

"Might I be informed what this quest entails?"

"Really? Oh, very well."
~~~

Crumbwell described the trading mission that was required of William, whose jaw dropped deeper with each sentence. By the end, his lower mandible hung low enough to dredge a river.

"Is that clear now?"

He shut his mouth and swallowed. "Mubble fubbles," he moaned to nobody in particular.

"What?"

"Oh, quite clear, Your Grace. I *think*."

"Excellent." Crumbwell disappeared inside the scriptorium and left William to ponder his situation. In the space of one week, he'd gone from arriving at Ebury as a complete nobody to sitting in the King's grandest palace as a knight of the realm and being tasked with travelling halfway across the great continent of Yorpia on an important trade mission. Wouldn't Verity and everyone else in Coxwell appreciate that? Not that he'd yet earned any money or established himself in any way. Still, Trusca wasn't built in a day.

An hour later, Crumbwell appeared again with a clerk who held a sheaf of papers. William rose to his feet, wondering what was coming next. He bit his own cheek to check if it was real.

"Well now, let's first deal with your title. A knighthood generally comes with land and other property, but since you are yet unproven, that will have to wait[26]. Here this is the contract agreement. I'm sorry, it is written in Truscan, so you'll have to trust me when I tell you everything is in order and quite regular."

William took the document in hand and scanned down its contents. He'd expected it to be written on everyday paper[27], but the thickness and quality of the parchment they'd used surprised him. "You're paying me how much?"

"Why, is it not sufficient?"

It was more than William could think to earn in a lifetime as a messenger, and more than enough for him to return to free Verity. And he could just imagine everyone's faces when he went back as a knight of the realm! "Um, it's more than enough, my Lord." He continued reading to the end of the document. "But it says here that my title is temporary, to be rescinded on my return to the Kingdom or on the event of my death, whichever comes first. I've never heard of such an arrangement and, well, it's not acceptable."

"You read Truscan? How extraordinary! It changes nothing. That's the agreement. Take it or leave it."

William almost gave in, but a germ of doubt crept into his mind. If they could cheat him on a matter such as this, how else would they seek to beguile him?

"Sorry, I won't accept it, and I won't go on this quest." He folded his arms and stared down into the cold eyes of the First Minister. There was a lot at stake, so he found the courage to stand his ground. After what seemed an age, Crumbwell's mouth curled up at the edges in what might have been a smile, but for the evident irritation the rest of his face portrayed. "Very well. Clerk, you will prepare me a fresh copy of this licence removing the rescinding paragraph."

"My Lord," said the clerk, bowing.

"Next, we have letters and official documents of royal patronage and the letter of passage[28]. These should smooth your way past the various officials you will encounter, along with a few coins, of course. And this last one is the most important: it introduces you to Queen Nannua of the Janasà and establishes you as the King's representative to trade for a vial of aphrodisiac water in return for concessions to sell into the Anglonian markets for wine and other produce. Please sit a few minutes longer while I have your title redraughted."

"What about a knight's sword? And chain mail? And armour?"

Crumbwell smiled. "Do you have any training at all in the arts of combat? Fencing, archery, jousting?"

William shook his head.

"What about horsemanship? Anything at all useful to fighting?"

"Um, no. I'm a messenger."

"Of course. You're a messenger." He sniffed. "Very well. The danger with a sword is that, without instruction, you are more likely to injure yourself than anyone else. Chain-mail makes sense, but armour? Do you have any idea what a suit weighs? I thought not. Besides, it takes weeks to make anything that fits, and it's quite impractical for travelling. I think you'd better get used to the notion that your title is more ceremonial than useful."

The clerk returned with a money belt of coins and a fresh document, which William checked over and then signed. Just then, the jester character showed up. "Ah Feydor," said Crumbwell. "I've just furnished Sir William with everything he needs for his official mission. Can I leave to take care of anything else he requires?"

Feydor bowed. "Yes, of course, Your Grace."

"Very well. Sir William, I leave you in the... capable hands of Feydor. Good luck with your travels. And Feydor, take him to the barber. His beard is a disgrace to the realm." He smiled, made a mock bow, and turned back into the scriptorium.

"Sir William. Come, we have much to discuss," said Feydor as he placed an arm around William and led the way toward the nearest exit. The arm felt as reassuring as the wing of a vulture around the shoulder of a rabbit.

"What about a squire?" asked William. "A knight always has a squire."

"Umm... did you have someone in mind?"

He hesitated. He had someone in mind. Much as Ridkin irritated him, the boy knew how to handle himself. He took a leap of faith. "There's Ridkin. Ridkin Fairchild. We could ask him to go with me."

"That's not how things work here. The royal court commands people to do things. It doesn't ask them, pretty please with pink ribbons. Do you understand that?"

"I suppose. Good luck commanding Ridkin."

Feydor's face lit up. "I do love a challenge. Where is this Ridkin?"

William led the jester to the palace gate and looked about for his companion, who, he noted, had their horses with him again. He bade Feydor to wait and approached Ridkin, who was chatting with a pair of women waiting in the line for alms, the three of them thick with the guttural Ludnam accent. It omitted half the consonants while mangling, to the point of obliteration, the ones that remained. The pair of them laughed at something Ridkin said. Once again, he envied Ridkin's effortless ability to talk to people. Was this a skill that could be studied?

Ridkin's back was to William, but one woman spotted him standing there listening. "Pardon me sir, you must be the one what he calls William." She said it with a kind smile and a sparkle in her eye. "Called you a right toff, he did. Well, that's as may be, but you're a nice-looking boy. What do you think, Agnes?"

"I wouldn't kick him out of *my* cot." William blushed seven shades of crimson.

"Your friend says you're a proper one for your books. Care to read to me at bedtime?"

She winked.

"If you wish it, good mistress," he replied, uncertain. "Do you mean this very eve?"

"Shut up William," said Ridkin. "You're not supposed to answer that kind of question."

"Ah, the lady is being rhetorical."

"Retor what?"

"Come on, Janet, we ain't got all day." The two curtseyed and left.

Ridkin turned and said, "William, you've been in there for hours. I didn't know whether to wait or nadger off. Did you deliver the message?"

"Um, yeah, that and a lot more. A few things happened. I got lost. I know that's not a surprise, but I sort of stumbled into the King's court and got dragged off to a dungeon. They were about to crush all my teeth when a jester rescued me."

"Are you having a laugh? Expect me to believe that?"

"Wait. It gets crazier. The jester got His Majesty to command me on a quest to Sardonica. You and I are to ready ourselves for a long journey. Thomas Crumbwell, that's the First Minister - I met him too - he's given us letters of introduction and enough money to get there."

"Sorry, but what's this got to do with yours truly?" asked Ridkin.

"You're coming with me, of course. This gentleman over here is Feydor. He will explain everything."

He pointed to Feydor, who bowed and waved while grinning over his bauble.

Ridkin spun around to walk away, but he ran into two burly guards who escorted him back to the gate and presented him to the jester. "Thank you, gentlemen. So, Ridkin Fairchild. Ever been to parts foreign?"

~~~

The light flickered, throwing garish and appropriately witchy shadows of the room's two occupants onto the walls. The stump of a freshly cut tree stood on the central stone dais, the smell of pine and wood sap still fresh in the air. A yellow-green image of his brother Jasper's face hung suspended above the chunk of timber, and his disembodied voice echoed around the room. "Good morrow, mother," said Jasper. "How may I serve?"

This, a trunk call, was his mother's preferred way to speak over a distance.

"Hear that, Feydor?" asked his mother, Imelda. "That's what a proper son says to his poor mother."

Feydor suppressed the urge to use sarcasm as a response to this. Jasper had none of the pressures he was under, what with the King, the priesthood and the ever more ridiculous demands she made on him.

As Filthy chittered away on Feydor's shoulder, Imelda continued. "I need you to meet up with a pair of travellers on their way to Ianua and guide them to the citadel of the Janasà in Sardonica." She described the other details of Feydor's plan, while giving the jester none of the credit for any of it. He took the lack of recognition in his stride; after all, this was his mother through and through.

"Why would the Janasà let us near?"

"They are looking for a mortal man, pale of skin, blonde of hair, and so on, to extract their crystal from its cavern. I'm guessing they will welcome anyone that fits the bill. Feydor, tell him who I've got lined up."

Feydor described William and Ridkin.

"A perfect plan, mother," said Jasper with apparent enthusiasm. "Your genius is undimmed."

Knowing Jasper as he did, he said, "By the way, the King knighted William."
~~~

"Really? A knight?" replied the disembodied voice. Even from a distance, Jasper's face looked like thunder. "And where did this William learn swordcraft, archery, jousting?"

This was Jasper's Achilles heel. Not being of high birth, they had refused him entry to knight school, despite being as good as any actual knight with a whole range of weapons.

"That's just the thing. He didn't. He's a messenger, although, in truth, not even that. Thomas Crumbwell suggested it as a joke, but the King took it seriously. I'm sorry, Jasper."

Imelda stepped in. "Jasper, you'll do this for me and do it well. Once the mission is done and I have the crystal, you can kill William or anything else you want to do with him. Until then, he's off limits. Understood?"

When Jasper didn't at first reply, she said again, louder, "Do you understand me, Jasper?"

"Yes, mother."

Feydor held Filthy just a bit too hard, and the creature responded by biting his thumb, causing him to let go. The monkey leapt toward Jasper's flickering green image. Before anyone could stop him, he jumped at the tree-stump and a loud crack was followed by a puff of acrid smoke as the connection was cut. The creature made a shrill shriek. Feydor smiled. Surely now Imelda would smite the beast and get him off his back. Instead, she sent a bolt of energy at Feydor, who yelped in surprise.

"There, there, Filthy," she cooed. She picked him up and held him like a babe in her arms. "Did that nasty Feydor let you get hurt? Diddums. Don't worry, mummy's going to punish him. I promise she is."

# Six

Early the following morning, the newly beardless William bobbed along on Milly down the Putnam Road toward the city walls. Progress was slow through the crowds, even more so given the liveried soldiers that flanked them as escorts. Ridkin had fiercely resisted joining William on the journey, but it turned out Feydor knew Travis, the man Ridkin owed money to, and had used a range of bribes and threats to ensure the young man's compliance.

"You know, he even threatened my mam?" said Ridkin, shaking his head. "I mean, who does that?"

"Sorry, it's my fault. I shouldn't have mentioned you."

"Well, I'm stuck with you now. May as well make the most of it. Who knows, it might turn out to be fun?"

Leaving Ludnam via Southgate they followed the Great South Road as it bore them through a dense area of low-grade dwellings that became ever poorer and rundown as they went. The stench of poverty hung like a threat in the air, making William reach unthinking for the money belt beneath his heavy woollen cloak. It contained more gold than he'd seen in his lifetime. The horses trudged through the foul puddles, kicking up a spray of sludge, and William offered a prayer of thanks to be a few feet above it. Every so often, they came across entire families camped at the sides of the road, huddled under thin blankets, faces bent with cold, hunger, and hopelessness. Children ran about playing games, their filthy hair in knots, their skin thick with dirt and their bare feet splashing in the muck. To them, the terrible conditions must have seemed horribly normal.

"Priest on a pony," said William. "Tell me this isn't happening."

"Welcome to my world," replied Ridkin. "Or at least what used to be my world. A right pen and ink[29], ain't it? Do you blame me for getting out?"

As they left the city limits, the escorts turned back, and they were on their own. William realised his shoulders had been clinging to his neck and tried to breathe the tension of the last few days away. The road took them up a hill and past a row of decomposing corpses hanging from gibbets, each with a neat notice nailed to the frame beneath giving the man's name and his crime.

"Wait," said William, who, spying the scrawny, near-naked body of a child, dismounted to get a closer look. He stared in horror.

"What's it say?"

"This is Terrence Stevenson, eight years old[30], executed for stealing a lord's loaf. How's that possible?"

Ridkin shrugged. "What's so surprising?" he asked.

"It's unjust."

"So? There's the few what makes the rules and the rest of us what takes them. That's how it is."

"Well, it shouldn't be. There must be something I can do to change it. I'm a knight of the realm now."

Ridkin scoffed. "Yeah, good luck with that."

The flat, straight road, built centuries earlier by the Truscans during their long occupation of Anglonia, carried every class of traveller: farmers with turnips and other vegetables to sell in the city, pilgrims heading for or returning from the continent of Yorpia, priests, soldiers, and merchants. Everyone looked busy, purposeful, confident, and William felt every inch the proud knight on his way to foreign lands. Until his horse stumbled and he fell off, causing Ridkin to howl with laughter. William remounted, his pride hurt, and his cloak mucky, and said nothing.

They paused for a water stop in the town of Standingbourne and as they set off, two women approached on horseback.

"Hail kind sirs," said the elder of them. "Please pretend as like you know us. Those two coves behind have followed us down from Ludnam, and I don't much like the look of them." She unfurled a smile that started as a line and expanded in all directions, pulleys and guys sliding into place, until it seemed wider than her head, full of even white teeth[31]. For a moment, it lit the space around her like a shooting star, then faded.

"Sorry?" said William, transfixed by the rosy fullness of her mouth.

"Don't be thick William, two ruffians are making the ladies uncomfortable. Hi, I'm Ridkin. This here's Sir William."

"A knight? Perfect!" exclaimed the woman, clapping once. "You can protect us. I'm Helena, and this is our Matilda. Greet the gentlemen, Tilda." She nudged the girl with her elbow.

"Alright pet?" said Matilda, smiling.

"Not so familiar, Tilda! It's not seemly." said her mother, looking stern.

Matilda scowled. "Oh, very well. Good morrow, kind sirs." She put on a smile and performed as much of a curtsey as she could muster from her saddle. "Happen that's how they speak in these parts, mother."

"Who is it what's bothering you?" asked Ridkin. "The dodgy pair thirty paces back?"

William turned in his mount and saw a pair of rough looking types following on horses not far behind. One was tall in his saddle with an eye patch, riding a white stallion, and the other, smaller, sporting a flat hat with a feather on a grey mare. Both tapped their hats in greeting, and William made as if to speak with them, but Ridkin stayed his reins.

"Don't Will," he said. "I seen their sort before, the type as rides about on the roads out of the city looking for easy prey to rob, or worse. If we ignore them, they'll get bored soon enough and drop back."

William took in the two women, both in modest travelling attire, long skirts, and woollen mantles with their long hair pinned up under bonnets, as per the custom. "Mistress Helena, excuse my boldness, but you do not look at all old enough to have such a daughter as this."

Matilda snorted. Helena smiled, touching a strand of loose hair below her bonnet. "That's too kind, sir. From where do you gentlemen hail?"

She spoke well, with a distinct but gentle northern accent, her voice deep in pitch and flowing like cool water over stones. While her face was far from perfect, it being a smidge too long with a nose a touch too broad beneath eyes too far apart, she was attractive, nonetheless. Not in the same league as Verity, of course, but he liked the way her bright eyes for a moment captured his own, and he felt at once comfortable with her. Her daughter had the same eyes but also a button nose that shone pink in the cool air and little sticky-out ears. William supposed she'd be a beauty a few years on.

"I'm from the castle at Ebury. My name's Sir William of Coxwell. This is my squire Ridkin."

"Have you long been a knight?" asked Helena. "And please forgive me, but you are not dressed in the manner of one who is knighted."

Ridkin sniggered. "The King dubbed him not two days since, and they never bothered to give him chain mail and stuff."

"All the same, I'm sure you trained many a year for the honour. Are we to call you Sir William?"

"Sorry. A simple William will do."

"Has tha' slain many dragons, Simple William?" asked Matilda. "Happen one made that cut on your cheek."

He couldn't help but reach to feel the healing gash.

"Tilda, show more respect," said Helena to her daughter.

"We're slaying our first dragons next week," said Ridkin, glancing over his shoulder. "Look, let's concentrate on getting some distance from those two." He sped up to a canter and nodded with satisfaction as the men fell behind. "I'll be happier when we gets to a town."

They reached Trotbury as dusk stole the best of the light and stashed it away for the next day. The two pairs split off and bade each other a pleasant evening.

~~~

The Old Squire's Inn appeared comfortable enough, its whitewashed exterior tidy and its façade decked with a winter web of bare ivy. Fresh lavender scented rushes covered the floor, and there were separate sleeping quarters available, at least for travellers who could pay a little more for them.

"Now *this* is an inn, wouldn't you say?" asked William, nodding to himself.

"Well, I'd be saying the chuffing obvious," replied Ridkin, a slight sneer on his face.
~~~

"You have a disarming eloquence."

"Yeah. Whatever." He batted the comment away. "Let's get something down our necks."

They jostled their way through a throng of other guests and settled themselves on either side of a long bench with jugs of fresh, aromatic ale.

William sat and fidgeted, tapping his fingers on the table, as yet unsure what their relationship was. A knight was a far superior rank to a squire, so why didn't he feel confident in addressing Ridkin? Not that the younger man made it easy. Before he could ponder the matter further, their earlier travel companions, Helena and Matilda, arrived.

"Gentlemen, may we join you?" asked Helena. William and Ridkin shuffled up to make room.

Ridkin glanced around. "Those are the same pair watching you again." To William, he said, "Give me a couple of groats, will you? I'm going to sort them out." He rose to his feet and wandered outside, leaving William, who, unsure of what to say, shut his mouth and waited.

Ridkin re-entered the inn and meandered over to the serving bench. The young man bought two jars of ale and sidled up to the men, offering them the drinks and engaging them in indistinct chatter. They laughed at something Ridkin said and slapped him on the back.

Ridkin sat with them again. "They won't be bothering you now," he said.

"What did you do?" asked William.

"I just got a little something from the stable-lads. Something what we give to horses when they've a colic."

"And?"

"I slipped it in their ales, didn't I?"

"So, they will be discomforted?" asked William.

"Yeah, I should say so," replied Ridkin, sniggering.

A serving boy brought a large jug of ale over with fresh mugs for the new arrivals. "There's potage followed by venison stew. If you want it," he said.

"What if we don't want it?" said Matilda. "The stew, that is."

The server stared, expressionless, and Matilda giggled to herself.

All four agreed to what was on offer, and the boy left them to talk.

"So, what, pray thee, are a knight and his squire doing in these parts?" asked Helena.

"We are on important business, a long and arduous quest, for the King, no less," William told her.

Ridkin objected. "Will, you can't go blabbing that to all and sundry. You'll attract attention."

"What is this important business for the King? And why am I sensing all is not well in the realm?" asked Helena.

"Go on, then," said Ridkin. "You may as well tell them."

"A week ago, I started a new job as a messenger to Lord Ebury..."

"*Apprentice* messenger," cut in Ridkin.

"Alright, apprentice messenger. Ridkin and I took a letter from the Earl to the King and got caught up in something I don't really understand, orchestrated by, as far as I can tell, a ridiculous court jester. And now I'm on one of those old-fashioned quests to a distant land. Although, rather than a quest, they called it a trading mission, whatever that means. Ridkin here, as you may have worked out, isn't so happy to be my squire."

"Too right," said Ridkin. "I'm not here by choice."

"It sounds exciting," said Matilda. "What quest? What distant land?"

"The King needs something from the island of Sardonica, something of a delicate personal nature. I don't think I can say any more than that."

"We may as well tell them the whole story," said Ridkin. "See, they sold us some cock and bull about how the King wants aphrodisiac water to help sort out his love life. And this pillock here swallowed every word of it."

"I see." A look of sceptical surprise played itself over Helena's face.

"And listen, here's the daftest bit," said Ridkin, shaking his head. "We are to knock oh-so politely on the door of the Queen of the Janasà in her mountain citadel and kindly ask her for some passion inflaming water. I mean, have you ever heard anything so dumb? Magic doesn't exist and the Janasà are just children's tales."

If Ridkin had expected confirmation from the two women, it didn't arrive. Instead, a pregnant pause long enough to deliver triplets broke only when Helena told him, "Magic is real, Ridkin, as real as the bench we are sitting on. As are the Janasà."

"What *are* Janasà, anyway, when they're at home?" asked Ridkin.

"Strange green creatures. Waist high and none too pretty at that."

"Ever seen one?" Ridkin challenged.

"Well, no."

"How do you know they're real, then? And aphrodisiac water? Can you honestly say that's a thing?"

"I don't have to justify myself to you," replied Helena. "Come, Tilda, we'll leave these fine gentlemen to their ale." She stood and turned, then stopped in her tracks, looking concerned towards the serving bench where the two ruffians were still standing, staring in their direction. "Perhaps we should just stay here for a bit," she said, looking worried, and sat back down.

"Ridkin," asked William. "Why are the two stooges still there? Are you sure you gave them a good dose of that horse cure?"

"Of course, I'm sure. They must have worked out the drinks were dodgy. It's fine, we can still deal with them. Anyway, about magic. I ain't never seen it and it don't exist, leastways not in the part of Ludnam where I was born."

"You've not said much," said Helena to William. "What do *you* think? Is there magic in the world?"

"He only believes what he's read in old books," said Ridkin.

"Let him speak."

"Definitely not. The universe functions according to great laws." William was warming to one of his favourite topics. "Anything that looks magical is just stuff we don't understand yet; laws we haven't uncovered."

"So, it might exist?" asked Helena. "Except that you, William, don't understand it. Is that what you're saying?"

"But it wouldn't be magic. Give me an example of *actual* magic. Have you ever seen any?"

"It's real. That's all I'll say to the likes of those who won't listen."

"And what of your travels?" said Ridkin, moving the conversation away and onto safer ground. "Where are you going and on what business?"

Matilda answered first. "We're heading for Trusca. That's in Italica, in case you didn't know. Actually, it's still in Italica even if you did know.

Anyway, we are looking for my father, who we've not heard owt from since two winters past."

"Are you worried about him?" asked William.

"Well, of course," replied Helena. "I worry if he might be in trouble, or worse. And whether we'll have brass[32] enough to live on if we can't find him."

"What will you do when you find him?" asked Ridkin, interested.

"Bring him home, of course," said a confident Matilda. Helena looked less certain, but said nothing.

"What's he like, your father?"

"Father's a master mason. One of the best. And wherever he goes, he finds interesting things to bring home. Carved bones, simple pieces of jewellery. And lots of amazing stones and crystals. Here, let me show you."

She reached to her waist and lifted the small purse she had hanging there. She spilled the coloured stones over the bench, little rocks of all sizes and hues. "They can tell your destiny. If you let them." She frowned at her mother as she said this.

"They're proper nice," said Ridkin "So many colours."

The serving boy brought more ale over, along with trenchers[33] of venison stew. As Ridkin noisily tucked in, Matilda scooped her stones into their pouch.

"You'll have to cross Gallia to get to Italica. How are you getting there?" asked William.

"We'll take a ship to Gallia then seek the pilgrim trail. We'll find plenty of company, so I've heard."

"We're doing the same," said Ridkin. "Why don't you travel with us?"

"Can we sail with them, mummy? Please? What harm can it do?"

"Well, perhaps we can. If it's not too much trouble."

"They're welcome, right Sir William?" asked Ridkin.

"Of course," replied William, who wasn't feeling so sure.

Ridkin and Matilda slipped into comfortable conversation, with Matilda talking about her stones, and Ridkin of his love for horses. In contrast, William struggled. The early warmth and playful interest Helena had shown had turned into a reserved distance. She looked about, biting her nails, and touching her scalp as though checking for invisible loose strands of hair. He reached for small talk.

"The climate in these parts seems more clement than further north, do you not agree?" he tried.

"Indeed," she replied.

Not very helpful. Out of ideas, he fell in to listening to the younger pair. By now, Matilda had emptied her pouch out again and was nudging and turning the little stones around for viewing.

"What's that turquoise one?" asked Ridkin. "It's not the biggest, but it reflects the firelight in an interesting way."

"Happen it might be amethyst or sapphire. I can't rightly say, but it's my favourite."

"And you say you can predict a fortune with them?" asked Ridkin.

"Aye. Should I tell you yours?"

Helena was quick to interrupt. "I'm sorry. My daughter is so easily distracted by anything mystical. Why, last year she thought she saw the future in the flight of birds."

"I did!"

"Sorry, Mistress Helena, but I want to know. My fortune, I mean," said Ridkin. "Please go ahead, Mistress Matilda."

Despite himself, William was fascinated to discover what the stones would tell him about his surly squire. It seemed harmless enough, and who could say? It might be revealing. Matilda scooped them into a cupped palm, breathed over them, and, while looking Ridkin in the eyes, let them fall.

"The art is to understand that what falls toward the centre tells me the main influencing forces in your life. Let's start around the edges. These larger stones tell me you have a tough exterior born from bad experiences."

"That's right enough," said Ridkin.

"Then see how the brighter colours have fallen a little closer to the middle, like. They suggest you have hidden depths of passion and compassion. Is that true?" She smiled, encouraging him to respond.

"I don't know what you mean," replied Ridkin, speaking behind his hand.

"And happen you will live a long and interesting life." She stared at the duller stones, which had formed a star pattern in the middle. "Oh…" she said and looked up at Ridkin. A flash of understanding passed between them. Matilda looked about to say something important, but held back. "We should speak alone about this."

"Do a reading for Sir William," said Helena.

"But you don't believe in my crystals," said Matilda.

"Humour me this one time. I should like to see what lies in store for our bold knight errant."

"You don't want to know about me," said William, who moved to rise from the table.

It surprised him that Helena touched his arm to stop him. "Tilda, go ahead."

Matilda gathered the stones once more into her hands, breathed on them, and gazed into William's eyes as they cascaded. Time appeared to freeze for an instant and the background conversation fell away as the coloured objects tumbled, intertwined, and rolled, appearing to be pulled into position as if strung on thread with the turquoise one at the centre. He had the impossible impression that they knew where to finish, and that somehow, he himself influenced their motion. A preposterous idea. A yellow stone slid toward him across the table and stopped right on the edge, almost falling before settling. The room hubbub returned, but he dismissed the notion that something other than a simple physical process could be involved. Matilda watched him, an intent look in her eyes like she knew what he'd been thinking.

"Well," she began, leaning forward, "it seems as like the stones have responded to you. How very curious." Her voice sounded older and wiser than before.

"What do they say?" he asked, unable to hide his interest.

"Much. I can see right away you are an ordered person. You like *a place for all things and all things in their proper place*. And you seek always to understand how the world works."

"True enough. I enjoy working in a library." He laughed, trying to lighten the mood. "Although it is odd that the colours and sizes have aligned so."

"You will live long and have children. You will have but one true love, and you will experience much darkness before prevailing."

He supposed that kind of prediction to be the standard patter for a fortune teller, but the tone of authority in her voice kept him curious enough to ask, "What about the one there on the edge?"

"I'm coming to that. Its separation from the other stones means you will love someone far away, and its aspect tells me you will make an important choice. William of Coxwell, you are an intriguing man."

She softened, yawned, and giggled self-consciously, the shy youngster back in the room.

William wanted to dismiss his impression as the silly superstition it surely was. Fortune tellers, like all charlatans, stuck to vague, general predictions, or else prompted their victims for the clues that would make their stories more convincing. And yet, a doubt rolled around in his mind. He hadn't done or said anything to prompt Matilda, and falling objects didn't drop into ordered patterns by chance. That's what the texts of the Grecan mathematicians had convincingly written. Had Matilda somehow made this happen by the way she'd dropped the stones? He'd felt an irresistible urge to look into her eyes at that precise moment, so perhaps, but he didn't think so.

Helena sat, looking right through him.

"Mistress Helena, did you learn what you expected?" he asked.

She brought her focus back into the room and unleashed her smile. "I expected nothing."

"What do the stones say of yourself, anyway?" asked William.

"Mother won't let me tell her fortune, will you, mummy?"

"Certainly not. Please don't take any of this seriously. It's just a parlour trick of my daughter's. That's enough for now Tilda. Gentlemen, we need to rest for the morrow."

"Let us walk you to your room," said Ridkin. "Those men disappeared a while ago, but they won't be far away."

~~~
~~~

William awoke to a cockerel giving of its best and sat up. He twisted to find Ridkin's cot already empty, and in a state of panic that the boy might have upped and left him, raced for the stables. There he discovered Matilda and Helena fussing over their horses, but no Ridkin.

"Good morrow, mistresses. Have you seen Ridkin?"

"Isn't he with you?" asked Helena.

"He was. Look, his horse is still here, so he can't be far away."

He circled around the stables and checked the outhouses that backed onto them. Then he wandered back through the inn, checking for signs of the boy and out into the street beyond. Nothing.

Down in the stables, he took his saddle, and that of Ridkin and ineptly set about fixing them to the horses. "Let me help," said Matilda, who seemed much more accustomed to the task.

The cock crowed again as sunlight shone through a gap in the thatch, picking out the dull metal of the saddle clasps.

"Does he normally do this?" asked Helena. "Disappear off, like?"

"Not since I've known him. I wonder what's happened."

Minutes later, Ridkin arrived, a broad smile on his face and a bruise on his cheek. "Sorry about that," he said, smiling. "I just had to deal with those two thugs from last night. Seems they figured out my trick with their drinks and didn't touch them. I guessed something of the sort so came out before dawn and set up a little welcome for them."

"Where are they now? Are they alive?"

"They're laid out in a field over yonder. I've given them something to remember me by. Right, come on." He looked at the three concerned faces. "What's up? Bit worried, were you?"

"Yes, we *were*," said Matilda. "They could've hurt you. Or killed you. Let me see that bruise." She dabbed at his cheek with a piece of linen she'd produced from a pocket.

"I've had worse," he replied, smiling with a shrug.

"Right, if we've done with beating folk up, let's get to the coast," said William.

They mounted and then guided the horses out of the yard and onto the road, heading due south. Ridkin and Matilda dropped some distance behind

Helena and William, chatting in animated whispers. "What are they talking about?" asked William. "Did something happen between them last night? I mean, when Matilda read the crystals."

"I don't know. Tilda won't talk about it."

"Why were you so keen for her to read mine?"

"Oh, call it feminine curiosity. And I like to watch folk."

"What have you decided about me?"

"That you're inexperienced, naïve perhaps, but a good man. And I'm an excellent judge of character. Mostly."

She fell silent for some minutes. What should he do? What could he say?

"I'm sorry. I must seem rather odd to you."

"Not at all," he replied.

"Don't be so polite. If I'm distant, it's because I'm wed and not the kind as to encourage other men. Even if I quite like them." She smiled.

"Oh, of course, I understand. I wasn't… I mean I didn't… mubble fubbles, I'm making a hash of things."

She laughed. "Mubble fubbles? That's so endearing. Do you have your own sweetheart?"

"I do. She's called Verity Bull, and I left her behind in Coxwell, where we both grew up. I'm trying to make something of myself so I can buy out her indenture and wed her."

"Goodness. Let's hope this Verity Bull appreciates you."

"I think she does, but it's only since solstice last that we've been courting. We aren't that close yet, but she's so pretty and I hope we can be together."

"Courting is an old way of saying it. I take it tha' knows a pretty face isn't everything. Is she your only experience with girls?"

"Yes. I'm afraid so. Why?"

"I'm sorry. It's none of my business."

"That's alright. You know, you're very nice."

She paused, looking at him askance. "Please don't try to flatter me," she said, with a sharper edge to her voice. "Besides, no lady likes to be described as *nice*." Then she softened. "If you get to know me, you'll find I'm not all that nice at all. And quite dull. Just a poor married woman in search of her missing husband. What are your folk like? Are they alive?"

He told her about his mother dying, while birthing what would have been his brother, and of being taken in by the monks, and of his father's recent passing and of his unconventional upbringing.

"So, you had no mother figure in your life like, and you grew up around men. That would explain a lot."

"What would it explain?"

"Oh, nothing. Please ignore me. Come on, let's drop back and see what those two are talking about."

She was a puzzle; one moment warm and interested, the next cold and avoidant.

As the morning wore on, they came across the first houses of a small town. A sign announced they had reached the burgh of Oakford, but there was no obvious trace of anyone around. As they continued toward the centre, the reason became apparent: everyone had crowded into the market square, in the middle of which someone had constructed a pyre of branches and dry wood. And there atop stood a woman, bound to a stake.

Helena gasped. "Oh, Sun and Moons, it's a witch trial[34]," she said.

A trial was indeed going on, and the outcome looked predetermined. She showed signs of a severe beating; her face a mess of cuts and livid patches. One eye had closed up, swollen and red. She'd lost part of an ear and her hands hung misshapen at her wrists, evidently with the fingers broken. William had seen nothing like it in his life. "By all that's sacred," he said, "this is wrong."

The woman's accuser stood on a platform and shouted, "Witch, what hast thou to say for thyself?"

Perhaps the man thought using old words added weight to his accusations.

"I am no witch, Richard Fitzpatrick. You speak false. You tried to have your way with me, and when I threatened to speak with your wife, you made up this cock and bull nonsense about me."

"But a witch, thou most surely art. Did'st thou not seek to seduce me and half the men in the town, and once spurned, did'st thou not cause women to miscarry and crops to fail?"

Before she could respond, he turned to the crowd and shouted, "Citizens of Oakford, who here doth agree that Margaret Downey is a witch and shall be burned?"

"Aye," chorused the townsfolk. "Burn her, Burn her."

A burly man in a leather apron, acting as executioner at the front of the platform, touched a torch to some kindling, and a fire started. The woman's face was a mask of terror.

"You can't. No! What about my children?" A flame caught hold on her bloodstained skirts. "No!" she wailed. "Please don't do this. I've done nothing. I swear it by Lord Sola and his Moons."

Helena turned away, her face contorted in what William assumed to be disgust. He felt sickened enough himself, but when he glanced back at her, did he detect something closer to concentration? Before the flames could advance any further, the woman let out another moan and collapsed forward against her restraints, lifeless.

The executioner got as close as he could before saying in surprise, "She's dead. I declare she's dead already."

Helena sagged and William caught her before she could fall.

"Lady Helena, are you well?"

"Sorry," she said. "I felt quite faint there. I've seen such a burning before and have no wish to watch another. Believe me, there's no worse spectacle. And that poor woman was no witch. I swear it by all the stars in the sky."

~~~

Laddà was attending to her queen in the depths of the citadel of Nuorrù. She'd been so proud to be made Nannua's First Hand, but, a year into the role, she wasn't so enamoured with it.

"Laddà, I'm not happy."

"Gracious Queen?"

"I want my crystal, and I want it now. Give me it!"

"But my Queen…"

Queen Nannua was always at her most irritable while laying eggs. She squeezed out a steady stream of cherry sized sticky green spheres, which
~~~

were scooped up by lines of worker Janasà and carried away to the fertilising chambers. Laddà couldn't stop herself visualising how there would soon be tiny males crawling all over them in a sexualised frenzy, trying to reach as many as possible before expiring with exhaustion. The whole notion disgusted her.

The Queen was having a moan. "We can't just wait for the Anointed One to come wandering across our plain and knock on our door. We must go out into the world and look for him."

"I will prepare myself at once, My Queen."

"No, not you. I need you here. Send squads to the mainland. Sniff him out."

"But My Queen, there are a great many human males that fulfil the descriptions in the scriptures spread across the continent of Yorpia. We cannot bring them all to you."

"I spoke with the scholars after my feed this morning, and they tell me they have a new interpretation of the Janasarium. They think the Anointed One will have an odour."

"An odour, My Queen?" All males had a heavy, disgusting odour, but she didn't voice that to Queen Nannua.

"Yes. You know what an odour is. A smell. A scent. Something we can detect in the air."

"Yes. My Queen. How can we *know* the right odour?"

"A Janasà will know when she has found it. It is written."

Ridiculous. All manner of things were written in the *Janasarium*. You didn't send good Janasà on dangerous missions for all of them. "Very well, My Queen. I could suggest five squads with orders to look for the right smell. Is this what you would have me do?" She hoped that hadn't sounded sarcastic.

"Excellent. I'd like Quaggià to lead the first squad. Make it so."

Laddà had misgivings about the impetuous Quaggià; her nose was dodgy, her judgement worse. But she was the Queen's favourite at the tournaments, and now wasn't the time to object. She bowed to leave. "My Queen. Consider it done."

A worker sidled up with flowing tubes of royal jelly that she stuffed into the Queen's feeding ducts. Laddà was grateful she didn't need to witness what would come next.

# ✦ Seven ✦

With William on his way, Feydor could attend to other matters. He met the man known as Walter Travis in a low-ceilinged tavern in the Cheap Side district. The notorious gang-leader had declared himself delighted with the delicate nymph figurine that Feydor had filched for him the week before from one of the hundred or more bedrooms of the palace.

"My old mother was dead chuffed with it," Travis told him.

The item was gaudy and badly executed, most likely a knocked off copy of something pulled out of a ruined Truscan villa somewhere in Anglonia. But if someone was happy to pay good coin for it, who was he to complain?

"To what do I owe the pleasure of meeting you in person, you old devil?" He slapped Feydor on the back, causing him to spray sour ale over the rough oak bench.

"I need a favour please, Mr Travis," began Feydor, once he'd recovered his breath.

"It's Walt to my mates," said Travis, smiling. "What kind of favour? Need someone to have a bit of an accident? Bumping off, like? Just say the word."

"Nothing like that, no. I want a certain item placed in safe keeping."

"What item? Nicked, I hope?"

"No. Stop thinking the worst of me. It belonged to my aunt Agata. Here, take a butcher's[35], if you like."

He placed something small and glinting onto the man's outstretched palm: a tiny figure of a butterfly cast in poor quality bronze with a securing clasp at the back.

"It's just a brooch. It's tatt. I'd 'ave trouble selling it," Travis said.

"Whatever you do, don't sell it. Please. Just hide it somewhere very safe."

"Don't s'pose you'd care to explain why?"

"If it's all the same to you, no."

"You know, this smells fishy to me. A dangerous kind of fishy. You're a friend, Feydor, but not that good of a friend."

"I could pay you."

Travis turned to look Feydor in the eye. "Is that so? Right, tell me now. What's really going on here? Thing is, the City Watch are paying me a lot of attention just lately. How do I know it's not been lifted from some important gent? One who might cast me in the slammer for having it."

"No, it's nothing like that. I promise!" He'd not expected resistance like this.

"Then what? What's the fuss about?"

Curses. He was going to have to come clean. "Walt, I promise it's nothing like that. It's…" He sighed. This could go very wrong. He looked about, checking for eavesdroppers and kept his voice down. "Look, it's magical. Alright? Nothing heavy, but… my life could depend on its safekeeping. There, I've said it."

Travis frowned and shook his head. Then burst out laughing. "Just kidding with you. Lawks, your face. 'Course I'll take care of it." He tapped his nose. "Mum's the word[36]."

The tension disappeared from Feydor's shoulders. "Thanks Walt. I owe you."

He emptied his ale jug, shook hands with Travis, and headed out into the oppressive Ludnam gloom, relieved at the step he'd just taken.

~~~

A linen wrapped package awaited Feydor on his return from meeting Travis. He peeled off the covering and pulled out a bundle of letters bound by a single grey ribbon. Atop, he found a short, scribbled note from the woman. *I discovered these in my brother Silas's possessions and thought you should have them. Pay careful attention to the last of them. Mary.*

That was all.
~~~

There were a dozen sheets of fine parchment in the collection. Feydor untied them and examined the first one. The letter was from his father, Alfredo the jester, to Silas the alchemist and included the following paragraph:

*Thank you for your letter I received yesterday. Are you yet close to that breakthrough with base metal? It was good to hear about Mary's joyful event. Who'd have thought she'd produce twins?*

The twins were called Fraser and Irvine and, thanks to their maladjusted mother, had become well known rabble rousers in Ludnam's gaudy west end. The letter continued:

*This morning brings us great joy. 'Melda has given birth to a large but healthy boy child, and we are naming him Feydor after her great grandfather. He arrived with a full shock of red hair and the most extraordinary piercing green eyes. Already he has a firm grip and can support himself in a sitting position, something the midwife tells us is very unusual, especially given his weight. It disturbs me to report, however, that 'Melda showed no sign of emotion at his arrival and seemed relieved to pass him off to a wet nurse to be taken care of. I, on the other hand, find myself one minute smiling, the next, crying, such is the tide of sentiment that has engulfed me.*

*Yours in jesting, Alfredo*

Feydor felt sad to read his father's words and note how the man had missed the big moments in his life. He'd have been so proud that his first-born son had reached the pinnacle of the profession. In another letter, he found this:

*Today, my joy has multiplied a hundredfold with the arrival of our third child, Morwena. To my surprise, 'Melda shows the full range of affections for the girl, who, like her two older brothers, has red hair and green eyes. It is most puzzling, as if she were, in fact, saving all her maternal love for the birth of a girl. I tried to discuss the matter with her, but it turned into a huge row, after which I found myself banished from the house. I fear for the wellbeing of Feydor and Jasper and will tomorrow try to persuade*

*'Melda to let me take care of them. Jasper is a singular boy given to bouts of wild rage, and I worry that without my firm hand, he may go out of control.*

*Yours, as ever in jesting, Alfredo*

That last comment made sense. His brother's thirst for fighting was insatiable; even at five years old, he'd challenged other children to duels. His mother would hear nothing bad said against him, though. He opened the final missive in the bundle, disappointed that there weren't more.

*'Melda and I fought over the children last night. She wishes to send the younger two to a relative in the country and to focus all her efforts on instructing Feydor, who is now almost eight years of age. Things came to a head today: she is set on the bizarre notion of castrating the boy in order to, as she put it, ensure his mind stays on his eventual role as a jester to the nobility. I am beside myself with fear for him. The very idea of harming our son in this way is barbarous beyond words. I have no option but to oppose her with every fibre of my being, while, for her part, she swears that if I stand against her in this, she will destroy me. I believe this may well be the last you hear from me.*

*Yours, not much longer in jesting, Alfredo*

Feydor sat in shocked silence. Even the monkey rested with its head leaning into his leg, seeming to sense his state of distress. His poor father! This explained the sudden disappearance of the man from his life and threw into relief the true awfulness of his cold, callous mother. He swore by every star in the firmament that he would avenge his death. Feydor would have to pick the time and place and he'd still need Mary's help, even then, but kill her, he would.

~~~

A limited magical ability had been a part of Feydor, as far back as could remember. His talents, although nothing like those of his mother, were real. It had been his great aunt Agata who'd first noticed it, when he'd made his younger sister turn vomit green for stealing his favourite toy soldier. Fascinated, of course, he'd not known what was going on. He'd prodded
~~~

and poked at his magic, much as a dog might puzzle at the discovery that it could lick its back end. Agata, a decent enough dark witch, if such a thing could exist, had taken him aside and explained how he shouldn't feel afraid or ashamed, but needed to keep his talent hidden, especially from his mother, who would have beaten it out of him. She told him many things about the art, for art was how she saw it. How it was unknown among males, and how his aura might glow, smell even, for several hours after using magic and be apparent to those with the sight to see it. And if he wanted to conceal it, he'd need to be oh-so-careful about where and when to use it. Secretive and crafty by nature, Feydor loved everything about it.

He soon came to learn about the nature of magic and that those women, for they were all women who practised it, fell into three groups, or levels. First there was the *dabbler*, who could perform minor works, but nothing of any significant impact. Although there was no hard and fast rule, a dabbler could generate curses, move objects from one place to another, and enact showy theatrical tricks. She could not, however, do more useful things such as cure the sick. Then came those who called themselves actual *witches*. A witch could enact a wide range of charms and incantations, cause or ease suffering, generate storms, and generally be a nuisance. She could influence the thoughts and intentions of others, but only in special cases, control them. Finally, there were the *adepts*. An adept was rare, only coming along every few generations. She could destroy a city, raise mountains, and even shape mother nature herself. There hadn't been the most feared type of practitioner, a *dark adept* in centuries.

It wasn't clear how he, as a male, could do his dabbler level magic. Agata had supposed his castration might have had something to do with it, but who could say?

His mother coveted the Nuragic Crystal because she supposed it would give her near adept powers and would make her a terrifying prospect. She'd take control of the kingdom and bend it to her own whims. As the only person who could stop her, it was vital that he wasn't sidelined by the machinations of that pathetic Lord High Priest.

So, to business. The King and Stackpole were up to something, and that something had to concern himself. He took out from the secret cubbyhole beneath his cot, a small rosewood box containing what looked like a collection of dead scarab beetles. He selected one of the inert insects and muttered a few words in what might have been an ancient language. The creature wiggled a leg. A few more soft phrases and it moved another, then an antenna, and within a few minutes, scuttled about on the back of his arm, with an action not unlike the gambolling of a young lamb. "Are you Feydor's good little boy? There, there, yes," he cooed to the scarab, which gave at least the impression of pleasure at the sound. Hiding the bug in his palm, he headed for the palace cellars.

The cellars occupied a footprint somewhat larger than that of the palace itself, extending as far south as the river, and north to the city wall. However, at some point, someone had bricked off the section below the royal chambers and filled it with dense stone. Feydor had hollowed this out with a charm, forming cavities beneath what he calculated to be the King's privy and bedroom. Another device kept the entrance concealed. He breathed onto the scarab and whispered, "Be a good boy now and Feydor will find you some nice ants to munch." The animal jumped from his hand and disappeared into a crevice while he settled down to listen, as anything the creature heard would echo right into Feydor's head.

The first few minutes frustrated him, as the mental connection had to establish itself and then the bug's own primitive thoughts needed to be filtered out, which were related to wood, fungus, and hot lady beetles. However, as he adjusted to the stream of consciousness, he soon learned that King Inglebert had the loathsome oleaginous Lord High Priest with him, and they were discussing the King's lack of an heir.

"Your Grace, may you always prosper, worry not. I have, as we speak, a hundred acolytes praying for your fecundity."

"Excellent. And this mission to Sardonica? Will the waters of that land aid our cause?"

"Your Grace, I regret that the Fool most likely has tricked us. I've never heard of any such waters."

"Now that I think about it, the idea sounds preposterous, but it costs us nothing for this Coxwell character to at least try to gain some of it. *However...*" the King paused, perhaps for effect, or else to pick at his wart.

"While I cannot deny his talents, I grow tired of Feydor's endless meddling in matters politic. His opinions, were they to catch on, could cause us great harm."

"I quite agree, your Grace, may the moons caress your glorious shadow. There are other less opinionated jesters in the land. Would you have me deal with him?"

"What do you propose?"

"We could try him for treason. After a suitable period of racking, I'm sure he'd admit to any accusation you wanted to level."

"Hmm, interesting. A deserving outcome. Any other suggestions?"

"A simple banishment might be the easiest thing to expedite. Somewhere the sun rarely shines like outer Albia, or what's that island out to the west, Emeraldia?"

"Yes, Emeraldia. I went there once. Never stopped raining. Perfect."

The faintest of coughs interrupted them both, and the voice of First Minister Thomas Crumbwell appeared. "Your Grace, there is a delegation from the guild of merchants for an audience with you. Should I ask them to return on a future occasion?"

"No, absolutely not. I want to discuss their tax contributions. Lord High Priest, we will consider the Fool again tomorrow."

"Your Grace."

Feydor could almost hear the lickspittle unctuously bowing, before receding footsteps and a closing door told Feydor they'd gone. What a strange quirk of timing that he should have begun listening during the exact part of their conversation that related to himself. So, he had only until the morning to stop the King banishing him to the dreaded Emeraldia, where even the dirt was green. To be sure.

What grated on his sense of injustice was that, in offending the King, he'd only voiced what he'd heard the merchants, the artisans, and the common folk say as he visited the alehouses of the city. That the King was bankrupting the realm for the sake of his own vanity.

"Lord Sola on a donkey," he muttered to himself as he collected the beetle and hurried back to his chambers, dodging bustling pages, maids, guards, and servers as he went. He couldn't let it happen. The ignominy.

His mother would be livid, and she'd punish him in one of those excruciating methods she reserved for such occasions. Much worse, he'd lose face among the jester community. There'd be many laughing their little stockings off at the very notion of the fall and humiliation of the great Fool, Feydor Foolson. He knew he shouldn't care what others thought of him; after all, what right has a man whose job it is to be laughed at to possess such vanity? But he was quite simply the best man alive at what he did, and there was no point denying it.

Boglets. Well, in his world, setbacks only existed to challenge a person, and you showed your true mettle by how you dealt with them. A plan formed in his mind, a plan that would solve the immediate problem while causing significant suffering to the would-be perpetrator, otherwise known as the King of Anglonia. But first he desired to make progress on a bigger, more important matter, one close to his heart. He changed into drab city clothing, grabbed Filthy, and made his way toward the kitchens with a hunger to wake the Stars.

~~~

In the great kitchen, Feydor did a dance and a curtsey to the staff, grabbed a chunk of rye bread, and found his way outside. Exiting the palace from the south gate, he set off toward the Ludnam Bridge[37] and beyond it, the hilly area south of the river Timmes, known as Bell End. Feydor's delicate gait, a kind of toe pointed shuffle, was ideal for working his way through the streets of the city, which were packed with farmers, merchants, soldiers, hawkers, prostitutes, and ordinary folk going about their business. In places, the boiling throng shoved him off course, or else forced him to swerve his significant bulk around such obstacles as random traders, stalled carts, and open street brawls. Ludnam Bridge itself was an improbable strip of stone across the river, comprising eight limestone arches loaded with layer upon layer of houses, shops, workshops and even a small temple. The whole top-heavy shebang looked so unstable it could topple over at any moment and jettison its cloying burden into the river.
~~~

He had directions to brow the hill that climbed away from the south bank and then look for an imposing whitewashed building where cousin Mary resided. Heavy rains that morning had washed the worst of the soot and grime from the air and Feydor took a moment to stop, turn, and enjoy the sweep of the river, which gave the impression of having entwined itself through the bridge and buildings, rather than the other way around. The river itself was dotted with floating traffic and was almost as densely jammed as the streets through which he'd just had to plough, from the tiniest rowed boats for hire, or *wherries*, to a variety of larger vessels, some oared, some with sails, some with both. Ludnam was a contradiction, a kind of organised chaos that somehow allowed the fast-growing population to function.

Approaching the broad main façade of Mary's place of habitation, he rapped the knocker with a display of theatrical aplomb; no skulking about the tradesman's entrance for Feydor. A few seconds later, the door opened, revealing a short kilt clad middle-aged servant who appraised Feydor from head to toe, not attempting to mask his distaste. Even out of his work outfit, the Fool made a striking, if not disconcerting, sight, and the scratching and shrieking noise coming from his basket didn't much help.

"Can I assist you?" The man said, with a thick Albian accent.

"This is where I will find Mary Grieve?"

"Is that a question?"

"Why would it not be?"

"What is it you want with her?"

"Is it any concern of yours?" Feydor could play this game all day.

The man sniffed. "Wait there."

The door had already closed. Five minutes later, Mary reopened it and looked out, bleary-eyed and dishevelled at the new arrival.

"Och," she said. "What are *you* doing here?"

"I'm here to tell you something."

"Well now, you'd better come in and stop spoiling the street. What the Stars do you have in that basket?"

Feydor undid the clasp to Filthy's container, and the monkey leapt out and onto his shoulder. Spotting Mary standing in the hallway, it arched its back, bared its teeth, and hissed at her. She didn't bat an eyelid. The black cat behind her, however, went rigid with its fur on end while Filthy raced around screeching on Feydor's head and shoulders. She bent to stroke the cat. "Shh, Mite[38], it's only a wicked wee beastie. He won't be here long." She turned to address Feydor. "Is this rank creature anything to do with Imelda?" Before he could answer, she went on, "Look, it's nae a good time. Tell me what you have to say and go."

She folded her arms and glared at him. A pale, chinless face appeared at the top of the stairs and called down. "Who's this, Mary?"

"Nothing for you to be concerned about, dearest. I'll be with you again in two shakes of my tail. Go back to bed, Sweetums!"

"Sweetums? And is that who I think it is?" asked Feydor, fascinated.

"Look, a girl does what she has to do. It could be a lot worse. Aye, it's Prince Albert right enough, and I've got him eating out of my hand now, so don't you go shoving your oar in."

Used as he was to the ways of the women in his family, his mind still boggled, but before he could say anything more, she continued, "Well, you'd best come into the wee parlour here, and spit it out. I can't leave his nibbs alone for too long."

With the door closed, she turned, arms folded, towards him. "Well?"

Mary, Feydor observed, hadn't aged well. Her face resembled a rising dough, pudgy and uneven like a focaccia loaf, and her little, dark, olive-shaped eyes completed the illusion. Except that a loaf doesn't in the general order of things, have prominent hair infested moles, not even in Ludnam.

"Are you and the prince a thing?" he asked.

"What do you care? But aye, I'm grooming him. Your whelk of a wee king might have an accident one day and need a replacement."

"Still scheming? I'm impressed."

"I don't give a half-sucked turnip what impresses you. Scheming is what I do. I'm a witch."

They sat at opposite sides of a table, Mary hunched forward and agitated, while Feydor reclined with his arms and legs crossed.

"Come on. Spit out the toad. Something about those letters?" she asked.

"The letters, yes, and thank you for sending them. But first, I have tidings that will interest you."

"Oh aye?" she replied, at once suspicious. "I cannae imagine what you could say that would interest me. Unless it concerns *her*."

She was always so obsessed with his mother.

"It does concern her. But tell me, why is it you and my mother hate each other so much?"

He already knew the answer, but winding her up was such fun.

"That whoor cheated me of my place as head of the clan, right enough. But I'm too tired to be angry right now, not that I won't still have my revenge. This is the new me: slow and steady wins the race. She's still a whoor though." This last comment amused Feydor, given how Mary appeared to be living immorally with the Bonnie Wee Prince Albert. "Anyhow, why do you still have anything to do with her after what she did to you when you were still but a wee bairn?"

"Because she compels it. I despise her more than I could say in a thousand moons. I know it was her that castrated me. That's bad enough. But if I understand father's last letter, he died trying to stop her from doing it, and that's something I'm still yet to wrap my noggin around. I swear on all the Stars, I *will* destroy her. Whatever it takes."

"Aye well. I'm with you on that." There was a long pause before she thought of something. When she continued, her voice had softened. "I was there when she did it, you ken? The castration. She just grabbed your sack and pulled it away, and when you screamed the place down, she sat and ate her supper. I think she fed your plums to the dogs."

Feydor's internal balance pitched. At that moment, he wanted to escape, to run from Ludnam and never return. "I remember nothing about it," he said, his voice barely above a whisper.

"Aye, she wiped the memory from your pretty wee head. What counts now is how you go from here."

That surprised him. She'd never made such obvious sense or shown anything like empathy before.

"I suppose the wee beastie there is your mother's idea of a joke." She nodded at Filthy, who was, it seemed, looking for something in Feydor's ear. He batted its paw away.

"It's a curse, that's what it is." He scowled as the animal now curled up to lick its own arse.

"So," she started. "I'm sure you didnae come here to pass the time of day. What do you want?"

With his emotions back under control, he said, "very well. My mother believes, no insists, she has located the Nuragic crystal."

Mary scoffed and snorted, setting Filthy into another frenzy. "Nurragù? No! That's a pile of shite, and you know it!"

"Maybe, maybe not. Don't you want to hear more?"

She appeared undecided. "This just sounds like one of your wee schemes to me. How do I know I can trust you?"

"You can't. I don't know how real this is myself."

She paused. "She doesnae realise you are here talking to me, does she?"

"Not unless this devil on my shoulder can tell her."

She focused her full attention on the monkey. "Hmm. He doesnae appear to have that talent. Look, give me a wee moment." She left the room, closing the door behind her and was gone for several minutes. When she returned, she picked up the thread. "I'm busy today. The wee prince is expecting me to take care of someone for him."

"In what sense, take care of?"

"Never you mind. Can you meet on the morrow?"

"Hmm. The King is hunting again…, so yes."

"I'll get a message to you. Now shoo, fleckle off, and take that infernal beastie with you before I fry its arse."

~~~

As he scurried home from Bell End, he first made for the market at Port Bellow, where there was a bookstall that sold amusing volumes. Arriving, he set to rummaging among the disorganised wares, his hand almost of its own volition coming across a volume entitled "Mrs Burton's Second Little
~~~

Book of Most Diverting Curses." Excellent. Just the ticket. The wealthy classes loved to place this kind of book in their privies, to show off their broad-mindedness and wit. A guest might peruse a few pages while completing his or her ablutions and enjoy a good chuckle, forming splendid opinions of their hosts. *What a card Lord Lionel is!* they would say to each other. *I split my sides last time I went to siege*[39] *at his palace.* Popular titles in the genre included *One hundred things to do with a dead stoat in Gallesia* or *Unspeakable acts to commit with a rabbit.*

Mrs Burton's books contained methods to inflict embarrassing ills on another person, such as causing his britches to drop at awkward moments in public, or deafening anal eruptions to rip out. Obviously, none of them worked, but a dabbler with a sprinkling of magical talent could make such curses do something, and Feydor, being a dabbler, had such abilities, even if he'd not had the training to develop them.

He'd found volume one in the series a few weeks earlier and, although most of the curses had been pretty dull, he'd been able to give the King a huge wart on his nose. Not as payback for a perceived slight or injustice against him. Those were everyday occurrences, after all. No, he'd cursed against the King's rampant vanity *just because he could.*

Feydor paid what the merchant wanted for the book. An exorbitant sum, but it would be more than worth it. Hiding the purchase under his cloak, he returned to his room, pulling it out onto his cot in eager anticipation. He dived in. *Make that his eyes swiveleth in opposing directions*, sounded entertaining, *Make that her ears poureth forth smoke whenever she fibbeth*, more so. But then he hit gold: *Give him an astriction of the vitals to vex the Stars.* Yes, perfect. A literal binding spell. In other words, bung him up something chronic. He read the list of steps needed to perform the curse and scurried down to the extensive kitchens to see if he could find some of the more exotic animal parts called for.

The curse had to be uttered under starlight, and he had to avoid any chance that someone might discover what he was up to. Furthermore, the fact that fire was involved meant that to enact the curse within the palace grounds would draw unwanted attention. He put everything he needed into the deep pockets of his mantle and exited into the darkness outside. Curfew had arrived, but he knew where the city watchmen would patrol at that time of the evening, and avoiding detection, he reached a wooded area of Martin's field. Under cover of the dark, and with just the twin crescent moons to provide pale light, he muttered the enchantment.

*First set a fire of elm and oak,*
*Take there a creature that doth croak,*
*Stuff it with jelly from calf's foot and skin,*
*Sow up its arse with thread, strong and thin,*

It went on like this for a whole page, citing the usual ingredients. Why did they always want the eye of a newt? Then:

*Burn the wee beast till its flesh be but muck,*
*Speak out the name of he to be stuck,*
*Spin on your toes then jump oe'r the blaze,*
*And the man shall not shite for the rest of his days.*

There was the faintest green glow that surrounded his hands, and only for a few seconds. Anyone unfamiliar with magic would have missed it.

He put out the fire, sweeping the ashes under a bush, and snuck back into the palace. If all went well, his Majesty would soon be in ten shades of agony, unable to empty his bowel and incapable of issuing the orders that would see Feydor toppled from his position. He stopped for just a moment to wonder whether his action might be reversible, but dismissed the thought. His kind of magic was never permanent. Was it?

~~~

Feydor slept like a babe, then rose with the birdsong, dressed himself in city attire, and wandered into the servant's dining hall where he found breakfast in full swing. Along the far wall, a row of trestles groaned under the weight of food. Not the regular servant slops that passed for nourishment in the palace, however, but the remains of the previous night's
~~~

kingly feast that Inglebert had thrown for the visiting ambassadors and envoys. The King liked a bit of ostentation to show just how beneficent the Anglonian monarch could be. Feydor as a rule didn't break his fast with lark's tongues or quail's eyeballs or any of the myriad gastronomic delights on offer, but today, he offered a prayer of thanks to the thousands of dead creatures who'd given everything to make the cornucopia possible, and stuffed down anything he could reach, only stopping from time to time to slip Filthy odd pieces of fruit. After an hour of hard eating, he experienced bloating and griping, but still he pushed on till his jaw ached.

Among the palace staff that came and went, he noted the presence of Serjeant Pollock, the gate guard he'd tussled with two days earlier, the one who'd tried to hurt him. An idea sprang to mind. Smiling, he stood, spun on his toes, made a hop and a skip, and rubbed with satisfaction his now empty stomach. Pollock, however, clutched his middle, screamed, and ran for the privy block. Feydor cartwheeled around the room in celebration, and bowed to his fellow diners, who stared in fixed disbelief. Then he once more sat to eat.

He spied one of the King's pages and motioned for the man to join him. "Good morrow, master Porritt. You look cheerful. Is all well in your house?"

"The wife is fine. Thank you, Feydor. I can't say the same for His Grace. According to the tidings, he has a great pain of the colic this morrow and is refusing all counsel."

"Indeed? Something he ate, perhaps?" said Feydor, performing his best imitation of concern.

"The word is, Stackpole fed him too much turnip," said Porritt, biting into a crown of peacock and ocelot. "I also heard he barely touched his food last night and excused himself from the banquet before the eighth course. Can you believe it?"

So the curse had worked. Not that he'd doubted it for a moment.

Another page brought him a slip of parchment. Unfolding it, Feydor nodded at the curt summons it conveyed, then snatched his cloak and made for the palace gates. As he walked, he thought about how this next encounter with Mary would pan out. She'd feign disinterest, while pumping him for as much information about the crystal and Coxwell as possible, so she could make her own plans without him. He had no desire to allow that to happen.

Thirty minutes later, he found the Wounded Ferret ale house in Coven Garden and entered the gloomy interior in search of his conceited, scheming relative. The place struck Feydor as a perfect venue for meeting a witch, what with the dim light and the stench of something decaying. His sensitive nose picked out notes of sweat, rotten meat, mould, but above all of that, a hint of burning flesh. He shuddered.

Mary's welcome was as graceful, eloquent, and effusive as ever. "You took your time getting here, carrot head."

"Carrot head? Not very original. At least I don't have a face like a smacked arse," he responded.

"I'll have you know I still turn heads."

"Turn them into what? Stone?"

"Ha ha. I'm not rising to it. I told you, this is the new me. Plan, plot, prepare, strike. She won't know what's hit her." She took a draught of her ale. "Now, ya ken those two old fools over there?" She gestured toward the far end of the room. He could make out nothing in the relative gloom, but nodded. "I have a wee surprise coming to them," she said, almost spitting with distaste. "They took me for a common besom and tried to take me upstairs."

"Besom?"

"A cheap whoor! But it's fine. Right about now, they'll be about to boak." Sure enough, two men hurtled past their bench, diving for the exit from where he heard them retching. "Perhaps they'll live, perhaps they won't. Go and fetch me another ale."

He went and fetched two fresh jars, although, based on the sour aroma of vinegar, there was nothing fresh about the brew. He eased his ample derriere onto the bench and faced her. "Can you explain something to me, something mother won't tell me?"

"Go on."

"Why is it she can't or won't use her magic to take the crystal? It would save us all a cartload of trouble."

"Because magic won't work in Sardonica, at least not the kind she and I use."

"Dark magic..."

She waved as if batting away a swarm of midges. "Yes, call it that, if you will. Once you get further east than Gallia, only the white stuff does anything." She twisted her mouth in disgust.

"So, no dark magic. How come?"

"There's a kind of wood-sprite that has blocked it these last few hundred years. The Ninfiné. A complete pain in the fundament, but it would take a determined adept to overcome them."

She supped again and placed her elbows down on the bench. "But that's not why I've dragged my carcass here. Tell me more about this crystal and how Imelda thinks she can lay her hands on it. Then indulge me with what it is you think you want from me."

He smiled. The fish had nibbled the bait, and he just needed to reel it in. He summarised how he'd hatched plans with his mother, then spotted William as the perfect mark for his deception. How the King had fallen for the story about the aphrodisiac, knighted William, and sent him on his way. Then he noted how he himself had pressed William's travelling companion into being his squire.

"What of their backgrounds? What manner of men are we dealing with?"

"William, I understand, grew up with some dreary order of monks near Ebury. He is of poor stock, but well educated, and speaks the old tongue. I think he will scrub up tidy enough to be credible with the people he must convince. As for his squire, he is local, has a foul attitude and a moat-load of street sense. I had someone find his family in Chiswell and they sound a sorry scum, the sort that's always in and out of the clinker. And get this: he isn't at all what he seems, in fact he was born with a hearth rather than a poker." He pointed downwards.

"What?"

"The candle holder rather than the candle. The ring rather than the spear. Think about it. I can be patient."

She appeared to puzzle what he meant before saying, "Ah, the squire's a squiress?"

"Bravo. And she's pretty convincing in the role of a boy. Not enough to fool me, of course, but I doubt Coxwell will ever notice."

"And they both believe the story you confected?"

"The King's aphrodisiac water? Coxwell does for sure. He's as keen as the proverbial and wants to prove himself. The other one would never have gone with him had I not made it difficult to refuse."

"Why did you do that?"

"Just so I could wipe the smug look off his face. But tell me, why is it you persist with that accent? I mean, Stars Above, you've even got tartan woven into your cloak, unless my eyes deceive me. You were born here in Ludnam, am I mistaken?"

"Aye, but Albia is my spirit birthplace. The smell of the heather, the sound of the pipes, the bracing breeze…" It was Feydor's turn to scoff, but she continued. "I don't need to justify myself. Explain to me why should I help you? Why should I take this crystal fantasy seriously?" She stared across at him intently. "An' let me get a proper look at you. I need to work out if you're lying."

"You know, it's really very simple. I had no choice but to give her a plan, but I've no intention of letting her get that crystal. Lord Sola on a donkey. Can you imagine what she'd do with it?"

"And you think I can, what? Grab it for myself?"

"You want it, right? And you're more than capable of beating her to the prize." This was a barefaced lie, but it suited him to flatter her. "You're the smartest, most stylish witch I know, but you need me."

"Waesucks, why?"

"Because I can stay close to her and tell you what she's up to. You'll lead her a merry jig as she works out how you are second guessing her every move. It'll be fun. So why not? Why don't you and I combine our talents on this?"

He gave her a moment to think through her options, then played his next card. "Or perhaps I should go to our distant cousin in Cymria? She'd work with me in a heartbeat."

"Hah, Dark Gladys? She's a pathetic impostor. She can barely rub two spells together."

"Are you sure about that?"

They were by now facing off, their raised voices drawing attention from the remaining men in the room.

Now for the clincher. "Working together, pooling our minds, we can do more than beat her to the crystal. I know how we can take her down. Destroy her utterly. You could take your deserved place unopposed as head witch in the family."

"I see. Right. Let me think."

Feydor settled and waited. It turned out he'd done enough. "Right. Let's say I agree. What would you have me do?"

"Coxwell is due to sail for Gallia on the morrow. They will be at sea for two or three days. Can you sink their vessel before they reach safe harbour?"

She nodded. "Sure. Brooding storms are my thing. I'll hole their ship and smash it to splinters."

"Good. One last item: we need to complete the plan. Once we've stopped Coxwell and Jasper from reaching Sardonica, we still have to grab the crystal for ourselves. But how? If we can't use magic, is there someone we can send to do the job? The twins, perhaps?"

He'd thought about this ahead of their conversation. Fraser and Irvine were as likely a pair as any to succeed. Irvine had a sly streak, and could talk himself into or out of anything, but lacked his brother's physical prowess and attractiveness to the women. Fraser, though, had balls enough for both of them. Feydor suspected they had different fathers, despite being born only minutes apart. Together, they could be a force.

She mulled it over. "Fraser and Irvine? Hmm. I think they'd enjoy that."

"Can you keep them out of trouble?" he asked, thinking of their reputation as frequenters of taverns and their prodigious appetite for prostitutes.

"They can be good boys when they need to."

"Last question: When can they leave?"

"First thing on the morrow, I'd say. Right, I have to go find them. Now avaunt. Be away with ye!"

Feydor nodded, donning his cloak. He hoped he wasn't making a mistake.

# Eight

They reached the modest port at Favershal in the early afternoon and found only one vessel bound for Gallia, The *Big Black Cow*[40]. A one-legged man stood on the quayside directing a swarm of what William understood to be jackdores or something, loading supplies onto the ship via a system of pulleys. William negotiated passage with the ship's master, Captain Dogwash[41], for the four of them while Ridkin sold their horses.

"Don't like the look of this heap of sticks," said a doubtful looking Ridkin when he joined the others on the quay. "It looks ready to sink at the first sign of wind."

Dogwash looked mortally offended, his hands raised, chin protruded. "Nonsense, my friend, she's as tight as a drum. Look, see all the new timbers around the waterline? That's a good shipwright did that work. She needs a lick of tar, for sure, but she's seaworthy. Besides, there's no other ship due to sail this week. Well?"

William weighed up the options. Ridkin had a point. The patchwork sails and stained timbers looked like they might have seen better days. On the other hand, the clock was ticking. He'd used up more than a week already of his six months and he was keen to get going.

"It's only a short voyage," said Dogwash, "and see yonder sky. Nary a cloud in sight. I'll get you there in a jiffy."

"Sold!" said William, heading for the gangplank. "Ridkin, stay if you want, but I'm boarding." Ridkin remained rooted to the spot, gently shaking his head. "Have you forgotten Crumbwell's threat?" asked William.

"I'll catch you up," replied the younger man. "Just as soon as something more solid shows up."

Helena and Matilda followed behind William. A deckhand helped them over the lip of the ship's side. "Don't be a scared-y cat, Ridkin," said Matilda, smiling. "Happen we'll be there before we know it."

"Chuffing hell." Ridkin frowned, then reached for the guardrail. "You'll all be the death of me. Right, let's get this over with."

Once aboard, the ship didn't look so bad. Doors and hatches looked solid enough and the single main mast, more than the width of a firkin, appeared reassuring, and two rows of oars were tidy in their racking. William reckoned the whole vessel to be a seventy paces long and thirty wide. He had no way to judge its good or bad points, but the relaxed way the deckhands went about their business was reassuring. He nodded his satisfaction.

A deckhand showed them to the guest quarters below deck, a cramped dark place that smelt of many things, none of them pleasing. He decided he would do everything to avoid spending time confined in there and climbed back to the deck to watch the final loading, while the others sat on stools and played with the shove penny board they found in a corner.

William took out his two books from his pack and opened the Treatise on Kings, but wasn't in the mood and instead made a tour of the deck, looking for where he might sit. That done, he settled on a low railing to mull things over. Had all of his precious volumes made it to the castle at Ebury and had Ant put them in his room? Had news about his quest even reached the castle? Was he doing the right thing by coming on this mission? He didn't know. Did anyone ever know they were doing the right thing? The great Grecan philosophers would have at least known how to think about it. He cleaved to two of them in particular: Epicurious and Epictightus. Both offered fascinating ways to achieve atheraxia, an inner peace, or a healthy balance in life, although by very different paths.

William had first learned of Epictightus, who held that almost everything in life was outside of your control, whether on account of the gods or some other higher power, and so the best thing was to live a virtuous life. You had to accept what you couldn't influence, that is, your destiny, and to use your mind to overcome damaging emotions through discipline and introspection, thus achieving inner peace. And you needed wisdom to recognise what could or could not be controlled. He had thrilled at the idea of using his reasoning to gain contentment, right up to the time when he'd learned about Epicurious.

To Epicurious, the gods or other higher powers either did not exist, or were unconcerned with mere mortals, and, therefore, destiny did not exist. Instead, you were free from the fear of god, of death, and of divine retribution; you could thus live your best life by taking responsibility for your own choices, while avoiding those things that made you uncomfortable, including excess. This philosophy didn't take scripture as a guide to life, rather, it used knowledge and reason to decide what was right. He'd been even more in thrall to this line of thought.

No surprise that the priesthood feared this second philosophy, and he'd had to find books about it in the forbidden section of the library. Spiriting away volumes in the dead of night had added a certain excitement to his studies, but that, in itself, meant nothing. He hoped that in completing his quest, he'd learn which of these was the best model for his own life.

Helena joined him on the bench. "What's our knight errant planning up here on his own?"

"Nothing. I'm thinking about Epicurious."

"Who?"

"A Grecan philosopher. He said we should think of our setbacks as the gods testing us. If we prove worthy and meet challenges with reason, then we avoid adding our own harm to that of others. Right now, I hope I'm not putting the rest of you in danger."

"You love your books, don't you? I've heard of these fine old men, for men is what they all were, but what did their women folk think while they washed and cleaned and mended for them?"

"Who knows? It's not recorded whether women didn't write philosophy because they weren't allowed or because they weren't interested. Personally, I can't see why a woman wouldn't be interested in the same things as a man."

"Do you understand 'owt about women, Sir William? What with you growing up with monks an' all? A woman can think as well as any man, but, as she sweats her brow to raise a dozen bairns and support a worthless lubbock of a husband, she sees the uselessness of it. Any road, most people, women included, *know* what's true; why can't you just feel what's right and leave it be? Put your books aside, Sir William, and trust in thy heart."

"But... not *all* women, surely?" he began. Why was she being like this? He felt the argument slipping away; one he should win easily. Logic had to be the master of emotion, right?

Well, he'd show this woman how wrong she was, but, before he could marshal another thought, Dogwash pegged his way past them, barking orders to men who'd climbed high into the masts to furl sails or whatever it was mariners did to catch the wind.

"Ahoy, you're right in the way there. Until we get full sail..." He gestured toward the ladder that led below deck.

They went below to find the others as the vessel rocked sideways.

"Hi William," said Ridkin, for once with no apparent hint of his usual disdain.

"Mummy, I've talked with Ridkin like, and we think we should stick together as far as Trusca. Say you agree. Please." Matilda made a sign of supplication with her hands.

"Well, pet, we need to ask our brave knight if he agrees. William, do you want to consult any books on the matter?"

Her sarcasm stung William like a flick on the ear. "I'm not sure about that." He glared at her. "I think this is more a call for intuition, don't you, madam?"

"I ain't sure what's been going on between you two," said Ridkin, "but I don't like it a jot. Why don't we stay together for a few days and see where it takes us?"

The ship rolled one way, then the other, unbalancing everyone, and launching them toward the starry side, or whatever the term was. Loud retorts came from deeper below as the old wooden hull rode the waves. William hit the wall of the cabin first and then Helena landed against him. For a moment, her warm weight leant against him, and a pleasing waft of pressed linen and wildflowers filled his nose. His sense of overwhelming embarrassment, however, cancelled out all pleasure in the contact.

She apologised first. "I'm so sorry, Sir William. Ahem."

Seeming as awkward as him, she soon righted herself, and he slipped past her, taking the stairs for the deck. Then the world jolted again, requiring him to focus on staying upright. By now, the ship was slicing a groove through the water, its main sails filled with air. From the stern, with Lord Sola setting to the west, it made a wonderful sight.

As the evening wore into the night, fatigue engulfed him and he fell into a shallow sleep, rocked by the gentle motion of the ship as it skimmed the waves.

Dawn broke, revealing a canopy of darkening clouds, as the wind picked up further in strength. A crew member handed him a bowl of congealed cold broth, which he couldn't bring himself to eat. By midday, the wind had changed direction, now blowing from the southwest, and the swell had grown, causing the ship to wallow and rise in a steady rhythm. At the top of every rising, the inevitable slow falling away made William want to heave. Rain arrived to lash him, and he hunkered into a ball on the deck with his cloak and a dirty tarpaulin wrapped around him. Everything stank of something, tar, fish oil, or worse, making him feel awful. Helena came out and gave him stale, dry bread.

"This should help settle your stomach. We might not agree on 'owt, but we can still be civil."

He tried nibbling the bread, and it helped. A little. She then produced a flask containing what she declared was sailor's rum. "It's dead rough, but it'll help, like. Just sip, mind."

He took a swig and part choked. "Are you sure we're supposed to drink this stuff or tan leather with it?" It didn't stop him from taking another nip, though.

She looked out into the darkening sky, worry lines showing across her face.

"What's your intuition telling you about this wind?" he asked.

For a moment, he worried she'd take it as sarcasm, but she replied, "It's telling me as how there's a big storm approaching. So much for plain sailing." She went silent before vanishing below, leaving him to cope as best he could.

He spent the second night in pure misery. Icy sea water sprayed over him, his hands ached with the effort of clinging onto whatever he could grip, and exhaustion had set in. He had a major fight going on with his intestines, which seemingly wanted to reach up out of his throat and strangle him. The deck rocked harder, forcing him to lunge for something solid to hold on to.

At last dawn broke, but it brought with it ever darker clouds that streamed in from the distance and the looming storm threw squalls of leaden rain and hail at the ship. Waves smashed across the bows, sending frigid spray in all directions.

William had heard of how ships often got into trouble along the Gallian coast. How far away could that be? This looked dangerous. As the day continued, the sky darkened further, and as the wind became a gale, concern showed in the faces of the sailors. He found Dogwash on the bridge, wrestling with the wheel and barking instructions that were uselessly ripped from his mouth to be lost to the roar of blasting air.

"Are we safe?" William shouted, his mouth close to the other's ear. "Aren't those rocks I can see way off over there?"

William caught snatches of his reply. "They are. I'm aiming… beach… to starboard." The ship heaved in the opposite direction. "Do you believe … gods? …pray to them."

William looked out seawards. Was it a trick of the light or had a wall of water formed out on the horizon? It was hard to tell when the sea looked so much like the sky. The wall was moving closer though, in the precise way walls don't, gathering speed and height as it approached. He thought he saw a face in the wave. The puffy face of a woman. It was strange how the mind could conjure up human faces in everyday things. Every now and again, some deluded soul would swear blind that he'd seen King Inglebert's image in a lump of rye bread, a turnip, or even a cow's arse. Pure invention. However, he wasn't so sure he was inventing *this* face. It winked at him.

The water towered high above them and hung in the air before crashing down onto the wooden decks. As William clung to the rail, desperate to not get washed overboard, there was a percussive crack that shook the whole ship and the main mast crashed to the deck, spilling sails and a heavy rope, which thrashed whiplike across at him. He ducked under it. When the rail gave way, he slipped across the bucking deck toward the broiling water. His foot caught in some fallen rigging, and he hung, headfirst, suspended over the waves. Hands grasped his feet, and he looked up past them to see Ridkin and Matilda holding tight, mouthing something at him that got lost in the noise of the wind and the spray. As he swung with the waves, he cast his mind back to a passage he'd read somewhere about swimming. Not that he'd ever tried it, but it couldn't be all that difficult, could it? He'd once watched the lads from his village diving into the brook during the warmer summer months, and all they did to stay afloat was swish their arm about a bit. He wriggled his foot, kicked himself loose, and half-dived, half-fell.

William slammed, stunned, into a wall of frigid water and sank.

What had possessed him to dive into boiling waves in the middle of a storm? And now that he had, why didn't he rise? He was doing the right things, wasn't he? He pushed and flapped, but the harder he thrashed, the less control he had. Where was the logic in it? He bobbed up and down in a slow arc, with just the top of his head occasionally cresting the surface. With fresh resolve, he kicked out with all his strength and… sank again, his cloak dragging on his movements.

A certain natural buoyancy brought him most of the way back up again, but not far enough. He craned his neck up, uselessly gasping for air.

And he sank again.

The more he agitated, the more he slipped downward. It made no sense. The sky taunted him so close through the foam, but it may as well have been a mile distant. He managed another tantalising brush with the surface, then…

He sank again.

Powerless to hold his breath any longer, he took in a gulp of water and went still deeper. The salty bitterness of the brine made him want to retch, but he held that back. A taste of blood told him he must have bitten his tongue.

He sank again.

With his mounting exhaustion, everything slowed and each tiny detail of the light, of every bubble of gas around him, became ever more vivid. The sensation of cold and wet inside his stiff clothes chafed against his skin. The liquid in his ears muffled all sound, dulling the noise of the waves above and the shifting pebbles below. He made one more desperate bid, kicking with every last ounce of strength he could muster. It worked. He rose, yes, his face reached the air… thank the Stars. But before he could take a full breath…'

He sank away again.

All he got as reward for his efforts was a lung-full of seawater. Time slowed further. As his life force ebbed away, he sensed rather than saw the distorted face of an old woman and a rasping voice that spoke his name and told him, "Let go, let go…"

He felt ready to die.

~~~

Feydor and Mary sat together, hunched over an occulem, a kind of small vanity mirror in which they watched the events unfolding on the Gallian coast several hundred miles away. Filthy lurked somewhere behind Feydor, still not comfortable with his proximity to Mary, as if Imelda had bred into him her hatred for her cousin.

This morning, a level of privacy had been important, so here they were in the extensive, if gloomy and rather damp smelling, wine cellar of Prince Albert's Bell End residence.

"Where is The Bonnie Prince of Bell End, anyway?" asked Feydor.

"Och, gadding about town, trying to be noticed. He's kenned that he's the nearest in line to be the next king, should something happen to Inglebert, and it's gone to his wee head."

Feydor had to take his hat off to her for getting her claws into royal blood; she could yet become an improbable consort to the King of Anglonia. He looked about the room in undisguised distaste. The place was filthy and a complete mess to boot. And at the epicentre of the disorder was the occulem surrounded by tools, bottles, retorts, clamps, jars, and open
~~~

crates. His hands were clenching and unclenching with the urge to leap up and get tidying it all.

William had just spent the previous two minutes submersed. He looked all but beaten. Mary leaned forward over the mirror, intent on her victim. "Och, he's fading. He willnae be lasting much longer. Come on, William, let's have a wee sleep. All will pass....let go...let go..." William, his face grey and lips blue, drifted down, inert.

Mary's black cat, Mite, wandered in with the body of a still thrashing mouse in its mouth. The moment it spotted Filthy, it dropped the rodent, arched its back, and hissed like a beast possessed. The mouse scuttled away under the nearest cupboard while Mary, absentminded, lifted the irate moggie to her lap to calm it while she concentrated on the occulem.

Filthy the monkey wasn't taking this lightly. He gave out a shrill, piercing and unworldly scream, leaping onto Feydor's shoulders and launching himself at the cat, fangs bared, spitting, and hissing. Mary swatted him away in mid-flight with her arm, sending him flying toward the cluttered table on which the occulem stood. Filthy crashed onto the table, knocking an array of bottles, ornaments, and figurines, one into the other, in a domino cascade of glass and spilt liquids. Vial after vial, vessel after vessel, propelled splintering glass across the bench and over the floor, where it further fragmented and spread. In weird slow motion, the last thing to fall was the little viewing mirror, which teetered one way, then the other, seemed to almost settle, then... tipped over the edge. It spun in mid-air three times while Mary made a desperate acrobatic lunge for it. Slipping between her fumbling hands, it hit the floor, and smashed into a thousand shards with a loud *thwock*, a sound like the air being sucked out of the room. Filthy scampered behind a chair while Mite raced out the door.

"No..." she screamed, incandescent. "It took me years to get my hands on that. This is your fault, carrot brain. Where is that bastard animal? Let me at it. I'll wring its neck, I swear it." She unleashed a bolt of white, which the monkey dodged. He hid behind his master.

"How's it my fault?" protested Feydor. "You frighten the poor creature at the best of times, but to let that cat..."

She screamed her frustration, then sat arms folded, nostrils flared, shooting a baleful stare in his direction that would cut stone. At last, her breathing returned to something approaching normal.

Feydor broke the silence. "So, I assume we are now blind. We don't know whether William is dead or alive."

"Och, dinnae worry yourself, he has to be dead. You saw him sinking away there. You'll pay for a new occulem, mind, and they don't come cheap."

"If we destroy Imelda, I'll buy ten of them for you. What if William isn't dead?"

"He's dead alright, now leave me before you do any more damage. I need to think without your damnable furball glowering at me."

He stood. "By the way, what news have you of the twins?"

"Fraser and Irvine left yesterday on a ship for Gallia and should be arriving there about now. Nae bother. They're good lads. They'll do what's necessary."

Feydor refrained from commenting. Never had the word *good* been applied to less fitting men. The pair of them were outright vile, pitiless, and vindictive. Which, of course, made them perfect for their roles in stealing the crystal.

~~~

As William sank little by little, drifting towards unconsciousness, Ridkin's face loomed into view, the proportions distorted, either by the light or by William's fuddled senses. His thoughts swirled like mist out of reach, and he scarcely perceived that his descent into the darkness had reversed. Ridkin held William in a bear hug and kicked hard for the surface until they hit the air. William spat water and gulped what he could into his lungs. And then resumed his total panic, lashing out with his arms, forcing Ridkin to let go again. Down he slipped. Ridkin pulled him up and lost him. Exhaustion came like a weight tied to their ankles, the current dragging them both away from safety. When they next surfaced, William gasped, "Leave me, save yourself!"
~~~

As Ridkin too weakened, another body appeared and took William into its arms from behind. In this position, William couldn't struggle, and he, together with the mystery saviour, floated to the surface.

"Matilda!" shouted Ridkin in amazement.

"Help me," she called.

Between them, William's inert bulk became easier to handle, and within minutes, they lay breathless on the sand among fragments of smashed timber, while waves broke around them. William heaved gut wrenching coughs from deep in his chest as his lungs fought to replace water with air. He vomited and collapsed, gasping.

Matilda spoke soft reassurances into his ear: "Calm yourself, trust your body, breathe full and slow. Count with me. In two, three, out two, three…" And, yes, his panic subsided, his breathing became slower and more confident. Alive!

"Where did you learn to do that?" Ridkin asked Matilda as he caught his breath.

"From father, o' course," as if to say how silly of you not to realise that.

Helena ran over to help them to their feet, and they staggered away from the waves. Around them stood or sat the rest of the crew, although, of the captain, there was no sign. "He stayed to get everyone off the ship," said Ridkin. "It looks like he never made it."

People arrived dressed in unfamiliar peasant clothes, ready to help with warm cloaks and dry blankets. They didn't speak any language that William could understand, but it didn't matter. The dialect of compassion is universal. The villagers took the four friends and the crew up and away from the beach and sat them sheltered outside a tiny temple, giving them beakers of hot broth and honey sweet biscuits. They were relieved to be out of the tearing wind and rain, but the storm soon lost its force and exited stage left, leaving the sky cloudless again.

Helena stood, shaking her head and looking out to sea, leaving William puzzled, but before he could ask her why, a panicked realisation came across him.

"But my books! What will I read?"

"You wouldn't be reading nuffing with yer arse sat on the bottom of the bay, Will," said Ridkin.

Coming to his senses, William turned to Ridkin and Matilda and said, "You both saved my life. How can I ever thank you?"

"Don't get carried away," said Matilda. "Happen we'd both have done it for anyone," then added, "but when we held you on the ship, why did you wriggle from our grip?"

"I read a description of swimming once. It seemed easy enough…"

"For the love of the Stars," said Matilda, rolling her eyes. "This lickspittle's books will be the end of him. And of us, I shouldn't wonder."

~~~

Based on books William had read in the monastery library, Willliam predicted it would take perhaps four weeks to travel the distance to Ianua. He had Ridkin and Matilda make for the nearest town to buy mules and provisions, and as soon as they returned, the group set off to find the pilgrim trail, the famous Via Frangipani[42], that led all the way to Trusca itself. He calculated it would run through a hilly region, three or more leagues to the east, and if they crossed the low line of hills visible in that direction, they were certain to stumble on it. To Ridkin's evident annoyance, but William's delight, he turned out to be correct.

At an inn in the first town they came across a large group of merchants bound for Mediola in western Italica. They were friends and associates of long-standing, well used to making the journey through Gallia and onto the silk road, and in consequence full of exciting stories and strange, improbable tales.

Their fellow guests included traders in spices, textiles, carpets, arms, and many other things besides. They had a minstrel and a puppeteer for entertainment, and for the soul, a travelling friar. And with this being the city of Bordax, they had plenty of excellent food and wine. William felt alive and carefree, ready to confront the challenges ahead. He pushed the recent near death experience to the back of his mind, confident he had the most troubling part of the journey behind him.
~~~

He wanted to hear all about Italica from the group. Not the poetic descriptions of the books he'd read, but the *real* Italica. He learned that it wasn't a country at all, but a mish-mash of ducal states, run by nobles and the priesthood, each with its own distinctive dialect[43] and cuisine. Wars broke out over the most trivial of issues, which could range from a perceived slight to an opportunistic grab for tax yielding territory. On one famous occasion, a five-year conflict had arisen over how best to make lasagna[44]. Recently, Duke Cosimo had come to power and brought together most of the western states in an alliance that centred around a mania for documentation and record keeping. All transactions, all building projects, births, marriages, deaths, and who knows what else had to be recorded. They called it Red Ribbon[45], since the documents were bound up with the stuff. The trouble was, there were neither the scriveners to do the scribing, nor paper on which to do it.

One man told him, "Duke Cosimo is bad news. They say he's part Janasà himself."

"That's just false tidings," said another, "put about by his enemies."

"Why else would he be so short and ugly?" asked the first.

The second man nodded. "Well... people in Sardonica are shorter than in Italica, so maybe it's happened. Me? I find it hard to believe."

William had to ask, "What *about* the Janasà? What are they *like*?"

A man replied, saying, "Ugly as wild boars. It's said that when the gods finished making our arses, they used what remained to make the Janasà. They are vermin like rats, and like rats, the more you cut them down, the more they come back stronger than ever."

"Aye, and they hate humans as much as we hate them," said another.

"If it weren't for the Ninfiné, they'd have taken over all Yorpia by now."

"That's just hearsay,"

"No, brother. They keep themselves to themselves, but sure enough, where the Ninfiné are, the Janasà stay away."

"But who is or who are the Ninfiné?" said William

"Fairies. Wood nymphs. Nonsense. Mark my words. The Janasà have a master plan to take over the world. Whatever it takes. Ain't no fairies can stop them."

"I saw a Ninfiné eat a Janasà. I swear it."

"What had you been drinking, brother?"

And on and on. It all sounded ridiculous to William. He'd just have to find out for himself.

~~~

Feydor opened the door to his chambers and heard a rustling sound like a leaf as his foot scrunched on a piece of parchment. Not paper, but actual parchment. On examination, it bore a short message written with an ornate, cursive script. The text read, *Meet me at the main temple at sundown. IS*. IS? That had to be Ignatius Stackpole. What could that conniving, viscid, vomitive, lickspittle puke-stocking want with Feydor?

When he rolled up at the palace temple gates, a man Feydor knew as Robert Pyke, a rough, weasel-like, bruiser of a character and Stackpole's minder, ushered him to the anteroom at the back. There, the priest had installed a small library with soft chairs and softer candles. A female minstrel in a white tunic plucked a lute in the background. A fountain gurgled nearby, and a canary chirped away in a silvery cage. Pyke offered him wine from a decanter, which Feydor hesitated to accept. It could contain poison, but in the curious mood he was in, he took it. Boglets and be damned.

Stackpole materialised behind him, giving him the briefest of starts. "Ah Feydor, may Lord Sola shine brightly on you this fine morning."

Feydor, for a moment off balance, collected his wits. This was how the insufferable goose-saddler spoke when he wanted something. He joined in the game. "Well met, Your Grace. May the light of Uranus[46] be upon you."

"Uranus indeed. Is this what you call a joke, my dear Fool? How very droll."

Stackpole had arrived at court the summer before, after the mysterious demise of his predecessor, who had, according to the record, been caught *in flagrante delicto* with an entire coterie of young acolytes in their shared bedchamber and been executed on the spot. As Feydor recalled it, Stackpole had been the one to uncover this cesspit of depravity at the heart of the
~~~

priesthood, and it had shocked the royal court, given that the perpetrator had a strong reputation for excessive piety. Stackpole was a short, rounded man, whose face had long since surrendered the fight against the dense hair that sprouted from his nose, ears, and eyebrows. It made Feydor want to reach out and rummage for the cheeks and lips he knew to be hidden in the hirsute depths of his visage.

"How can I be of help, Lord High Priest? A diverting entertainment perchance?" Feydor couldn't resist shaking the bells on his bauble, and Filthy gave a good impression of laughter.

The priest scowled. "Must you take this creature everywhere?"

"Filthy is but a harmless little mite, Your Grace."

Stackpole stared at Filthy. "Harmless? I'm not too sure of that. Please be seated."

It was time to move things along. "Was there something in particular you wished to discuss, Lord High Priest?"

"Oh, come now, Ignatius is my name. We can be on familiar terms, you and I, can we not?"

Feydor wanted to say *when all seven hells freeze over,* but held his tongue. Instead, he nodded.

"You know," began Stackpole, easing himself back into his chair and stroking his beard. "I have thought much about the King - may the firmament bestow its light upon him - and have motive to think his recent illness to be an unnatural act, or indeed a crime against nature."

"Somebody poisoned him, perchance? - May his haemorrhoids be forever small." Darn it, what did the priest know?

"Not poison as such, no. This resembles more of a curse."

Feydor didn't miss a beat. "Is that so, My Lord? What makes you think thus?"

"After so many years as a priest, I've learned to see the signs, the little clues." He tapped his nose to convey what? Wisdom? The man wouldn't know wisdom if it bit his arse. "Magic has a certain aura to it, you know. A glow. An aroma even."

Boglets! If the priest could genuinely perceive the glow of magic… he, Feydor, would need to be a lot more careful about how he used it. "Really?" he replied, feigning a yawn. "How interesting."

"And what's more, the charts confirm it." Stackpole sat back and folded his arms as if to say this was all the proof needed.

"Isn't astrology a mere superstition for the simple-minded? And is it not a sin against the Stars?"

"For most purposes, yes, but if you are someone who has access to the true charts, they are most instructive, and astrology is permitted to those of us who carry the heavy burden of guarding the flock."

"I see," said Feydor. "And you are such a shepherd?"

The priest smiled.

Feydor asked, "So, if someone has cursed the King - may his birthdays all come at once - then who do you think is behind it?"

"I cannot be certain, but I will state that such acts against nature cannot and will not be tolerated. Do you understand me?"

"I believe I grasp your general drift. What else do your charts portend? Will the King - may maidens swoon at his every breath - recover?" Feydor couldn't help but betray his interest.

"They aren't all that specific."

They never were. It meant you could make up anything you wanted to justify yourself.

"But the message I am reading," Stackpole went on, "is that there will be a new king - may the Moons have mercy upon King Inglebert - before the year is out."

"Ah."

"Feydor, let me be frank. If, hypothetically of course, a new king were to be needed, then I aim to be that king. I'm what this land needs; a complete exorcism of witches, and everything that goes with them. We shall have a kingdom once and for all free of superstition and magic."

Good luck with that, thought Feydor. "How very perspicacious you are. But what is it you want of me, your Grace? I am but a simple Fool."

"Don't play the pillock with me. Meseems you are the least foolish person at court, myself excluded, of course. I observe people, Feydor, and I see how you are the same. We can work together to safeguard the realm."

"Is that so?"

"There'd be an ennoblement and land in it for you, of course. Lord Fool, something of the sort, and you can have the county of Nuffolk. There's nothing there, anyway, beyond marshes and bogs. What I need is for you to be my eyes and my ears. I want to know everything there is to discover about my rivals."

"Who are?" said Feydor, feigning ignorance.

"Oh, two relative inconsequentials, not worth the effort to mention."

"Please indulge me."

"One is the current Earl of Ebury, an insignificant fellow, but popular among the northern nobles and the lower orders."

"Sir John Scratchface. Interesting. And the other?"

"The Albian Prince Albert, who by birth has a gossamer thread of a claim to the throne. Both are inestimable gentlemen to be sure - may Lord Sola bless their days with boundless happiness - but unsuited to such a high and sacred office. Would you not agree?"

"It is not for one such as I to comment. However, I take it you wish me to spy on these men?"

The man winced. "To spy is such a distasteful expression, but it conveys the general idea, yes."

"I see. If I decline?"

"I'll have you banished."

Of course. Well, Feydor had no intention of spying or anything else for the priestly dolt; he'd have preferred to boil his own head before furthering the man's narcissistic dreams. Still, he'd have to play this with the utmost care.

Stackpole stood and escorted Feydor to the exit, followed by an attentive Pyke. "I'm so glad we could have this little conversation. Now, not a word to anyone, and be sure to update me as soon as you've seen Albert again. Good day Feydor, may the Stars bless your every waking step."

He wanted to reply, *may your manly member shrivel and fall off with the pox; may you trip over your own weeping ball-sack; may your sad arse be filled with festering boils*… But instead, he bowed. "As to yours, Your Grace."

# Nine

Feydor was not at all at the top of his caper on account of his father's final letter. *That* letter. The one he'd written before going to his death. It had robbed Feydor of his peace of mind, thrown him off balance, invaded his dreams. The night before, he'd cried. For pity's sake! They'd beat the crying out of him when he was eight years old, trained him to contain his emotions. To control them. To shape them. This, *this*, was too big. Horrible. And yet… Deep down he'd known he had to let the hurt work itself out and then, only then, to plan his revenge.

He shouldn't have come, not in this frame of mind, but a nagging doubt that William might have survived Mary's storm had nibbled away at his resolve. And facing his mother was the only way to find out whether William yet lived.

Today he had Filthy sitting on his shoulder, having dispensed with the basket that only got in the way of working his rotund form through the crowded streets. A hawker tugged at Feydor's cloak to offer him some chestnuts, but the creature hissed and spat so much that the man withdrew. Interesting. Was his pet defending him or did it just hate strangers? He passed blind Harry on his usual street corner and pressed a gold coin into his hand. "Buy yourself a meal fit for a prince, Harry," he said and pushed on up Cheap Side. "Boglets, I must be going soft," he muttered to himself.

As he dragged himself into the Castle And Ball, Rod, the landlord, beckoned him over. "A word in your shell-like," he said, his voice nasal, flat and inexpressive.

Everything about Rod sang, if not chorused, in a four-part contrapuntal madrigal of negativity. The publican had never so much as welcomed a guest, attempted to make light small talk with one, cracked the mildest of smiles, or, heaven forbid, made eye contact in a *Hail stranger well met. What will you have?* sort of a way. He was a tavern half-empty kind of guy. Except that the tavern was, for the most part, entirely empty. A corpse in full rigor mortis was less, well, stiff, it had more people skills and at least with a cadaver, there would be the chance of a smile, albeit a rictus one. Over the years, the tavern had lurched, teetered and then dived headlong from a lively trade in ale and pies down to an obstinate trickle of forlorn drinkers, themselves so joyless as to render them as welcome anywhere else as a haemorrhoid at a farting contest. The year before, his establishment had come, by some significant margin, bottom in a poll of Ludnam's Jolliest Taverns, a scraping-the-bottom-of the-firkin kind of achievement, of which Rod felt a mischievous and ill-conceived pride.

"Yes, Rodnye. Is it important? I'm not in the mood today."

"Sorry Feydor, but could you please ask your mother to keep the noise down just a tinsy-winsy bit?" He mimed something tiny with two fingers of his right hand. "She's making a racket like a dozen banshees up there at night. Also, the tannery next door has been complaining about the stench. Whatever she's doing, can she stop it, please?"

Tanneries used human waste to soften leather and the dense, acrid stink could strip the bark off a tree at a thousand paces. He should be impressed, but he wasn't in the mood. "Why's it my problem? Ask her yourself or go forth…"

Rod interrupted him. "Blimey, you're in a good mood today. Of course, I could speak to her myself, if I wished to die in torment."

For Rod to die in excruciating agony would be a relief to everyone, including Rod himself, if only he thought about it. He gave Rod his best withering stare and trudged up the stairs to Imelda's sanctum. "Is there news on Coxwell?" he snapped, Rod's complaints already out of mind.

Today she had again dressed head to toe in black, in her usual unique style that revealed much more of her ample bosom than Feydor could ever have wanted to see.

"No greeting, Feydor?" she said. "How are you, my boy? Morwena tells me Coxwell is progressing well."

There. He'd known it. Coxwell lived. He forced himself to be civil. He even attempted a smile. "Indeed mother?"

He walked to the only chair, but before he could sit, he needed to pick up the piece of fabric on the seat; The Drowning Hood. This was her favourite torture device. Something was very wrong.

"You've been a naughty little jester, haven't you Feydor? Such a fool!" She smiled at her own wit.

Could he have actually slipped up? Had Mary ratted on him? "I don't know what you mean, mother. I've always tried to serve you."

"Hah, is that so? Think! What have you done that I didn't condone? Take your time."

He couldn't resist goading her. "Um, I had oatmeal for breakfast three days this week?"

She slapped him hard enough across the face to rock his chair back onto its rear legs before it settled to the floor. Her amulet glowed like amber.

"I'll get to the point, since I don't want to play this game all day. Do you have anything to do with his Majesty and his current malaise?"

"Um, no, mother,"

She whacked him again, on the other cheek, even harder than the first. Then she turned to her desk and picked up a pair of books. She held one up to him.

"Ah," he said.

"Is that all you have to say?"

"Would sorry be enough?"

She kicked his kneecap, making him grab his leg.

"So, you found some diverting little volumes containing party curses and made them work for you? I'd congratulate you if I weren't so angry. There's one page in particular I want you to look at."

She pointed out the curse that Feydor had enacted to bind up His Majesty's vitals.

"How...How did you find these?" he asked.

"I had someone go through your chambers and these are what he discovered, along with a bunch of stolen stuff that you had no right taking for yourself. I knew you were up to something, and here is the proof. You used a pale imitation of magic to curse the King. I didn't know you had it in you, but that aside, let's get this clear: you stick to jesting, I do the magic."

Although Feydor didn't believe in the Sun and Moons religious stuff, he nonetheless offered a silent prayer of thanks to Great Sola, that she'd uncovered his attempts at cursing, rather than his full-on betrayal of her to Mary. Curses, though, he needed to find a better hiding place if he wanted to keep things private from the vile old sow.

"What have you got to say for yourself?"

He lost all patience, and for once, dared to raise his voice to her. "Say for myself? I'll tell you what I've got to say for myself. The King and that conniving half-wit priest Stackpole were about to banish me to Emeraldia, and I needed to act fast. There wasn't the time to involve you."

"Watch your tongue, nit brain. The fact you had the book in the first place is disobedient. And anyway, you should have told me. I won't tolerate you messing with magic." Her dark amulet glowed red. Was she *enjoying* this? "Put it on," she said, pointing at the Drowning Hood. "I'm going to give you a lesson in obedience."

He did as he was told, it being useless to resist, and waited for his punishment. Filthy scampered away to a safe distance. He didn't need to wait long before the familiar and dreaded feeling of drowning began, or at least what he thought of as drowning. It was like being in the depths of a life-sucking dark lake, unable to breathe, and getting dragged downward into a frigid trench, while harpy shrieks filled his ears. Sneering ghoulish faces leered out from the darkness as though lit by flickering torches and danced in a circle around him. His limbs were on fire and his lungs full of gelid, cloying water. The smell and taste of rotting algae rose and made him panic and retch. And yet, for once, he didn't care. He grinned to himself and pumped his fist. She knew nothing of his deeper betrayal! Let her have her five minutes of pleasure at his expense, because in that moment of darkest torment, he gathered his hatred for her and forced it down into a stoppered flask. And with it, the torture dissolved. He took control of his mind and drove out the banshees, the algae, the burning... He was sitting in a room above a tavern with a hood over his head. What was the fuss about?

She pulled away the hood, showing no sign of having noticed his little victory. "I forgive you and your frail, masculine flesh. Besides, you've made me realise we need to consider the royal succession."

"What is it you want me to do about that?"

"Do about it? Find out what's going on, pillock. What's being said behind closed doors? Who's conspiring with whom to succeed him? I shouldn't have to explain this stuff to you."

He nodded.

Down in the tavern again, Feydor passed Rod wiping a bench down, which was a first. That said, the rag he was using looked like it'd wiped a hog's arse. "How'd it go, Feydor? Did you ask her about the smell?"

"Get stood on," he snapped back with more venom than he'd intended. "Sorry, Rod, but I've more important concerns just now."

~~~

For the first few days of the trek across Gallia, William and the three others wallowed in warming sunshine under azure skies. The stiff breeze whipped in fresh from the northwest, and the few puff balls of high cloud there were, scudded along like white-robed acolytes running late for temple duty. Dense conifers lined the ancient road, the sharp smell of spring pine oil needled their noses, and noisy rabbles of squabbling geese passed over in tick-shape formation migrating north toward Anglonia. William had read how these birds mated for life, so he imagined their noise to be the familiar bickering of old married couples. What did they have to argue about? Plumages not groomed? Goslings not disciplined? Whatever the problem, they made a rare old racket about it.

The lengthening days brought cherry trees, rhododendrons, and sweet-smelling magnolias into vivid bloom. Birds squeaked, chirped and squawked in ever greater numbers. Bees and insects bustled about in the meadows and hedgerows, and the sun god Sola continued to spread his beneficence. William, experiencing optimism for the first time since leaving Ebury, pushed the trauma of his experiences at sea to the back of his mind.
~~~

For three days, the road worked upwards almost without break, snaking across tree covered hillsides, searching for the best way to surmount the tallest of them. In the far distance surged the white tipped peaks of the high Alpian mountains, the improbable gateway into Italica.

On the fourth day, the sky darkened, but rather than turning into another full-blown storm, the weather set itself to downpour mode. It took less than a day for the firm road surface to turn into a bog that made progress on foot next to impossible and on mule-back not much better. The rain leeched all the colour from the landscape, driving it into the relentless mud. Wetness worked its way through heavy cloaks, and chafed the skin, before penetrating inside the bones and gnawing away at the very spirit of a person. Their stops became longer owing to the time it took to dry out clothes and the reluctance of the travellers to abandon shelter. At least there were plenty of inns to choose from, and often they also found castles[47], monastic refuges and even private dwellings, their occupants happy to take in wet, bedraggled, and demoralised wayfarers. If he doubted that the gods rewarded such charity, or even existed, he wasn't about to complain about receiving it.

After seven days of gelid soaking, the deluge at long last eased, the skies cleared, and the flies came out to play, swarming around people's eyes and mouths. William swatted them away for several hours, but gave up after that, letting them do what they would, much as the mules were obliged to. In the evening, the twin waning moons straddled the luminescent ribbon of the Milky Way, which looked like painters had whitewashed it onto the darkness. What kind of scaffolding reached high enough for someone to paint the sky? The Ancient Grecans believed it comprised countless stars, squished together to appear like a brush-stroke, but how could there be so many?

He lay on a canvas sheet spread on the damp ground and gazed up, marvelling at what he could see, the cool earth pressing into his back. He'd read much about the stars and their wandering companions, the planets. Helena joined him, and together they tried to spot the north star, Jumpiter, OBrian, the Hoe, and so on. William didn't recognise every constellation, so he made up his own. "Look, just there. That's the Weeping Wench. And over there, you can see The Praying Monk and the Sleeping Bishop."

Helena took all this in and said, "You are so clever William, how do you know of these things?"

"It's all in books. There's The Soldier, and right there…"

"Yes?"

"That's the Angry Gnome."

She glared at him, her eyes narrowed. "You're making these up! Making fun of me!" Gone, the smile. "Just because you're cleverer than me, there's no reason to rub it in. I am *not* stupid. Nasty man."

She stood up and walked away, leaving William befuddled and feeling sorry for himself.

~~~

As the journey wore on, William looked for distractions. He started telling the story of Don Creosote to Ridkin, who listened with keen attention, as did Helena and Matilda, a short distance behind them.

"Will, what manner of man writes such a tale?" asked Ridkin.

"I know little about him, other than he wrote it in prison. And it took him years."

"But why? Why go to the bother? Alright, I guess there wasn't nothing else to do, but still…"

"Because in writing the story, he wanted to say something. Something about what it is to truly want one thing, the wrong thing, while deep down needing something very different. And that, by making mistakes, changing into a better person. There's a moral to the tale that we can use in our own lives. That's how I understand it, at any rate."

"Sounds like a load of old tosh to me."

"Aren't you interested in what happens to Don Creosote?"

"S'all right. If you likes that kind of thing."

William hesitated before asking a question that had bothered him since leaving Ebury. "Can you tell me? What is it you hate so much about me?"
~~~

"I don't hate you. But just listen to yourself. You talk all fancy with big words and ideas that I can't understand. It's like you're better than the rest of us. Go on, admit it."

"Why? Because I can read? I could teach you to read, you know."

"Wait, no. Don't you dare. Make yourself feel all good inside by teaching the poor bumpkin letters?" Ridkin, while not shouting, was speaking with force. "You can tickle right off, Sir Know-it-all." And he dropped back to continue riding some distance behind.

William turned to Helena and asked, "What did I do? I just offered to teach him to read. Isn't that a good thing?"

"My sense was he's angry," said Helena.

"I got that, mistress. But why be angry with *me*?"

"Perhaps he isn't," said Matilda. "He might be afraid, but he makes it look like he's upset. Have you thought about that?"

"You're talking in riddles, Mistress."

"Think about it. What might Ridkin fear so much that he won't do what's good for him?" she asked.

"No clue there. Sorry."

The girl paused before responding. "He might fear failure. Not having the noggin and losing face. That would be the worst thing for him to confront."

"You think?"

"I do, yes. It sounds like one of the morals in your book. Happen you need to find another way. Make him see as how it's worth the risk."

"Tilda's right," said Helena. "You're the logical one, like. I'm sure you'll work it out."

Both refused to be drawn any further on the topic, leaving William to think. Was there any truth in what they'd said? Even if there were, he couldn't see how to deal with it. Well, like his old father had often said, a problem slept on was a problem ignored for a few hours. He'd leave it be for now. But was there a moral here he could apply? That was the second time he'd said the wrong thing: the first was when he'd joked with Helena about the stars, and now this. Except that, for now at least, he was just as confused as ever. He could only hope it would get more obvious with time.

~~~

Feydor's concerns about the threat Stackpole posed grew by the day. After all, he'd failed to do the priest's bidding by not furnishing him with so much as a single morsel of covert information. The holy hairball wouldn't ignore this and therefore had to be up to something, and it wasn't in Feydor's nature to just let things happen. He needed to know what the creep was planning and the best option by far would be to bug him where he felt most at ease: the temple. However, how to get one of his scarabs secreted there without arousing suspicion?

That today was International Maiden's Day, an important festival held in celebration of the fairer sex was too good an opportunity to miss. Every woman related to the palace would converge on the temple for prayers of thanks for the bounteous wonders of femininity. This seemed like a hollow show of solidarity, given how the ludicrous and hypocritical priesthood considered women and their lustful natures to be the font of all evil[48].

Well, Ruthenia's ladies-in-waiting were international women, or at least women from the Kingdom of Luthenia, and they would want to attend the event. Acting on an idea, he scampered toward the Queen's wing of the palace and knocked on Lady Rasa's door.

"One moment," she called out. The door opened. "Feydor, I don't expect today. What you want?"

"I have a small favour to ask of you. I hope you don't mind beetles."

She looked at him, confused.

"You know, little black things with legs."

Her eyes widened. "You Anglonians eat insects? But I'm rude. Come in."

He followed her over the threshold and into the parlour. "We don't eat insects, no. You misunderstand me. See this? Give me your hand."

He took from a pocket a folded linen 'kerchief and pressed it into her palm. "All I need you to do is place this somewhere out of sight in the temple today. Not the 'kerchief. What it contains. No, don't look now. It's a scarab. Just release it and let it do what it wants. Can you do that for me?"
~~~

She looked doubtful. "Why? Why you want this thing?"

"I can't explain it now, but if you do it, I will entertain you tonight. Just you."

"In that case, of course." She smiled broadly.

While Feydor himself took minimal joy in lying with a woman, he found, quite oddly, that he enjoyed giving them pleasure in much the same way he loved making other people laugh. And they were generally grateful enough to do him small or even quite large favours in return. "Excellent. Until this merry eve." He bowed and walked away, happy that the first step of his plan was in motion.

Two hours later, he received news that Rasa had placed his bug. Now he just needed to wait.

~~~

In the central Gallian town of Senapia, William's party found a sprawling market in full swing. Customers jostled between jammed in stalls laden with anything and everything you could want to buy. Except books. There were meats, cheeses, vegetables of every colour and shape, trinkets, cooking pots, firewood, and garments. Lots of garments. Did Gallian men and women spend all day changing from one costume to another? At last, at one small stall hidden in an alleyway, he hit gold; it sold books. Stories, poetry, almanacks, travel guides, scriptures; it had everything. He bought several volumes, including even the second part of the Don Creosote story, and a much older, altogether more interesting one. No more than a span tall, it had a red cover and embossed yellow lettering. Inside, the text was tightly formed, and the letters weren't easy to recognise. Parts he could read; passages in old Grecan and Truscan were easy enough. The bulk of it, however, made no sense at all. Yes, there were letters grouped together to form something like words, but not words that made sense. It had margins decorated with fine drawings of living things, both plants and animals, and dense descriptions, all of them incomprehensible. The scribe in him instantly recognised the work of a master when he saw it. He had to have
~~~

it. Ridkin stopped him from paying full price, then wandered off saying he wanted to try some local sweetbreads.

A little further down the street, William found himself being taken in by a man shuffling three cups on a low plank of wood, taking bets on which one had a bean under it. He soon lost a substantial sum.

Ridkin returned to his shoulder. "Will, watch out. It's a con. A trick. These crooks'd steal your grandmother."

"What do you mean, a trick? It was plain as my nose which cup contained the bean."

"It's never, ever, where you think it is. That's the whole point. You don't have a clue, do you?"

"So, he'd have taken all my money?"

"Every groat."

"Is anybody honest in this world?"

"Nobody. Not even you. Not all the time, like every waking hour of every day. You're lying to yourself if you think different. It don't make no sense to lie to yourself, not in my book. And for Lord Sola's sake, stop pretending the King gives a rat's whisker about your quest."

"But if I don't believe the King, what's the point? I've got to believe in something."

"I only know what I can see and touch for myself. You should start thinking the same way… If you ask me."

But he did believe in something. He believed in reason and that it would change the world for the better. Somebody had to think that way.

~~~

The common mosquito has a complex apparatus of mouthparts comprising six separate components that permit the animal to penetrate skin, find blood vessels and draw the fluid from within. Besides these six pieces, there is a seventh less obvious one that's not described in books: Malice. Mosquitoes are an ancient genus that, over many millennia, has evolved a visceral hatred for breathing animals and for humans in particular, on account of the perpetual war we wage against them. So, they hide away
~~~

in nooks and crannies within our houses, and wait for the most silent moments of the night and then, only then, they attack with that whining buzz that invokes expectant terror in the victim. Furthermore, the fluid that we think they inject into our veins to keep the blood from clotting is, in fact, designed to cause the worst possible welts, which can persist for days, making the victim rub and scratch day and night.

"Shine a light!" shouted William. "A purple pox on every damnable insect that bites."

As the evening gloom had gathered strength, the mosquitoes had arrived in numbers. They had lined up on the ceiling, ready to take a turn at diving at him. They easily eluded his many futile attempts at self-defence, to the point where it was useless to try to hold them away. There were swarms of them! Could they do a waggle dance the way a bee could? He had angry red welts everywhere. His welts had angry red welts everywhere. Soon, all his blood would have been sucked out and that would have been an end to it.

For some reason, the blood of a tall mortal man, pale of skin, blonde of hair and weak of heart, far from home, was perfect for female mosquitos who wished to feed their young. For some other reason, everyone else in his party found this hilarious.

That night, William dreamt of faces. First Verity came to him, arms outstretched, begging for his return. *Time is precious. Please save me. Hurry!*

"I'll be there. I promise!"

She faded to be replaced by his father, shaking his head in reproach. "Nay lad, you'll never amount to 'owt," said the old man. "Useless lump. Always stuck with yer nose in a book. I should o' drowned you when I had the chance."

"I'm sorry, father, I'm trying my best."

Next came his mother. She seemed to be telling him something; her mouth moved, but no words came out. "Mummy," he called out. His memories of her were so vague and so sparse; he wanted to speak to her, to listen to her, to be held by her, but like the others, her image vanished.

The procession of familiar faces stopped, and in their place, that of an old woman like the one from the storm, came into view and loomed out over him. He'd pushed her out of his mind since that day of his near-death experience, but now she appeared to him as vivid as if she were in the room and leaning over him. This time, instead of seeming to want him dead, she murmured softly in the way, he supposed, that a mother soothes a young child in the night. Lost memories of his own mother swirled in his head and wove themselves into the dream. The woman transformed into his mother, and he reached out to her to be picked up and nuzzled into her neck and shoulder. And everything felt *real.* Natural. Good. However, a voice in the back of his mind objected. This was illogical. Implausible. Impossible. It couldn't *be* his mother, and much as trusting the image of her *felt* right, he couldn't do it. His imagination had to be playing tricks on him. He blocked out his mother, who resolved back into an old woman. He blanked her out as well and awoke with a start. The moment of waking normally revealed to the dreamer that his experience had been just that. A dream. This had been different. He shuddered.

It couldn't have been real. Twice now he'd imagined seeing an old woman, with a hooked nose and pudgy face. A *witch?* Where did that idea come from? He didn't believe in witches or in strange faces manifesting themselves within waves. His imagination must have made it all up. The mind saw faces in everything. By force of will, he dismissed his visions and sat up, wishing he had a candle handy to read by and could distract himself with his new book purchase. Frustrated, he lay down again and practised his Truscan declensions and conjugations. It never failed; the next instant daylight played on his lidded eyes, and he awoke, going into his favourite cat-like stretch, ready for another day's travel.

~~~

The four tired and, it has to be said, smelly travellers dragged themselves, or at least their mules did, into Ianua, the first significant city on the Italican pilgrim trail to Trusca. For the last few leagues, the route had tracked close to the coast and taken them over a succession of high passes, always with the azure ocean to their right, glimmering in the early spring sunshine. William understood Ianua to be an ancient and important
~~~

port serving the entire coastline of the Middle Sea, although reaching it from the north would test the hardiest of travellers.

On arrival at the gates, they'd needed to fill out several documents, stating origin, nationality, immediate parentage, and purpose of visit. And of course they'd had to pay taxes.

"What's all this for?" asked William, referring to the mountain of paper.

An official dressed in elaborate formal attire, complete with gold braid, peered through his eyeglass at William. "Orders of the Duke. All travellers are to be documented, checked and taxed[49]. Oh, I see you are an Anglonian knight. Knights pay an extra ducat in tax. It also says here that your occupation is *On A Very Important Quest.* This is hardly a profession, but I will let that pass. You have, I presume, the requisite Questing Permit as described in city ordinance two fifty-one b?" He lowered his reading glass. "Have you even read special city ordinance two fifty-one b?"

"No," replied William, "nor indeed special city ordinance two fifty-one a."

"That would be difficult, since it was deprecated earlier this year. Hmm, now let me see… in all, that will be 25 ducats in taxes and fines. Payable at once."

William sighed and handed over the coins. "Right, let's find an inn and celebrate arriving here alive."

An hour later, the four set out and found a suitable tavern near the port area with outdoor tables for guests wanting to enjoy the fresh salty air and space inside for those that preferred the dense fug of sweaty men with their wine. The women chose the outdoor space, while William and Ridkin wandered in.

The red wine William bought came as a whole new experience. Rich fruit, a warming sensation on the throat, and a delightful alcohol kick had him in awe and he downed the first one as though it were water and asked for a second. Ridkin, meanwhile, stuck to ale, wanting *nothing to do with any foreign muck, thank you very much.*

As had been the case in the hostelries of Anglonia, William couldn't help but get involved in the conversations that flowed around him, trying to express his knowledge and opinions. Most folk showed surprise to hear this man with a strange flat accent speaking in their tongue and had no problem listening and acknowledging his points. However, one well dressed and very inebriated man took exception and started a loud argument.

"You're in my city," said the man, using his finger to poke at William's chest, "and I don't like smart-arse foreigners. Drink your wine and get out."

"Let's be reasonable," said William. "Tell me what troubles you."

Ridkin stepped closer, his arms hanging loose, ready to step in and haul William out. "Will, we should scarper. Make ourselves scarce."

A much larger man also stood near, one with fists like shovels and a three-day stubble on his chin.

"What troubles me," replied the man, "is smelly foreigners in my face."

"But we can have a conversation, a reasoned argument, can't we? As gentlemen and scholars. There's no need to get nasty."

"Reason is shit. A pox on scholars. Go back to your damned frigid wasteland, Anglonian." He pushed William with the flat of his hand, knocking him off his feet and to the floor. Ridkin picked him up and pulled him towards the door. Too late. William was incensed.

"Reason is everything we have as human beings," he shouted.

A punch landed on his jaw, sending him reeling to the ground. Reaching to his waist, he jumped up, pulled out his dagger, and waved it in the man's direction.

"Will, no!" cried Ridkin.

The wine in William's system had taken hold, and he advanced, by mistake, catching the man's cheek with his blade and drawing blood.

"Priest on a donkey!" screamed Ridkin, taking advantage of the man's shock to drag William toward the exit.

"Don't just stand there, Paulo," the man yelled, "get the bastard. He'll pay for this."

His barrel of a companion made a grab for William, as Ridkin crashed through the door and ran out into the street, pulling a complaining William behind him.

"Let me back in!" shouted William. "I'll explain. Make him understand."

The man-bear charged out and called three others standing nearby to join in the chase. William lurched past a worried-looking Helena, while

Ridkin steered them both into an alley twenty paces along the road. Ridkin spun around to face all four pursuers, sword in hand, and braced for a fight.

The injured man ran up, urging the others forward. William's earlier bravura evaporated. "Mubble…" He stopped as the five men all drew swords and advanced on Ridkin. William looked behind and had a sinking feeling. There was no way out of the alley.

"Sun and Moons, Will," said Ridkin. "What fresh hell have you got us into?"

# Ten

As angry locals closed in, William and Ridkin receded until their shoulders touched the rough stone of the wall behind. William wafted his dagger toward the mob, trying to appear confident he could use it, while Ridkin at least looked like he might know what to do with his. "Sorry Ridkin. I'm never arguing with anyone again."

"It's a bit late for that, Will. I could maybe take one or two of them out, but these guys mean business."

William steeled himself for the worst, but it never arrived. Instead, there was a commotion from the opening to the alley, as five armed men ran from the street shouting at William's attackers.

One of these new arrivals detached themselves from the melee, and, with the noise of grunts, clashing metalwork and shouts behind, announced herself, "Hi. I'm Morwena Foolson. Pleased to meet you. My brother, Feydor, sent us."

She turned to watch the fighting, while brushing flecks of dust off her immaculate maroon tunic. Under her helmet, stray locks of vivid red hair hung down, as though placed to frame her perfect oval face. William's gaze was drawn to the tiny black piercing on the right side of her nose, which looked to have a miniature spider design carved into it. As one local separated off and ran at William, she made a rapid sweep of her sword, taking out the man's throat, before resuming her conversation. "He asked us to escort you to your destination, and from what's going on here, it's just as well."

By now, more Ianuans had shown up to join the local men and William's would-be rescuers had a fight on their hands. Morwena turned and leapt into the fracas, but as even William could tell, Morwena's men had superior poise and technique and, outnumbered as they were, she and her friends looked assured of victory. They worked as a team, controlling the limited space to pick men off one by one. In no time, the scene was one of carnage, with men lying, some still moaning, in pools of their own gore. The man with whom William had rowed, however, had disappeared.

A tall red-haired man posed, twirled, and thrusted, his flowing locks streaming behind him. He had an ease of movement and an economy of effort that demanded admiration. His two opponents took turns to advance and withdraw, the first going to the middle of his man, the second aiming for the head. He brushed them aside with aplomb before, in quick succession, stabbing them through their hearts. You didn't need to understand their dialect to get the sense of what they shouted as they fell.

Another of Morwena's men stood a full head taller than William and double his width, a veritable bear of a man with long, black, matted hair and a shaggy beard. He lifted a man from the ground and hurled him back toward the street before slashing across the throat of another, sending up a fountain of blood.

At last, the battle finished, the red-headed fighter introduced himself. "William Coxwell? Jasper Foolson." He wiped the blood on his hand off onto the coat of a man on the ground and held it out for William to shake. He had a grip like stone.

Morwena used a 'kerchief to dab the blood off her pointed leather boots. "Come on, there'll be more coming soon, and we need to get out of here." She led them out of the alley, where Helena and Matilda stood in open-mouthed shock. A short distance away, a man held the reins of several horses, enough for the fighters, William and Ridkin, but not for the two women.

"Wait," said William. "I'm not leaving these two here. They're not safe. Don't you have any more horses?"

"What, am I an effing magician who can knit them from thin air? I never had no instructions about escorting any women. Besides, they'll slow us down."

Helena bristled. "I can ride at least as well as Sir William!"

"Much better than me," said William. "Anyway, without them, I'm going nowhere."

"Me neither," said Ridkin.

The man Jasper frowned. "I don't have time for this rubbish. We have to leave. Now. Do I have to effing carry you away?"

"Go without me then." William stood defiant, arms folded, doing his best to look resolute.

The fighter laughed and faced up to him, his nose a finger's breadth from William's face, before Morwena touched his arm and told him, "Calm yourself, brother. The girl can ride with me, and Big Ger can take the other one."

Before Helena could react, the huge fighter scooped her up and onto his horse and, in one bound, joined her. Morwena helped Matilda up onto hers, and in moments, they were heading down the street toward the nearest city gate.

A dozen watchmen sprinted after them, with the man from the tavern spurring them on. He shouted at the top of his voice toward the gate, something William couldn't catch, and two men ran out to close the huge wooden barrier, just as Jasper at the head of the riders reached them and cut them down. The riders streamed out, sped up, and were heading away across the flat land for a rising road that led into trees.

~~~

Two maids were standing outside the chambers of one of Queen Ruthenia's ladies-in-waiting.

"There's two of 'em in there with him, I swear it," said one.

"What're they doin'?" asked the other.

"What do you think they're doin'?"

Inside the room, a woman was shrieking. "Sounds like the Lady Rasa," said the first maid.

"Who's the other? Lady Lina?" asked the second.

"They've been at it for hours. It's shameful, that's what I calls it."

"Shouldn't be allowed."
~~~

"Wait. They've stopped."

As the door opened, the two maids scuttled away.

"Boglets," said an exhausted-looking court jester as he spilled out of the room and swayed toward the main hall.

Having completed his profitable task, Feydor[50] made his way toward his own rooms. Why was it they needed his tender ministries? Why couldn't they just sort it out amongst themselves? The truth was, if he didn't need them for his own ends, he wouldn't be doing it.

He passed The Lord High Priest, Ignatius Stackpole.

"Good morrow, Lord Fool, may the Moons light your days and nights," said the priest, who smirked while executing a mock bow.

"Beshrew thyself, may your piles fester," muttered Feydor under his breath as he bowed. Aloud, he said, "Lord High Priest, may the Stars shine on your passage." Even he winced at that one. "I hope the season finds you well."

"Ah, the season indeed."

The slimeball slithered past with a demented smile plastered over his face. Feydor allowed himself the lightest of smiles of his own for the fact that the halfwit holy man had no idea what debaucheries went on under his nose. And to think the realm entrusted the disgusting creep with the morality of its people. He shuddered.

Once again ensconced back in his own chamber, Feydor tipped out the contents of his purse and counted a dozen gold pieces. Not bad for a couple of hours' work. Queen Ruthenia's ladies always paid well, and it amused him to be pocketing their noble, but dull as ditch-water, husbands' wealth, while being so warmly appreciated.

Having re-bagged the coins, he donned his cloak and left the palace through the side entrance on his way to Usury Alley. The Swift brothers there gave a good rate of interest and provided a safe-haven for his earnings. He nodded to himself. Yes, his retirement fund was building into a decent sum, thank you very much.

~~~
~~~

Feydor fumed. For three frustrating weeks of squatting down in the damp cellars, the bug had yielded nothing of interest beyond the disturbing amount of self-abuse The Lord High Priest appeared to enjoy, which wasn't what Feydor needed right now. His back ached. He'd run through half his stock of beetles and was fast running out of excuses to have more put in the temple. Could he have been wrong? Had Stackpole lost interest in harming him? Unlikely, but possible.

And then, bullseye. Later, he would recall the conversation almost verbatim.

*"Pyke, I need you to take care of, how can I put it, a delicate matter?"* This was Stackpole's dreary, nasal monotone. Stars above, Feydor would cut off what remained of his genitalia rather than listen to the man conduct a ceremony in the Temple. Although you'd never find Feydor Foolson in a temple in a month of Lunadays, anyway, not if he could help it.

*"Name it your Grace,"* replied his factotum and vicious fixer, Pyke. Feydor imagined the dangerous rake bowing as he spoke.

*"Take this and place it under the Fool's cot. Then send me word when it's done."*

*"But this figure doth belong to the King," objected Pyke.*

*"That doth be the whole point, dullard. I intend to search the Fool's rooms and, when this is found, have him thrown in the Tower."*

So that was their plan.

*"And your plan to become king? You promised me a knighthood."*

*"That and much wealth besides. I just want the jester out of the way, then I'll make my move. He always seems to know too much."*

*"Very good, Your Grace. As soon as the Fool vacates his rooms, it will be done."*

That was it. A short but critical exchange that Feydor could have missed. It was a crude but deadly plan. His mind spun in delicate loops as he worked through the options. And out popped the answer. He climbed the steps that led back to the ground level and hurried along several corridors to reach the familiar door of the Lady Rasa, his top client when it came to love's labours, whether lost, found, or anything in between.

"I hate to call in another favour, but..." he muttered at the inert lump of wood as he knocked, pressing down against the surging emotions he felt.

A muffled response suggested the presence within of someone who has just woken up and a half minute later, a yawning Rasa opened it. "So early, My Fool. I not ready for you, but if you come..." she beckoned.

Feydor shook his head. "No, no. I'm not here for a tryst, my sweet nymph. Another time, I promise." He smiled apologetically.

"Sometime you are of the teasing me, yes? Come in and tell Rasa what you need. Is about ugly priest, yes?"

"Regrettably, yes."

Luthenian beauty, Queen Ruthenia, and all her ladies-in-waiting, Rasa included, shared the same tall upright frame, piercing blue-grey eyes and a flawless complexion. Not that he'd had the pleasure of examining Her Majesty in quite the same detail as some of her ladies. Perhaps one day. Eunuchs were not beyond appreciating the human form, whether male or female.

He recomposed himself and explained what he needed twice using different phrases and asked her to repeat it back to him. Satisfied, he made for the grand salon, where anyone and everyone would see him relaxing away from his room. For sure, Pyke would use the opportunity to plant the figurine. He could have headed back much sooner, but delayed, lingering to cause the priest, and whoever else he had enlisted into his scheme, the maximum frustration in waiting. As the midday bell tolled, he stood, made a spectacle of stretching, and began a gentle, circuitous saunter, taking in as much of the palace and its grounds as possible before, an hour later, at last, turning for home. A great many people brushed past him, pretending to be about their business, but failing to hide their true intention, which was to track his progress.

At last, he reached his door and inserted the key. Then he appeared to change his mind, causing a guard he recognised, now disguised as a page, to bump into him. "Sorry," said the man, avoiding Feydor's direct gaze.

Here came the crucial part. He'd have thirty seconds to enter, lock the door, locate the figure and hold it behind his back before the priest burst in to make his theatrical arrest. No time like the present.

He opened the door, darted in, and relocked it in one fluid movement. Then, over to his cot to find the item. Boglets. Not there. Trust that lug Pyke to not follow instructions. Quick, where else? He hurried to the cupboard and hurled its contents to the floor. Nothing. Crap. And in a state of total panic, he froze. Filthy sat looking up at him on his cot, his head tilted to the side as if expressing concern. A key sounded in the lock. The priest must have got a spare from somewhere. As the door swung open, Filthy leaped to the top of the fourposter and grabbed whatever was there before swallowing it and landing on Feydor's shoulder. How had the creature swallowed something that *big*?

"Stand still," commanded the hirsute Lord High Priest. "I have a royal warrant to search this room for stolen property. A gold figurine is missing from the King's own chambers. Proceed."

The dreadful Pyke lurked smirking near the door, rubbing his knuckles, ready in case Feydor made a run for it.

A man brought a portable step into view and climbed up to the canopy of the bed. He felt above. Then he tried again. "Nothing, Your Grace," he said.

"What. Look again. Turn this room inside out. Search the Fool. I know it's here."

Three soldiers went through the room, turning everything over and ripping the stuffing from his chair and mattress. Then they roughly checked his person.

"Still nothing, your Grace."

Stackpole looked at Feydor, his eyes narrowing. "I don't know how you did it, Fool, but I'll catch you out, one way or another. Count the days until I do. Come," he commanded, and the search party traipsed out, dispirited.

Feydor looked down at his pet with concern as it began retching. Surely it wasn't about to vomit up the statue? It was. "Good… boy?" he muttered. The item spilled with a metallic clang onto the wooden floor, covered in half digested nuts and stinking to the Stars. Feydor scooped it up, wiped it on the underside of his tunic, wrapped his hand around it, and raced to the door. He hesitated for just a moment. What if the priest really could sense the use of magic? Boglets, it was just too good an opportunity to miss and could well get the man out of his hair for the foreseeable future. He called to the receding backs of the searchers, "Wait, I think I know where it is, that which you seek."

He closed his eyes and concentrated. The figurine vanished from his fist. "Guards," he said, relishing what was about to follow. "Surely you should also search His Grace. How do we know he himself isn't responsible for the theft?"

"What nonsense is this?" asked the priest. All eyes turned to him. He stared at Feydor, an odd expression on his face.

"Your Grace," said the serjeant, an eyebrow raised in expectation.

The priest sighed and rubbed at his moustache. Feydor could almost see a waterwheel grinding away in his head as he looked for an excuse not to submit. Then he shrugged. "Oh, very well, I can't see it will cause any harm. Go ahead. You're wasting your time. And once you are done with that, arrest the Fool for wasting *my* time."

Two guards stepped forward and patted Stackpole down. It took no time at all to find a lump in the man's cassock and to pull out the gold figure of Venusia, the late Truscan deity. Stackpole's jaw dropped open almost to the point of dislocation.

"Your Grace, I am sorry to say you are under arrest for theft. Take him away."

"What? But it's him." He was pointing at the jester, his pleading eyes wide. "Him I tell you. Can't you see? He performed magic right before your eyes!" As he was bundled off, he shouted backwards over his shoulder, "I swear by the Stars I will kill you, Feydor. I swear it!!"

Feydor caressed his new best simian friend on the head and tickled him behind the ears before carrying him off toward the kitchens. "I'm going to feed you on nuts and fruits till you burst," he told him.

~~~

Jasper led William and the others at a brisk canter into the wooded hills south of Ianua. The trail ran flat and level through a forest of resinous scotch pine and, although they made good progress, the two overloaded
~~~

horses soon tired and slowed. After three hours, soldiers from the valley had gained on them, and it was clear they either needed to hide or turn around and fight.

"How many of them are there?" Jasper asked his man, Wymond.

"Fifteen, maybe twenty."

"Can six of you cope with a small army?" asked William.

"Hmmph, depends. I'd back my men in most fights," replied Jasper.

Coming across a fork in the path, Jasper and Morwena looked at each other and nodded. It was like they read each other's minds.

"Right, Coxwell. Morwena will take you and your friends off to the left out of sight while the rest of us lead the chasing party away on the other track. We'll sort 'em. Go."

Morwena had Matilda and Helena dismount, and as Jasper and his men sped to the right, she led the rest of them left.

Minutes later, in a small clearing just off the path, she found a loose branch and used it to cover their tracks. She returned a couple of minutes later. "Complete silence now until the riders have passed the fork."

A thudding of hooves approached and then moved away; the chasing pack had taken the right fork as Jasper had intended. The four travellers began all at once to question the woman.

Ridkin got in first. "What's really going on here?" he asked.

She explained how Feydor had contacted herself, Jasper, and the fighting men with them, to ask for help in guiding William and Ridkin to the citadel of the Janasà. She wouldn't say how the message had arrived from Ludnam, nor could she justify Feydor's peculiar interest in the quest's success, save for a vague reference to serving the King of Anglonia in his moment of need. They'd received word (again without describing how) that the travellers had arrived in Ianua, and having gone to meet them, extricated them from the melee in the alley. The man William had cut rejoiced under the name of Ludovico da Ianua, and was the son of the local bigwig Duke Cosimo, which was why so many soldiers had chased after them. What was worse was that Jasper had history with the Duke, although Morwena refused to elaborate.

Throughout this exchange, Ridkin questioned and doubted everything. At the end of the account, he said, "I'm not buying this. It all sounds dangerous, fishier than a cockle bed. I say we thank our hosts and make our own separate way to Trusca and beyond. If these guys have a reputation, we might even be safer that way."

Morwena fixed him in the eye. "How far do you think you'll get with the Duke's men scouring the roads for you? They'll be setting up roadblocks. Do you know how to find ways around those? Could you fight your way out of a tricky situation? No, I thought not. We know this land, and you'll not find a better group of fighters than Jasper's."

"And my friends?" William nodded at Helena and Matilda. "Without them, it's not happening. Bring them along and deliver them to Trusca, and I will come with you. Otherwise, we'll take our chances alone."

"It's alright William," said Helena. "If travelling with you is going to cause problems, we can go on without you."

"No Helena. You're much safer with all of us. We travel as a foursome, with or without these fine folk." He met Morwena's stare.

Finally, Morwena broke away. "You should listen to your friend here, but I'll do my best to persuade Jasper. He has a point. Without more horses, they'll slow us down."

"We'll get horses," said William. "I have money. For now, we'll stay with you, but no promises. If we don't like the look of your brother, we'll go our own way. Are we all agreed?"

The other three nodded.

~~~

"So, dear cousin, what have you done to arrest our bold knight's progress?" Feydor, sitting in Mary's parlour, had just arrived at the house in Bell End and came straight to the point. "Mother tells me William got into a mess in Ianua. He stabbed the son of Duke Cosimo, of all people, which would have been perfect except that my brother showed up and hauled him out of trouble. So, with our little bird still in play, what are you going to do to clip his wings?"
~~~

Mary chuckled to herself. "Waesucks. Jasper really is a wee force of nature."

Feydor fixed her in the eyes. "I mean it. We need action. Are your twins anywhere close yet?"

"There was… a slight delay." She gave the smallest of frowns, then smiled to indicate it was nothing. "They got picked on in Senapia and I had to sort things out. They're just a couple of days behind William, but they won't attack. I don't want them taking on Jasper in a straight fight, at least not without a wee army to back them up. My boys are tough, but he's a maniac. There is something else up my sleeve, though. Last night I tried to reach into his mind."

This was new. "William's? Did you find one?"

"Ha ha. Yes, I found one. An oddly strong one for such a wee man. He reasoned his way out of the attack. Extraordinary."

"So, is that it? Are we stymied? This is deeply disappointing. I hope you have more than one string to your bow. Something guaranteed to take him out of the game."

"I don't see you doing very much to help. Let me try it again with another member of their party. Who else is travelling with him right now? I might exploit one of his companions and turn them against him."

He thought about it for a moment. "There's the boy Ridkin. I told you about him before, right?"

"Aye, you did. Remind me, what's he like?"

Feydor stared out of the shutter and watched a gong cart trundle past. "Streetwise, cynical, hard-headed. Too much so. I wish now I'd not made him go with William, but he was pissing me off. To be honest, I can't see you succeeding with him."

Mary nodded. "Right"

Feydor couldn't help but ask, "Tell me, how does this mind control thing work?"

"Well, it's hard to explain. I have a set of stones that I arrange in the right shape and then I come to the target in their sleep and pretend to be a relative. Preferably someone they haven't seen for a long time and they miss.

I can pick up the impression of the person easily enough and then form the image in their minds. I'm only using what's already there."

Filthy yawned, then curled up in Feydor's lap. He was careful to keep his fingers well away from the animal's mouth. "And then?"

"I lead them to their safest place, somewhere perhaps they knew as a child, and then I get them to open a door into my world where I encourage them to take a bite of something sweet. And from then, it's only moments before I have complete and total control. I can listen to their thoughts, see with their eyes, and make them do things they'd never otherwise imagine doing. You wouldnae understand. You're just a man; you have no magic."

He protested. "I have magic, I can assure you."

Mary wafted a dismissive hand towards him. "Aye, but you're just a wee *dabbler;* It's not *real* magic. You ken?"

Feydor did not *ken*, but let it go.

"Is there *anyone* else with William who I can corrupt?" she asked.

He nodded. "Possibly. Morwena says there are two women with them, a mother and her daughter. What of it?"

"What can you tell me about them?" she asked.

"Morwena couldn't say much about the mother, who seems like a closed book. The girl, however, is young and impressionable. Likes to mess around with crystals. Apparently, she thinks they predict the future. I mean, as if pregnant sows might sprout wings and fly. Do you think you can get into her head?"

"Hmm. She sounds perfect. What's she called?"

"I heard the name Matilda, although that could be the mother. Does it matter?"

Mary shrugged. "Not really. I'll try it tonight. Now leave me in peace and take your wee pest with you."

As Feydor wandered away into the city gloom, he pondered the way in which Mary had, throughout that encounter, been touching something hidden up her sleeve. A dagger, perchance? It would be just like Mary, with her twins in place, to want to remove himself from the picture and take the crystal for herself. Well, she'd have to get up very early in the morning to catch *him* out. Still, he'd have no qualms now about doing away with her when the time came.

~~~

William sat with his back against a tree, looking again at his strangely coded book. He'd always been a sucker for puzzles, and this one was too intriguing to ignore.

Ciphers had been in use since ancient times. Would simple transpositions of letters up or down the Truscan alphabet reveal the meaning? It didn't help that in old Truscan, different versions of an alphabet had existed, so this could take a while.

Ridkin came across and interrupted his train of thought by kicking his feet. "Wanna hear something dead dodgy?" Before William could react, he went on, "I just snuck into the trees to answer a call of nature and heard voices."

Irritated at the interruption, he answered. "So?"

"When I crept closer, I only saw one person. Morwena. That's not the best bit. Get this. She was talking to a tree stump. I couldn't get nearer without her spotting me, but later, when I checked, the wood was fresh cut. What's that about then? You're the brainy one."

"No idea."

"Follow me, I'll show you."

Checking that Morwena was busy with the horses, they slipped into the woods. Ridkin headed toward the south, then looped around to a small gap in the trees where the trunk lay on the ground, its cut stump exposed, just as Ridkin had described. William crouched and touched a dark residue covering its surface, a greenish black powder the consistency of milled flour. He sniffed it and caught a whiff of something not quite cabbage and not quite sulphur.

"Never seen anything like it," he pronounced. "And you say she spoke into thin air?"
~~~

"As far as I could tell. Must be magic. I know…" Then he put his hands on his hips, mimicking William. "*It's just stuff we don't understand yet.* Why can't there be things we will never understand? Explain that."

"Very good. It's obvious I can't." He went thoughtful for a moment. "Maybe she used whatever this powder is to communicate with someone. Who? And how?"

Ridkin shook his head and looked away. "Search me. But I'm curious."

"Curious gets you killed, so I've heard. Any road, let's get back to the others before we're missed."

When they returned, Morwena and Matilda were locked in conversation on the other side of the clearing, just out of earshot. The younger woman listened with rapt concentration to what Morwena was saying. From time to time, Morwena assumed a pose as if using a sword, or engaged in manual combat.

Catching sight of William and Ridkin, Morwena called out, "What are you two up to?"

"Can't we even pee in peace?" asked Ridkin.

"Not if you go too far away. Stay close."

"How long *do* we have to wait for Jasper?" William asked.

"As long as it takes. There are Janasà in these woods and we need Jasper and the others."

"Janasà? How exciting," said Matilda, bouncing about on her toes. "Can we look for some?"

"No Tilda, we don't want to do that," said her mother, who looked horrified. "Everyone knows as how they're dangerous."

"How do you know, mother? You've never met one."

Helena shrugged.

"I've heard enough. There are no weird green creatures running around." Ridkin stabbed at the air to make his point. "There's something else going on here. Tell us or we're leaving."

By now Ridkin and Morwena were facing each other, only an arm's length apart. William felt the tension rising in his gut and an involuntary jump in his heartbeat.

"No. You stay here till my brother returns."

"And you're going to stop us, how?"

"Any way I need to."

Ridkin stood with his arms at his sides and flexed his fingers. Without warning, his arm shot out to strike Morwena, who dodged to the side and grabbed it in a lock, her shoulder pushing against the back of the boy's elbow. Ridkin moaned and tried to wriggle free. Morwena tightened the hold.

"I'm going to release you in a moment," she said. "Let's try to be civil here."

She let go, shoving his arm away. "Alright, alright," he said, rubbing at his elbow joint.

"Next time, I won't go so easy on you."

Helena placed a palm on Ridkin's chest. "Calm yourself," she said, her voice soft and reassuring.

"We can make camp here," said Morwena. "If Jasper doesn't show on the morrow, we'll move on, but I'll be staying with you. Agreed?"

"Yes," said William, pursing his lips. "We get it. Danger."

Matilda changed the subject. "I'm freezing. Let's build a fire." She set off into the trees to gather dead wood. "Come on Ridkin." The tension ebbed away.

William said to Morwena, "I'm sorry for my friend's temper."

"It was nothing. Just don't even think of sneaking off during the night. I'm a light sleeper."

"I believe you're telling the truth," he replied. He'd just referred to Ridkin as his friend, but was that really the case? He wasn't sure. "Is there something going on? Something I'm not getting?" he asked her.

"I don't know what you mean." She continued, "This fire is out of sight of the main trail. It shouldn't attract anyone or anything into paying us a visit."

As dusk gathered, the darkness seeped out of the surrounding woods and swirled around them. The sky hung moonless, and as the light faded, stars sprung into existence, one by one, like glinting crystals of ice. They took it in turns to add logs to the fire, aware that without it, they could freeze. As their surroundings darkened further, voices floated in from the main track, and Morwena crept out of the clearing to see who it was.

"Brother," she shouted. "You're well."

"Of course," came the reply. "Takes more than a few blokes with swords to stop me."

Seconds later, she led a grinning Jasper and his men into view. "Warm yourself and tell me what happened."

"Not much to say. We carried on half a league till we found higher ground and caught 'em by surprise, like. They were good, but not good enough. We lost Johannes. Sorry, you were fond of him. That's why we took a while getting back. He deserved a decent burial, and so did Cosimo's men, come to that."

Morwenna's mouth turned down, and she shook her head. "No! Johannes was a good man. Did you kill them all?"

"All but one. A smaller, rat-faced little so and so. Top swordsman, mind. He got away and escaped on horseback, heading north. I reckon Cosimo will know by the morrow which way we came. Thing is, he's not the sort to give up. But hey, at least I picked up a couple of spare horses for the women. Those dead guys won't be needing them. Right, where's this sprat I'm supposed to coddle?" He looked about and, spotting William, he walked over. Then his pinhole eyes fixed on William's. "I know you're not a real knight. You're just a lily-livered fool that's out of his depth. Let's get one thing clear. You keep out of my effing way and do what you're told and maybe, maybe I'll let you live." Looking about, he added, "Now what food have we got?"

~~~

Morwena introduced Matilda and the others to Jasper's group of fighting men. There was Big Ger, the gentle and thoughtful giant who'd so easily scooped Helena up onto his horse, and to whom William took an instant liking. Then came Jacopo, a short, stocky, dark complexioned Italican who came from the area and acted as a guide. There was Tymothy
~~~

the Loud, who was tall, shy and never spoke, and Wymond the Weird, so called because of the strange carvings of animals he made at every camp.

Everything about Morwena fascinated Matilda. Here was a woman that she could admire, perhaps even emulate. Matilda had no intention of assuming the kind of role that the priesthood expected women to conform to. Neither did she much fancy bringing a succession of children into the world[51]. It was so stupid that celibate men should dictate to everyone else what they could or couldn't do with their own bodies. Not long aware of the sensitivities of hers, she couldn't see why women shouldn't enjoy physical contact, her mother excluded, of course. In the short conversations she'd had with Morwena, it was clear already that the woman saw no such limitations to what she could do with her life, or what she could experience. Dammit, the woman seemed so *alive*.

They spent their second day looping around the villages and hamlets they found along the winding and little-used hill path they were following through the woods. Late in the afternoon, their guide, Jacopo, announced they were not so far from his home village and went on ahead to check it was safe to go there. He returned an hour later, shaking his head. "The place is full of Cosimo's men. We'll have to sleep in the open again."

They found a convenient clearing near running water and set up camp.

"It's cold enough to freeze the proverbials off a bronze monkey," announced William to nobody in particular as he waited for the campfire to heat up.

Jacopo, Wymond, and Big Ger scouted around the area. "It might be my imagination, but I saw something green running between the trees," said Wymond when he returned.

"Green? Could be Janasà," said Jasper. "Let's make a stockade around the camp."

They cut down trees, burying the trunks in a defensive circle and sharpening their exposed ends. Jasper explained this is what the old Truscans always did when making camp. Everyone pitched in as much as they could. It made Matilda feel part of a team, and she enjoyed the sensation of well-being it gave her.

That night, despite several layers of cover, Matilda shivered so hard that it hurt. After an hour of this, she was on the point of giving up on the idea of sleep when a wave of warmth washed over her. "Mother?" she whispered, but Helena continued snoring next to her, unaware of this change. While it puzzled her, Matilda was too tired by the lateness of the hour and the day's exertions to care very much and drifted off into a relieved and, at first, untroubled slumber.

She dreamed of her father, whose face during waking hours had all but vanished from her memory. In her dream state, his features appeared with a blade-like clarity, and warm waves of comfort washed into her mind. His smell came to her just as she recalled it, a mixture of pulverised stone and the rosewater scent he favoured. She was a little girl again, sensing the fatherly touch of his hand on her head, and the warmth of his solid body, safe and reassuring. She missed him.

Snuggling down deeper under the rough covers, she relaxed. It felt so natural to let go and trust in this wispy-soft, balm-like blanket of security, as if nothing could ever hurt her again.

Was that her Great Granny Prentice calling her name? It was just as the old woman had always summoned her from the orchard games she played as an eight-year-old. There'd be fruit pie or honeyed oatmeal, and a beaker of refreshing water drawn from the cool darkness of their well. How she missed the taste and refreshing sensation of that water. She yearned for other things half forgotten. Jemima, the carved wooden doll she'd played with until their dog gnawed it to a pulp. Of milking their goat, Eustace, and helping her mother to curdle, and press into blocks, its pungent cheese. Of clear mid-winter nights when the distant St Elmo's fire poked from beyond the horizon, forming ghost-like fingers of green and blue that reached and danced across the sky before giving way to new forms resembling animals, trees, and spirits.

The dream turned to something closer to a trance. She thought of the strange motionless display adults sometimes put on at travelling fairs when they had consumed the local mushrooms. She floated down the path that led from their kitchen door, through the herb garden with its pungent scents of sage and tarragon, and towards the apple orchard, coming across a wall she couldn't recall existing. An ancient rotting gate blocked the way. The only right thing to do was open it. She had to see what lay beyond. Had to, with every shred of her being. She pulled the handle, which felt warm in her hand, and passed into another garden, this one walled, the aroma of jasmine and roses strong and almost acrid. In the centre sat an old woman she didn't recognise. The woman's shawl, stockings, boots, and cowl made her think of the many kindly widows that she'd known in her home village.

"Come, child," said the woman, her voice harsh, but only in that way old women often speak. "Step around that I might see thee."

The woman's pale face was pudgy, her dark eyes sunk back into the skull, the long hair under her cowl a brilliant red. "Here, child, take this cake. I made it myself with honey from my hives. It's sweeter than anything you ever tried. Take it."

Matilda took a bite, and the world changed around her.

Where there'd been warmth and comfort, now there was only darkness and the biting cold of the night. The woman's smile no longer comforted but threatened from the blackness of her cloak. "Come to me," she rasped. Fear gripped Matilda's gut like a garrotte. She tried to resist, but there was nothing to hold on to. Helpless, her body poured like liquid into the woman's hands, her chest constricted as though weighed down by the pressing torture[52].

A clamour of shouts and screams jolted her out of the trance. Noise came from every direction, and she experienced the entire process of the last half hour unravelling in just seconds. In her mind, she passed out from the walled garden, drifted without steps back up the kitchen path, and again stood on the threshold to their cottage.

She jerked awake. The screams were real, along with the grunting of men fighting and the clash of iron striking iron. The camp was under attack! Something moved close by, a greenish figure half her height but at least twice her girth, with a garish face that flickered into and out of focus in the dim light of the fire. It carried, two handed, a heavy object… an axe? The space filled with an odd clicking sound and the smell of damp earth swirled under Matilda's nose. Could this be one of those Janasà that Jasper had spoken of? There wasn't time to ask it, as the creature shrieked a noise like a bird of prey and raised its weapon.

Matilda screamed.

# ✦ Eleven ✦

Matilda scrambled out from under her covers with an agility that surprised her, unsheathing the dagger she wore at her side. The creature swung its axe at her head and she dodged left. The draught of the axe whooshed close by her cheek before it sank into the bedding under which, an instant earlier, she'd been sleeping.

"Mother!" she shouted, as she stumbled, trying to stand. "Wake up. Now. Whoa..."

The creature lifted its weapon again, seeming not to look at her while hoisting it over and behind its head with both hands and starting its swing in one fluid action. Helena, awoken and energised, jumped from her improvised cot and grabbed at the axe's wooden shaft, and for a moment she had enough of a grip to stop the swing, but the monster jabbed back an elbow, catching her low in the gut and making her double up and fall back. Another sweep began. Matilda just had time to react and thrust her knife out flat, with her full momentum moving forward in the way her father had taught her. However, rather than the blade sinking into soft flesh, it hit something solid and recoiled in her hand so that the sharp edge sunk into her gripping palm. She dropped it, crying more in shock than in pain. The attacker paused.

"Help!" she yelled. Where were Jasper and his men when you needed them? "Help!"

Helena muttered some incomprehensible words, and the creature spun around to face her. It took a step towards her, and as it did so, raised its arms. The steady clicking noise coming from the creature's head increased in intensity. Matilda grabbed at her heavy riding mantle and, ducking under the axe at the top of its backswing, threw it over the attacker's skull.

Matilda's cloak muffled the click, click, click of the attacker as it writhed to shake itself free and stepped too close to the fire. The tail of the cloak dipped low and burst into flames, which engulfed the head as it emitted a high-pitched wail. Helena stared at it, muttering something indistinct again. What was she up to? The thing paused still for the briefest of moments and shrugged off the flaming cover before turning again to Matilda, and surprising her with a horizontal slash of its axe at her body that cut a gash across her nightshirt. She fell back and toward the fire. The thing loomed over her prone body as its blade began a sweep from the other direction. Time slowed down as the axe head bore towards her scalp. Her reflexes took over, and she scuttled backward, crouching below the swing. But now, backed up against the flames, she could go no further. Fire licked at her hair. She needed to get away, but where to?

Another huge slash began. Once more, everything slowed, enough for her to lean sideways and watch in fascination as the blade once more brushed past her cheek. That was really close!

Someone shouted, "Take that, wart face!" from behind the creature, who looked down to find a sword tip poking out from its stomach. It spun around, sweeping its blade towards its assailant, but as it turned, William came into view, doing his best to cling onto the handle of the sword. As it paused in its spin, William planted his feet and twisted the weapon, provoking a piercing squeal. It reached behind itself with an arm action that shouldn't have been possible, punching William toward the fire. Had Matilda not caught him, he'd have gone into the flames. Instead, he spotted Matilda's knife on the ground and, in a single motion, gathered and thrust it into the creature's right eye. It howled like a banshee, grasping at the handle.

Jasper and Big Ger arrived, their swords held out towards it. It took a moment for the creature to register their presence, then it advanced on them, Matilda's knife still stuck in its head, looping its axe in front and pushing the men back. Helena took Matilda's hand to get out of the way and stepped a safe distance behind, as the fight unfolded. William joined them.

The two mercenaries ducked and dodged the creature's whirling weapon, which became a blur of motion, backing them up against the fire. It lunged forward and Jasper's attempted parry connected with the fast-moving axe. The sword leapt out of his hand and landed several feet away. He escaped by a finger width a slash across his body. "Loop behind it, Jacopo. Morwena, help us out here," he shouted. William retrieved Jasper's sword and handed it to him, as the four humans formed a ring around it.

If the attacker was at all troubled by its predicament, it gave no sign of it. The clicking noise increased. It closed its remaining narrow eye and appeared to go into a trance, its whirring arms forming a defensive pattern that kept the men at bay. All watched, mouths open, then without warning, it twisted and swung at Big Ger, who ducked to his left and as the axe passed toward the ground, Ger grabbed the shaft of the weapon and yanked it out of the thing's grip, sending it beyond the fire. It paused, then, reaching to its belt, and pulled out a dagger. Before it could take guard, Helena lunged out from between the men and rammed a sword into its throat. It shrieked a curdling cry of pain and gurgled before collapsing. As she withdrew the blade, dark sulphurous liquid fountained above the heads of the men. Jasper stood on its head until the thing convulsed and quietened, its left leg hanging in the fire. The flames caught its clothes and, in seconds, the camp filled with the stench of burning fat as its flesh fizzed and popped. Jasper rolled its body into the fire as Helena turned her back and walked away.

~~~

The first signs of dawn were encroaching. Matilda sat on the ground, stunned at the action of her mother. Who'd have expected it? Not her. She looked around; four more of the monsters lay dead, scattered about the clearing. What were those things? Now that she could see more, she got a better look at them. Smooth, almost feminine facial skin with a greenish hue. A helmet and body armour of something not unlike leather. Where ears should be, bony bumps poked through the helmet, covered in the same green hide as the face. What stood out were the oversized and taught muscled hands. That and the six fingers on both hands. The men dragged
~~~

another one onto the fire, which leapt up and enveloped it. A smell of burning fat filled the camp space.

"Janasà," declared Jasper. "See all of you. It's not safe in these woods. Ger, Jacopo, you were on watch. What effing happened? Did you fall asleep?"

"Jasper," said Ger, "I swear on my mother's life, I didn't. It all went so quick. One moment, I'm sitting here sharpening my knife, the next, something rushes past me and starts swinging at us."

"Jacopo?"

"The same. I saw nothing until they were on us."

"What did they want?" asked Helena.

"You or your daughter, I'd say," replied Jasper. "Four of them made a protective ring so that one could go after you. With those axe skills, I don't know how she didn't kill you both."

"*She*?" asked William, surprised.

"Had to be female," said Morwena. "The males are just for breeding."

"You mean sort of like bees?" asked William.

"I wouldn't know about that," said Morwena, shaking her head doubtfully.

"Why are you going on about bees? Why was it they attacked Matilda and me?"

"No idea, mistress," said Jasper. "We can hardly ask it now, can we? Maybe you smell different? Come on, let's get these things burned. I don't want them springing back to life or no nonsense like that. Ger, give me a hand with this one, will you?"

William watched as Morwena pulled Matilda aside and tended to the girl's hand. It seemed odd she would gravitate to the red-headed fighter rather than her own mother in such a moment, but what did William know of how young women thought?

~~~

Leaving the five Janasà attackers roaring away on the fire, the travellers broke camp, stashing their belongings onto their horses. For the first couple
~~~

of hours, nobody spoke. They must have all had their own reasons for that, but Matilda had so many unanswered questions. She'd expected her first contact with the Janasà to be exciting, but it had been horrific. She could have died. How *hadn't* she died? Perhaps what made the least sense was the behaviour of her own mother. The woman had been talking in not much more than a whisper and in what had to be a foreign tongue. And she'd seen with her own eyes how the Janasà's arms had slowed down, giving her time to dodge that axe. Yet, when confronted with Jasper and the others, its weapon had become a blur of movement, enough to keep four well-trained swordsmen at bay. And then who'd come from nowhere and killed the thing off? Her mother, of course. Like what? And whose sword was that, anyway? She'd always refused to touch the things.

So here she was, staring at her mother's back as it bobbed from side to side on her horse. In her head she was screaming *what did you do there, mother?* She recalled for the hundredth time that night when her father had vanished from her life. She'd been at her Great Granny's for the day, and on her return, Helena had said all matter-of-fact that he'd gone to Trusca for work and wouldn't be home for many months. And to be fair, they'd received letters from him for the first few years. Letters that spoke little about anything, but at least they appeared to be written in his hand. And there'd been money sent via the priests' system of exchanging currency: *Praypal.* So it made no sense to accuse Helena of sending him away. Matilda, however, had a hardening belief that important things had been kept from her, and were still being kept from her.

The slash across her front, 'twas but a scratch, but the cut on her palm still oozed blood into the balled square of linen Morwena had pressed into it. And it stung. Not that there was any point in complaining. The more worrying thing was the threat of disease. People died from wounds that became poisoned. Morwena had wanted to press a hot coal into it; she'd insisted that could prevent the poison taking hold. However, Matilda had once burnt her hand as a child touching a hot kettle and the pain had been intense. She'd leave it a day or two before deciding.

With a jolt, she remembered the dream she'd had just before the attack. She almost never recalled anything of dreams more than a few minutes after waking. With this one, however, the exact sequence, the colours, the touch of the grass beneath her bare feet, the smell of the orchard, and the ugly clarity of that face all played themselves over again in her mind, vivid and troubling. The old woman was the clearest part of the whole thing. Without a trace of a doubt, she'd been looking into the face of a witch, and it *hadn't been a dream*. This vile woman had got inside her head, invaded her very mind. Violated her private thoughts. Yes, violated seemed the right word for it. She'd always felt deep down how magic existed, despite having no direct experience. And everyone knew magic came from witches, right? So, she reasoned, a witch had attacked her. And she'd only escaped because some terrifying *thing* had tried to kill her and broken the dream. Moments longer, it would have been too late.

Without thinking, she reached to her waist and traced the outline of the stones in her pouch. She felt heat. Odd. She let the reins drop and emptied them into her good palm. The turquoise one jumped out at her. *Shocked* her. It was glowing. That wasn't possible. She twisted her head, then her hand. Not just a trick of the light. No, it gave off a faint flickering glow, as if it were a candle inside a lantern. She touched it with her index finger and nudged it. Turning it over, she dropped it into her injured hand, and she almost fell out of her saddle, as, for just a couple of seconds, it flashed brighter. Then as she watched, the bleeding stopped, the wound came together, and new skin formed over the gash. A minute later, it was like new. She looked about to check who else had seen it. Nobody was paying any attention. Her palm tingled with warmth. For now, she'd keep the blood-soaked dressing pressed against the healed wound. This would be her secret. At least until she decided what it meant.

So, she thought it through. She could list three remarkable things. The first was that a witch had trespassed into her dream, tricked her with memories of her childhood, and almost succeeded in possessing her. She shuddered to think how that could have turned out. Then a creature, a vicious green axe wielding apparition straight from a nightmare, had come to her in her sleep and launched a deadly assault against her. And just now, most extraordinary of all, her crystal not only had its own puzzling inner light, but it had healed a knife wound right before her eyes.

What did she conclude from all this? She was *special.* Goodness! These things, each bizarre by itself, taken together, were a pattern. She should share it with someone. Her mother. Yet she didn't want to do that. If the woman could play games and hide things from her, then she would have her own secrets and say nothing.

Should she mention it to William? He'd have an explanation of some kind, one written by a centuries-dead Grecan with a weird name. Perhaps she'd look for a way to speak with him alone. Perhaps. Thinking of William, she couldn't make up her mind about him. On one hand, the pathetic know-it-all annoyed her. He always had an opinion to *interject*, a dumb argument to *expound*, or, as she'd once heard him put it, a *partition* to *discourse.* He didn't preach; he *proselytised.* Priest on a donkey. She'd not even heard of half the words he came up with and had a suspicion he invented a lot of them. On the other hand, he'd saved her life, so she should be grateful, but hadn't she also saved *his*? That meant they were quits, didn't it? She was free to despise him.

She replaced her crystals in their pouch and spurred her horse forward to find Ridkin. Ridkin would distract her from her troubling thoughts.

~~~

Ridkin rode alongside William. They'd left behind the scene of the attack a few hours earlier and had made steady progress under clear skies and early morning sunshine.

"What you did back there was great Will. I never imagined you'd have it in you."

"What the Janasà thing? Wasn't me that killed it. Helena did."

"No, but I didn't see you as a man of action."

"Sometimes you just know you have to do something. Do what's right. You must have had moments like that."

"Do what's right? I wish." The younger man shuddered, then changed the subject. "What was that noise it made all about?"

"The clicking?" said William. "Oh, that's easy."

"Um, to you, maybe. Go on…"
~~~

"Bats."

Ridkin arched an eyebrow. "Sorry?"

"I wonder whether Janasà spend a lot of time underground or in caves like bats. Where there's no light. Bats make clicks and then listen to the echoes. It's like they see in the dark."

"Is that what bats do? Neat."

William went on. "Didn't you notice how it could still *see* us, even with a knife in one eye? It makes me wonder, though. Are you sure you and the others want to continue with me? I attract danger. Our ship sinking. That fight I got into in Ianua. The Janasà."

"Jasper reckons the Janasà were after the women, not you. As for continuing, Helena and Matilda are determined to reach Trusca to find Tilda's father. And now they realise they are safer as part of the group."

"And yourself? You could duck out of this. I can't believe the jester would ever find out if you kept away from Ludnam."

Ridkin went silent for a long while. Finally, he began, "It's hard to put into words. You're all like… you're a kind of family. I've never belonged anywhere. Damn it, I even like *you* a bit now. Only a bit, mind. I still fink your books are stupid. And you like people, *but only as an idea*. For all that, you ain't so bad for a posh bloke."

"I'll take that as a compliment."

"Can I ask you something?"

William shrugged, "Sure, go ahead."

"Why is it you're so obsessed? With books and all."

Was he obsessed? He smiled. It didn't feel such a bad thing to be. "I don't know. The best way I can describe it is that I've no choice. Reading makes me feel *safe*. Does nothing make *you* feel safe?"

Ridkin appeared to think about that. He reached forward to touch the ear of his mount. "Horses. Horses make me feel safe."

"There you go. They don't argue, right? Neither do my books. Not exactly, anyway. There's one thing bothering me, though. If those few Janasà could cause us so much trouble, what's a city full of them going to be like?"

~~~

Just south of Ziti, toward Ninfia, they crossed a narrow wooden bridge over a slow, wide river and stopped to appreciate the fresh air. Life woke up much earlier here than at home. The trees would still be bare back in Matilda's village, the fields either frozen or waterlogged, the people miserable. Here, wildflowers rioted, clamoured, and jostled for the brush of insects to caress them, while flowering bushes begged the warm breeze to carry their essences to others of their kind. The placid water popped with darting flies and fish reaching to snatch them from below or birds swooping to scoop them up from above. As a nod to the season, however, and despite the calor of the morning, a fine mist hung over the sandy banks.

"What infernal heat," moaned William as he stripped off another layer of clothes.

"This is nothing," Morwena replied. "Wait a few weeks, you'll be begging for the Ludnam rain."

"That's hard to believe," said Helena. "Jasper, can't we stop, please? Just for a while."

Jasper looked around in that peculiar darting way that Matilda had grown used to.

"If we take ourselves off the track. There's a meadow. We can sort the horses. Not for long, mind."

They followed a line of trees off to the north and found a path along a creek that fed the river proper, a perfect spot to bathe and enjoy the air.

"Come on Tilda, get your feet out," said Helena. "The water is lovely on your toes."

Matilda groaned inwardly at her mother's fussing. "I'm going further. I want to see where this goes."

"Are you sure? I think you should stay with me. It could be dangerous."

"How could it be dangerous? There's nobody here. Listen. Just the birds and the wind. Happen you're just trying to control me."

"Matilda. Have some respect!"

Ignoring the reproach, she carried on along the path, leaving a tutting Helena with her feet dangling in the water. The ground here was
~~~

waterlogged and full of reeds, and, out of sight of her mother, she untied and slipped off her own shoes. As she followed another bend in the track, the river itself disappeared from view and she found a small mist-covered lake filled with rushes. Here, nothing stirred, save for the cool vapour, which swirled as if propelled by a hidden force. White gossamer tendrils curled around and clung to her legs, passing through her clothes to her skin. Something soft brushed her nose and cheeks, like walking through spider webs in a forest. She felt a presence and wondered whether to be afraid. The twisting mist sped up, and an outline emerged from within, at first ethereal and diffuse, then coalescing into a female form more delicate than anything she could have imagined. Its skin shimmered, and its eyes shone with a mild white flame. Extending above and behind it, two pairs of butterfly-like wings flexed in the sunshine, giving off a rainbow of translucent light. And the music! Soft high notes climbed and cascaded in flowing arpeggios while an undercurrent of counter harmony balanced it. It was like the voices of two lovers entwining and exploring each other. She'd heard nothing like it in her life. She felt herself pulled toward it, but resisted.

"Do not be afraid, child," a voice spoke, or perhaps sang, in her mind, as the music shifted to support it. "We are Ninfiné."

She'd had enough of voices in her head, although she had to admit to the creature's beauty and couldn't help but murmur, "You're, you're gorgeous."

"It is well you sense us this way. We don't have true physical form in your world. You are Matilda, the Crystal Bearer."

What? Surely, they didn't mean…

"How is it you know my name?" she asked.

"We come with a message and a warning."

"Right…"

"We see you have doubts, but you are strong of mind and good of heart. Stay true to your calling." The music became lighter. "When the time is right, you will follow your destiny."

Her thoughts flashed back to the face of the witch.

"Wait, how do I know as I can trust you? You're not *her* in another guise, are you?"

The Nine Fine, or whatever they called themselves, went quiet. The music stopped. A lone fly buzzed close by.

"Well?" prompted Matilda.

The melody resumed, a little quieter. It appeared to reflect their mood. "We are the Ninfiné. You are the Crystal Bearer."

"You said that already. What's your warning, then?"

"Guard against malign spirits."

"Oh great! Bravo. *Now* you tell me." A realisation came over her. "Wait, Crystal Bearer. What crystal?"

"The one you carry with you."

They had to mean the blue one. Yes! She'd known it meant something big. "What's this crystal *for*, anyway? Happen you'd best come out with it."

The mist swirled about some more and the image began to fade.

"No! Don't go! I'm sorry I was rude. Please don't go, things have been happening, like. I don't understand anything. Can't you stay and explain it all? Please…"

"We cannot. Trust in your destiny, child. You will not fail."

And it or she or they were gone.

"But…" she called after them. "I have questions. It doesn't make sense. If you can hear me, come back," she shouted, but the mist had evaporated and the sounds of insects, birds, and the faint breeze returned.

What should she make of what just happened? Her destiny? Crystal Bearer? Why her, anyway? Did every young woman in Italica get visited by such visions? And what about that useless warning? For pity's sake. Malign spirits indeed!

She waded away, stomping through the water to find the others, wondering what, in fact, to make of her entire experience since leaving home. Who could she trust? Her own mother, no. She didn't doubt her to be a good person, but she concealed important things. In Matilda's opinion, she was adult enough to be treated as one, and she'd just have to force her mother to be fair to her. And the woman seemed so sappy about that stupid William.

William was a puzzle, both confused and certain at the same time. Confused about the world around him, and yet certain of his ability to solve any challenge with his ridiculous reason. Even someone her age could see the folly in that. And the doe-eyed way he looked at her mother made her feel both queasy and angry inside.

She could at least trust Ridkin and Morwena. Ridkin seemed sincere. Her friend Ridkin, who concealed his inner identity behind a wall of bravura, but underneath, had a good heart. Morwena too. She gave her a model of how a woman could make her own choices. The fact she could use a sword better than most men helped, of course. But she still couldn't, or wouldn't, tell either of them what she was thinking. What she was experiencing. They just wouldn't understand. They'd make a fuss, mother would get involved, and then nothing would be her own any more.

She felt ever more convinced that she needed her own identity, separate from that of her mother, and with it, the freedom to choose her own path. And much as she'd been in awe of the Ninfiné, she was suspicious; what if that witch had sent them? And like her mother ever since her father had left, *they* weren't giving her a choice, either. She didn't like how she, or was it *they,* had shown up, given her a meaningless title, a useless warning, and then vanished without answering her questions. The arrogance of it.

"Did you have a pleasant walk, darling?" asked Helena, her head tilted back to enjoy the sunshine.

"Happen it were alright. Can we get going, please?"

~~~

When evening came, they found an old barn in which to shelter from the elements. Jasper and his men used the lengthening daylight to practise a kind of Grecan wrestling that involved removing everything but their britches and grappling each other to the ground. Morwena lay on a fallen tree trunk, unconcerned with it all. Ridkin and Matilda had ventured off, they said, to investigate a nearby ruin, which left William and Helena alone. William sat in a hayloft taking advantage of the sunlight streaming through gaps in the timber roof to pour over his strange tome, which he'd now
~~~

worked out had a title that meant something like *Little Grimoire*. From out of the corner of his eye, he saw Helena below, who'd plonked herself on a battered milking stool and was trying to comb imaginary knots from her mane of auburn curls. He'd not seen her before with her hair down and he took a moment to savour the sight of it and the way the sunlight appeared to shine through it.

He turned his attention back to the book. The first section said nothing much of interest in plain language. Most of it was simple descriptions of the herbs to be found in a particular mountain forest some way to the south of where they were now. The second part, however, contained coded text. This had to describe something important; why go to the trouble for example to list a recipe for nettle soup? He'd thought he'd worked out the cipher now. The reason it had taken him so long was that the writer had been cunning indeed. The right-hand pages used a different cipher to the left-hand ones. He'd cracked the left-hand side: he had to shift letters to the left by three, four or five places. There was no pattern to it, so he had to use trial and error until it came together. This didn't work on the right-hand side, though. He tried alternative approaches until, *eureka;* he solved it. Moving two, three or five places to the right yielded well-formed middle Truscan, a tongue last used over eight hundred years earlier, but still comprehensible to the scholar in him.

That he had no pen and paper to write out the decoded phrases presented no problem, given his picture-perfect memory. So, while not a simple proposition, he composed complete sentences in one part of his mind while he read the garbled text with the other. What emerged fascinated him.

The book spoke of a crystal with an odd name, Nurragù. It also had the name that translated as something like Life Crystal, but there was no detail on what that meant. This was hidden deep under a mountain in a magical land, described here with an archaic title that he knew to be the modern island of Sardonica. It told of how the crystal had been closed up in a cavern centuries before and set with a guardian in the form of an enormous cat whose name was something like Two Cats Fighting. This creature guarded a pit at the end of a maze of caverns and would only grant passage to a pale man who'd journeyed far and who could answer three riddles.

Had not the King tasked him with travelling to the same place in Sardonica? Aristopholes maintained that coincidences never happened. When events coalesced in this way, they were invariably intentional or significant. He'd make his own mind up about that, but it was food for thought, along with the way both the shipwreck and his troubling dream had struck him as actual attacks. And now this odd grimoire had come into his hands. Was destiny playing a game with him? He dismissed the notion. Total nonsense. The world worked on cause and effect, nothing magical, nothing mysterious or Hand of Fate about it.

On the other hand, if his experiences were part of someone's attempts to destroy him, was he putting his friends in danger? Ridkin, Helena, Matilda, each in their own way had put their trust in him, and in so doing, placed themselves in harm's way. Perhaps he should turn back now, stop, reason, try to make sense of the world. It was just so complicated.

He was jogged from his reverie by Helena, who'd climbed the ladder to his loft and crawled across to where he sat to avoid the low roof. "William," she said, "can I talk to you?" A shaft of sunlight picked out different shades of brown in her hair, and she was wearing a smile full of teeth like reflecting moons. She smelt of a wonderful mix of pressed linen, rosewater, and something floral. He felt quite stirred.

"Um, y-yes, of course," he mumbled. Why was he suddenly nervous? "W-Would you like to know what I've found in this book?"

"No, William. Put the book down."

He closed and placed it on the rafters, then turned toward her. Before he could react, her face filled his field of view, and a pair of ruby red lips planted themselves on his open mouth. She held her mouth on his for several seconds and seemed to expect him to do something. Like what? Not that he found the experience in the least bit unpleasant, nor was he at all tempted to push her away. Ridkin and Matilda entered the main barn area below, excited about what they'd seen in the ruins. She pulled back.

"Mubble fubbles," said William, making Helena giggle. "What was that for?"

"For being all brave like and helping to save Tilda from that Janasà."

"You're the one that killed it."

"True, but you played a role. You bought us valuable time at great risk."

"I couldn't have done anything else, I promise you."

"I don't care. Thank you." She touched his hand, unleashed again the full blaze of her smile, and then wriggled away over to the ladder before disappearing below.

His heart raced, and his breathing came like he'd been running outside. How curious. The velvety sensation of her lips on his stayed chiselled in his mind. The softness of them, the hint of warm moisture from her mouth. His scalp tingled. Verity had never done that. She'd not even wanted to hold his hand for fear of *falling down with child*, as she'd described it, despite his assurances that procreation didn't work that way. And in any case, her mouth was narrow, her lips thin, and he couldn't recall her ever smiling, at least not in the way Helena did. And yet the kiss was a betrayal. A betrayal of Verity and of the promise he'd made to her.

Thinking of the kiss, he said to himself, *A simple* Thank You *would have sufficed.*

# ✦ Twelve ✦

Dawn broke, catching Matilda between sleep and wakefulness. The previous evening, they'd arrived at the castle belonging to some friend of Jasper's. It turned out the fighter had spent a lot of time in Italica and knew a lot of people. If it meant a safe, dry place to get her head down, it was fine with her, and this castle was better than fine. It looked like something from another age, like from a fable or a legend, or some such. Full of extravagant crenellations and all those other buttressy, castley things you'd expect.

She'd chatted away to Ridkin and Morwena late into the night about the wonderful things the flame-headed woman had experienced, all the places she'd been, about her hopes to give up the mercenary life with Jasper and settle down. Maybe she might even have children. But what Matilda loved best about her were the stories. She'd danced with princes, fought alongside knights, taken and discarded lovers where she found them. The woman was alive. She'd never met one before so determined to live her own life. A vague plan was forming in her mind. She still wanted to see her father again and force her mother to accept her part in his disappearance, but after that, Matilda was going to go her own way in life. She just didn't know yet what that meant.

She didn't, as a rule, wake at dawn without good reason, but thoughts of what the Ninfiné had told her were never far from reach. Being a bearer and fulfilling her destiny? It didn't and couldn't make sense. Could it? She sat up, stretched, and opened her crystal pouch, reaching inside for the blue one, expecting it to have returned to normal, but… it hadn't. It still glowed with that same odd light, like one of those wandering stars that crept across the sky at night. And if anything, it was even warmer to the touch than before, and the healed skin on her palm was still intact. She considered telling William about it, but it was *her* crystal and *her* secret. Something to cherish, something to make her feel different. That said, the man for once might be useful to her.

After returning the crystal to its pouch, she wrapped her cloak over her shoulders and wandered out to the main hall looking for company. A comforting, herby smell of baking focaccia hung in the air, making her mouth water. She found the doltish William already there, sweeping up the old rushes in slow, methodical strokes. Had destiny caused the very person with whom she wanted to talk to be there at that moment?

"Don't they have folk for that?" asked Matilda.

"I'm sure they do. My father used to do this every morning, for hours on end. It's a wonder he didn't wear the flags out."

Matilda smiled a little despite herself. "Happen you miss him?" she asked, thinking of her own father.

"You want the truth? I didn't know the man, at least not for the last ten years. I regret that now, more than I can say. When I have children, I won't let them be strangers. I won't be like him. You're fortunate to still have your mother."

She thought of telling him how her mother frustrated her, but wasn't ready for the inevitable lecture she'd receive. He finished one side of the room with a last flourish and leant the broom against the wall, but, hesitating about what to do with the pile of rushes, he left it for someone else. "I'm going for a walk. Would you come with me?"

Matilda hesitated. She'd wanted to speak to William, but wasn't at all sure about this almost paternal response she was getting. But then what could really go wrong here? She followed the man through a corridor, and out to a terrace that gave onto a valley with a fast-flowing river far below. The local bird population chorused with frenzied intensity.

"The noise…," said William. "Isn't that amazing?"

"Why do they make that din?" Now that she stopped to listen, she had to admit it was impressive.

"Not sure. It's the males trying to get the attention of the females, perhaps. *Look at my plumage*, shouts one. *My song is better than his*, calls another." He inclined a little towards her. "You've had a troubled look about you since the Janasà attack. How is your hand now, by the way?"

She reached down to touch the linen dressing and told a little lie. "It doesn't hurt much and there's no bleeding."

"Good. Now tell me about anything you want. I'm good with secrets and nobody will hear anything we say above this racket."

Matilda said nothing, working out how much she could or wanted to tell him.

He interrupted her thoughts. "It's alright, you don't have to say anything. Let's just walk down here and enjoy the sunshine."

He set off for a set of steps that led to a pathway down into the trees toward the tumbling river off in the distance. He clasped his hands behind his back and she scurried to keep up with his long strides. He slowed a little, and they continued side by side for a dozen paces before, "It's about my destiny," she said.

He inclined toward her and smiled. "Oh, good topic. I'm intrigued. Go on."

"Well, not just my destiny. Everyone's destiny. What do you think it's all about? Didn't your old Grecans have 'owt to say about it?"

"They had plenty to say about it. Can you be more specific?"

"Where does it come from? How is it decided?"

"What do *you* think destiny is?" asked William, using the same technique that the brothers had often used on him.

"It's… umm… I don't rightly know."

When it became clear she wasn't about to play that game, he began, "I have spent much of my time thinking about this. The ancients, and the stoics in particular, considered destiny to be that which *must* happen. A flow of moments one after the other stretching to an infinite horizon of time, each leading inexorably to the next. And we are all an inevitable part of that flow, not separate from it."

"Wait," she stopped. "Happen that means we have no more choice than a tree or a rock?"

He paused in his step for a moment. "Yes. I think that's the general idea."

He resumed his slow meander. Now seemed the ideal time to ask him about her encounter, but… and yet… Instead, she asked, "Suppose someone told me to follow my destiny? Isn't that pointless? Wasn't I already destined to do that? What would happen, like, if I did something that wasn't written in it?"

"Ah, a thought experiment. Well, let's see. The Stoics might say that the world would make you fulfil your destiny. If not one way, then another. It would guide you."

He paused and watched her.

"And you believe this yourself?" she asked him.

He broke into a broad grin. "Sun and Moons, no. I'm just telling you what Epididymes thought. I think either destiny is real and can't be denied, or it doesn't exist at all. There's no logic in there being just a bit of destiny hanging about the place that we can follow if we get the urge." He wafted his hands upward to emphasise the idea. "On this matter, I cleave more to the followers of Epicurious who thought themselves free to make their own choices."

"I've always thought of destiny as real," she answered. "But what *is* it, I mean, like, what's it *made* of?"

William laughed in a way that was almost cute, and it was interesting to see him so animated. "That's a deep question, and one I can't answer. I know of some Grecans who proposed something called Fate Spinners." With one hand, he mimed something spinning beneath him. "Maybe they were correct, but I can't tell you to believe it."

"But if that's true, what's the point of bothering to make an effort? Why battle through life if it's all going to happen, anyway? Happen I could return now to my bed with a barrel of wine and leave destiny to sort itself out."

"Destiny would find you, and you would do what you must."

"That's just… *stupid*."

"You always have a choice. It's what the Grecans called a paradox."

"Hah, a single choice to do what I must. That's no choice at all. It's all an excuse to do what you want anyway, and pretend it comes from a higher calling."

"That's very perceptive. You know, destiny or not, you should always do what *you* think you must. You have to answer to your own conscience."

"But I don't know what I must do!" she wailed. "This is impossible. Why did I bother asking you? You and your stupid learning, 'tis no help at all!" She turned and stomped away toward the castle.

~~~

The following afternoon, they found welcome at a hilltop monastery with stupendous views across a wide valley, at the other side of which, high mountains soared skywards, still bearing late snows. Matilda and Ridkin, once again, made an excuse to go off together into the trees and Jasper and his crew got into their usual fighting practice, leaving William and Helena in the monastery. Not that they were alone, of course. The monks made sure they were never alone for more than a few minutes, perhaps fearing contamination from wanton acts of passion. Fat chance of that!

Ever since that kiss, William had been a bag of tense agitation. Why had Helena done that? Did she kiss everyone to whom she was grateful? Was it a northern thing? That seemed unlikely. In his experience, northerners weren't the most demonstrative sort. He'd once heard one say, *I'm from the North. We don't do excitement*[53]*. We're what you call taciturn.*

Verity depended on him to save her from Rowbotham, and time was running by fast. And marrying her was the reason he'd agreed to make this quest. But he could no longer form her image in his mind. That his memory refused to do his will was strange, but even stranger came his illogical desire to experience another kiss. What was wrong with him? If you loved someone, none of this should happen, but there was nobody he could ask about it.

Not that Verity was the only reason he'd wanted to do this. The idea of completing a kingly quest and returning in triumph as a knight of the realm was at least as important. Not for the sake of fatuous vanity; the ancients would have poured scorn on such prideful displays. The nub of it was that he didn't want to turn out like his father, a man who'd died sad and broken, having allowed life to grind him into the ground. For his last months, the
~~~

old man had refused human contact, and William had found him that fateful morning hanging from a beam, covered in his own mess. A stained letter had lain on the dresser, the writing all but illegible. *Do not be like me.* That was all. He assumed the message to be for himself, but hadn't then understood the meaning. Now, with the perspective of time, it seemed so obvious. "I won't, father. Be like you. I promise."

His mind drifted back to the kiss. Sun and Moons. Well, there was nothing for it. He needed to talk to her and sort this out.

The monks had a special separate dormitory for women guests. William wandered through the building to look for it. Finding the door ajar, he knocked and entered to see her sitting on her cot, her hair squeezed tightly under a cap with not a hint of her dazzling smile below her hazel eyes.

"Ah, William."

"Helena?"

"Come in. What troubles thee?" she asked.

She gestured for him to sit on the cot opposite. "It's about what happened the other day," he said, his brow furrowed. "That kiss."

"Ah. That. I'm sorry it shouldn't never have happened. I weren't thinking straight that day."

"Oh, thank the Stars," said William, demonstrating a relief that he didn't entirely feel.

"I'm here to find my husband, and you're here for Verity. There's nowt else to discuss on the matter."

"So why did it happen?" he asked. "Why did you do it, and why didn't I resist?"

"Must there always be reasons? Explanations? Logic? Some things defy all of that. But we've had this argument before." She looked into his eyes for affirmation, but clearly didn't see it. She sighed. "Look, I wanted to show gratitude, and I got carried away and all. And you… you've no experience of these things and didn't know what was happening. Is that reason enough for you?"

"Yes." He paused. "Can I ask you one thing please, mistress Helena?"

"Yes…" she said, looking uncertain of where this was going.

"Did I do it right?"

She went silent for just a moment, looking thoughtful, then smiled in that way of hers that could doubtless stop a small army in its tracks. "The kiss? If that's what's bothering you, aye, you did at that. Now be off with you."

~~~

Fraser Grieve rode with his brother Irvine into Trusca and made for an address in a well-heeled residential area where they expected to find a palazzo belonging to Duke Cosimo. He showed the major-domo that greeted them the letter from Cosimo, and the man ushered them inside, leaving their horses for a groom to handle.

Cosimo's son, Ludovico, treated them matter-of-factly, the deep scar on his cheek still livid. "So you gentlemen think you know where I can find this son of a whore, Coxwell? We have unfinished business."

"Aye, we've a good idea of where to look. When we find him, where can we hold him? Here?"

"Here? Moons and Stars, no. My family has a castello outside the city. Much more appropriate. Just know I want to be the first to draw his blood. Understood?"

"Nae problem. Leave it to us."

An hour later, having eaten and rested up, the two of them contacted their mother via trunk call to update her on progress.

Her face, rendered even more sallow than normal in the green light of the call, hung above a segment of a newly cut tree. "You can expect Coxwell and his friends very soon, perhaps even tomorrow. Don't mess with him, though. Let Ludovico do as he wishes, then kill him. I need you in Sardonica as soon as possible. Got it?"

"Oh aye, mother. Dunnae bother your wee noggin over it."

But where was the pleasure of that? No, they had something rather more complicated in mind: they'd have fun hurting the guy, messing with his head, breaking his bones one by one. And *then* kill him.

A short while after that, a man came to the residence carrying a wicker box. Opening it, Irvine took out an enormous rat. "Look at this evil
~~~

bastard," he said to his brother as he held it by the tail. As it swung about, it squealed, writhed and gyrated like its life depended on it. Which, in a way, it did.

Fraser gripped the terrified animal by the scruff of the neck. "Pass the branding iron. Let's find out how loud it can squeak."

~~~

Nearer to Trusca, the Infernal City, dense woodland was replaced by vineyards and olive groves. The nicer towns and villages were found on hilltops and the poorer accommodation in the surrounding valleys. "Shit runs downhill," was Ridkin's eloquent interpretation.

By now, spring was well under way in these parts and the temperature had edged up a touch toward uncomfortable. Not that Anglonian wind and rain would have been better, mind; William much preferred being too warm over too cold.

Their first sighting of the city came as they browed a larger hill. A sprawl of distant habitation was visible across a plain of fields in varying shades of yellow and green. Lancing through it was the dead straight road, and beside it, an equally direct viaduct, built by the Truscans a thousand years earlier, and still in use.

"All roads lead to Trusca," announced William. "So they say."

"Who's they?" asked Ridkin. "Cos they ain't been down shite-brook[54] in Black Chapel. That don't lead here, I can tell you, it leads to a lake of…"

"I get the picture," said William, smiling. It was easy to be in a good mood in the warm weather with such a beautiful landscape to appreciate. The city was immense and packed from the first dwellings all the way to the centre, with its fine temples and monuments. It took more than a day to navigate there, and they soon sold off their horses to work their way through the throng. Despite Jasper and Morwena hiding their conspicuous red hair, they still felt nervous about being spotted by Cosimo's men[55], with good reason, as it turned out later.

William explained to anyone who would listen, that is nobody, about the thousand years of history, of how the twins Truscula and Tresca,
~~~

descendants of Aenus, had been abandoned as babies and raised by wolves before establishing the city. Of how Truscula had killed his brother over a woman and founded Trusca. He'd read about the ancient Truscan buildings, many still standing twelve centuries after the old Truscans had left them. He'd been looking forward to seeing the great Flavianid[56] amphitheatre, and it didn't disappoint. It loomed over him taller than any construction he'd ever seen, and with a perimeter larger than most cities, a genuine wonder. The old builders had covered the multi-arched façade with brilliant white travertine marble[57], and it still gleamed in the morning sunshine. William stood and tried to visualise the crowds streaming toward it to witness the spectacles that the Truscan emperors had staged to keep their idle poor entertained.

"You can go in," said Jasper, who claimed to have been to Trusca many times.

William wandered beneath one of the high arches and into a curving corridor, at the inside of which wide stone stairs led upward. He took four flights of steps until he exited out into the light and looked down into the middle of the oval central space. Filled now with nothing more than market stalls, it nonetheless struck him with wonder. The thought that gladiators had battled each other to the death here while a crowd numbering many tens of thousands shouted on, beggared belief. And not to mention the ingenious and spectacular executions of the criminals and non-conformists. He recalled the sense of amazement when he'd first read the accounts. Could it be true the ancients had even staged a mock naval battle in that arena?[58]

Then they moved on to what remained of the old Forum, the governing hub of an empire that had stretched for thousands of miles in every direction, and the Pantheron, a marble clad temple with a massive dome, still the largest such standing structure in the world. William insisted on going inside and someone charged him a whole ducat for the pleasure of watching, as priests wafted incense and chanted their nonsense while their gaunt and emaciated believers cowered in reverence. He'd hoped Trusca, the very centre of the religion of the Sun and Moons might be different, better than the towns in his own country, but if anything, it was worse.

"Come, Bookman," commanded Jasper, who'd taken to calling William by this nickname. "Done with gawping for now?"

Jacopo approached. "We're being followed," he said.

"How many of them?"

"I counted two. Fifty paces back."

"You're sure?"

"I seen 'em as well," said Wymond.

"Right, let's split up. Morwena, stay with William and the others and head toward the Ovaltine[59]. Jacopo, you go with Wymond; Ger, stay with me. We'll loop around them and give them a surprise they won't forget."

Morwena led them away from the historic centre, down a side street to the south before they picked up the wider Via Dolorosa. The road coursed upwards for a mile or more before leading to a meadow. After half an hour, Jasper and the others caught them up.

"All sorted," he said. "They're floating down the Tigra now. Still, it shows we have to be careful. No wandering off anyone."

"How did they spot us?" asked Morwena.

Jasper shrugged. "No idea. It's like they knew what to look out for, though."

Behind them, the city sprawled off toward the horizon, while before them stood an impressive villa not much smaller than the palace at Eastminster, from which William had set out two months earlier. "This is it," said Jasper, smiling to himself. "Palazzo Sevrio on the Ovaltine Hill."

He walked past the broad twin oak doors and around to the side, where he found a more modest entrance and knocked. A full half minute later, the door opened, and a face peered out. "Signor Foolson, what fair wind?" exclaimed a man. He looked them over. "*Entrate tutti*," he said, waving them into a marble lined atrium. Muscular statues filled alcoves in the walls, and a huge painting of an ancient battle dominated the ample space from its commanding position on the far wall. William surmised the depiction had to be of the Battle of Thermopola in which a small band of Grecans had defended their country from a vast invading horde from the East. So the legend went.

The man asked them to wait in an enormous library. This room struck William with more awe than all the ancient buildings combined. Shelves dense with books lined every wall, from the floor to the ceiling at least forty feet above. The supporting columns likewise bristled with yet more shelves crammed with yet more volumes. It would take a lifetime to read everything here. So many words. So many worlds described, lives experienced, wisdom expounded. Then there was the ceiling. And what a ceiling! It depicted Truscan deities in situations related to writing. There was Zetus pointing out to Pane some lines written on a tablet. Mercurio sped across the sky with a trail of words behind him. Some of the characters had crumbled, but William could make out the words of a Grecan poem about learning. Lower down, the great philosophers read treatises to each other, their faces impassioned with the power of their words. He recognised Aristolopheles by the beard. Behind these details, the sky was rendered in a piercing shade of blue and at the centre of everything floated great Lord Sola, flanked by His Moons, Luna and Runa. William was captivated[60].

A cough announced the arrival of their hostess, a middle-aged woman of surprising beauty, despite the prominent Truscan nose that dominated her face. She put William in mind of the great empresses from the ancient times, with dark flowing hair, elegant, looped earrings, a bare upper chest that sported a jewelled necklace, and an extravagant blue dress that brushed the floor. Matilda swooned and Morwena ahh'd her approval. William was pretty much blind to anything concerning fashion, but even he was impressed.

"Ottavia," said Jasper. "You're even lovelier than I remember you."

"Signor Jasper, how you flatter," she replied. "Please present me to your friends."

Jasper introduced each of them in turn to the Lady Ottavia di Medici, finishing with William. "This sad looking turnip here with his mouth agape is *Sir* William. Though we call him Bookman."

"Sir William, indeed? I see you are interested in my late husband's library."

"It's staggering," said William, adding, "Though I'm sorry for your loss."

"Infatti," she responded, inclining her head to show agreement. "Come onto the terrace. We can take wine, and you can explain the purpose of your visit."

"Jasper," said William, trying to draw the man aside. "I need to talk to you."

"I told you to stay out of my way, Bookman."

"But this is important. I want to get a proper look at this library. It could contain something that helps us with the Janasà."

"Not a chance. As soon as I've taken care of something, we leave. I don't want to skunk around here a moment longer than we effing well have to, what with the place crawling with Cosimo's men."

This was the longest Jasper had ever spoken to him.

"Then I'll have to work through the night. I can't pass this opportunity up."

~~~

Aided by a goodly quantity of excellent red wine, Helena and Ottavia were getting on a storm. Long after Matilda and everyone else had gone to their beds, the two women had slipped into an unforced, almost sisterly conversation. Helena's nerves regarding the possible meeting with her husband had been building for days, and, if she cared to admit it, had contributed to why she'd been so cold with William. Here with this beautiful and sophisticated woman, she felt the tension ebbing away.

"I feel like I've known you a long while," said Helena.

"Altrettanto," agreed Ottavia. "Likewise."

"Have you always lived in Trusca?"

"Sola above, no. I'm a simple mountain girl from the north. I married many places above my station and, as you can see, have much to be grateful for. My husband died five years ago, and I've been battling the priesthood ever since to keep this house. It doesn't sit well with them that a mere woman can inherit so much. They keep trying to foist men onto me *to protect me*, as they put it. I need no protection, save from the robed ones themselves."
~~~

"Why's that?" asked Helena, not entirely surprised.

"Let's say the hands of the gods get everywhere, given a chance."

Helena burst out laughing.

"Your Matilda is a fine young woman," said Ottavia.

"Aye, that's right enough, but she's vulnerable, impressionable, and she has too much of her father in her…"

She paused long enough for Ottavia to ask, "Meaning?"

"I mean, she can be horribly judgemental, but the biggest thing is how secretive she is. She complains about me concealing things, but she's so much worse herself, and gets so angry when I challenge her."

"Would you mind me suggesting you might need to stand back?" Ottavia reached out and touched Helena's arm, then looked into her eyes. "Give her the space to grow. Let her find herself."

"Are you saying I over-mother her?" asked Helena.

"It's not for me to say. Be careful though; she's of that age where she can take against you, much as I once did with my own parents. Think about it."

She'd never have taken this from anyone else, but Ottavia wasn't just anyone else. "You may just have a point," she conceded.

"You can tell me to mind my own business if you wish…" She looked at Helena, her head conspiratorially close, "but what's going on with your daughter and your husband?"

Helena wondered if she could tell this near stranger the truth about that. Maybe some of it. "Well… let's just say we had a falling out. He'd just lost another job after drinking too much and tangling with the sheriff. Tilda was with her granny, thank the Stars, but it came to blows." She'd actually used magic to keep him from really hurting her, and it had been much more than blows, but she wasn't about to tell Ottavia about that. "So, I made him pack his things and leave."

"That was brave of you. What then?" She smiled in encouragement.

"I lied to Tilda. I told her how he'd had to leave for an offer of well-paid work he couldn't refuse, and well, here we are now. Tilda is adamant she wants to find Ralph, and it has been easiest for me to go along with it. And to be honest, I do wonder if a reconciliation might be possible."

How easily the lies came. She couldn't reveal her real motive for making this crazy journey. Because not long after Ralph had gone, she'd realised he'd taken her mother's magical amulet and now she rather wanted it back. To avoid Ottavia probing further, she changed the subject. "There, I've told you my story. What about you? Do you and Jasper have 'owt special between you?"

"Stars above, no," said Ottavia. "And in any case, he's a bit, you know…"

"I don't know. What?"

"My dear. Jasper doesn't lie with women."

Helena blushed. "How do you know that?"

"Because my husband was the same way. Let's just say they got very close and we can draw a veil over it. One has to be careful discussing it even here; the priesthood has eyes and ears everywhere. Not that it isn't rife within their own ranks. It's not natural making all those men be celibate."

"Is all this true?" asked Helena, amazed at what she was hearing.

"Oh yes. As for your party, I must say, I find the tall, fair one quite dreamy. What's his name? Will?"

"William. What do you mean by dreamy?"

Ottavia was having none of it. "You can't fool me. I saw the way he looked at you, and I get the idea you like him, too. Am I wrong?"

Helena sighed. "No, you're not wrong, but it can't happen. I already said, as how I'm here to find my husband, who I've heard nowt from these past two years. Until I know different, I'm a married woman. Some things aren't proper."

"Well, I think I may be able to help you with your husband. I have a man. A man who knows people in the city. You tell me your Ralph was a stone mason, so chances are my man can find someone who knows what happened to him and, if he still lives, where."

"Seriously? I thought I'd be months in the finding of him. That's too kind."

"Nonsense. I'll introduce him on the morrow."

~~~
~~~

True to his word, William, in self-declared monk mode, worked through the night, looking for anything that might support his quest. While he found plenty of references to the Janasà, there was nothing at all about an aphrodisiac anywhere, never mind on the island of Sardonica. He ploughed on, his eyes stinging in the weak flickering candlelight and his frustration mounting. He did find several mentions that appeared interesting. Some were about the Nurragù crystal, while others talked about the folklore of Sardonica and the beliefs of the Janasà.

As the night wore on, he came across one text a little different from the others. This one was in a small volume with a thin cover of a kind of hide like leather, but not leather, and pages that were in various stages of disintegration. He resolved to flag it to the librarian for copying, but soon became engrossed in the fantastical descriptions. Written in Grecan, it spoke of strange centaur-like beasts that ate the flesh of men in the mountains of an island far to the south, and of small burrowing creatures, little bigger than hares, with odd magical abilities. This then was a Grecan mythology that he'd not seen mentioned anywhere before. Such myths were entertaining and little else. The final pages were the most worn and difficult to decipher, but contained by far the most interesting information. They described, in faded lettering, three great artefacts of magical importance: these were the Crystal of Life, the Book of Tales, and a third that he couldn't make out at all. Together, they were known as the Tripletta, and they represented the solution to a grave threat to the world and all of civilisation. Amazing. Where did such stories come from?

He put all this aside and carried on his search.

Not long before dawn, he must have slipped off into the realm of Orpheus. He dreamed of that face again, the face of the woman from the storm. She had another woman in a cage. Was it Verity? It looked like her from behind, but as she turned to face him, it wasn't Verity it all. It was Helena. Then the scene shifted to a clifftop in a howling gale and William was in the cage, and Helena had switched back to Verity, who was looking in from the outside and singing a nursery rhyme about algebra. Verity kicked the cage toward the cliff, and it teetered on the edge. He pleaded with her. *I'm sorry, I haven't given up on you. I promise I'll get there.*

"Will! Will! Wake up!" Ridkin was shaking him hard. He woke up with a start with his head on a desk.

Looking up, he was still in the library. "Hnnnuu rbbbu," he said, not at his bushiest with just an hour or two's sleep. "Look..." He slapped his own face to knock the stupor out of him. "Look at all this I found." He pointed at a stack of volumes several hands deep.

"Where's that dolcop knight?" shouted Jasper, striding into the room, with Morwena a pace behind. "We ride in one hour. Be there, or I'll slit your throat."

He turned to leave, but William called him back.

"For the love of the Stars, turn around and look what I've got here," screamed William, surprised at himself for the anger he felt. "What's wrong with you? It's not just about swinging a sword around like it's your manly member!"

Ridkin put his hand over his eyes. Jasper turned again, and as he advanced, drew his sword. "What was that, Bookman?"

"Jasper, don't, he's tired," pleaded Ridkin.

Morwena touched his arm. "Wait, brother. Let's at least look at what he's found."

William prayed some of it might be interesting to the red-headed maniac in front of him.

"See, this one talks about Janasà culture. Ways to speak with them. Ways to persuade them."

"Right. I don't need or want any of that."

"And this. This is about how to navigate there. The words to use, the stuff you need to wear to survive the jungles there."

"I can get all that from the islanders. What else have you got? I'm getting bored."

In desperation, William squeaked out, "There's this crystal the books all talk about."

The room went silent. William held his breath. He noticed birds singing outside and a clock mechanism clacking away on the far wall. Morwena tugged at Jasper's sleeve. "Brother..." she said. "He might have something useful."

Jasper sheathed his sword and pulled up a chair. “Show me.”

# Thirteen

The gravel path crunched under the shoes of the three women as they wandered through Ottavia's extensive gardens in the early morning Truscan sunshine. They stopped at the northern end of the pathway to admire the view over the distant city. Helena had just learned that the rest of the travellers were going to stay a little longer while William researched the Janasà. At least he'd found a use for his peculiar talent and she felt happy for him. It didn't matter, he'd soon be far away, and she could forget about any feelings she might have for him.

Giobbo approached, bowing low to Ottavia before addressing Helena. However, she understood little of his dialect.

Ottavia translated. "He found your man. Outside of the city, in a terrible place they call Tromba di Nerone."

The concerned expression on Ottavia's face led Helena to ask, "What is it about this Tromba that I need to know?"

Ottavia glanced at Matilda then looked at Helena with her eyebrows raised as if to say *should I continue?* Matilda showed no intention of going anywhere and folded her arms in defiance. Helena nodded her assent.

"This district is Trusca's dark spot, where a man might go to buy a woman's favours. Do you know what I'm saying?"

"Is that allowed?" asked Helena. "Don't the priests forbid this?"

"Allowed? Of course not, but it's the robed ones who run the place just the same.[61]"

"What?"

"See, here's how it works. There are always men who want sex and women desperate enough to sell it. Having one district where this happens means control, and who do you think controls the city? The priesthood.

They take a cut, in theory, to help feed the poor. Reality is, they spend the money on… other things. Those simple priests have the finest houses, I can tell you. The women have to wear red bonnets and are called Nerone's Geese. I don't know why. When they die, they bury them in sinner's graves and pretend they never existed. Same goes for their children. Sins of the parents and all that. I wish it were otherwise."

The first rays of doubt shone on Helena's resolve. What could Ralph be doing living among prostitutes?

"Is it safe for me and Tilda to go there?" she asked.

"Not alone, no. I fear you'd both end up on your backs with a red bonnet on. You'll need protection."

"How much does it cost?"

"Let me take care of that. The money's not important. The main thing is that your husband may be involved in some dirty business. It's hard to think of any other reason for him living there."

"That's kind of you. When can we leave?"

"This afternoon."

"One more thing. Does my husband know about us? Being here, like?" asked Helena.

She spoke with Giobbo. "He thought it best not to tell him. He says not all husbands wish to be found."

"Is he at home?"

She checked. "As Giobbo understands it, yes. He warns you. The experience won't be pleasant."

"Tilda, are you ready for this?"

"We've come this far. I want to see him."

Approaching Tromba, Helena, Matilda, and their guide passed a ruined temple and a disordered cemetery full of unmarked graves for *the outcast dead*. In other words, the remains of the women who plied their trade in the town. With them, as well as Giobbo, there were a pair of off duty watchmen and a translator. The road led into a narrow street lined with unloved, whitewashed houses, many with boarded up shutters and crumbling brickwork. Smaller streets jutted off in both directions, crammed with buildings in similar states of disrepair. Filth and litter lay everywhere. The town reeked of neglect. Matilda thought she'd seen poverty before, but this took the oat cake.

Arriving at the address, an unremarkable part ruin, Giobbo knocked on the door, and a scab faced girl of about twelve answered, dressed in ill matched and filthy clothes.

"Too early," she said, and slammed the door.

Helena stepped ahead of Giobbo and knocked again, harder.

The same girl opened up again. "What?" she shouted, but before she could give further vent to her annoyance, Helena asked, "Is Ralph Jarvis here?"

Giobbo translated for her. The girl softened her expression and nodded, but still shut the door on them again. After another minute, a woman of about Helena's age dressed in a stained grey smock reopened it. A red cowl only hid a part of the knotted unwashed hair that tumbled down over her pockmarked bare shoulders. She wore her plume of stale body odour like a mantle.

"You want Raffa?" she said.

"Raffa, or Ralph, yes."

"He's busy," she replied, her voice devoid of emotion.

"I'll wait. May we come in?"

"I suppose. I am sorry. My daughter thinks you want sell girl."

Matilda's eyes widened.

The woman showed Helena and Matilda into a cramped, airless space with young girls slouched around in various states of undress. On sighting newcomers, they reached for their cowls. From above, they heard a rhythmic banging on bare timbers that, anywhere but here, might have been a carpenter at work.

"Through here," said the woman.

Passing into a passageway, the woman opened another door to a dingy smaller room in which a man sat sideways on to a desk. Before him, a much younger woman knelt, but on seeing Helena, stood up, wiping her mouth and rushed past them out the door as he adjusted his britches. Helena struggled in the gloom to make out his features, but when her eyes accustomed themselves to the low light, she realised with a jolt: Ralph.

Ralph, or Raffa as they called him, staggered to his feet, cursing in a mix of the local dialect and Anglonian. He approached Helena. "What the hell do you do-gooders want, disturbing a man in his home? I don't need saving. Get out, get out!" Before he could come closer, he collapsed into fits of coughing. Fine drops of blood sprayed down the front of his filthy shirt.

"Daddy?" asked Matilda.

A flash of puzzlement followed by recognition ran across Ralph's face. "Who's that? Tilda? Tilda, my angel, what? Is that you? I mean, why?" he said, as he dragged a hand over his thinning, greasy hair and sighed to Helena, "you could've warned me, at least." He looked like a man twice his age, exhausted and defeated, a picture of despair.

"I couldn't risk you refusing to see us," said Helena.

"Right, happen I might have done. Look. Let me sort things out here. I can meet you in the taverna on the main piazza." He pushed them out.

Helena and Matilda made their way out and down to the taverna. They found an almost clean bench and ordered watered down wine. Helena asked Giobbo and the others to wait outside and keep watch. She hoped her husband wouldn't do a runner, but she needn't have worried. After what she guessed to be about twenty minutes, Ralph appeared. He'd attempted to clean himself up, but some things can't be masked. His skin had greyed and scabbed with the pockmarks, and fluid leaked from one eye. He'd lost most of his teeth, and those that remained had browned. It broke Helena's heart to see how old and sick he looked. She reminded herself why she'd come and set herself to see it through. The worry now was how much he'd reveal to Matilda.

"Tilda, can you please wait outside? I need to talk to your mother."

"No, daddy," said Matilda, as tears welled up. "Mother keeps so much from me. I couldn't bear it if you did the same. What you tell mother, you can tell me."

Ralph looked at Helena for agreement. She shrugged, suddenly feeling too tired to argue with her daughter.

"If you're sure..." he turned to address Helena. "How dare you come to me like this and bring our daughter into it? What happened between us four years ago were final and done with. There's no going back on it. What did you think you could achieve? Because you won't get owt from me." He'd gone red in the face and collapsed into yet another coughing fit.

Helena seethed as she waited for him to calm. "I'm doing it for Tilda." It was like they'd never been apart, so soon did the familiar feeling of rage come to her. She couldn't risk having it all spill out in front of her daughter, so fought down her urge to drop all of her anger and frustration on him in a torrent of ire. Instead, she said, "You don't know and don't care what she's been through since you stopped writing."

Ralph dismissed her with a wave in that annoying way she remembered so well and looked at his daughter. He ran his hand back through his greasy hair. "Tilda, happen you've become quite the woman. I've missed so much."

"What are you *doing* here, daddy? This place is horrid."

He lifted his palms to her in a show of guilt. "It's how I earn a crust. Sorry I won't gild the lily."

Matilda's reaction was of anger. "I can't believe it." Then she looked around at Helena. "This is *your* fault, I *know* it!"

Before Helena could think, he replied, "Nay, pet, this is of my doing. It's like this. I came away to make good honest coin and found it. For two years, my work was in demand. Folk paid well for it, like. Then I made a mistake."

He paused. "Go on," said Matilda.

"Arch I made collapsed on me and two mates, like. They both died. All on account of something I did, and it were tough to live with, that's Sola's truth. I started drinking. Your mother'll tell thee, I'm not good with the drink in me. I got into a fight and took a kicking. They broke my back. Truth is, I wanted them to hurt me. I deserved it, like. Paid a good chunk of my savings to get cared for, but after that, couldn't lift the heavy slabs no more. Nobody wants a mason as can't work stone."

"Then what? How did you get like this?"

"Simple. The drink again. As I used up me money, I drank bad wine and worse grappa, and then stopped eating to afford more of it. When I began begging, they threw me out of the city, and I washed up here. They look after me well enough, but the place has mould, and something attacked my chest." And as if to illustrate this last point, his lungs chose that moment to kick off with another body wracking fit of coughing. "Then this priest came along and he heard me speaking Anglonian. Said he had a business proposal. Turned out he wanted me to sell these girls to merchants and other travellers from Anglonia. They pay good coin for a Truscan wench. I'm not proud of myself, but you try living here without a trade."

"But you were my world, daddy; how could you leave us? You didn't even say goodbye. Don't you know how that hurt? Well, it's *her* fault. You'd never have left if she hadn't made you. Don't deny it."

He looked up at Helena. "I have to tell her. She's a grown lass, she 'as a right to know."

"Ralph, no. Please don't." Helena put on her best pleading expression.

"There're things your mother doesn't know," he said to them both.

"Wait. What do you mean?" asked Helena, alarmed.

He shook his head. "You've no idea, have you? I was up to all kinds of no-good back home. Upset the wrong folk and had to disappear. Yes, she told me to go, but I were leaving anyway."

"But I came all this way to take you home. Please come home," said Matilda.

"Can't. Ever. You have to accept that."

"We could move to another county."

"No, child. This is my life, or what's left of it. At any road, I'm too weak to travel."

"Oh, daddy…"

She reached to hug him, but he palmed her back. He stood and walked outside with Matilda and then Helena in pursuit. "Daddy…"

"Don't get close." He shouted in warning. He continued in a softer voice. "Sorry, pet, but what I have spreads, so they say. And as hard as it sounds, please don't come back, because I won't be here. I'm going to put some things in order and then make my peace."

"No! It's never that bad."

"It is. Please go and try to remember me as I was. In the good times. And Tilda… I always loved you. Never doubt it."

There were tears in his eyes as he turned and shambled away and into the brothel, closing the door behind him. Helena and Matilda stood speechless in the street. A breeze wafted a foul smell from somewhere at the end of the road, and a dog barked in the distance.

"I don't feel safe here," said Matilda.

"Wait with Giobbo. I'll only be a moment," she said to Matilda in a tone that allowed no discussion. The girl looked shocked. None of this could be what she'd have expected. On the verge of tears, she nodded and offered no argument.

Helena went in after her husband. "Ralph," she called, once they were alone.

He raised his voice. "Let's cut the crap. Why are you here, Helena?"

"You know full well."

He stood implacable. He was going to make her beg. "Do I? Explain it."

She held out her hand. "Give it back. It's not yours."

"Ah, of course." He paused long enough for a sly smile to creep across his face. "It's important to you, isn't it? To do with that magic you do, is it? Tell me, does Tilda know owt about what you are?"

She stared hard at him. "She knows nowt, and I aim to keep it that way."

"Just as I thought." He looked in no hurry to do anything.

"I can *make* you give it back."

"And let Tilda see that? What's it worth?"

She glanced down at his groin. "Tell me you don't want *that*."

"Moons and Stars, no! I'd rather take any of these girls before I'd touch you now. I need brass. Brought any?"

She'd been ready for something of the sort. She rummaged under her kirtle and took out a money pouch, offering him the whole thing, a handsome sum. As he reached to take it, she held it back. "There are a hundred ducats in here. Give me the amulet, and it's yours. You'll never have to hear from me again."

He weighed it up for a moment, nodded, then leant down to his ankle with a pocketknife. He slit the leather band there and brought up a white stone. "You'd better not be lying."

They made the exchange. "Are we done? Goodbye Helena and good riddance." He turned and disappeared into another room.

~~~

William sat at a desk in the great library, working through a pile of accounts of the ancient lore surrounding the Janasà. It was hard to find much that didn't also reference some supposed magic relating to the crystal, Nurragù, and its cat-like guardian, and despite himself, he found it interesting. He'd already discovered some further fascinating aspects of the legend. For instance, that, in the right hands, the object gave its bearer the power to both give and take life, to heal the sick, and promote fertility. That was quite an impressive list. Where on earth did these ridiculous tales come from?

The nagging thought remained that his quest might be linked with Nurragù. Just from the way that Jasper and Morwena seemed so interested in it. What wasn't he understanding? The questions mounted. He listed the most vexing on a piece of parchment, enjoying the feel of the fine quill as it travelled across the page, as though wafted on warm air.

*One. If my quest be of the crystal, why then does my contract with the King revolve around aphrodisiac water?*
*Two. Why are Jasper Foolson and his strange sister so keen to see me reach my goal, even to the point of risking their lives? And come to think of it, what's in it for the jester chap?*
*Three. What does the image of that old woman's face mean?*

He wasn't so sure about this last question; it might be his imagination. People didn't project their faces onto waves, did they? Or try to enter your mind at night.
~~~

He picked up the next volume, marvelling at how the library clerk appeared to know where every book rested and what its subject matter related to. More to the point, where in each work to find the relevant passages. The man must have a memory that matched his own. He flicked to the bookmarked page and read it.

The beast that protected the crystal went by the name Bisgattù, which he took to mean something like two cats. So why elsewhere did the literature only mention one such cat? He pressed on, the translation slow and difficult to be sure of. The cat possessed great magic. Well, of course it did. It was a legendary cat. And it could only be passed if a man, or, he assumed, a woman, could answer three riddles, riddles that related to the nature of things, the order of the universe. He liked riddles. However, to answer incorrectly would cause swift death. Minor stakes, then. The rest of the account made little sense; maybe the description itself was a riddle? He sighed and reached for the next reference.

This one told that the crystal had been stolen from its resting place by a capricious spirit, who crept past the cat as it slept and having gained its prize, lost it in a distant land. Who made this stuff up? Why did one account contradict the next?

Bored at last with that topic, he switched to focus again on the Janasà of Sardonica. The first new reference he found had been written a hundred or more years earlier, and said they were gentle. Peace-loving in nature. Try telling that to the ones they'd burned. The next, more recent account, gave the same general idea. Why then were they so often described as violent and dangerous, and why had a group attacked them? He felt puzzled, but also more hopeful. Perhaps their journey to Nuorrù might not be so dangerous after all?

With wonderful timing, Jasper came in and got straight to the point. "What have you uncovered then, Bookman? It'd better be worth the delay."

"I don't want to spend any longer here than I have to."

"Right. The sappy Verity girl you're always going on about."

"She's not sappy!"

"Whatever. Spill the beans, come on."

William outlined his research so far. "What is it about this crystal that interests you? I thought this quest was about an aphrodisiac for the King."

"A what?" Jasper looked puzzled for a moment. "Oh, *that* aphrodisiac." He smirked.

"Is there more than one?" asked William. "Anyway, I've found nothing about it. Not a word. Should I keep looking?"

"Um. You don't need to do that. I'm sure it'll be good. I mean, you've learned a ton about the Janasà already."

He drummed his fingers on the desk. Jasper never looked comfortable confined to one place.

"Jasper," said William.

"Hmm?"

"Why do you hate me?"

Jasper was slow to respond. "I don't hate you. Not as such. Well, a bit. Yes, I actually hate your guts. What of it?"

"Why?"

"Because you are what he can't be." It was Morwena, who'd crept in where William hadn't seen her. "He's dreamt his whole life about becoming a knight, and you got it handed to you on a silver platter."

"But he can have mine. Take it."

"It doesn't work like that, Bookman," said Jasper. "I don't come from the right stock. They'd never accept me. But I'm the best there is! It's madness."

Morwena placed her hand on his shoulder. "Come on brother. It's not William's fault. Maybe it's time to move on?"

"It's so unfair!"

She led him out, still complaining. William shook his head. All that fuss over waving a sword around. Now where was he?

He stood, stretched, and wandered to the end of the room, looking for the clerk. He wanted something more contemporary and written in plain language as a relief from deciphering legends. The door to the library opened, and a voice called his name. Helena.

As he stepped toward her, she ran forward and wrapped her arms around him. "Oh William, I've been so stupid." She burst into tears.

With considerable caution, he placed one hand on the small of her back and, with his other, without knowing why, pulled her head to his shoulder. For once, he knew what to say: nothing. A minute later, she stepped away.

"What happened?" he asked.

She looked into his eyes and erupted into tears again. This time, he held her longer until the sobbing subsided. "You don't have to tell me anything."

She sniffed and wiped her eyes. "It was difficult seeing Ralph. He's sick, very sick with his lungs. He looks to have one foot in the grave already."

"That sounds awful."

"But he was horrible. He's covered in pox and he keeps… he keeps red women."

Before he could ask how a woman could be red, she continued. "And he said he'd left to get away from me. Not for work. Because of *me*. And I realised I'd never loved him. And…"

"Yes?"

"That's it. It's done with and I have to forget him."

He worried she was about to kiss him again. Instead, to his relief, she turned away, her face unreadable, and left him with his books.

~~~

That evening, Helena found William again in the library and had an interesting proposal for him.

"You know the amphitheatre we passed yesterday on the way here?"

"The Flavianid? How could I not? It was stunning."

"Ottavia suggested something to me."

"Go on…"

She hesitated.

"Tell me, please," he said. "What's the worst that can happen? I *can* say no."

"Well…It's a tradition for couples to visit it when there's a double full moon and to make a wish[62]. I know it's nonsense and we're not even a couple, but I don't want to miss the chance to see it."
~~~

Her eyes glinted in the candlelight. He should really refuse. For Verity. On the other hand, the prospect of seeing the huge arena by moonlight was so tempting. "But it wouldn't be proper."

"Can we not for once forget about what's proper? It's set to be cloudless tonight and I won't go alone and there's nobody else I'd rather share it with. Please."

She smiled and his resistance teetered and then crumbled into a heap of rubble like a badly built arch. He was beginning to think he'd do anything just to bask in the warmth of that smile!

Shortly before midnight, William and Helena arrived at the ancient arena, being careful to avoid being seen by Matilda or Ridkin, who wouldn't have understood. Ottavia had insisted two of her men accompany them as protection, both dark, taciturn, and well-armed, so they were safe enough. The cook had given them a small hamper to carry containing honied cakes and fruit.

They reached the ruin and followed the same broad stairway upwards as before. Their escorts stayed halfway, and one of them pointed at how to continue higher. A hundred or more steps further, they came out onto the highest level and looked over the doubly moonlit spectacle laid out like a fine table. Both of them wore capes against the chill night air. The structure was eerily silent inside, and their every movement echoed across the open space. The ancients had known a thing or two about sound.

They settled on a flat stone and Helena unpacked the hamper while William stood up to get a better look and marvel at the design of the construction.

"Please William. Just come and sit with me." He sat a body width away. "You can get closer than that. I won't bite." He shuffled up close enough to feel a hint of her body warmth.

"Penny for your thoughts," she said, taking his arm. His heart skipped a beat.

"Um. This place is magical," he said, trying not to give away what he was actually thinking.

She glanced at him, eyebrows raised.

"Not *magic* magic. I mean, there's a wonderful, indescribable beauty to it, despite what happened here centuries ago. That should be all the magic the world needs."

"My word, you're an actual romantic. Who'd have thought it?"

She passed him an oat biscuit and some kind of local thing, round with cheese in it. She looked out over the scene, and he stole a glance at her. The moonlight caught her face side-on in an almost perfectly sculpted silhouette. How did he come to be sitting so close to a woman such as this?

She pulled his face toward her and looked into his eyes. The world stopped. As she moved her head closer, he held his breath, realising his helplessness with her. She got closer still. She looked about to… "Wait. What was that?" she asked. She stood up, craning her neck all around. "Did you hear it? Like someone trying to mask a sneeze."

"No."

"Shh. Listen." Footsteps echoed before receding down the stairwell.

"They've gone. Um, relax," he said, conscious he might never get another chance with her like this.

"Come on, it's late. We need to get back." Helena was packing, the moment lost.

On the way to street level, she asked Ottavia's men if they'd seen anything.

"Nothing, save a cowled figure hurrying by. Didn't see his face."

Another mystery to add to the others.

~~~

Back at the villa, Helena and William sat together on the terrace to sip wine and appreciate the torch-lit city view.

"Thank you for being there, William. I needed to spend time with a normal man."

"Normal?" he asked, eyebrows raised.

"As normal as any of us," she replied, shuddering at the thought of what she'd discovered the day before. She banished from her mind the whole, *is*
~~~

*it my fault?* thing. She hadn't made Ralph do the bad things he'd done, and there was no reason to feel guilty.

She wanted to focus on the now, and with her was a man she could respect, however strange, however imperfect. And after all this time alone, didn't she *deserve* a bit of human comfort? She set down her wine and stood. Walking around the low table between them, she planted her mouth on his. It was up to him now. He could block her out or accept her. His choice.

She led William around the bench and on up to her room.

A while later, she lay awake listening to his gentle breathing, a whirlpool of emotions making her heart race. She'd never sleep unless she could calm her mind, but that was unlikely. This needed to be thought through to its conclusion, regardless of where it took her. She'd made so many mistakes with Ralph, but with William, there was a world of possibilities. She was still young, still fit enough to make a full marriage with him with all the wonder that could bring. And this time around, the man might love her for who she was, not because magic had made him do it. This time around, she couldn't risk messing things up. William had to know the truth about her, in all its awfulness, so he could decide with that ridiculous logical mind of his what he wanted to do. She'd lay it all out for him and hope it didn't change the way he felt about her. It could go very wrong, but at least her conscience would be clear. She drifted off into a deep sleep, happy she'd made the right decision. What would be would be.

She awoke with gentle early morning sunlight having replaced that of the moons, and with William looking for all the world like a sleeping child. She listened to the birdsong pouring in through the open window. A fly buzzed somewhere around the ceiling. She dreaded what she was about to do, to say, but resolved to get it over with.

"William…" she whispered.

"Hmmm," he answered, half asleep.

"I've something I need to tell you. About me."

"Hmmm."

"Something you might not like."

"Hmmm. Let me sleep." He rolled over away from her.

She shook him. "You need to listen." She shook him again.

Finally, he turned back to her and pressed up on one elbow to look her in the face. "Can't it wait?"

She wished it could. "I'm. I'm really… curse the Stars, it's like this. I'm not like other women."

"Of course you're not," he said, mistaking the cue and caressing her arm. "You're truly very special."

"Aye. Special right enough, William, but not in a way you'll want to hear."

She decided it might be easier if she demonstrated something, something to pique his curiosity. She pointed a finger at the ceiling and a series of sparks streamed out of it that danced about the room before disappearing.

"Neat trick," he said, impressed. "How did you do that?"

"You're not getting it, are you?"

She made the blankets fly off the bed and turn into a cascade of rose petals that fell around them.

A puzzled frown came over his forehead. "That's all these are right? Tricks that anyone could learn to do?"

"No, William. Only a witch can do owt like this. Truth is, I'm a witch, a white one, or perhaps an off-white one, but a witch all the same."

As he turned to sit up with his legs to the floor, he looked troubled. She waited for his response and at last it came. "I'm not sure what that even is. Explain it to me."

And it all poured out. She'd not intended to go so far, but once she began, it was like a wave that needed to exhaust itself onto the rocks. She told him of her young woman's infatuation for Ralph, that he'd been uninterested, and how she'd used her magic to ensnare him, and how it had turned out wrong. About the rows, about the sense Ralph had of being a caged beast without understanding the reasons, and of that fateful last day when she'd told him the truth and he'd left her. How she could tell Matilda nothing of the story. And her relief at the news that he'd misled her all along and had *wanted* to leave her.

And that was it. The wave had broken. She searched in his eyes for a sign of comprehension, of acceptance and saw something more akin to fear. He grabbed his clothes from the chair and moved to go. "I… I don't know you at all. You've done something to me. Made me want you, tricked me into betraying Verity. I can't stay."

He hurried across to open the door, and she came up behind him, trying to close it. "No, it's not like that. Please William. Stop and talk. We can work this out."

"Mistress, we cannot." He'd raised his voice a couple of notches.

Matilda appeared through the gap in the door. "What's going on Mother? What are you doing in her room, William?" Seeing her mother naked, she put her hand to her mouth and wailed, "Oh My Stars! You were doing… *that!*" She looked about to mime an action, then thrust her hands to her side. "And so soon after we saw father. You're despicable." She stamped off and made for the stairs.

William grabbed his clothes, hurriedly putting his britches on and getting into, inevitably, a tangle. As he stepped out to leave, he turned for just a moment. "I'm sorry." He looked about to say something more, then softly shook his head, closed the door behind him, and left her.

~~~

William struck out into the city to clear his head, surrounded by the bustling sounds of Truscan folk starting their days, forgetting for the moment the risk of being seen around Trusca. So, here he was striding down the Via Perplessa, too consumed with himself to care where he might be going. Tall waves of anger curled up, white-capped with a sense of injustice, before crashing onto the beach of his mind and washing away all possibility of rationality like so much flotsam. Then came a sucking undertow of doubt and regret, before the cycle resumed with undying intensity.

He was angry with himself, with Helena, with the jester, and with the world.

He couldn't believe that at the first sign of feminine affection, he'd banished all thought of Verity and dived headlong into a night of what had seemed gentle, thoughtful passion with a woman he clearly didn't know at all. Guilt washed over him, permeating the cracks in his shell of logic and
~~~

seeping into his core. This was *horrible*. How could he ever respect himself again after this, and how could he marry Verity, knowing his own nature as an adulterer? He'd have to return and buy out her indemnity and then leave Coxwell forever. Oh, the shame of it.

He directed the bulk of his anger at Helena. She was the one who'd led him down this path. It was she who had seduced him, played with his inexperienced nature, and made him betray Verity. And then after that, she'd done some kind of elaborate conjuring trick. How? Why? Had she been taunting him? How could he have slept with such a woman?

And he felt scared. Scared of what it would mean to accept what she'd told him. That she was a witch. That she'd bewitched Ralph into marrying her. If so, she must have bewitched him as well, made him do things he hadn't meant to, made him *trust* her.

But then, none of that could be true. Could it?

He needed to be alone. Walk, walk, walk. Calm himself. Find the space to think. It didn't take long for him to realise he was lost. No matter, he could ask for directions to Ottavia's villa, but the only people around looked threatening. They stared at him with cold eyes, like they were weighing up whether they could rob him. Or worse. This was a bad neighbourhood, with high tenements, blocks of crumbling stone and some grey substance that bound the stones together[63]. Everything looked grey, dark and unloved. The place stank of stale human occupation and hopelessness. He turned to retrace his steps, but only got more lost.

He passed a pair of red hooded women, their faces thick with some garish paste to whiten their skin, and crude rouge painted onto their lips. "Good day, mister," said the older of the two. "Fancy spending some sexy time with two lovely girls?"

Thinking aloud to himself, he said almost under his breath, "Why, do you know any like that?"

The younger one got there first, narrowing her eyes. "Oh, very funny, mister." She spat on the ground, glaring at him.

He mumbled an apology and pushed off in the opposite direction. Maybe he'd acted in haste, by not staying to listen to Helena. After all, if he didn't believe in magic, how could he blame her for practising it? And it wasn't like she flaunted it. On the other hand, if she were a witch, his whole understanding of the world would have to change, and he'd have to review everything he'd ever believed.

Turning a corner, he bumped into something large and unyielding. Not to mention smelly. This something punched him hard in the gut, knocking him to the floor, then hauled him over a bony shoulder. He tried to shout for help, but couldn't draw enough air into his lungs.

"Where's that cart?" said the voice of a youngish man in a mix of Albian and Ludnam accents.

"It's coming. You ken?" said another reedier voice with the same accent.

Wheels ground on cobbles and a single horse clopped near. "Right. Get him in the cart." William landed on his back with a jarring thud that once again knocked the breath out of him. "Where's the sack?" said the first voice.

"Yer sittin' on it."

"Oh aye, right."

Someone stuffed something in William's mouth, yanked a bag down over his head, then tied his hands and feet before covering him in a scratchy woollen blanket.

"Right. Go!"

The cart sped away over the rough cobbles jostling him this way and that. He'd been taken.

# Fourteen

Matilda barged into Helena's room without knocking, her anger spilling out of her like an overboiling kettle. The door slammed back against the wall. "How long has it been going on, mother?" she demanded.

Helena half sat up from her cot, and stared at her daughter standing over her, hands on hips as if she were the parent. "You mean William?" She lay back again, staring unfocused at the ceiling. "There's nowt going on, Tilda darling."

"Don't come the innocent like I'm a child. I saw you. Naked! And so soon after father."

"It happened, and it's over. There's an end to it."

"You're… *You're impossible!* Just stop it. Speak to me like an adult."

"As you wish." Helena sighed and stood up. "Truth be told, I don't know what I were thinking. It were a mistake. It would never work."

"Of course it would never work."

"I'm sorry. It were only the once, and it's over now, good and proper." She held up her arms toward her daughter. "Come here, lass."

Matilda rushed over to her mother, sat beside her, and accepted her embrace. She sobbed.

"Why? Why did you betray father? Right after we saw him and all."

She hadn't thought of it as betraying him, but wasn't about to argue the point. "I didn't mean to. I wanted someone to be with last evening, someone who I thought would understand how I felt. And then… let's just say that one thing led to another."

"Did he press himself on you? I'll rip his head off if he did."

"*No!* Calm yourself. It were nothing like that. He'd never lay a finger on me."

"Promise me you won't go with him again, mother. Promise. I couldn't bear it." She looked up, expecting an answer.

After a moment's hesitation, Helena replied, "Of course, pet. I promise." She pulled Matilda's head to her shoulder and let her cry herself out.

For a moment, it crossed her mind that she should confess all. The truth that Ralph hadn't revealed. About her being a witch. She dismissed it at once. Spilling the beans to William hadn't worked out so well. How would it help matters to reveal everything to her daughter?

"We're not right for each other. All that useless learning has filled his head with stuff and nonsense. It's alright, I don't need anyone else. Besides, I have you."

"Where's he gone, anyway?" said Matilda, pulling away.

"He'll be in the library, I'll warrant. That's where he'd live, given half a chance."

"But he were tearing off toward the city, just now. In a right stinking mood he were. Looked straight through me like I weren't there."

Helena felt a pang of concern. More than likely, he'd already be in trouble. "I need to look for him."

"No mother. He'll turn up when he's calmed down. What got into him to go off like that, any road?"

Helena lightly shook her head. "I can't rightly say." Which was partly true, at least. "I'm going to ask Ottavia if she can help…"

Worried sick, she looked out for William's return all day. When he didn't show up for the evening meal, her concern turned into outright panic. If something bad had happened to him, it would be her fault.

The idea of using magic to find him she ruled out right away. Too dangerous, too unpredictable. No, the better solution would be to tell Jasper. Get him to help. He'd know what to do. And he'd have the wherewithal to do it. Although why he cared so much about William's fate troubled her. She'd never believed for one second in the aphrodisiac water story, so what was it really all about? That could wait. Regardless of what she felt or not for William, she didn't want any harm to come to him. He didn't deserve that.

~~~

William's three captors said nothing as the speeding cart jolted over rough street cobbles, the clatter of hooves echoing off the buildings as they tore at speed through the streets. They appeared to be climbing, then the echoing stopped, and he assumed they'd left the city, although in which direction he couldn't tell. After at least an hour of uncomfortable lurching and banging, the cart tilted sideways, almost tipping, and then slowed as the sound of the horses echoed around some kind of courtyard. They came to a stop, then someone hoisted him up, lifted him over the now familiar bony shoulder, and carried him off down a flight of steps. From the echoes of his bearer's footsteps, they were in a narrow stone floored space.

"Open this door," said the voice of whoever was carrying him.

A door creaked open as metal grated on metal and a second pair of hands helped drop him to the floor. Footsteps receded before the door slammed shut and a lock turned closed with an ominous *click*.

With his wrists and feet bound, he groped with his arms to pull the hood off. A narrow sliver of light from under the door illuminated the room. Not that it revealed a huge amount. The space measured no more than three paces square with a low roof, and stank of mould. Beneath him, a thin mattress promised little comfort. It crunched under his weight, a sound like straw. He rolled himself to the wall and levered himself to a standing position, bowing his head just enough to fit under the ceiling. Shuffling over to the door, he used outstretched fingers to check the lock, then did a full circuit of the walls in the vain hope there might be loose bricks or some such through which he could escape. Having found nothing, he made his way back to the mattress, colliding with a wooden pail and grazing his forehead against the brick wall.

He slid into a sitting position and started shivering, partly on account of the cold and partly from sheer terror. What was happening? He tried to think. Always choose the simplest logical explanation. Except at that
~~~

moment, there were no logical explanations to choose from. Was this about Duke Cosimo and his son wanting to exact revenge? If so, why did the two voices he'd heard speak good Anglonian? Or was this in some nonsensical way related to the vision of that old woman again? Impossible. There had to be a third reason, although it eluded him. Unless they intended to just leave him there to starve, someone would come to feed him, maybe even talk to him. He'd argue with them, explain who he was. It might all just be a misunderstanding, right?

He didn't have to wait for too long before the door opened and a short man entered, holding a bowl of broth while a second remained framed in the doorway. Neither spoke. "Can you at least unbind me?" he asked in Anglonian, not thinking of the tongue the man might use.

He held out his hands and nodded at the bindings. A ray of understanding crossed the man's face. He exchanged words in dialect with his accomplice, who handed him a knife.

"Thank you," said William in Truscan, as the man severed the tight cords.

"You are Anglonian, yes?"

"Yes. I'm William. Where am I? Can you tell me what's going on?"

The man hesitated. The second one nodded. "You are at the Trusca residence of Duke Cosimo. What you are here for, I couldn't say. My job is just to bring you food and take away your pail."

Having freed William's bindings, the man turned to leave. Then stopped in the doorway. He appeared thoughtful for a moment, then placed his candle on the floor inside the door, which he closed with a loud click. A key scraped in the lock.

"I suppose a blanket's out of the question," William called to the silence.

~~~

"William has disappeared, mother," said Jasper, talking to the green image of Imelda as it hovered over a cut tree stump. Darkness circled around him in the little clearing south of Ottavia's villa, where they'd found the space to call her.
~~~

"Why are you bringing this to me? Have you turned sluggen? You're the ones in Trusca. Go find him. I'm…"

Morwena interrupted, "It's dark now, for one thing. For another, he's been missing since this morning and Ottavia's people have found no trace of him in the city. We need help."

She huffed. "Do I have to do everything in this family? Curses. Leave it with me. I'll let you know as soon as I find anything."

The image vanished.

"Who's rattled her cage?" asked Jasper. "Anyway, do you think she can trace him?"

"If anyone can, *she* can," said his sister, trying to look convincing. "I just hope it's not Cosimo that's taken him. He'll be dead by now."

An hour later, Imelda's face again loomed out of the timber. "I've picked up a trace. He's in a large stone building about a half a league southeast of where you are. And he's still alive. That's all I can say from this far away."

Morwena replied. "Maybe Ottavia's people will know of a place like that. It could be a castle or a prison. We can head out there at first light."

"Good. Make sure you free him."

"Why not just leave him?" asked Jasper. "I mean, we can find some other dolt than Coxwell to talk to Queen Nannua. What does Feydor say?"

"Feydor?" she replied. "I don't know. He's been acting strangely these last few days."

Jasper scoffed. "Sounds normal for Feydor."

"This is different. He's been distant, uncommunicative. When he comes here, he just wants to know where William is. Anyway, let's not change our plans unless we have to. Check out where he's being held and report back. And be careful. I don't want you taking risks tomorrow."

Her image swirled and disappeared into the tree stump with a sound like water running down a hole.

~~~

William awoke from a fitful night's slumber to the sound of distant birdsong. Faint daylight penetrated through the gap under the door. He'd
~~~

spent an uncomfortable night shivering on the thin straw mattress. By now, he felt sure Jasper would know of his having disappeared. Not that this gave him cause for optimism. Assuming the wild fighter considered it worth the effort to look for him, finding his location so far out of the city and launching a rescue bid looked unlikely.

He heard keys in the lock, and the door opened. As bright daylight burst through, three men entered: two of them younger than himself, both with pockmarked faces and red hair. The third, shorter man looked familiar. With a rush, he recognised the man he'd cut back in Ianua. The gash on his face had almost healed, but he'd carry a scar for life. None of them appeared to be there for a friendly chat.

They made him stand. He wanted to ask a thousand questions. Before he could think of the first, the Italican began, "Your name is William of Coxwell, is that correct?" He spoke Anglonian, with a thick, hesitant Truscan accent, every word bearing a surplus rising vowel sound at the end.

William kept silent and received a kick to the shins from the larger red-headed one. "Answer when you're spoken to. Have ye no manners?"

"Yes. I am William of Coxwell. What do you want with me?"

"I am Ludovico of Ianua, and a week ago, you inflicted this cut on my face. The only reason you aren't already dead is that my father urges leniency. He says I have to accept my own share of blame on account of being drunk."

He shrugged, holding his hand toward the two redheads. The smaller of them handed him a knife.

"I believe in the old ways. A nose for a nose, a scratch for a scratch." The bigger of the twins held William's arms uncomfortably tight behind his back as Ludovico lifted the knife up and made a long gash in William's right cheek. William held his breath, expecting further mutilation or to be stabbed, but the man looked at the wound and tilted his head. "There. I'd expected it to be more satisfying than that."

Blood trickled down William's face and ran onto his front. "He's all yours," called Ludovico to the younger men as he handed them back their knife and left the room.

The smaller of the two remaining men addressed William. "How rude of us not to introduce ourselves," he said. "I'm Irvine Grieve and this here's my twin brother, Fraser. Yes, I know we don't look alike. Trust me. We think the same. And right now, we want to hurt you."

"But why? What have I done?"

"Exist," chuckled the one called Irvine. "You will soon wish you didn't. Well now, it's your great misfortune to be on a quest that my mother wishes to be brought to an end. We have orders to stop you reaching Sardonica. But first, we want to indulge in some fun. Do you like a little fun, William of Coxwell?"

When William didn't answer, he continued, "Alas, for you, the fun will be all ours."

William protested. "What quest? I'm on no quest."

"You're a shocking liar, Sir William. Fraser, what do you think?"

"Terrible liar," said Fraser. Releasing William's arms, he took his left hand, grabbed a finger and snapped it back hard, generating a crack that echoed round the room and shocked William's entire arm.

He squealed. His world turned to pain, and he clutched his hand. The man punched him hard in the stomach before pushing him to the ground. He gasped for breath and writhed on the floor until he could say, "My quest is for the King of Anglonia. It's just for some curative water. Nothing to concern anyone. Anyone at all."

"Ah, so he believes the story about the water," said Irvine. "You're such a wee sap, Coxwell. There's no water that we know of. It's about the crystal, you fool. *The Crystal.* You cannae be allowed to reach it."

He levered himself into a sitting position and leaned his back against the wall, taking a moment to compose himself. The pain almost made him faint. He held the damaged hand to the side of his head and whimpered.

"You mean Nurragù? *That* crystal? Like, seriously?" he asked.

"Not as stupid as you look," replied Irvine. "Yes, *that* crystal. My brother and I are to go in your place to Sardonica and steal the crystal for my witch mother and my weird uncle Feydor."

"What? The *jester* Feydor?" asked William.

The man smirked. "There could only be one Feydor."

His hand throbbed like the furies. "But it was him who set me up for this journey. Why would he want to stop me?"

"A wee change of plan. He's working with our mother now."

"What do you mean? This crystal doesn't even exist. It can't do. It's just a legend, a myth."

The brothers laughed. "Then why is our mother prepared to kill to stop you? No, the crystal is real enough. And it's the reason for your quest."

"But my quest is…"

"For the King of Anglonia," said Irvine, mimicking William's accent.

"Except that it's not," said Fraser. "They all lied to you, fool. Can't you understand that? You've been plucked like a well-tuned lute, my friend."

"But…"

"We'll be back every hour or two to break another bone. Or worse. You'll be begging to die before we've done with you."

"But why?"

They left the room and slammed the door behind them.

"Why? Why?" he shouted after them in the near darkness.

He collapsed down onto his backside, the pain from his face and hand bringing him close to tears.

~~~

Horses and riders milled about in the stable yard where Matilda stood watching Jasper, Morwena, Jacopo, and Wymond, gathering in readiness to ride out to where William was. Apparently, he was at a castle belonging to Cosimo near the town of Frasciatti, although nobody could or would explain how they knew that.

"What's your plan? Why not take Big Ger?" Matilda asked Jasper.

He was checking over his horse and his weapons: a short sword *in the old Truscan style*, as he'd put it, and two daggers, one stashed into his belt and the other down inside the leg of a boot. "We'll scout the place for now," he told her. "Work out what we're up against. No way I'm going in blind. As for Ger, I've asked him to look after you and your mother."
~~~

Morwena came up from behind Matilda and gave her a hug. "Don't look so worried," said the woman to her. "It's just a recce to check the lie of the land. We'll return on the morrow at the latest."

"Why bother to save him?" she asked. "He can't be worth it."

Morwena mounted and answered, "You know, Jasper. When he's fixed on something, he keeps at it."

"How do you even know William's there, like?"

"We don't. We're just going to look around, to see whether there's a chance we could free him."

"And if it's too dangerous?"

Morwena shrugged.

"Right, Let's move," commanded Jasper.

The four riders headed out. Matilda watched them disappear until only the dust they had kicked up remained hanging over the track. She had the distinct impression Morwena had lied, or at least held back the truth. And she'd not answered her question: *Why bother with pathetic William*? She wandered inside the villa to look for her mother, who'd been behaving even more oddly than normal since William's disappearance. She found her in a long ground floor room with a dozen enormous windows that gave onto the gardens. Not that the woman showed any interest in the view as she sat hunched forward, chewing on her nails. For the first time, Matilda thought her mother looked *old*. A few grey hairs, a hint of puffiness under the eyes, and of course, her posture and demeanour spoke of it. More than anything, though, Matilda sensed something deeper.

Her mother looked up, unsmiling. "Hello, darling."

"Are you sure you've finished with him?" Matilda asked, meaning William.

Helena's mood turned. "I told you I had, didn't I?" she snapped.

"Touchy! Sorry I asked."

To take her mind off things, she forced herself to think of her father. Not that this topic was any less disquieting. He could be dead already; it would be a kindness if he were, given the shocking state she'd seen him in. But for her mother to have taken William to her bed so soon after seeing her father so sick! They should be there with him, feeding him, keeping him clean and warm. Had he lied about not wanting to be found again? She didn't know.

Back inside the villa, she drifted into the great library where Ridkin sat at a reading bench, mouthing the words of a book to himself one at a time. He was the one person she could think of who'd never hidden things from her.

"Hi, Ridkin. How's the reading?"

"Could use some help," replied her friend.

Glad of the distraction, she pulled up a stool and got involved.

~~~

"Are you hungry, Sir William?" asked the guard who'd freed his bindings.

William, sitting on his mattress with his back against the wall, cracked open a bleary eye and tried to focus on the man. He'd slept little, what with the pain and the cold, and was groggy and miserable.

"My name is Teo," said the guard. He handed William a blanket and put a bowl of something hot on the floor in the centre of the room.

"I'd shake your hand," replied William. "only…" he held up his injured limb.

The guard called Teo winced, then handed William's waste pail to his companion and received an empty one in return.

"How… do… you… do?" said Teo, in faltering Anglonian, before offering a questioning smile.

William's head snapped up. "Mustn't grumble," he replied, the obligatory response of an Anglonian when asked *how are you?*

Reverting to Truscan, Teo asked, "Is there anything I can get you?"

"Other than the key to the door? I don't know. Perhaps a book?" Not that he actually felt like reading at that moment.

"I dare not bring you a key. If your two countrymen found I'd given one to you… well, you understand how it would get ugly."

"Uglier than things are already? Oh, I see. For you. By the way, they are from Albia, not Anglonia. They're no countrymen of mine."
~~~

Teo bowed and turned to leave. William, desperate for conversation, tried to stall him. "You are interested in my country?" he asked.

"Yes. My poor Bella, before I met her, worked for a short time in Anglonia in a tavern serving bread with hot cheese. She had fond memories of her visit there and spoke your language well. Sadly, she died in labour just last year. Then my son Antonio passed the month after that. I'd love to go to Anglonia. Ludnam Bridge. The Tower of Ludnam. Eastminster Palace."

"Right now, I'd love to go there as well," said William. Then added, "I'm sorry for your losses."

Teo smiled. "Thank you. Tell me. Do you eat turnips at every meal?"

Despite his pain, William couldn't suppress a smile. "Almost every meal."

"Could you teach me all your banter?"

"All of it?" He shifted his weight on his backside and grimaced as a jolt shot down his left side. When it eased, he said, "You want to learn to spout ale house nonsense?"

"I wish to learn everything about your culture."

"Culture? Hmph. If you ever find any of that, let me know."

Footsteps sounded outside the cell. "I'll see what I can do about a book," whispered Teo, stepping aside as the twins entered. Fraser mimed a walking action to the guard, using two down-pointing fingers.

"So, Sir William. I trust you had an uncomfortable night. You know, I was just telling my brother how fortunate you are to have our undivided attention. It's time to break something else. What'll it be?" This was Irvine, the smaller, sparkier of the two.

"Go stick your ugly heads up a sow's arse," replied William. "Tickle off and die."

"There's no need to be like that," said Fraser. "Let's get a wee look at your hand."

"No!" William jumped up and hid his damaged limb under folded arms. He whimpered at the pain of brushing the broken finger.

Fraser approached, and William dodged to the side. "What sport!" said the man.

This time, they both came forward, flanking him and driving back into the wall.

"Please, no. Not again. I can't stand it. We can talk this over like gentlemen. This has to be a mistake. Nobody should want to hurt me."

"Oh, but we do. Want to hurt you. A lot."

"Why? Give me a single argument that makes an ounce of sense. Even Prometheus knew the reason for his torment. Tell me!"

"Won't," declared Irvine. "There doesnae have to be a reason, does there, brother?"

"Nope," said Fraser.

"I get it! You're both *solipsists*. You think everyone else's suffering is imaginary. That has to be the explanation."

The twins laughed. "He thinks we're imagining him? Oh, that's grand," said Fraser. "No, we do it because we *enjoy* your suffering. It's as simple as that. Now give me your wee hand."

He tried to resist. He did. It made no difference. The man's sheer strength made the result a foregone conclusion, and as soon as he had the damaged hand in his grip, he squeezed.

William's agony increased. Fraser yanked at the already broken finger this way and that, grinning as he watched William writhe.

"Please no. You don't have to do this," he said, barely above a whisper. Their eyes locked. There was no shred of compassion there, no hint of doubt. He stared into an abyss full of contempt and held the gaze long enough for the abyss to stare back. If hatred could run like water, it washed over William, drenching him to the bone. This creature before him lacked what he could only think of as a soul. Here before him stood a wild, chaotic, demonic, *unthinking* monster dressed in human form, with no empathy and beyond all reasoning. He abandoned hope, just as the big man grabbed another finger and bent it back. Another cracking noise rang around the tiny room and William screamed again.

~~~
~~~

Helena debated with herself long and hard. Should she use magic to save William? *Could* she use it that way? With no clear answer, and with no particular expectation, Helena took her mother's amulet from the linen sac she'd place it in and stared into the white stone at its centre. She'd spent no time with it back in Anglonia, having been still in that frame of mind where she'd wanted nothing to do with magic or anything that came with it. It was luck that she'd noticed its absence at all; she'd knocked the tinder box that contained it off a shelf and when it spilled open, it was empty. Had Ralph worked out its importance to her, or had he stolen it just to spite her? That was probably it.

The stone was stained with soot. No surprise there, her mother had died in a fire. She wetted some linen and wiped some of the muck off. What had her mother chosen to store in it? She focused. Focused hard. And pulled back. She'd had a moment of revelation. A sense that it contained power and a lot of it. That it could still hold so much, so long after her mother's passing, attested to the woman's life force. There must have been a lot she hadn't known about her mother, but there was nobody alive she could ask about it. She'd have to work it out for herself.

She put the stone with her own, closed her eyes and opened her other sense, *the* sense, the one she'd tried to suppress for so many years. Yes, she'd performed the odd magical act here and there throughout her life, like saving that poor woman accused of witchcraft from a terrible fate. But that, and the magic she'd done to convince William, were just dabbler level parlour tricks, simple adjustments to reality. Nothing like what she was about to attempt here.

As she opened herself up, she experienced what she could only think of as an *awakening*. It started with a tingling in her extremities and soon snowballed into a gushing flood of liquid fire. It burst through every locked door, every bulwark, and every levee she'd constructed over the years, filling everything it touched with light. Too much. Way too much. She broke off, sweating and gasping for breath, her heart beating loud in her ears.

What she'd practised in her youth got nowhere close to what had just happened. The sheer scale of the difference between her previous experiences and this astonished, terrified, and perplexed her in equal measures. This was almost adept level power.

She tried again with the same result and this time she collapsed, exhausted. Well, that was the end of that. She couldn't control it. What damage might she do if she even attempted it again? She couldn't take the risk, not even to save William. His hopes rested on Jasper and his band now.

~~~

William's hand throbbed with each pulse of his speeding heart. He'd never known pain like it and never dreamt it could be this blinding. Desperate, and close to despair, he clung onto the knowledge that as long as Jasper and his fighters were out there, they'd find him. Then those twins would get what was coming to them.

The only thing that had kept him sane was the company of the guard, Teo. The man buzzed with thoughts about visiting Anglonia and he seemed more than happy to sit chatting with William and plying him with good grappa that at least made a dent in the pain.

Now that his earlier anger had dissipated, his reason returned. It shocked him how easily his conscious mind could be taken over with rage. This was what the Stoics had warned against; that by allowing emotions to take over one's entire being, the damage was multiplied many-fold. You couldn't control what the world did to you, but you could learn to control how it affected you. Except he'd had no control. None whatsoever. He'd failed as a stoic. And then a cascade of cause and effect had begun, and he'd ended up in this cellar in the most abject state. His hand twitched involuntarily, and another blast of pain shot up his arm and into his shoulders. He whimpered.

Anger had transitioned into denial. He was a victim in all this. From the moment they had forced him out of the monastery, right up until now, things had happened to him. Been done to him. Wrought upon him. He had the overwhelming sense that somebody or something was the architect of all his suffering, sapping at his resolve to be true to his learning and to Verity. All he'd ever done was try to do the right thing, but stuff beyond his
~~~

control got in the way. It wasn't his fault that his father had died lonely and afraid. It couldn't be his fault that his ship had run onto the rocks and many sailors had died. Neither was it his fault that one of Jasper's men had died saving his life in Ianua. Well, maybe that kind of was his fault, in that he'd picked a fight there, but he didn't ask to be rescued, did he? And it wasn't his fault either that Helena had come into his life and so beguiled him that he'd betrayed Verity.

Verity again! His mind kept coming back to her. He tried to work out how much time he had left to save her, but the pain made it difficult to calculate. Maybe he had three months? Four? Time was slipping away, and being stuck in a locked cellar didn't help.

There was noise in the distance, the sound of men fighting. Little by little, the clamour of shouting and weapons clashing got closer. Men screamed. Jasper? A jolt of optimism engulfed him, making the pain a touch more bearable. Come on Jasper, you can do it!

The fighting sounded almost on top of him. Doors slammed, shouting echoed along corridors above and down to his cell door. Any minute now, that door would swing open, and in would swagger a triumphant Jasper, ready to whisk him away to safety. He stood, expectant.

Then silence. He waited. What had happened? If there was a god in the universe, he'd pray to it every hour, if he could just get out of this hellhole. And he waited. Finally, he slunk to his mattress and lay there, his damaged hand hanging over the edge. The pain returned worse than before.

After an eternity, footsteps approached. The excited voices that neared him weren't those of Jasper and the others, but the Albian maniacs. The cell door creaked open, and an object landed on the floor, rolling unevenly across the narrow space. With utter horror, he recognised it. A head. Red hair. A face. A spider piercing on the side of the nose. Morwena!

The twins entered. Fraser kicked the head toward William and blood drops sprayed onto his legs. Irvine followed on, holding two more heads by the hair. "Your rescue has failed, Sir William," he said, as he dropped the heads with Morwena's. He recognised them as having belonged to the quiet Jacopo and Wymond The Weird. "Sadly, we must leave for Sardonica to complete our quest. We can no longer stay and entertain you. However, we'll leave these three here for company."

"Are you completely sick? You don't need to do this. There has to be something I can offer you. Name it!"

"There's nothing we want from you, other than your pain, your horror, and your slow death."

"Look, take me with you. You'll never get past the cat without me," said William.

"Yes, the cat. We're nae afraid of a wee pussy," said Fraser. "Miaow, Miaow." He mimed a scratching action. "Rather than kill you now, though, we'll lock you in with three rotting heads and leave you to starve. It should be quite a party."

Teo and the other guard entered, bringing a pail of water and a barrel of grain.

"This should keep you alive for a couple of weeks at least," said Fraser. "Aren't you going to thank us?"

"Thank you? Spawn of every evil that's ever walked this earth. I hate you. I hate the very air you breathe. I hate the stones on which you walk. If there's any justice in this life, may both your members wither away and drop off with the pox that they might be free of you," said William.

"Ungrateful, do you ken, brother?"

"Aye. Listen, pal, dinnae think someone else will let you out. We're taking all the copies of the key," said Irvine, who stepped to deliver a kick to William's midriff, causing him to fold over, gasping.

By the time he'd recovered enough to haul himself to a sitting position, they'd slammed the door and gone.

"Bastards," he shouted. "Bastards!"

# Fifteen

Queen Nannua's voice had entered the anger register. "Laddà, I am becoming impatient. What news of Quaggià?"

Laddà knew to tread with great care in responding, lest she be smote down unto oblivion, as Nannua liked to put it. The Queen had grandiose affectations and a vocabulary to support them.

"There is nothing new to report, My Gracious Queen. Quaggià sent word that she had picked up an interesting scent and was tracking a party of humans south of the city they call Ianua."

Laddà hadn't been keen on the appointment of Quaggià. Although she had by far the best axe technique among all the protectorate, she also had a tendency to attack rather than talk. And she hated human females for betraying their gender by *consorting* with the males of their species. It made Laddà shudder to think of it, but while the very notion of humanity disgusted her, she didn't feel the need to slaughter them over it.

"Alas, that was the last message. Should I send a search party, My Queen?"

Nannua sighed and ignored the question. "Can nobody do anything right around here? Do I have to go myself to carry out such a simple instruction?"

Laddà treated this as rhetorical. The obvious answer was that the Queen struggled to so much as waddle down a tunnel, such was her vast bulk, never mind cross the middle sea. She'd binged on royal jelly for the last month, and it could have that effect. "Your Grace?" she enquired.

"Curse the rocks," said the Queen. "Bring me the scholars again. There must be *something* in the Janasarium we've missed. Some way to bring the crystal forth from the ground without waiting for a foul, stinking *Anointed One* to show up."

"I will fetch them at once, Your Most Majestic Grace."

*Majestic, my stone arse*, was an approximation of what she actually thought. She knew it irked the Queen to think of depending on anything male to bring to fruition her lifelong dream: that of holding the crystal. But humans weren't like Janasà, were they? She bowed to the floor and hurried up the spiral passage to the library level. The scholars wouldn't thank her for the summons, not one bit.

~~~

Imelda received Jasper's trunk call mid-morning. She'd been amusing herself all night with a pair of gentlemen friends half her age. As she dismissed them, exhausted and broken, she made the connection and listened. "I hope you have good tidings. Tell me you've located Coxwell."

"We located him."

"And?"

He hesitated. "I don't know how to say this. Please believe I have only ever tried to serve you."

"What? Spit it out. I haven't got all night."

"It's Morwena. She's dead."

A cold veil descended over the witch. She paused for what seemed an eternity, and Jasper knew not to interrupt her thoughts. At last she asked, her voice little more than a whisper, "How did it happen?"

"You'll never guess who was holding Coxwell, so I'll come right out and tell you. Mary's sons, Fraser and Irvine, along with a small army of mercenaries they must have found in the bowels of Trusca. They were expecting us. We were looking for a weak spot in the walls when they jumped us. Twelve bastard swordsmen to four of us, with the twins cheering them on like demented ghouls. I was lucky to get out myself. It's best we forget about Coxwell. By the time I can raise enough men, he'll be long dead, if he isn't already. I swear Mary is behind this mother, but how did she *know* how and where to take Coxwell? And why?"
~~~

Imelda broke off the connection, too upset to continue. *Mary.* She should have dealt with her pathetic, damnable cousin years ago. And now this. What was going on? Did she know about the crystal? The only logical conclusion was that Mary had heard about their plans to take it and come up with a plan of her own. Did her own slug faced son, Feydor, have anything to do with it? It would explain the strangeness of his recent behaviour. Dark magic crackled from her hands, singeing the wood of the bench. She swore by all that was evil that she'd make someone suffer for this, starting with her cousin.

An hour later, she went down into the tavern below, not caring who saw her dressed as she was, in little more than her black undergarments. A rare customer of Rod's asked her if she were offering herself for hire.

She parked herself on the bench next to him. "I believe I just might be."

"How much?" he asked.

"More than your life is worth…"

~~~

The previous night had been freezing. William had faced a tough choice: he could have either chosen to drape his only blanket over the heads of his dead companions or to wrap it around himself to stay warm. He'd covered them. The expressions on those faces, accusing and reproachful, had been too much to bear, even in the near pitch dark. The untameable side of his mind imagined the skulls rising and floating above him as they chanted, *This is your fault! We died trying to save you. This is your fault…*

Not that covering them made much difference. He couldn't unsee what he'd seen. Pretending they weren't there didn't work, nor that the world hadn't gone crazy, or that absolute evil didn't exist. Because now he knew it did.

He wished he could roll back time and still be a nobody at the bottom of the pile at Ebury Castle, with nobody expecting much of anything from him. It had been a lot simpler. And less deadly.

How would his death come? He hoped it would be quick, so he wouldn't have to cope with the putrefying, fetid remains of Morwena and the others.
~~~

He could choose to not eat or drink and be gone within the week. That sounded oddly attractive.

With the bleakness of his predicament, many things had become clearer. For starters, he'd been as much to blame for his tryst with Helena as she was. He couldn't honestly say she'd bewitched him into it. He'd wanted to do it. Been more than willing. And how was her little demonstration of apparent magic something to be feared? With the presence of death so close, and the certainty of his own, it all seemed so insignificant. He'd do anything now to be back in that room and to listen to her. To understand who she was, and what she'd done. To experience again the comfort of her arms. The sound of her voice.

So if what had happened wasn't her fault, why had he so soon forgotten Verity? What did it tell him about his feelings for her? Why did he care about the girl, anyway? He tried to list what he loved about her, and it shocked him that there wasn't much. Yes, she was quite pretty, but only a fool would marry for that alone. In fact, she was shallow and dull without an original thought or opinion to call her own. Could it be that he'd been in love with the *idea* of Verity much more than the person?

Of course, none of it mattered now. He'd never see Helena again and have the chance to say how sorry he was for panicking and running out on her. He'd never know Verity either, for that matter, so her fate was sealed and she'd be married to Edmond Rowbotham by the autumn. Would the man provide well for her? Would she find happiness given time? He hoped so. Nor would he ever see Ridkin again. Steady but infuriating Ridkin, a man he'd come to trust and depend on, always there to bring him down to earth. And he'd never see Anglonia again with its endless rolling green hills and oak forests or smell its fields after a summer rain. He'd also never complain again about the frigid rain and mud, its rotten food, its bad ale, the inequality of its class system, and the stifling restrictions of its priesthood. Nor the state of the roads, the lack of provision of education to the poor, the bewildering and random actions of those who dispensed justice, the absence of sanitation, the shocking ignorance of the medics... Not even the turnips would trouble him now.

Moons and Stars, he'd exchange his current situation for all that in a heartbeat. Exhausted and despite his throbbing hand, he fell into something close to sleep.

Someone was making a scratching, scraping noise, fiddling with a key in the lock of his cell door. He forced himself onto his elbows, feeling tense and worried about what might be about to happen next. Had those two monsters returned to heap further misery on his head? The noise stopped for a moment, then restarted. At last, the lock clicked, and the door creaked open. He held his breath. And there, entering the cell, came the guard, Teo.

"Signor William," he began. "Are you alright?"

"How… how did you get in?"

"I have spare keys to many rooms here." He held up a key. "Lucky for you, I have this one."

William dragged himself to a stoop and shuffled over before hugging him for joy. Hug him? He'd have borne his babies if he'd been in possession of a uterus.

Teo pulled away. "I'm sorry I couldn't come last night. I needed to be sure those other two had gone. They left for Sardonica at first light, and it's just the servants that remain, so here I am."

Before William had time to think of questions, or indeed to hug the man again, Teo hurried him out of the cell, leaving the door ajar. "I've asked my friend to bury the heads of those unfortunates. They were your friends, yes?"

"I suppose they were, yes."

Teo draped a hooded cloak over William's shoulders and covered his head with the cowl. "Quickly now. My brother is waiting outside with a cart. I don't know who might try to stop you, so you must go in haste." He led William up a flight of stone steps and into the courtyard above. "This is my brother," said Teo. "He will get you away from this place."

The man helped William into the back of the cart, pulling a blanket over him.

"Good luck. See you in Anglonia one day," said Teo.

With a barked instruction to the horse, they were off. Gliding over smooth cobbles, they picked up speed and swerved twice before settling down at a steady pace. It crossed William's mind that he didn't know where they were going, but that was fine. Anywhere had to be better than the tiny cell he'd left behind.

~~~

A rare customer sat in the corner of the Castle and Ball tavern in Oldiegate, Ludnam. Rare, as in one of the few remaining customers prepared to brave the depressive atmosphere of the establishment. Rare also, because women almost never sat alone in a tavern, not unless touting for the wrong type of business. But rarer still because this particular person didn't, as a rule, drink intoxicating liquor.

The landlord, Rod, was sitting opposite Imelda. "Sorry for your loss," he said. For once, his aspect of extreme negativity suited the occasion to a tee. She wanted to bathe in a lake of melancholy, to immerse herself in her anguish, to feel, actually feel inside, the gut-wrenching sorrow of grief. So she breathed Rod's loathing of life and disdain for joy deep into her lungs, savouring every last mote of darkness, as it spread round her body like icy fire. She ached to pour it into a bath and dive in. If she drowned in the process, so much the better.

She gave Rod the faintest of nods to acknowledge him.

They were the perfect pair for the occasion. Him with his natural demeanour of unrelenting gloom. She with her standard black on black mode of attire, which resembled that of a mute, a professional mourner hired to stand in silent vigil over a coffin. She would only need to walk into a crowded market holding a sickle to send an entire crowd screaming for cover.

She fiddled with the black amulet hung around her neck, with at its centre, a piece of polished obsidian. It was her witch's heart-stone that she wore at all times, essential to her existence, and was the means by which she could do everything she did. Every witch used theirs in a personal, unique way. Some to remember and organise everyday tasks, such as appointments
~~~

and birthdays; how banal. Others as a place to put their darkest thoughts as a respite from them; all well and good for those with a conscience. And some, like Imelda, as a way to pass on to the next generation the secrets of their craft, a kind of record containing the essence of their power. Imelda had always wanted Morwena to have it, convinced that her daughter would then understand her true calling and take up the black cloak of witchcraft in the murky footsteps of her mother.

But Morwena had died, and with her death, Imelda's own hopes for a meaningful legacy had passed into the dark realm. Yes, she could use magic to make her old womb succour another life, but the results would be demonic and useless for her purposes. Her sons? No man could ever wear a witch's amulet and live to tell the tale. Imelda's bloodline as a witch ended with her daughter, much as Feydor's as a Fool would end with him.

She closed her eyes. The words of the musician and inveterate minister of gloom, John Dowling, came to her:

*In darkness, let me dwell; the ground shall sorrow be,*

*The roof despair, to bar all cheerful light from me;*[64]

It felt so good to channel such desolation, the only truth at the centre of her existence. She'd heard it said that without life, there is no sadness, and without sadness, there is no life. Who made up such nonsense? Instead, to her, sadness in the form of grief had terrifying potential as a powerful weapon. An idea formed in her mind. Well, not so much an idea, but a volition. A scintilla of something visceral. From deep within her soul, she found a kernel of anger and turned it toward the person responsible: that ever interfering, jealous bitch of a witch, her cousin Mary. As to the possibility that her own flesh and blood, Feydor, had betrayed her, she'd get to him after she'd killed Mary. Her bile grew yellow and livid, and turned into a tiny flame. It took hold. She used the bellows of her grief to fan it into a raging inferno. Mary would burn slowly in the heat of a thousand suns. She placed all this in her amulet and opened her eyes, now free of concern. She smiled.

Rod's face turned into a mask of relief. "Priest on a donkey, woman, you had me worried good and proper there."

~~~

The disc of the sun merged into the distant tree line as the air cooled. All afternoon, her mother had been pacing back and forth outside the villa, insisting William still lived and that she wouldn't abandon him to his fate. Not that Matilda could tell what use that could be because he was that kind of stupid man who was bound to get into trouble, sooner or later. What on earth did her mother see in him? How could she bear to do *that* with him? It made her feel physically sick just thinking about it. And now his stupidity in getting taken by Cosimo's men had led to the death of three of the people she most admired in the world. Especially Morwena, who'd treated her as an equal and shown her how a woman could be every bit as strong as a man.

She heard shouting from outside, around to the front of the villa, and rose to investigate. To her astonishment, there was William standing next to a man she didn't know. Helena stood facing him. Matilda sensed their mutual attraction, and their awkwardness about it.

William held up his hand and unwound the linen wrap that covered it. It revealed hideous injuries. Two of his fingers pointed off in crazy directions and the knuckles had gone black and swollen to the size and colour of beets.

"Oh, my Stars, William. What happened to you?" asked Helena.

William stood, glazed over, and collapsed. Helena rushed over to fuss over him while Ottavia instructed her servants to fetch the medic. Ridkin and a footman helped carry William inside the house. How typical. Even unconscious, William made the world revolve around him.

She wandered past everyone else and climbed up to her chamber to be alone with her crystal and to think. Whichever way she looked at it, her destiny was linked to the little blue stone, and its fate rested on the island of Sardonica. She felt no option but to go there, but it posed other questions. For one thing, how would she persuade her mother it was a good idea? Sure, she was old enough not to need permission, however, she didn't want the drama of arguing with the woman. For another thing, it would mean travelling in the same direction as William, and she didn't relish
~~~

spending more time in his company than necessary. Nor did she want the challenge of keeping him away from Helena. She smiled to herself. The crystal in her possession could very likely relieve William of his obvious agony, but did she want to reveal its power to everyone? Not likely. And in any case, he needed to suffer a lot more yet for causing Morwena's death.

~~~

Feydor helped himself to a hearty breakfast of trout and pheasant, along with sweet breads and ale, while Filthy filled his face with nuts and fruit. The little Monkey was putting on timber around the middle, but Feydor was fine with that.

As he left the dining hall, he spotted a copy of The Daily Tidings, a pamphlet of the type used to disseminate lies, false tidings in fact, along with interesting titbits of banality, gossip, or other such frivolities, although sometimes it contained something useful or even, Stars forbid, actually true. This one announced:

*Strange ball of fire espied south of the river during the hours of darkness. House destroyed and everyone in it. This journal understands Gallian infiltrators to be responsible. We must all be vigilant in the face of such affronts.*

These were the tidings he'd been half expecting; his mother was making her move against Mary, although the obviously false bit about Gallian skulduggery made him smile. The big question was whether his mother might have guessed at his own betrayal of her.

He spent the next hour asking guards and officials for any information they could provide, but when nobody knew any details, he donned his cloak and prepared to go and check for himself. However, before he could leave the palace, he ran into a breathless messenger, one from the office of the First Minister.

"What's the rush? What's occurred?" he demanded from the man.

"The house of Prince Albert. It's gone. Witnesses say a fireball rolled up from the river and swallowed it."

"Bodies?" asked Feydor.
~~~

"None found. Excuse me, I must reach the privy council. There's foul play afoot."

No bodies? Could Mary still be alive?

He drifted back to his rooms, concerned for his cousin, not because of any particular affection he had for her, Moons and Stars forbid, but because they still had unfinished business.

Hours later, he emerged with Filthy and headed to the kitchens to sate both their renewed hungers. The palace was rife with tidings; Firstly, Inglebert was on the cusp of death. Well, that seemed believable enough. Secondly, Stackpole was pleading his case with the other nobles to be released from the Tower. Feydor didn't see how that would work; after all, the nobles hated each other with a passion, but you never could tell. Feydor would need to keep an eye on the situation. And lastly, John Scratchface had apparently formed an alliance of northern nobles and now led a massive army on its way to take advantage of Inglebert's continued decline and seize control of the capital. Supposedly, as many as fifty thousand men at arms, complete with siege engines, cavalry, and infantry, were camped a deuce of leagues to the north. Thomas Crumbwell appeared to be busy organising the city's defences, but word was, he was doing too little, too late. Feydor smiled to himself; *Long Live King John* had a certain ring to it.

~~~

Helena found William in bed, with a medic attending to his hand, arguing about the man's desire to bleed him.

"Get away from me, quack! How under the seven hells is sucking my blood supposed to do anything useful?"

"But this is the standard treatment for, well, everything[65]. Please don't obstruct me."

"If he doesn't want bleeding, don't do it. If there's nothing else…" Helena indicated the door.

The man shrugged. "No skin off my nose." He packed his things away and left.

"Thank you," said William.
~~~

It was the day after his improbable return, and, with the help of laudanum, he'd apparently been as comfortable during the night as could be hoped. He had a small vial of oil of poppy by his side that he took sips from every so often. "It doesn't stop the pain, but it makes it more bearable."

During bouts of wakefulness, he'd given a full account of everything that had happened after his kidnapping. It sounded awful.

"Helena, I'm so sorry," he began. "I should never have rushed off like that."

"True. You had us all proper worried for you."

He reached out for her, but she pushed him away. She'd made a promise to Matilda that she intended to keep. She had to stay strong. "It's my fault, William," she said. "I were weak. I wanted comforting and look what happened. You were right to be upset."

"Don't blame yourself. I overreacted. Should have listened to what you were telling me, tried to understand. I see that now."

"That's as may be, but on the morrow, I'll be taking Tilda home to Anglonia. Ottavia will lend me brass enough for the journey." She told herself she didn't feel anything for him. "It's best we part ways now."

"But I still want to know you better."

"That wouldn't be right. It's too late at any road. I suppose you plan to continue your quest now?"

William frowned. "I think I need to. Those twins knew everything about my plans. They said the aphrodisiac story was false tidings and what's going on here has to do with a crystal. The one I was reading about here in the library."

"Don't you think you should leave it be? Go home. Forget about all that. If there's one thing I can tell you, it's that it's dangerous to continue. You might never return."

"I get that. I do. This isn't for the King. And I've decided I'm not doing it for Verity either. I'll do my best to get back and save her, but I'm clear we won't ever wed."

"Then who *are* you doing it for?"

"Myself." He put a hand to his chest. "I want to prove to myself that I can mean something in the world."

He went quiet, as though he was drifting away in his own thoughts. She turned as if to leave. He snapped out of the trance and sighed. "How's Tilda? Jasper? Please, at least tell me that."

She half turned back towards him. "Tilda's distant. Different. But she'll be right soon enough. Jasper's not been out of his room since he returned. Has his food taken in to him. I never had him down as such a sensitive type, but there it is."

"I can't get the sight of it out of my mind." He looked up at her, his eyes red at the edges. "Her head, I mean, rolling and rolling. That was the worst thing. Poor woman!"

He tried to touch her hand, but she ignored him. "As regards Matilda, the less she knows of witching, the better." As she reached the door, she lingered for a moment. "So I'll thank you to say nowt about it to her or anyone else." Then she was gone.

~~~

"I'm going to Sardonica."

"Good morrow daughter," said Helena in reply to Matilda's abrupt entrance into Ottavia's breakfast room. She recognised the combative tension in her manner, the clenched fists, a hardness in the eyes. The girl must have built herself up for this encounter. Helena decided not to play that game.

"Say what you need to say. Let's get it over with," said Matilda, challenging.

Helena sighed. She didn't want to push too hard against her daughter. After all, she'd been shaken by the meeting with Ralph, and hadn't yet vented her understandable feelings over it. Added to that, the death of Morwena had been tough on her. Matilda had blamed William for that, loudly enough for the entire villa to hear. Poor William, he lacked the emotional defences to cope with an irate teenager.

"Why don't you tell me what I'm going to say?" said Helena.
~~~

A wary look came over Matilda's face. She'd be suspecting a trap. "You'll say it's too dangerous."

"It is."

"I heard William telling Ridkin, as how the Janasà will welcome him. They'll think he's some manner of hero from a legend. And Jasper is going. I'll be safe."

"How many are the Janasà, dear? Ten thousand? A hundred thousand? You recall as how one tried to kill you. How does William explain that?"

"He says as how it were a rogue group. They're not all like that, at least according to what he read in the library here." She paused. "You've not asked me why I'm going."

"Enlighten me."

Her daughter appeared to be weighing up what to say. She'd looked on the point of saying something important, but in the end, had held back.

"I have reasons, mother. I'm old enough now to decide for myself."

By convention, Matilda was right. Girls younger than her got married off to much older men all the time, a shameful thing in Helena's mind, but it happened. And the encounter with Ralph had taken a lot out of her. But all the same, Matilda's justifications for going to Sardonica made no sense. Her daughter had to be hiding something important, so she acquiesced. That said, there was no way she'd let Matilda go without her. She knew if push came to shove, she had magic enough to get them out of trouble. Assuming she dared use it.

"I won't stand in your way."

Surprise shone in Matilda's eyes. "Really?"

"I'm coming with you, mind."

The girl pouted. "But I were wanting to go on my own. You can't stop me!"

Helena weighed things up. She could for sure stop Matilda if she wanted to, although she'd have to use magic. "If you're daft enough to dance a merry jig with danger, so am I. I can't or won't stop you, but you can't stop me either."

Matilda looked at her, her eyes narrowed in a way that suggested she'd expected more resistance. It seemed they were both going to Sardonica.

# Sixteen

The order came through to Laddà from Queen Nannua to come at once to her private chambers at the deepest level of the citadel. As a member of the elite protectorate, Laddà took advantage of her status to gain access to the vertical shaft that ran from the ground above. Thirty levels down, she showed her spiral tattoo to the guard. As the only Janasà alive permitted to carry this emblem, she still felt considerable pride. The guards saluted and admitted her into the Queen's inner sanctum.

She looked about in the near total darkness, and said nothing, as protocol demanded. It would have also been against protocol for her to use her echo location to find the Queen. The Queen would acknowledge her when the Queen was good and ready.

"Come up to me," commanded a voice from above. Ah, she was hanging bat-like from the apex of the vaulted room. She made for the wall and used her suckers to climb up to where the Queen awaited. "Excuse my rudeness in not greeting you properly," said the Queen of the Janasà. "I call this Goblin Mode. That's just a little jest."

Laddà smelt the satisfaction signals the Queen was giving off, although she remained on her guard. Anything could happen next. "How can I be of service, Oh Queen of the Seven Earths? Oh, Guiding Light of all Janasà, Oh…"

"Yes, yes, all of that. Enough. I am, after all, the humblest of leaders. Laddà, you have proven yourself a most loyal servant."

"Your Grace is most kind."

"I have a task I wish you to perform as the custodian of the crystal caverns."

"Yes, My Queen?"

"I have received word that two Kindù are riding toward our city from the south, and Praise the Rocks, they have pale skin."

It took a moment for Laddà to get the significance of that last sentence. "Ah," she said. "They may be on their way to fulfil the legend. In that case, I'd better prepare a welcoming party."

"The legend, indeed. However, their hair coverings are red."

"And… not the white foretold?" Laddà needed to be sure she understood what the Queen intended.

"Indeed, not. I think it unlikely either of them is the Anointed One, but we need to be certain. Perhaps it would be wise to show them directly to the cavern and let Bisgattù decide their fate."

"Very well, my Queen. You are the wisest of all of us. Leave it with me." Laddà suckered back and did her best to perform a bow, which is difficult when your head is already hanging lower than the rest of you. She dropped to the floor, executed another bow, this time the right way up, and left the chamber. It would be interesting to see how these strangers fared. None of the others had survived so far.

~~~

Feydor received the summons soon after breakfast. A terse message read, *Still alive. Messenger will bring you to me.*

He'd first met the messenger at the former residence of Prince Albert, a broad humourless sort with a strong Albian accent, called Carter, who'd never hidden his disdain for the Fool. Feydor grabbed his cloak and followed the man out of the palace gates, where a cart stood minded by someone he recognised as another of Albert's men. Carter invited Feydor to sit behind him and, once outside the grounds, placed a hood over Feydor's head. "Stay low," he told him.

If the man's intent had been to avoid Feydor knowing their destination, it failed. A strong whiff of fish told him they were passing through Billygate. The clanging bell belonged to the temple at Camptown. Then, from the sound of the cobbles, they were exiting Ludnam through the Old Gate and were heading along the Great North Road. The journey continued
~~~

for a couple of hours before they pulled off onto a rough track and stopped a half hour further on. The chorus of woodland birds and the smell of damp moss confirmed where they were: they'd reached the famous Effing Forest.

Carter removed Feydor's hood and took him into a low-ceilinged wooden shack where Mary sat in a room containing nothing but a simple sleeping mat. She looked thinner than when he'd last seen her, her complexion sallow and red hair lank. She stank like she'd not bathed in a long time. "Did you bring food?" she asked Carter, who handed her a lump of bread from a sack. She grabbed it with both hands and thrust it at her mouth, chewing noisily. Feydor had to look away from the yellowing teeth and red gums.

"I've nae washed, nor eaten, nor slept a wink," she said, pausing between bites. "I'm scared fit to widdershins she might find me."

"How did you escape the fire?"

More chewing. "Luck. I went to Coven Garden to see a wee friend. Saw the fireball from the north of the river, as bright as the sun, so it was. Poor Albert - nobody should die like that. Except *her,* of course."

"There's still a chance that can happen. Look, we need the crystal. What can you tell me of the twins?"

"They're in Sardonica," she said, now picking at her teeth.

"Yes? And?"

"Last I heard, they had the towers of Nuorrù in sight."

"That's it? And what of William? They did kill him, right?"

"Well…"

"Please tell me they didn't go rogue." He sighed. "I'll drag it out of you if I have to. What did they do?" He had a bad feeling about this.

"They…" she looked away in distraction, her voice lowered. "They locked him up in a cellar with the heads of your sister and two of Jasper's men."

He reeled. "What the…?" He put his head in his hands. *Morwena*? The only person in his family who'd ever been kind to him. Tears welled up in his eyes. "No! They killed Morwena? How could you allow that to happen? I'll tear their balls off for this."

"She was collateral damage. Jasper and his men tried to free William."

"Who should have been dead already!" By now he was shouting.

Mary recoiled. "Look. He's already as good as dead, you ken? They took the only keys with them. Let the wee boys have their fun. They've worked so hard."

"They've never worked a day in their lives. I was a pillock to trust them. To trust you. I'll tell you now, if Coxwell survives this time, you'd better hope mother gets to you first or I'll peel your skin from your bones strip by strip. I'm going back to the city now. And don't think I can't find you again."

~~~

The human with the red fur on top was pouring red liquid into his mouth out of a large container. Had Filthy possessed words, the one for this container would have been glass. This pouring of the red liquid had been going on for some time, and the normally quiet Red Top had started making not very melodic streams of noises from his throat.

Filthy had the strongest of *bonds* with Red Top and he was sensitive to changes in his *scents*. These scents were clues to the inner state of Red Top, and Filthy had learned to read them. Red Top was at present giving off the smell of something that Filthy, had he had words, would have called *sadness*, while Filthy himself was feeling the simian equivalent of *empathy*. He put his little arms around Red Top's neck. When Red Top tried to stroke Filthy with his free hand, he bit his finger.

Filthy didn't like that every time Red Top held his hand near to him, he bit it. The trouble was, it was what a monkey like him *did*. Nobody complained that horses shat in the streets. What was the difference?

His empathy was starting to turn into what he might have wanted, had he had the words, to call *concern*. Red Top had been sending out distress smells since the day before, and this had culminated today in Red Top's current state. Filthy had to *do* something. He regurgitated some nuts and tried to press them into Red Top's mouth. The human coughed and made loud throat noises before trying to smash Filthy with a large stick. Then he
~~~

vomited a lot of warm red liquid over Filthy. The monkey tried to hold on to the earlier feeling of empathy. It was difficult.

Filthy *reasoned*, as much as he could be said to reason, that the red liquid was the cause of Red Top's state of being, and concluded that his best option was to prevent further pouring of said red liquid into Red Top's mouth. He leapt at the container of red liquid, sending it to the floor where it shattered, spilling its contents everywhere. He expected to be struck hard by Red Top for this act of what could have been described by a talking monkey as *altruism*, but nothing happened. Instead, Red Top slid off his cot and onto the floor, falling instantly asleep, and making a strange warbling sound at the back of his throat. Filthy had no word for *snoring*.

He curled up next to Red Top, secure in the knowledge that the human would reward him for his intervention when he awoke.

~~~

Ridkin, Helena, and Matilda stepped down the gangplank and onto a wharf at the Sardonican port of Caligulari. It was early on the morning of the fifth day after leaving Civitax, the main port of Trusca. Behind them came Jasper and his last remaining fighter, Big Ger. Taking up the rear was William, who'd been in a terrible state for much of the voyage. He kissed the ground and pronounced that it tasted like sheep. Violent storms had held them up for three days, storms that blasted them in one direction and then changed direction to thrust with equal insistence in the opposite. Even the iron stomached Ridkin had struggled.

Besides the nausea, William had experienced bouts of anxiety during their journey from Trusca, and any hopes he'd nursed that Helena might provide comfort had been dashed by her cold, confusing indifference. The nights had been the worst. In the darkness, he'd dreamt again and again of his place of torment, unable to erase that first sight of Morwena's head rolling over the stone floor as the blood sprayed up. Since that experience, his jerking, shaking hands had been living an apparently separate existence to the rest of him, and his sleep had been at best fitful and interrupted by terrifying dreams. Was it peculiar to himself, or was this how any man would
~~~

react to what had happened to him? He could recall no accounts of such traumas in anything he'd read.

With his uncomfortable decision to not return for Verity, he'd needed to think through his motives for continuing the mission. He'd finally got Jasper to admit the aphrodisiac water was a lie, but the man would say nothing about the crystal, and he was left to figure out for himself what it meant to him. Supposing he succeeded in bringing it out of the caverns, why would the Janasà ever let him take it away? And what would he do with it, anyway? Instead of continuing with the journey, he could just slink away to some backwater town and look for simple work. Scrivening for a county court, perhaps? But in that case, what had it all been for? He'd have nothing much to tell his children. *Hey kids, I went to parts foreign once.* He wanted more. Much more. He ached to be *relevant,* to *be someone*, and walking into the home of the Janasà was the biggest opportunity he could imagine of doing that.

They set out for the town proper in search of food and lodgings. Food they found easily enough, thanks to the universal property of the servers in tavernas and other such establishments, which was to understand any spoken language that existed on earth when a customer had money to spend. Finding an inn, however, proved to be another tale. The local dialect comprised more grunts than words, with every uttered syllable sounding like a curse. People spoke no Truscan and didn't hide their disdain for anyone that did.

They made for what appeared to be a market, hoping they'd find among the crowd at least one person who would help them, and were soon being jostled and poked by tiny old women dressed head to toe in black. The women elbowed their way toward the market stalls and cursed at anyone blocking their route to a bargain. Once there, they prodded the vegetables and shouted at the traders. Angry hand gestures played as much a part of the bargaining process as words. It took little to discern the meaning of a lot of the sign language. Slapping the side of the head with a flat palm meant, "Are you crazy? I'd never pay that much for a misshapen carrot." Placing the thumb under the chin and sweeping forward appeared to mean,

"If the ragu I make with this meat isn't delicious, my son will kill you. And how is your charming daughter, by the way?"

As Jasper's agitation grew toward boiling point and William feared a bloodbath, a blur of black rushed in from behind a mass of bodies and screeched to a halt, revealing itself to be a balding but powerful looking, well-balanced man dressed in a black tunic tied at the waist with a simple cord. His dark skin, two-day beard, firm chin, and heavy eyebrows gave him a serious business-like aspect.

Jasper further tensed, sensing a chance to fight, but then the man broke into a broad intelligent smile and said in passable Truscan, "Welcome to our city, dear travellers! I hope you are already enjoying the warm hospitality of these parts!" A sense of irony then. "Let me introduce myself. I am he whom they call Maloreddus on account of my ears," as if that explained everything. "You may call me Mallo for short."

William held out his hand to shake, but Mallo ignored that and instead kissed him on both cheeks. William experienced the man's rough cheeks against his with shock and alarm. Was this what women had to put up with from men? However, being Anglonian, his natural politeness prevented him from complaining, so he tried on his best smile and was the first to say, "Thank you for your welcome. Please pass on my esteem for your fellow citizens, since they have indeed been most accommodating."

"You speak false, but I like you," said Mallo.

The others all accepted Mallo's greeting, although Helena and Matilda also curtseyed, which Mallo found entertaining. "You must be Anglonian! How wonderful."

Jasper refused to get close. "Who are you?" he asked, recognising a fellow fighter, and not appreciating the competition.

"Why, I am the Ninja of Caligulari, can you not tell by my clothes? No? Perhaps I need to work on my costume a little more, but no matter. As well as fighting for justice in dark times, I guide visitors and arrange for lodging, entertainment, and anything else a guest may require. I can even draw your amusing likeness in charcoal, all for a small fee, of course. Now please tell me, what is the purpose of your visit here?"

William felt it was on him to explain. It was his quest, after all. "We are here to meet with Queen Nannua of the Janasà."

Everyone around them went silent at the mention of this name. Mallo stroked his chin in calm contemplation, and, sucking air through his teeth, said, "Are you serious? You must know this is dangerous? My advice would be to turn around and go home."

"I cannot. I have orders from the King of Anglonia." He neglected to mention anything about aphrodisiacs or crystals, rather than get laughed at.

"Is that so?" said Mallo. "I can guide you. For a fee. Now come, you will be hungry and have need of somewhere to wash after your journey," and without waiting for an answer, he set off with purpose away from the market, back toward the port.

William, confident as a representative of his king, stayed close to Mallo so that he could ask important questions. However, "Why are your ears so mashed up?" was the best he could come up with at that moment.

"I am known hereabouts as a superb grappler. I can wrestle to the ground a man the size of a bear and subdue him, but I cannot protect my ears. On the plus side, people here hold such appearances in high esteem, they think them a mark of a great champion. You will be safe with me. Now here, observe, I bring you to the finest hostelry in the city."

Someone must have once loved the dilapidated building, but not for many centuries.

"How can this be the finest place to stay?" asked William.

"By being the only place to stay," replied Mallo, with a beaming smile, "unless you like to sleep with sheep, of course."

The only place to stay turned out to be not as bad inside as out, with separate rooms for guests of varying sizes, all at a fee, with Mallo most likely taking a slice of the cash.

"This is alright," said Jasper, "now, here's a list of stuff we need. Can you sort it?"

Mallo scanned down the page and noted some things in a small book he carried. "A siege engine may be a little challenging," he observed, but he didn't show any great concern.

"My fee is fifty ducats for each day that I guide you. I suggest that is a good and fair price. You won't find anyone else here that will have any interest at all in travelling to the citadel."

"The citadel?" asked William, surprised, "We are visiting Nannua, not Kublai Khan!" He looked pleased with himself for this witticism, but nobody else seemed to notice it.

"The citadel is what the Queen calls her home in Nourù. She has grand ideas, the Queen, for one who is barely three feet tall."

Mallo approached the landlord and conversed in the standard grunts and imprecations of the local dialect, in what sounded like an angry exchange of views that seemed about to lead to a full-blown fight. Returning to William and the others, he said, "It pleases him to have you."

"That was him being pleased?" asked William.

"Of course. You would soon understand if he were otherwise."

Did the man only talk in riddles?

"Please take some time to relax," said Mallo. "This evening, I will find you a good taverna for the best food the city offers. It might be the last decent food you ever taste."

~~~

Mallo led William and the others on mule-back through the northern gate of the city and onto a rough track that wound through a landscape of lagoon and swampland. In the near distance, wooded hills stretched upwards, while much further off, a wall of grey and white-capped peaks like broken teeth, dared them to approach. Dense swarms of flamingos stood in the shallow water like pink ears of corn, their legs about to snap at the first sign of a strong breeze. Solitary red kites wheeled and screeched overhead, and William spotted a distant herd of wild horses. A heavy wet heat clung to the clothes of the travellers, and before long, everything they wore was drenched with their sweat. As the afternoon continued, William's arch nemeses, the huge local mosquitos[66], arrived in their thousands, eschewing the blood of the other riders for that of himself, their bites like
~~~

the stabbing of blunt darning needles. They treated his precious life fluid as a rare gourmet delicacy to be tasted and savoured over and over again.

Thankfully, Mallo had provided them all with wide-brimmed hats to keep off the worst of the harsh sunlight, but any exposed skin soon turned pink and then crimson under the onslaught. He also promised there would be at least some habitations along the way where they could find water, food, and bedding, although there'd be nights when they'd need to sleep out.

As dusk fell, they reached the foothills of the mountains and began a trail that climbed upwards. A short while later, they found a stone dwelling that Mallo called a nuraghe[67], and he declared it as the safest place to rest. The circular structure comprised a wall of even blocks, each the size of a man's head, with the whole thing measuring perhaps twenty paces across. Walls as high as four men supported a tidy roof of smaller corbelled stones. Mallo made a fire at the entrance to ward off the wild boar that he claimed inhabited the area, the smoke also helping keep at bay the mosquitos, while doing nothing to hold back the swarms of tiny red ants that crawled everywhere, biting chunks out of any exposed body parts.

"I've read about these buildings. They're ancient," said William.

Jasper sneered. "Bravo, Bookman. Even I can see that."

"Just looks like a pile of chuffing rocks to me," said Matilda.

"Aren't any of you interested?" asked William. "Don't you wonder about the people that built them? I mean, it takes real time and effort to move so much rock around. There has to be a reason for it all."

"Nobody knows," interrupted Mallo. "And it's bad luck to speak of it, but they are everywhere you go on this island." He paused. "And we are being watched."

"I thought so, too," said Jasper.

"Something green and fast moving?" asked Ridkin, fidgeting with his hands as he spoke, his pale blue eyes glinting.

Mallo nodded.

"The Janasà? Are we safe?" asked Helena.

Mallo said, "yes, the Janasà. And you would not be here if you prized your safety."

"This would be a good point," said William, "for anyone with doubts to turn back." He watched them all for a reaction. "I don't want to be responsible if anything happens to you."

After a long pause, Ridkin spoke first. "We talked about this before Will, after we were attacked. Nothing's changed for me. I ain't turning back after coming this far."

"Helena?" he asked. He half hoped she would turn around toward safety and half that she would stay with him. "You travelled to Trusca and found your husband. Go home. Why risk everything now?"

"She's doing it for me," said Matilda. "I want to reach Nuorrù. I can't explain why. And mother still insists I have to be protected." Her voice betrayed her disgust at this last sentiment.

"Jasper, Ger?"

"I have my reasons, Bookman." said Jasper, eloquent as ever.

"Mallo?" asked William.

"I will only take you as far as the last pass," answered Mallo, his face now grave. "After that, you're on your own, and may Lord Sola light your path."

The following morning, the forest thickened. They travelled along rough, overgrown pathways through dense forests of Holm Oaks and Cork, these latter often with gaping red gashes in their trunks, bringing to mind images of bodies slashed and bleeding[68]. William had spent another troubled night reliving the horror he'd left behind in Trusca, and the sight of the wounded trees did nothing to calm his racing thoughts.

Where the trees thinned out, huge rock formations stood proud of the land, part covered in moss, requiring everyone to dismount and lead their mules on foot. Aromatic bushes gripped the rocks as though hanging on by their fingernails, their bright flowers blanketed in butterflies and bees. They reached a broad valley[69] full of gigantic irregular boulders, some larger than houses, that looked as though a race of giant children had made hurling them in all directions into a gleeful game.

Beyond the giant's playground, a huge wild boar stood blocking the path, its black fur matted and swarming with flies. It stamped a front hoof and snorted. Sharp yellowed tusks protruded from the corners of its mouth and drool ran down from its snout. William looked about in alarm, the track behind being covered in roots and rocks was an impossibility to take at speed. If it charged them, they could be in trouble. Jasper and Ger drew their swords in readiness for a fight, but Mallo calmed them. "I've got this," he said, and cupped his hands, bringing them to his lips. He uttered a series of low grunts and whistles, while stamping his feet and approaching the squat animal, who stared back at him in something resembling disdain before sauntering off into the tangle of trees and underbrush.

When the trail flattened out, it also widened and William could ride abreast of Mallo. He asked, "What else can you tell me of the Janasà and their legends?"

Mallo showed no sign of having heard the question, but after a pause to wipe the sweat from his face, told them what he knew. "I've spent time with their kind. Most believe them to be dangerous and to mean only harm. This is not my experience. At least it wasn't until this new queen arrived."

"Queen Nannua?" asked William.

"Yes, her. She feeds her people with tales of how humankind have been their hateful enemies since the dawn of time, and kept them from their rightful place, whatever that means. I've even heard she wants to build a wall between us and their city, and make us pay for it! Who could believe such nonsense? The crystal, Nurragù, will make the land of the Janasà great again, she says. A glorious past that never existed. The truth is, they keep themselves to themselves and we leave them be. There's no need for any magical crystals."

"The crystal is the true purpose of my quest, as I now understand it." He looked at Jasper, who shrugged. "Every new thing I read contradicts everything else. What do you think it is?"

"The crystal? The legend my people tell is of a cat that has guarded the Crystal of Life for all of eternity."

"I've heard about this cat and the test of the riddles. But what I don't get is this: what stops the Janasà from defeating this cat and taking the crystal themselves? A curse?"

"I can tell you only what the legend says. Yes, there's supposed to be a curse. If a Janasà passes the challenge of the cat and tries to take it from its resting place, the crystal will turn into a giant butcher fly and slaughter every living creature on this island, everything[70]."

"So how is it that William will take it?" asked Helena.

"No idea," said Mallo. "Who even knows if any of this is true?"

"I don't know what to believe," said William. "It's just that… legends can contain a germ of truth. And my curiosity exceeds my fear." He said this last thing more to convince himself than the others. Who knew whether he'd get anywhere near any crystal that might exist?

# Seventeen

Feydor grew impatient to know what was going on in Sardonica, so took a horse and rode north to Effing Forest to find out what Mary knew about events on the island. He dismounted early, intending to cover the remaining fifty or so paces on foot.

The first sign of anything amiss was the noise, a deep growling roar that came from the direction of Mary's shack. What was the daft bat playing at? She'd get herself noticed.

He came out into the clearing of the forest as the entire structure lifted off the ground and burst into flames. Hot ash rained all around him, setting fire to the nearest trees. A stench of something like mustard traded punches with another of burning sulphur. Where the place had stood, two dark figures faced each other a dozen paces apart, firing bolts of power and screaming at each other.

It began to rain dead things. Birds, squirrels, mice, jellyfish. Jellyfish?

He heard his mother's voice. "My daughter is dead because of *you*."

"She was attacking my lads. They defended themselves."

The sky turned black. Sheet lightning arced over the clearing. The rain turned to poisonous toads that stung when they touched flesh.

"Morwena never loved you!" screamed Mary. "Nobody has ever loved you."

"Liar. My children all adore me."

"Feydor doesn't. He despises you. I told him what you did to his father."

"What! You had no right to do that!"

"It's him that told me about the crystal. Does that sound like he loves you?"

"No! You lie!"

"Ask him yourself. He's cowering over there."

Imelda broke her concentration for a moment to look over toward him, and Mary caught her with a lightning bolt. She was flung back with her cloak on fire. Mary approached and raised her arms to deliver another bolt, but was herself propelled through the air in the opposite direction. A sheet of power raced over Feydor's head with a roar and splintered an ancient oak behind, the fragments bursting into flame. Fire soon spread in all directions and Feydor found himself trapped between the witches and the blaze.

"Feydor!" shouted his mother. "You love me, not this cheap bitch."

"You're the cheap whoor, cousin," screamed Maray. "Always were and always will be."

A spinning ball of fire erupted between the two hags. Both reached out to shape it and push it toward the other, and at first it looked to be an even fight. The ball spun faster.

"How dare you! I've fought for this family for decades. Without me, you'd all be nothing."

The intensity of the fireball increased as both dug deep into their reserves, their faces contorted in bared-teethed stares. Feydor realised whoever lost this tussle would lose her life, and right now, Mary was buckling.

"Feydor, here, help me!" called Mary. "I'll give you more power than you ever dreamt. You'll have your *own* jester."

"No, help *me*!" shrieked Imelda. "She lies. I'll make you rich. Trust *me*!"

"How am I supposed to help anyone? You're the witches. I'm just the stupid jester."

"There's a wee charmed knife in the fold of my cloak," called Mary, her arms straining to keep the fireball back. "Quick. Take it."

Decision time. Now or never, then. Time to nail his colours to the mast and free himself from his mother's influence. He made the three steps over to where Mary stood. "Where is it?" he asked.

"It's at the front. Hurry, I can't hold her."

He reached. Imelda said something behind him and ice encased his hands. The weight of it was too much to support. "I can't" he shouted.

"Dig deep Feydor, find the power."

"Move one more muscle, Feydor and I swear I will kill you," warned Imelda.

He closed his eyes and concentrated. Moments later, the ice shattered. His hand stretched, almost of its own volition, and his fingers enclosed the knife.

"Right, throw it at her. It doesn't matter how, just hit her with it."

"No!" screeched Imelda. "Can't you see? I've made you what you are."

"Exactly," he said and hurled the blade at her.

The flat of the knife landed against her flank, and to begin with, nothing happened. But then her concentration broke and the flow of energy from her hands closed off. The full force of Mary's power surged into her chest. She screamed and fell on her back convulsing, yellow drool running down her chin and a rictus grin etched on her face. A rattle came from deep inside her throat, and as the breath left her, her head shrank and shrivelled as the pent-up years uncoiled.

Feydor looked on in complete horror.

"Och, dinnae mind that," said Mary, crossing the clearing to the convulsing body of the witch and retrieving her knife. "Now, where's that wee amulet of hers? I'm taking what's rightfully mine."

Mary felt Imelda's neck and found… Nothing. "Where is it?" she said, looking concerned. "It has to be here."

Something tugged at Feydor's cloak and he looked around to find Filthy there, holding up to him a black pebble on a length of chain.

"The wee bastard beastie," shouted Mary, and dived to grab at the stone. Too late. Feydor danced out of the way. "Don't be a winksop," she said. "No man can take a witch's amulet. Just hand it over."

He shrugged and spoke softly. "You forget. I am not a full man."

He grasped the amulet and drew some of its power. He threw a wall of heat at an unprepared Mary and the witch froze in mid-scream. She fell to the floor.

"Aren't you a bag of surprises?" he asked the monkey. He reached his hand down to scoop up the animal, who still took a customary nip out of Feydor's finger. For once, he didn't care.

Ten minutes later, a trussed-up Mary lay across the back of his saddle hidden under sackcloth, as he returned to Ludnam, with not even a thought for the end of his mother.

~~~

The morning after their third night travelling across Sardonica, the ground rose steeper and became rockier and more difficult for even the mules to continue along. At a waterfall, they found a collection of three dwellings and stopped to share food with the little people living there.

Jasper and Big Ger wandered off into the woods.

"Quick, Will," said Ridkin. "Let's see where they go."

They waited a minute, then followed at a distance for a hundred paces along a pathway, on either side of which there was a dense wall of thorny brush.

"Where are they?" asked William.

"They can't have left the path," said Ridkin. "Not without tearing down all this stuff."

"Shh! Wait. What can you hear?" asked William.

Jasper was speaking. It was indistinct, but Will caught a repeated word. *Mother*. They edged closer, then Ridkin pulled William back. "They'll see us. Let's just listen."

Jasper's voice. "Are you there, mother? Mother? Effing hell, where are you?"

Ger's deeper voice. "It's no good. She's not there."

"She's never not there," said Jasper. "Ever. I don't understand it."

"Could something have happened to her?"

"To her? Like what? Makes no effing sense."

There was a sound like water draining from a bucket. "Quick, before they return this way," said William.

"What do you think that was?" asked Ridkin.

"I'd say Jasper wanted to call his mother."

"Sarcasm, Will? Sometimes you piss me off."
~~~

"I wasn't being sarcastic. I'm thinking. His mother might be behind a lot of this."

They got back to the waterfall, and both men washed their heads in the cold water, drawing some off into their flasks.

Jasper and Ger returned, with Jasper showing an expression Will hadn't seen on him before: worry.

"Does this trail lead to the Janasà?" William asked Mallo, nodding ahead up the incline.

Mallo smiled. "This path leads to a high pass and then a wide plain. You will see the citadel ahead. After that…" He shrugged and turned his mule back down the trail.

~~~

Laddà headed out once again across the high plain that stretched from the central southern pass to the walls of her citadel. Queen Nannua had instructed her to go out to welcome the new group of humans that the scouts had spotted the day before toiling up the approaches to the plateau. This time, the Queen had expressed optimism; among the party of six was a white-haired, pale man who might just be the Anointed One. If it were so, it would be a great honour to receive him.

She noted, as far as was possible from a distance, that two of the six were females, at least based on their longer, flowing attire. The other four, of course, were all male.

Laddà had with her seven other members of the Queen's protectorate in full diamond battle formation. Laddà regarded this as an unnecessary precaution, although she understood the symbolism involved in such a show of strength.

As she neared their party, she felt and suppressed the familiar sense of distaste for being in the presence of anything male, regardless of the species. Among the Janasà, only the lowest caste, the egg tenders, needed to *touch* an occasional fledgling male. It was called the lowest caste for a
~~~

reason. Laddà hated everything about males and especially of her own kind. Their smell, their lack of facial hair, their physical weakness… everything.

She'd need to tolerate this new group of arrivals for the two days they would be present in the citadel. After which, crystal or not, they'd be dead.

"Greetings from the Queen of the Janasà," she said, lowering the register of her voice to that favoured by humankind. "You are most welcome here as our guests. May I present a white myrtle flower[71] as a symbol of our friendship?"

~~~

The Janasà that escorted them for the last stage of their journey had introduced herself as something like Ladder, it not being clear from the odd pronunciation and voice register she'd used. She sounded both high and low pitched at the same time, almost as though two voices spoke rather than one. And the sour, acrid smell of the creatures took William right back to the attack they'd experienced in Italica.

The approach he was taking was not without risk. What if he'd miscalculated? What if they turned out to be anything but friendly? By the end of the day, he'd either go down in history as a selfish fool who got a bunch of people killed, or as a wise scholar who'd taken a chance that would be seen as historic.

On first contact with the Janasà group, William had experienced a state of near panic, worrying about what was about to happen. It was one thing to have studied their beliefs and customs. It was quite another trusting what he'd inferred from those studies. He tried to convince himself that he had control of the situation. There was nothing to be concerned about. If he was right, the Janasà needed him.

The city of Nuorrù impressed William from the moment he saw it. Its many delicate gold tipped towers were arranged at perfect *golden* intervals apart, and as they neared it, the spiral arrangement of its spires around a central point became clear. Added to this, the light had a bright, *clean* quality unlike anything he'd experienced. Was that because of the altitude? The
~~~

effect, to William at least, was pleasing and reassuring. In different circumstances, he could live in a place like this.

"Why is it they're so welcoming?" Helena asked William.

"I'm not sure," he replied. "I didn't expect to gain entry quite this easily. And there's still a risk they will just kill us."

Helena looked across in alarm. He shrugged.

The main gate towered above them, the height of at least five men, William guessed. Why it stood so high had to be down to the impression it gave. Come to think of it, everything he'd seen so far seemed to be about appearances, about ostentation. In the centre of the gate, a large spiral had been drawn or painted in gold. Or was it *actual* gold? Hard to say.

Just inside the entrance, a small Janasà pointed at the mules and then at some nearby stables. Jasper told Big Ger to stay with the animals, as he put it, just in case. He wasn't so keen on the instruction to also leave their weapons, but William persuaded him they needed to do it.

"Come. I will show you your quarters," said Laddà. "These will be your home for the duration of your stay." William interpreted for the others; Laddà's use of old Truscan was difficult to follow, even for him.

They emerged into a vast marble clad atrium with, in the middle, a golden mosaic depicting an elaborate spiral[72], at least a dozen paces across. A fountain on one side sprayed water from the mouth of a child-like figure. A clicking noise from high up made William crane his neck towards the ceiling, where he noted, surprised, that there were Janasà in armour hanging from it like bats. He supposed they would drop to the ground, ready to fight in the unlikely event that William and his companions caused trouble. William counted a hundred paces before Laddà ushered them onto a wooden platform suspended by ropes that ran into a recess in the roof. The Janasà joined them, emitted a high whistle, and they plummeted.

"Sun and moons," shouted Ridkin. "Are they trying to kill us?"

"Amazing," said William. "I never imagined there could be such a clever way to move between levels."

Soft light emanated from each floor as they approached that expired on passing. The platform decelerated and arrived at its destination.

William looked up and to where they'd just come from. "Twenty-five levels," he pronounced. Matilda rolled her eyes.

Laddà led them down a low corridor, making William and the others hunch over to avoid head butting the ceiling. The end of the passage opened up into a larger area. "Your sleeping quarters," said the Janasà with something resembling a flourish. "Newly fitted, the best in the citadel."

Smaller Janasà filed in through the other end of the chamber with ladders and bedding, and they led the travellers to hexagonal open-sided cubicles stacked ten across and four deep, each with a spiral emblem carved above. The effect resembled the honeycomb of a beehive, and it struck William that Janasà society was more like that of bees than of men. He smiled. It might make a useful framework for him to understand more about these creatures. The scholar in him couldn't wait to record it all.

"Tonight, Queen Nannua will host a grand banquet. We have food from every corner of our land, and afterwards, you will be guests of honour at a cutting ceremony." Laddà bowed and left them.

"I don't want to go to no cutting ceremony," grumbled Ridkin. "What the Stars are they cutting? Us?"

~~~

Mary screeched in frustration. She'd made multiple attempts to break free of the wooden frame on which he'd bound her, but Feydor had done his homework and she was powerless. For now.

He'd spent the day working through his mother's papers and books, while Mary had whined and complained behind him. Her tone had gone from indignant to reasonable to pleading and back to enraged.

"Lickspittle. Let me free."

"Not a chance."

She tried another tack. "Feydor, dear Feydor. Be a nice wee jester and let your cousin free. I promise I'll be good."

"It's cousin once removed, as you once pointed out. And I trust you as far as I can spit."

"But you know I'll be nice to you."
~~~

"Shut up and let me read, will you?"

"But Feydor…"

He turned and unleashed a silencing charm on her before once again addressing the pile of books he'd pulled off his mother's shelves. It was amazing how easy powerful magic had become for him since he'd donned Imelda's amulet. He reached to his neck where he'd got it strung on a new leather strip and wondered how he'd ever coped in life without it.

His research was going well. He'd found in Mrs Biggins's Book of Common Spells, a way of materialising himself in Sardonica. And if he could get there, he could take the crystal for himself with no help from William. The problem was to materialise back out again. The magic he now commanded, a form of dark magic, didn't work over there and he had no intention of travelling home via land and sea, a journey of at least twelve weeks.

He pulled another volume out of the pile; this one was named the Grimorio Minore, the Little Grimoire. Which implied there could be a Grand Grimoire or some such, although his mother didn't appear to have possessed a copy. It was written in a kind of code with the words garbled. Someone had scribbled something in the margin of the first page. It looked like his mother's hand. It read, *cypher?* Ah. In what language? He spent an hour trying out the obvious ones; modern Anglonian, olde worlde Anglonian. Gallian. Modern Truscan. He cursed himself for not having paid more attention to his studies of old languages. Perhaps she'd written down somewhere how to decode the text. He turned the grimoire upside down and shook it. A sheet of parchment fluttered to the floor, from where Filthy scooped it up and stuffed it in his mouth.

"No…"

He dived for the monkey, who scampered away up the wall. Hmm. Ah, of course. He touched his mother's amulet and concentrated. Filthy froze and tipped over, falling headfirst. He caught him and wedged his fingers into its mouth, pulling out a soggy and torn piece of parchment. He placed it on the bench and smoothed out the creases, grimacing at the stickiness of Filthy's saliva. Ten minutes of careful study and he'd cracked it, while marvelling that his mother had read the book to him months ago without apparent difficulty. She must have memorised it. He put it all together and, sentence by painstaking sentence, read the coded sections. The decoded text was in perfectly understandable modern Truscan.

The most thumb-marked page read as his mother had described months earlier: a crystal hidden away that had remarkable powers. Nothing new then. He read on and found something interesting. A riddling cat appeared to be the most formidable of a set of protections. That didn't sound like much of a protection. If a traveller tried and failed to answer a riddle correctly, he would be torn asunder. A metaphor perhaps? He continued. The crystal could only be taken from its resting place by, and here he struggled with the translation, something like a Special One who would be tall, fair of skin and have white hair. That would rather rule *himself* out, then. He might be able to snatch it off William, though, should the man succeed in reaching it. That William might be able to pull off this seemingly impossible feat seemed unlikely, given how he had no notable qualities that Feydor could discern.

But supposing William passed the riddling test and met the conditions, could he himself perhaps get to Sardonica, steal the crystal from William as he came out of the caverns, and return?

He opened the next book, this one containing a variety of ways to mould time. How to slow it down, speed it up, reverse it for a brief period, even. And here, this looked interesting. A spell to delay an action. He assumed this got used by couples wanting to prolong their time in the bedroom. Pushing that thought aside, his mind twisted in loops as it sought inspiration. What was to say you couldn't combine spells? What if… It might work. He would test it first.

That left other issues to solve, like how to know where to materialise and how to find out what was going on there. It would be rather inconvenient if he were to arrive, for example, in the middle of a battle with swords swishing and arrows flying. Or inside the trunk of a tree. Ending his days encased in a lump of wood wasn't high on his pail list.

What *was* on his pail list then? Most men would have chosen something related to wealth, or travel, or sex. He'd never given it much thought, but using his mother's power to make his life easier would do just fine for now.

He pulled his attention to the matter at hand. He searched through his mother's other possessions. How untidy she'd been. She'd crammed things into trunks, down the back of cupboards, on high shelves. Doubtless there'd be secret compartments he hadn't found yet. He rummaged through it all. Bottles containing eyes, boxes holding bat wings, dishes of what, fingernails? Why fingernails? And then, on a high shelf sitting behind a row of books, his searching fingers stumbled across a small ebony box. That was an odd detail; ebony was a useful way to shield powerful magic. He gingerly released the clasp and pulled out...a mirror. Could this be an occulem? She'd told him she didn't need such articles. Liar! He brushed his sleeve over it and an image appeared. A dim and empty cell somewhere, perhaps underground. It must have, at some point, contained someone that his mother had wanted to watch. An occulem was just what he needed. He closed the box and smiled to think how his plan was coming together.

He sat back down and contemplated Mary. Then he had an idea. Where was that book of magical restraints he'd noticed earlier? There. After leafing through it for a few minutes, he stood before her and weaved a globe of light out of the air that he released toward her. It circled around Mary and closed up, enveloping her. Then he removed the other charms.

"What are you up to, Feydor? And when are you going to release me?"

"Never you mind what I'm up to. And I'll let you out once I have the crystal. I'm not risking you getting in the way. I don't need you or your sons now."

"But I told you. Dark magic won't work there."

"I've worked out how to get around that problem. This time tomorrow, I'll have the crystal."

He put the silence charm back in place, stuffed the occulem into his bag and called, "Come, Filthy. To the palace."

The monkey scampered after him. Only later did he wonder at the odd smile that had played over Mary's lips as he left her.

~~~
~~~

The Janasà gave William and the others costumes for the grand reception that almost fitted them. While broad enough in the body, nothing extended to encompass the human form, so the effect was one of children who have outgrown their clothes. In style, the outfits were all similar, with a rustic peasant look featuring bold, bright colour combinations. Ridkin complained about the whole thing.

"Just leave me here," he told the others. "Ridkin ain't the partying kind."

"Please Ridkin," begged Matilda. "You're my best friend, and I want you to be there."

When William caught sight of Jasper's garb, he burst out laughing. Jasper didn't take it well. He stood up menacingly close to William, who was wise enough to say a simple, "Sorry, Jasper."

Laddà returned and escorted them up three levels via stairways, the top of which gave onto a stage that overlooked a grand hall. The floor below soon filled out with a horde of Janasà, and it became apparent that banqueting here was a spectator affair. With assembly complete, a trio of Janasà came onto the stage sporting bag type arrangements with pipes into which they blew and made an uncomfortable high-pitched squeal that caused the two women and four men to hold their hands over their ears. After this, four more Janasà bore a fifth on a kind of litter, surrounded by gold drapes. As they lowered the litter to the floor, the curtain parted and a grotesque, corpulent Janasà dressed head to toe in gold placed her feet on the ground and was helped to a standing position by her bearers.

"Bow," Laddà instructed. All five did so. After a brief pause, chairs were dragged out before a shrill voice invited them, "Please be seated."

What followed was the most uncomfortable mealtime of William's life. Not only was the food almost, but not entirely, inedible, but the silent, watching stare of a thousand pairs of three-lidded eyes gave William the collywobbles. Course after course was brought out, each harder to chew on than the last while a group of small, child-sized Janasà made a noise that approximated to singing. William would never again moan about the excruciating sound of human children trying to sing together for as long as he lived.

The worst dish was a pungent cheese that contained actual live maggots squirming around[73]. It had a smell like rotting wood. William and the others refused to touch it, all except Ridkin, of course, who dived in and professed it delicious.

Without any announcement, the Queen stood and began a speech, the tattooed words of which she read off the bare back of a lackey. "Welcome, Oh Anointed One," she paused. "This night, the whole Janasà nation awaits that you bring us Nurragù." She shouted the last word, causing the entire hall to erupt into chants of "Nurragù, Nurragù, Nurragù."

William did his best to understand and translate for the others.

The Queen lifted her arms and stilled the throng. "Tomorrow, the Anointed One will enter the cavern of the crystal and confront Bisgattù." A collective hush settled over the crowd at the utterance of that name. A thousand hairy faces stared at him. "Stand, oh anointed one, that the Janasà nation may see you clearly."

William was prodded to his feet.

"He's not the Anointed One," whispered Ridkin under his breath. "He's just a very naughty knight[74]."

"Silence for the Queen of the Janasà. She who is the tallest, humblest Janasà in the nation of Janasà and affiliated minor, much more minor, races," proclaimed Laddà.

"And now," said the Queen, "the cutting ceremony."

All five looked about alarmed, but all that happened was that a group of six Janasà filed onto the dais, stripped to the waist, followed by six more holding long curved knives.

"What's this malarky about?" asked Ridkin.

William shrugged.

The children started up singing again and the bagpipe things played their impression of a live cat being gutted. When sudden silence descended, the knife bearers cut deep gouges across where breasts would be on a human, and an enormous cheer rang out from the crowd. They made William and the others bow before them, and then the whole thing was over.

As they led the five of them to their quarters, William muttered over and over, "incredible," and words like that until Matilda hissed at him to shut up.

"So, oh Anointed One, got any wise words for us?" asked Ridkin.

"There's no need for that," said Helena. "Let him be. He has a big day tomorrow."

William had to admit this appeared to be true. He had a date with a cat.

~~~

Feydor set off for the Castle and Ball, not relishing the task at hand. The decision to do away with Mary had seemed easy enough when he'd made it, but now it came to killing her in cold blood, he didn't feel so comfortable. He couldn't claim to be an innocent where these things were concerned, of course. However, there'd always been others to do the dirty work for him, but this… this might be tricky, one job he couldn't and wouldn't delegate. She'd be difficult, persuasive, and could do magic. Quite why he hadn't done it already, he couldn't say. Boglets. Best just get it over with.

He'd left Filthy behind at the palace playing with the Queen's Fool, Jane. This was the first time he'd been separated from the little monkey since his mother had first foisted the animal on him, and it felt odd not to have him there, but killing Mary might turn out to be tricky and he didn't want any distractions.

He reached the tavern mid-afternoon and greeted his favourite depressive landlord. "Good morrow, Rodnye."

"What do you want, fat face?"

"Just wondering. Is everything quiet upstairs?" He nodded up at the rooms above.

"Now that you mention it, no. There's been a right kerfuffle going on, banging and scraping. It's upsetting my customers."

"Have you had an actual customer since I last came by?"

Rodnye scowled. "Yes. Darren was here."

"Darren is deaf and won't have heard a thing. Oh, never mind."
~~~

He bounded up the stairs, two at a time, then paused halfway. The commotion Rod had mentioned might have been Mary breaking free of her confinement. Which meant she could be waiting to attack him, or, more likely, she could have set up traps. He half hoped she had; it was the kind of challenge he relished. Either way, the utmost caution was required.

He cracked the door open a fraction and peeped in, looking for signs of tampering. Nothing obvious. He opened up the rest of the way and threw his gloves into the room, expecting something to explode or knives to rain through the air, but no. Still nothing. As he crossed the threshold, he grabbed a broom and probed left to right, floor to ceiling, and triggered... nothing. However, there were no poison darts, no cascades of fire, no torrents of vitriol pouring down from above. How odd. Having satisfied himself all was for now safe, he relaxed and looked around. Boglets. The 'A' frame he'd at first used to restrain her lay shattered in pieces across the floor. A shutter at the far end flapped open in the breeze. She'd escaped through there, then. Boglets. Where under the Stars had she gone, and how had she broken free? He sat at his mother's desk to think. If he knew Mary at all, and he believed he knew her very well indeed, there was no way she wouldn't have set a deadly surprise for him somewhere, but what? Where? Maybe she'd put a charm on a cupboard or shelf that he might at some point later set off? He worked his way around and poked at every recess, corner, container, and flat surface. Next, he looked at books, plates, goblets, clothes-racks, and ...still nothing. He caught sight of a long grey hair on the floor. One of Mary's? He carefully pocketed it. Who could say whether it could be useful?

About at last to give up his search, a thought spliced itself sideways into his mind. What if she'd booby trapped the exit? She might have put something on the steps leading to the room that allowed him to pass upwards, but would unleash hell on his returning descent. Her mind worked like that.

He took one of Imelda's shoes and dropped it onto the top step. Nothing happened. Perhaps he'd been wrong, but tried one more shoe, this one aimed at the bottom of the stairs at around chest height. The stairwell exploded with an almighty crack, with the walls on both sides shattering outwards and a dense wall of flames spreading from the bottom to the top. The entire building trembled. Without stopping to think, he charged to the back shutter and set himself to dive out, but hesitated. What if? What if she'd anticipated his move? He yanked off his own boots and threw them out. Sure enough, another blast of fire leapt out and burned them to instant ash. As he jumped through what he hoped was now a safe gap, the room behind him fire-balled and fell into the tavern, which itself erupted into flames. The walls caved inwards, and the roof came down onto the whole shebang. He fell sprawling to his side, and a cascade of wood splinters, glass, dust, and other debris covered him. Curse the Stars and holy boglets. She'd almost got him.

The last thing to fall was his mother's black hat pin. It landed on his nose.

# Eighteen

The Janasà warrior arrived soon after a gong sounded and explained, "I will shortly take you to the crystal hall where you must pass the two-headed cat in order to reach the crystal."

"I have a book with me that tells of only *one* head on a beast that guards a crystal. And that head poses three riddles that the traveller must answer correctly or die. Here, I can show you."

Will reached into his travel pack and pulled out the Grimorio Minore.

Laddà took a quick glance at the page opened up to him. "The legend has been written and rewritten over the centuries. I tell you Bisgattù has two heads. I have seen it with my own ears."

"And the riddles? I read there would be three."

"One head will ask but one riddle. The other will ask for the answer to something deeper, an Eternal Enigma. Before you ask, the questions are different every time. The first thing you must do is choose."

"Choose what?"

"Whether to answer the riddle or the Eternal Enigma."

"What's an Eternal Enigma?" asked William, intrigued. It sounded fascinating.

The gong sounded again. "I'm sorry. I have to leave to make more preparations. Expect me again when the next gong sounds." She jumped up onto a wall and scuttled off into a recess in the ceiling.

"This place is mad," said Ridkin, when William translated what he'd been told. "Listen, Will. I know you well enough to say you will ask for the riddle. Do you believe you can answer it? Think about it; all our lives depend on you here."

William stared at Ridkin. "Thanks for that. I warned you all not to come. Remember."

"I'm not saying it for that. Just… think before you choose. And know this…"

"Yes?"

He clapped him on the shoulders and looked into his face. "I trust you, Will."

Jasper climbed down from his pod and patted William on his back. "Good luck, Bookman. You can *do* this. Say it. *I can do this.*"

"I can do this. I *think*."

"Hah–good joke," said Jasper, who punched him on the arm. William smiled for just a moment. The first pleasant thing Jasper had ever done with him had involved violence.

He sat on the floor with his book, looking for any last-minute clues it might give him. It didn't help. Many of the sentences contradicted themselves or made no sense. He stood as the next gong sounded, a sick feeling growing in his stomach.

"The mouth of the wolf, break a leg," said Ridkin, smiling.

Not the most reassuring wish he'd ever heard.

~~~

Laddà led the five travellers down a sloping passageway that curved around on itself, in yet another spiral, for at least twenty levels. In contrast to the clean, crisp mountain air of the citadel, the air down here had a stale, sulphurous, almost oily odour to it, not unlike the Janasà themselves. Warming as he traversed the levels, William peeled off the tunic he'd donned for the journey downwards and handed it to Ridkin, who'd also taken off his woollen jacket.

He'd spent the preceding night trying to convince himself he was up to the task. As much as his reasoning mind agreed with this, his emotional side said the opposite. It caused his breathing to quicken, his gut to tighten and his palms to become cold and sweaty.
~~~

And there it stood, the culmination of three months of sometimes hard and dangerous travel: a low narrow entrance to what had to be the cave system in which the two-faced moggie awaited them.

"You only," said the Janasà, pointing at William, its face unreadable. "The Anointed One."

William felt anything but anointed. Condemned One would be a better description. Another Janasà waited by, holding a torch, its flame contained and flickering within a mesh frame. She gave it to William. "Will you wait for me?" asked William of the others, not needing a response. A quick nod to Ridkin, and he crossed over and into the entrance.

They entered the first cavern, and William asked a question. "There's something I've been wondering."

"Is it important?" asked the Janasà. "We have some distance to travel, and you are not… equipped for it."

"It's important to me."

The Janasà turned to him. "Go on then."

"My King sent me here to trade for special water. Does it exist?"

"Special? What do you mean?"

"It was… An aphrodisiac."

"I don't understand the word."

William grasped for terms the Janasà might understand. "Something humans swallow to make them want very badly to produce children, or at least do what causes children."

"We have a myrtle berry preparation that makes our males vigorous."

William smiled, then mused on whether his body language meant anything here. "That sounds right."

The little creature gave an impression of thought. "You know, there is an unusual spring in these caves."

"Really?"

"Really. But the word you used afro…"

"Aphrodisiac."

"This word sounds very close to a word in our language. A word meaning *wart*. The water from this spring treats warts."

"Warts? You Janasà have warts, just like humans?" He couldn't help asking, "Where?"

"It is best you don't know where. Trust me."

William made the mental connection. Some visiting human had heard something spoken here and misunderstood its meaning. He broke into a low chuckle. "This means I travelled across a continent to find a medicament against warts. That's crazy." Then again, when he'd last seen the King, the man had been sporting a huge wart on his nose. He thought about it. "If we finish this. *Once* we finish this. Can I see this spring? It will please my king to bring some of this water back for him."

The creature shrugged. "Have you finished asking stupid questions?" it asked. It continued down the next passage without waiting for an answer.

The passageway led further downwards at varying rates. Where the slope became steep, carved steps made it easy to continue down. They passed through a succession of galleries, each linked to the next by more sloping passages. His guide emitted a steady stream of clicking sounds as she navigated the twists and turns, causing William to almost run to keep up. "Can we slow down, please?" he called. "You don't want to lose me before we've even begun." The Janasà ignored him, intent on its destination.

His innate fear of the unknown mingled with a new sense of anticipation. Now, for better or worse, he'd be doing what he'd set out to do all those months before. It didn't matter that he'd been misled. It ended here and now. He barely noticed his damaged hand. A facet of the excitement coursing through his blood, perhaps?

At one point, they entered a gallery part-filled with water. They waded on, the water almost up to the neck of the Janasà. Their splashing made bizarre echoes that bounced in all directions at once, like an entire army was in progress. While the floor rose, the roof tracked downward and became so low they had to shuffle along on their backs with noses raised to continue breathing. After what seemed an hour or more, Laddà stopped and disappeared from view. He caught up. Ah, a narrow gap off to the right. He squeezed through and the Janasà informed him, "The crystal caverns start here."

Cool air flowed out, so there had to be an opening to the surface somewhere up ahead. After a sharp turn to the left, the passage continued downward. Unlike the previous caves, the walls, floor, and ceiling were smooth. Not natural. He counted a hundred and fifty paces before the noise of rushing water came to him. After another sharp twist, the passage led to an underground river, too deep and turbulent to enter. With no bridge or other obvious means of crossing, it appeared their journey was done, however Laddà took William's torch, placing it in a holder slung across her bag and leapt upward to stick to the ceiling. He couldn't see exactly how.

"Hold on to my belt," commanded Laddà, shouting above the roar of the torrent.

William reached up and wrapped his good hand around some kind of knob or handle at the Janasà's waist. With the other, he gripped as best he could another handle on the opposite side, using just his thumb and index finger. The rest of his hand ached like the furies, but there was no time to be concerned about that. With William attached, the Janasà lifted herself upwards and made what resembled a walking action with her hands gripping the rock roof, while William swung around beneath with his feet dangling in the freezing, tumbling water. His nose pressed into the Janasà's soft midriff and a musky, but sulphurous smell filled his nostrils. Not unpleasant. After two dozen 'steps', the Janasà dunked William's feet to the floor, and it landed next to him.

"Almost there," said the Janasà, handing back the torch.

The still smooth and regular shaft now passed upward and gave onto what William could see in outline and dancing shadow as a vast gallery. Laddà pointed to the wall. A spiral design etched into the surface contained an animal figure within; a cat with two heads. They'd arrived at the moment of truth. A part of William still doubted that a cat existed down here. After all, what would it eat? The Janasà pressed him forward, but then stopped him before he stepped from solid rock and into thin air. He held his torch out and traced the outline of a huge void. The Janasà directed William's gaze off to the left. A pile of bones and debris lay there. Nothing remarkable. But wait. It looked like the half-chewed remains of something animal or human, which even in the dim torchlight had reddish hair.

"The twins!" William muttered in surprise. The realisation hit him like a punch to the gut. No doubt about it now. He could no longer pretend this was anything but a deadly quest, and his stomach tightened.

The rasping breath of something approached from far below, or was it two somethings, as of two men struck down with the lurgy? And there it was at last, looming high above, and spitting down on him gobs of hot saliva. It had mottled fur, sat on its haunches, and waved a pair of massive, clawed paws around as its heads surveyed the new arrival. Colossal heads, but nonetheless feline.

"Who approaches?" said two distinct voices in his head. This couldn't be real. Could it? Cats don't have two heads and don't speak right inside your mind. The whole situation couldn't be happening. Supernatural beasts far below the surface of the earth were something you read about in children's tales. He had to be hallucinating, right?

"We asked you a question," thundered the voices. "Speak or die."

Laddà poked William hard with her toe. That hurt!

"W-William of C-Coxwell."

"C-Coxwell? What kind of place is that to come from?"

Not that conversation again?

"It's in Anglonia."

"Do you believe yourself to be the Anointed One?" asked the giant kitties.

"He does," interrupted Laddà.

"Silence!" screamed the cats and a huge paw slashed at the Janasà, who dodged a short way back up the passage. "Speak the truth, William of C-Coxwell. Are you the Anointed One?"

"How would I know?" wailed William.

"He answers with truth," said voice one. "He can't know it."

"Agreed," said voice two. The pair of them were having a discussion in his head. Could this get any weirder?

"And now you will choose," said one.

"Between a riddle and an Eternal Enigma," said two.

William frowned and squinted at Bisgattù. "So… What *is* an Eternal Enigma?"

~~~

Matilda watched William vanish into the caverns. There was no way William would ever come out of there alive, not if a murderous riddling cat needed to be confronted. Of course, he didn't actually deserve to die. He hadn't an evil bone in his body, but… his death, however it came, would solve a problem. She could stop worrying about him and her mother getting all loved up over each other again.

There was another question: what about the crystal she clutched in her fist? The Ninfiné creatures said she had to *bear* it, but she still didn't understand what that meant. Was she supposed to carry the stone inside the caves, perhaps? The answer formed in her mind just as soon as she posed the question. The crystal knew where it belonged: the caves. It was pulling toward the opening even now. The cat would allow her to pass if she held the crystal. And she would know the way in and out again. She was the bearer. She'd be fine.

All the same, she was going to wait to see what happened to William. If he never emerged, there was no way she'd be following him, thank you very much. Alternatively, all being well, she'd have the job done in no time. Destiny fulfilled. Free to get on with her life.

It sounded very dull.

~~~

The voice of the cats in William's head stayed silent. A loud drip echoed around the chamber. Had that been there before?

"You hear the water clock? Good. If you wish to proceed further, you must choose. Riddle," said voice one.

"Or Eternal Enigma," said two. "You have six drips of the clock to decide. Your time starts now."

Drip…

Think. Could his unshakable belief in reason be flawed? If so, the riddle could be dangerous. As Ridkin had said, it could even be a trap.

Drip…

But what for the love of Lord Sola and his Moons was an Eternal Enigma? He'd never come across the term in any of his readings. It sounded simple enough, right? It could mean anything, though.

Drip …

Both options had to be difficult. Close to impossible. Perhaps it made no difference which one he chose. Riddle then.

Drip …

What about his love for Helena? Where had that thought come from? His feelings for her couldn't be understood from a book. And if logic couldn't explain everything, was the Eternal Enigma the right choice?

Drip …

If only Ridkin were here. Simple straight thinking Ridkin.

Drip.

"Time's up," said voice one, as the animal raised a paw to strike downwards.

"Eternal Enigma," William blurted out. "I choose the Eternal Enigma. Whatever it means."

"Brother," said voice one, "what question would you have the human answer?"

"My question…" It paused.

"Yes?" said William. He closed his eyes and crossed as many fingers as he could bear to move.

"Let me think…"

"Yes?" shouted William. "Come on, let's get this over with."

"Very well. Without speaking, without silence, how can you express the truth?[75]"

"Nice!" said voice two.

"Sun, Moons, Stars, and a Priest on a Donkey. *WHAT DOES THE QUESTION EVEN MEAN?*" he shouted, his voice reverberating around the chamber.

"We can't help you. You have ten further drips to provide an answer."

He panicked. This question had only one logical answer he could think of. It came down to whether truth existed in the absence of thought. That sounded both *eternal* and *enigmatic*. But what even was the question? He'd never see Helena and the others again.

Drip …

If he guessed wrongly, he could die. If he hesitated too long, he would die. *MUBBLE FUBBLES!*

Drip…

Perhaps, after all, death here would be alright. It would be swift. But wait. The others. Their fate might depend on him.

Drip…

Calm yourself. What could he deduce about this Eternal Enigma? Maybe that would at least point him in the right direction.

Drip…

He'd chosen the opposite of a riddle. And a riddle was something to be reasoned. So that meant…

Drip…

It meant the Eternal Enigma couldn't be answered with reason. It could only be contemplated. *Perceived.*

Drip…

Something unconscious then. *Felt* even. How to feel the answer?

Drip…

He looked for his own mind to close it down. He quelled the instinct to think. What was thinking?

Drip…

Agh! A thought! Stop it. Pull back. Open your mind. Connect with the unthinking.

Drip…

The idea welled up within him. No time to question it, no chance to test it. Nine drips down. Speak now or die anyway.

Drip…

"Like the sound of one hand clapping, truth has no meaning that can be expressed. To search for an answer is to fail already." He spoke with clarity, certitude. Little more than a whisper. "Truth has no *meaning*, nor does it require it. It only *is*. It does not need expression in order to exist and every man, or Janasà must experience it from within."

In the silence that followed, William counted his heartbeats. They sounded like a fist hammering on a door. Panic rose in him. Was this the prelude to his death? Why was the cat saying nothing?

"Brother. Is this the answer you sought?" asked the riddling voice.

"Dunno," said the enigmatic voice. "It sounds good, though. You may pass."

~~~

"Why ask a question you don't know the answer to?" asked voice one of the other.

"None of my questions have answers," replied the other.

"You need to think of some new ones that do."

The animal slunk away from view.

William blocked out the bickering conversation and focused on his next steps. The faint torchlight flickered, lighting the other side of the chasm. "Laddà," he called out. "Are you still there?"

"Right beside you," said the Janasà. "Would you like me to take you across?"

"Only if you want me to look for the…"

Laddà had already climbed part way up the wall and beckoned William to grab hold of her belt again. "Are you sure there's no other way?" asked William.

"Yes," came the emphatic response.

"Right."

As before, Laddà hauled him upwards. His damaged hand ached and throbbed, sending shocks of pain up his arm. Not that he intended for one moment to give up. He'd come too far in distance and in every other way imaginable. Once again, the Janasà climbed higher and then scuttled sideways and out over the void.

"Oh my giddy aunt," said William as his feet dangled over nothingness and his whole body swung one direction, then back the other. Not such a great idea. In fact, outright terrifying.
~~~

"If you relax a little, it'll go a lot easier," the mad scuttling creature told him.

"Relax? Are you having an absolute laugh? You stinky crazy… thing."

"I could drop you if you prefer," answered the Janasà.

"No, no. Stinky is good, anyway. Just get me across."

"There's a gap here," said Laddà. "I'll need to jump across."

"Jump? No way. You're not…"

The creature above him tensed, and they were airborne.

"Argh! I'm going to die," William shouted.

Laddà landed. If that's what you could say about someone that clung to a roof of sheer rock with a floor too distant to see.

William closed his eyes. "Tell me when it's over," he said.

"It *is* over. Put your feet down and stand."

He opened his eyes and looked down. The Janasà had spoken the truth. He wasn't falling through space.

"Give me a moment," said William.

Laddà jumped down and handed him the torch. "Right about now, we should see the crystal," said the Janasà.

With exquisite timing, a shaft of what appeared to be sunlight reached through a fissure in the roof ahead and picked out something reflective.

"This is as far as I go," said Laddà.

"It's safe?" asked William.

Laddà blinked. "Perhaps. Go. Before the light disappears."

His eyes adjusted to the brightness, and the smooth floor extended down to a recess in the rock, some fifty paces ahead. In that space, the most brilliant jewel glittered, inviting him to grasp it. At least that was what it looked and felt like. This new universe of feeling for the truth still confused him.

He stepped forward. Twenty paces further, his shin made a crunching, painful collision with something solid. Part blinded by reflected sunlight, he stooped to find a round stone platform, knee high and a pace across. Puzzled, his fingers traced the surface, expecting to find some other feature, but it was smooth and flat. The ideal place for a legendary crystal. He mentally shrugged and stepped around it.

Moving on another thirty paces, he reached the source of the reflected light. And there it was. Tiny. So much fuss for such a small thing. He crouched to get a better look, positioning himself to not block the light. The brightness of the reflection, however, made him squint. Impatient, he extended out with his good hand and… "Ow!"

He pulled his hand back. A bubble of blood formed on his finger. What the…? He reached again with a lighter touch and traced the form. Not a single crystal. Several irregular crystals. He unwrapped the linen from his injured hand and laid it out on his palm. Then picked up the items, placing them in the centre. He turned out of the direct sunlight and inspected. Writing. A flash of recognition brought a slow, wry smile to his lips. Oh boy, this was going to be interesting.

Laddà kept to her word. On the way back through the cave system, she took him off to a separate section and gave him some spring water in a tiny bottle that she produced from her belt. At least he'd have something to give the King on his return. He might even receive a reward that would set him up for life. He just needed to escape the citadel with that life intact.

~~~

Feydor sat hunched over Imelda's occulem, waiting for the perfect moment to relocate himself to Sardonica and grab the crystal. Hours had gone by since he'd watched William entering the cavern. He stretched his neck out and the vertebrae clicked loudly into place. He needed to stay awake. The window of opportunity would be brief. He yawned. He'd slept badly the night before, worrying about what could go wrong and how he'd deal with each eventuality. Partly that, and partly the sheer excitement of the potential prize at stake. As he waited, he drummed his fingers on the bench and went over for the umpteenth time the complex sequence of spells and other actions required to perform the grab he had in mind. A lesser mortal could never master the split-second precision it called for. Confident, he continued staring and found himself drifting off. He awoke with a jerk. Boglets, he'd almost fallen asleep.
~~~

He'd not uncovered a way, so far at least, to use magic to stave off fatigue or skip his sleep. If anything, magic required its practitioner to lie in slumber longer and more deeply. He reasoned the mind filled up throughout the day with disorder and dirt and needed to be emptied and refilled with clean *stuff*.

He touched the side of the occulem, and the scene pulled back. Five paces from the cavern, his mad brother stood waiting with the others. Another two paces behind them squatted a squad of battle Janasà, ready for any kind of threat. And well behind everyone else, on a golden throne, sat Queen Nannua, with her elite guards.

He glimpsed movement. He uttered the first incantation. This would initiate a time spell. On arrival, he'd have at most five seconds to snatch the crystal out of William's hands and vanish before the combat Janasà could react and put an axe through his head. Or his brother could make some predictably heroic gesture. And yes, there! There was William exiting the cavern with an odd smirk on his face, like the cat that got the cream. Not for long.

Feydor chanted the second spell and vanished from the room. And it worked! He'd calculated the trajectory to the exact inch and stood between an open-mouthed William and everyone else. He smirked at a wide-eyed Jasper.

"I'll take that," commanded Feydor with a voice he'd practised on Blind Harry. William, unresisting, proffered the blood-stained linen package he held before him.

"Sure, have it," said William, smiling. "Fill your boots."

Odd. But there was no time to discuss it. As an axe flew through the space in which he'd just stood, he rematerialised in his chamber and caught his breath. He'd done it! He'd done it! Relief coursed through his blood, and the weight of everything he'd been carrying these many years fell away. He'd never need to bow to a king again or hustle for trinkets to sell. Or anything else annoying, ever again. His hand shook as he laid the little parcel on his bench and peeled back the folds. And found nothing but shards of brown-coloured glass. What? He lifted the pieces to check beneath, probing with his fingers for a hidden fold. Nothing. Holy Boglets. What had gone wrong? Had the crystal morphed its form during the jump in space? Improbable, not without a magic more powerful than any he could muster. Wait, there was something inscribed on the largest two shards. Might this be a clue to the true location of the jewel?

He placed the fragments on the bench and nudged them together. The surfaces slotted into a perfect fit. A phrase. He traced the letters. Truscan. Not his strongest suit, but this looked simple enough. He mouthed the words and sagged in absolute astonishment.

*Ale of Italica.*

"HOLY EFFING BOGLETS!" he shouted.

There was a knock on his door. "What...?"

A boy's voice answered, "Message for you, Mr Foolson."

Putting aside the shards of glass, he hauled himself over to the door and unlocked it before cracking it open. A messenger bowed and handed over a piece of parchment, which Feydor snatched and carried inside, slamming and relocking the door behind him.

He broke the seal and unfolded the page. *Come at once. My chamber. Urgent. Rasa.*

It looked like her writing. He brushed the surface with his fingertips and got no suggestion that anyone other than her had written it.

Boglets. He'd better get over to her and find out what the problem was. What an odd message. In his agitated state, though, he didn't think to question it.

~~~

"Where is my crystal?" demanded Queen Nannua. She'd raised her considerable bulk out of her chair and, with the help of two of her personal guards, waddled over to William and Laddà. "I repeat, where is my crystal?"

"You saw what happened," said William. "Someone came from nowhere and took it."

"This was your plan?" she asked, now standing with her face close to William's midriff, trying to look threateningly into his eyes.
~~~

He only just managed not to smirk. "I had no plan. Other than to serve you, Oh Wondrous Queen."

"You lie. All your kind lies. You are vermin not to be trusted. When I find that crystal, I will erase you all from the earth."

She turned her back and walked away as serenely as her size permitted.

"Kill the males," she ordered, "and send the females to the mines."

~~~

Feydor raced to the suite of chambers occupied by Ruthenia's ladies-in-waiting and knocked on Rasa's door. He heard a faint muffled noise from within. He took a risk and opened it. Sat in the middle of the room, bound to a chair, a heavy gag over her mouth, the Lady Rasa stared up at Feydor and shook her head.

In two strides he was over to her, "My Lady," he said, as he removed the gag and fiddled with the knots.

"Feydor, I'm so sorry. He made me do it, I swear."

"Who, what?"

"That horrid priest. He came here and threatened he have Lina burned if I do not do it."

So, Stackpole had finally managed to get out of the Tower of Ludnam. How had he not known about that? "You mean he made you write the note?" he asked.

"Yes, the note. I'm sorry. What have I done?"

She shook as she burst into wild sobs. He frowned, then patted her on the shoulder. "It's alright, not your fault, my dear".

So, Stackpole was not only free, but had moved quickly to deceive him. Feydor Foolson, the greatest jester of them all, had fallen for a simple trick. And then, with an awful feeling in his bones, he remembered how he'd left his chamber. The occulem! He hadn't closed it down. If someone were to have entered his room, they'd have seen the occulem. Boglets. Caught with his britches down, his day was going from bad to worse.

He hurried back to his room, dark dread fermenting in his stomach. He knew what he'd find well before he got there. What remained of his
~~~

shattered door hung on its hinges and inside stood Stackpole, with a smug smile on his lips, wringing his hands in anticipation, and flanked by a pair of burly guards. More guards came up behind Feydor and took him by the shoulders.

"Ah Fool," he said, smiling. "Do join us."

Almost in a trance, Feydor found himself shoved into the centre of the room. The priest gestured toward the occulem where Feydor saw at once a scene of total mayhem in progress.

Smugness dripped off every one of the copious hairs on the priest's face. "This is forbidden magic, punishable by death."

"Ah," he replied.

~~~

Helena watched agog as the red-headed man in the attire of a jester vanished with whatever William had been holding when he'd emerged into the low light of the citadel. Without thinking, she ran to him and wrapped her arms around him in a tight embrace, her face moist. "You're safe! I were proper worried."

"Sorry, Helena," he said to her, as he brushed a tear from her cheek. "I don't care what you are and that I can't control how I feel. I want to be with you."

She held him tighter still.

"Um, William," started Ridkin. "I hate to break up the party but..."

William pulled back far enough to look around. A ring of squat, armed Janasà had formed about them. Jasper tried to grab an axe from one of them and landed on his backside. A heavy boot pressed downward on his chest, and a Janasà pushed a knife to his throat. More Janasà grabbed hold of the others and held them with arms behind backs.

Laddà shouted something, and the Janasà holding William stepped back. "I need to search you for the crystal." Two Janasà separated William and Helena.

As Laddà searched every part of William, his mouth and ears included, Helena looked about for a way out. Pointless. She had a simple choice: use
~~~

her magic to save them all or accept their death. A terrible choice. Who could say what worse thing would happen to them if she attempted it and lost control? And Matilda would know who or what she was. Time to decide. Laddà completed her search, then reached up to take William's head by the hair, kicking his legs from under him, and dropping him to his knees. Laddà had Jasper brought to kneel next to William. Kill the males, the Queen had said. William looked behind as Helena, Matilda, and Ridkin were pulled away to allow the assembled throng of Janasà to be spectators to the killings. Two of the biggest Janasà raised their axes high over William and Jasper, and Laddà began a murmured chant that the crowd took up. The sound pulsed. Somewhere behind, a drum struck up. How long did they have?

Helena closed her eyes and leant into that core of her she'd kept locked away all these years. Energy coursed over her, running in waves up and down her spine. Time slowed. Sweat ran down her face, drenching her front. Her hair stood on end like an untrimmed privet and heat burned from every pore in her skin. She screamed, but instead of withdrawing, she allowed it to continue. She opened up further and convulsed. Foam formed in her mouth, her lips pulled back to reveal her clenched teeth. You were supposed to take years to undergo this kind of change. She had seconds.

She must look like a wild beast to anyone else watching. And still it raged. All faces turned toward her. Axes paused in mid-swing. In this state, all she needed to do was accept who she was and bow to the simple logic of the situation. She only had to think of what she wanted for it to happen. The Janasà froze solid in blocks of ice and time resumed as normal. The trauma subsided, and she shook herself down like a wet dog. It couldn't have been an attractive look. Her skin cooled, her hair fell limp, and she turned to William, smiling.

"I want to be with you too, William Grey."

~~~

Matilda thought herself to be on a runaway cart. From the moment the puke-stocking William had emerged from the cavern, everything had gone
~~~

from totally boring to completely wild. First, a court jester had appeared out of nothing and grabbed whatever William was holding. Next, the Queen had ordered their executions, and Helena had grabbed William in a bear hug before acting like a rabid beast. And then the Janasà had transformed into blocks of ice and her mother had professed something like love for William. Typical! She couldn't leave him alone, could she? And she was a *witch*! She'd kept it from her for her whole life. It explained so much and yet nothing. A thousand questions formed at once. Anger rose inside her, starting as a low irritation, rising to a rage. Her self-control vanished. Something welled from deep within and took over her mind.

She turned to her mother. "You were a witch all along! I knew you were hiding things from me." Her voice wavered as she bit back tears. "Me, your own daughter. And father. He must have known. I… I hate you!"

She screamed and ran for the stairway, clutching her crystal, which now shone with a dazzling light like a thousand stars. Passing on the stairway an immobile Queen Nannua with her retinue of sycophantic helpers, she wafted the crystal in her face. "Look. I've got your crystal, your mad bitchness!"

Reaching the main atrium of the citadel, she burst breathlessly out into the open, clutching the jewel to her chest. Her aching legs powered her forward, and she tore out over the plain toward the high southern pass. If she never saw her mother again, it would be too soon.

# Nineteen

Two guards seized Feydor. One bundled him to the ground face down while the other bound his wrists and feet. He resisted the urge to panic, confident that he could break out of the hold any time he chose, so for now he waited to discover what Stackpole had to say.

"Feydor Foolson, former jester to King Inglebert, under the magical prohibition act signed into law by His Grace just yesterday, I arrest you on the charge of performing magic within the grounds of a royal residence. I further charge you with having performed a curse on His Majesty the King, causing him grievous ills. This is treason. You will be taken to the Tower of Ludnam to await trial at our leisure. What have you to say, Fool?"

Stackpole nodded to the guards to haul him upright. Feydor smirked. "The King hasn't been capable of signing anything for months."

Stackpole produced a document with a flourish. "Observe, is this not the King's signature and seal?"

"It's false. Anyway, do you think you can confine me, cretin?"

"Indeed, I do," replied Stackpole, who nodded to his faithful muscle, Robert Pyke. The man reached to Feydor's neck and grabbed the leather cord. And pulled away… his mother's amulet.

*Boglets*. How had they known about that?

Pyke took the little black stone and placed it inside a black box, closing the lid tight with a clasp.

"Take it to the witch woman now and inform her I have fulfilled my side of the bargain and trust she will do as promised," said Stackpole.

It didn't take a genius to work out who the witch woman might be. That he'd lost his most potent weapon against the priest was bad enough. That he'd lost it to Mary caused him to feel actual panic. It gave him no choice.

He'd have to openly perform his dabbler magic right there and then if he wanted to stop it from happening. He concentrated his thoughts on the feel of the amulet and muttered a word. Nothing happened. The box! It must have been made of ebony, the only material known to be impervious to magic. He tried a simple release spell to free his bindings. It didn't work. Boglets; what *had* Mary done?

"Do you have any idea what you are getting into by working with her?" asked Feydor.

"By *her*, you mean the witch known as Mary Grieve? We have a deal. I give her the amulet. She agrees to leave Anglonia for Emeraldia and never return."

"And you *trust* her?"

"Of course not. Let's just say I have something on her that will ensure her compliance. Pyke, take him downriver to The Traitor's Gate."

Feydor had to ask, "How did you know to search my room? You seemed very certain of finding something."

The priest tapped his nose twice. "I could smell the magic." As Feydor's eyes widened, he continued, "See, not so smart after all, are you? Get him out of my sight."

As Pyke and the guards Feydor him away in an uncomfortable shuffle, a dark blur jumped at the priest. The shape landed on his face and sank its teeth deep into his nose.

"Agh! Avaunt devil!" he shouted, trying to swat Filthy away. "Get this *thing* off me!"

Before the nearest guard could react, the monkey scampered down and onto Feydor's right shoulder.

"Pyke. When you reach the Tower, you can start by burning that creature."

As Feydor reached the end of the corridor, a page called out, "Lord Priest, the Queen bids you to come at once. The medic says the King will die within the hour!"

~~~
~~~

Deep under the Janasà citadel, Ridkin reacted first to Matilda's disappearance. "I should go after her."

"I should go as well," said William.

"Let her be, guys. It's just an effing teenage thing," said Jasper. "She'll be back."

"Shut up all of you," shouted Helena. "She's *my* daughter."

She wrapped her arms round her own shoulders and transformed into a pillar of white light, which swirled around on its axis before narrowing to a slit and vanishing with a soft *pop*.

William's jaw hit the floor. "What?"

They looked at each other in stunned silence. Ridkin pointed at the water that was pooling in the hollows of the stone floor under the static Janasà. "Um. Those chuffing ice blocks are melting."

"What? Crap. Run!" shouted Jasper. He led the way, leaving Ridkin and William to hammer up the dimly lit stairway behind him, dodging around blocks of fast thawing ice as they went.

William tripped over one and smashed his shin on the next. "Ouch! Priest on a donkey, I have to stop doing that." He hobbled on after Ridkin.

They reached the great atrium and raced on through the open gates.

"What about the mules?" asked William. "Who saw where Big Ger went with them?"

"It's this way," shouted Ridkin.

They discovered Big Ger with a pair of what had to be child Janasà, frozen like the others. He had the mules saddled and ready to go. He handed Jasper his sword, and the man kissed the blade before fixing it to his saddle.

"What's going on?" Ger asked. "I guessed there was something wrong. One moment, I'm playing with these cute little ones, the next, they're in ice blocks."

"No time to explain," said Jasper. "Let's get the eff out of here."

Where mules were perfect for carrying heavy loads over rough terrain, the downside of them was very obvious: they weren't bred for speed. The image of Jasper out ahead of the group, riding his mount as if in full gallop, while achieving little more than a trotting pace, would have been comical in any other situation. As it was, William once again felt terror at being in a kind of glacially slow danger over which he had no control.

They crossed the wide plain in what seemed an age and hit the rocky pass that would lead them back to Caligulari. They were three days from safety and would soon be pursued by angry green demons that could cross any terrain and even see in the dark. How the Moons and Stars were they going to get out of this one?

That the mules had struggled to get up speed on the flat of the plain was one thing, that they slowed further still, trying to pick their way down a steep stony track laden with a man in the saddle was another. "Enough of this. We're better off on foot," said Jasper. He dismounted and made quicker progress until he lost his footing and slid down a jagged section of rock. "Lord Sola on a cart!" he yelled. When Ridkin helped him stand again, he was shaking. William had never seen fear in the man's eyes before and found the effect contagious. He pushed the hollow feeling in his gut out of his mind and focused on the descent, one awkward step at a time.

An hour later, a noise like a swarm of arguing children came to them from further back along the trail. It had to be Janasà in pursuit. Moments after that, the first exploding axe landed not many paces behind the trailing William. Another one fell among the bushes off to his left and detonated like thunder.

"What devilry is this?" shouted Jasper. "Magic axes?"

"I think you'll find it's a simple natural reaction they've learned to harness," began William.

Jasper faced up to him, his face contorted with fear and rage. "For once in your pathetic life, shut the eff up!"

Ridkin pulled at his sleeve. "Jasper, we're wasting time. Come on."

William had to do something. Negotiate. That was it. There had to be something the Janasà wanted that he could offer. He turned around to look back up the trail as the leading pursuers appeared over the ridge. He waved at them to stop.

"What the…" said Jasper behind him.

The drooling, reddened face of Laddà was the first to come into focus. The little creature held up an arm and halted the chasing group. For a moment, nobody moved. William stepped forward to start the negotiation, just as an axe raced toward his head. Ridkin flattened him and the axe burst into flame a short distance further down the trail with a loud *thwock*.

Jasper grouped the four of them together and stood facing up the path with Big Ger at his side, swords in hand. Tears at the injustice of it all came into William's eyes. After everything he'd faced, all the threats on his life, the pain he'd experienced, the exhaustion he felt after such an emotional day and night, it was to end on a mountain trail with an axe exploding in his brain.

Jasper twisted his face to Ger. "Are you with me, friend?" he asked.

"Aye, to the end," replied Ger.

Both men stood forward, one foot in front of the other with swords pointing at the Janasà. "On three. One… Two… Woohoooo…" They were off and running at their pursuers.

~~~

John Scratchface looked down, hands on hips, from a hill overlooking the city of Ludnam, which, as usual, appeared to be drowning in its lake of smoke and fog. The last of the day lingered over the trees of Effing Forest, as if reluctant to miss whatever was about to happen next. A lone rider sped out from the Ludd Gate, a white standard in one hand and the gaudy crest of Ignatius Stackpole on his chest. Ah, the priest desired a truce, perhaps? He could desire what he wanted; The Earl of Ebury felt in no mood to give the city's remaining defenders time to organise themselves better.

"Ackroyd," he called. "Is there any news from the spies and scouts?"

Anthony Ackroyd scuttled up, his head bowing this way and that, a helmet perched between the antenna-like tufts over his ears. "Your Grace. Soldiers continue to desert the city in numbers. The only serious remaining resistance will come from the religious corp and the newly arrived mercenaries from Gallia."

The messenger reached them. "Your Grace," he said, bowing one knee before Ebury and the assembled nobles to either side. "I bear a message."
~~~

"No shit," said the Earl. "What else would you bear? Your donkey's arse?"

Guffaws of laughter broke out around him. The messenger handed a scroll of parchment to Ackroyd, who passed it to his master. Scratchface broke the seal and read aloud.

"To Lord John Scratchface, may his days always be long. I, King Ignatius, command you to lay down your weapons and bend the knee to me. If you agree to this, you may be permitted to live and to attend my coronation next Wigglesday."

"And there's a load of guff after that about how noble is House Stackpole. Have you ever heard of House Stackpole, Latimer? Anyone?"

To his right side, the young Earl of Stratfield, Sir Roger Latimer, sniggered. "Not I, my Lord."

Scratchface handed the parchment back to Ackroyd. "Draft me a letter, Anthony."

"Your Grace?" Ant motioned for a writing table and chair to be brought up and sat, quill in hand, expectantly.

"To Ignatius Stackpole, shriving upstart rantallion[76] of a priest, may your arse catch fire. Lord John Scratchface of Ebury notes your request and suggests you shove your coronation where the sun don't shine. There, that should do it."

Ackroyd finished the letter, added His Grace's seal and handed it to the messenger, who mounted and sped away back to the city.

"Tomorrow," shouted John. "I shall personally place the priest's shriving head on a pike. What say you all?"

The nobles cheered and chanted. "King John, King John, King John…"

~~~

William couldn't bear to watch Jasper and Ger get torn to pieces by the Janasà. He turned his head away and closed his eyes. Why then did everything go silent? He opened his eyes again. And opened them some more in surprise. Helena?
~~~

There was a sound like a whoosh and a crackle of fire. William scrunched his eyelids against the brightness of the light. When he next reopened them, the four of them were in the middle of a piazza in what he recognised as Caligulari. All of them were crouched with weapons in hand, facing a crowded market. Jasper continued his charge forward in full battle cry and sprawled, tripping over a stray dog. Ger stopped and helped Jasper up. Other than the dog, nobody showed the least sign of noticing them, or if they did, this was a regular occurrence.

"What the?" said Ridkin.

"I grew up around witches," said Jasper, dusting himself down. "I never picked Helena for one."

"Will, what happened?" Ridkin turned to William and repeated it louder. "WHAT JUST SHRIVING HAPPENED?"

"Yeah, Bookman, what *did* happen?"

It took a moment for William, still experiencing the tremors of several kinds of shock, to compose himself. He smiled inwardly at being the one they assumed would know. "I understand most of it. I think. See the tavern on the other side of the piazza? Give me some time. I'll meet you there when I'm ready."

He needed to get everything straight in his mind, so he passed out of the square and up an incline toward what looked like a ruined Truscan temple. The hill was steeper and longer than he'd expected, and he reached its crest out of breath and perspiring. What remained of the temple consisted only of discoloured and crumbling columns and a few shattered statues. He found a flat rock and sat facing back down toward the little fishing port and the Middle Sea beyond. In contrast to the events of the previous few hours, this was a picture of safe tranquillity. He felt the cool breeze on his face and breathed in the salt air. Just what he needed.

He didn't quite have all the pieces, and what he had was chaotic and difficult to organise. Starting with the simplest elements made the most sense. Not that much of anything about it was simple. He'd have to make some big assumptions in meshing it all together, but that felt justifiable.

The start of it all had been the jester, Feydor, and his witch mother's quest for a powerful crystal, the so-called Crystal of Life. They might have learned about it from the same grimoire as the one he'd come across in Gallia. But they'd masked this quest with another more innocuous one involving aphrodisiacal water and tasked himself, William, to carry it out. Only Jasper could explain how that was all supposed to work.

Based on what the maniac twins had said, Feydor had soon switched allegiance to the twins' mother, herself a witch, and it was she that had attacked him: once at sea, again in a dream, and a third time by capturing him in Trusca. Their aim had been to stop him from reaching Sardonica in any way they could, including torture and murder. The twins could then complete the quest for the crystal unimpeded. But, rather than killing him, they'd played out a sick game, hurting and leaving him to rot in a dungeon cell. What was worse, Morwena and two of Jasper's men had died trying to free him.

Meanwhile, Helena and Matilda had stumbled into the picture and become entangled in the whole mess. Helena, it turned out, was yet another witch and had kept the secret hidden from everyone, including her daughter, only revealing a part of the truth to William in Trusca, with disastrous results. Witches, it seemed, came along in threes. From what Helena had told him, her reluctance to reveal herself stemmed from having misused magic when she was little more than a child. He'd seen Matilda pushing against her mother and assumed it was normal. Was there more to it? Something to do with Matilda sensing important secrets withheld? He wasn't sure, but it could make sense.

How best to understand Matilda's part? She must have been carrying the crystal since before he'd met her. She'd toyed with her stones and crystals at the inn in Trotbury, using them to predict his and Ridkin's futures. Would she have played with something that important if she'd known its significance? He didn't think so. She had to have come to a realisation somehow later. One thing was clear: by the time he'd exited the caverns, she'd known. She'd even taunted the Queen of the Janasà with it. Why was she there at all? The only reason he could come up with was that she was intending to return the crystal to its home, which he assumed now was the plinth he'd banged his shin against in the caverns. How had she known any of that? Why had she changed her mind?

How best to understand his own part in it all? The Janasà clearly thought he was their Anointed One, the only being alive able to take the crystal from its cavern. A ridiculous notion, to be sure. Quite what the Janasà thought the crystal could do for them was unclear. It was a Crystal of Life, not of infinite power, unless there was something he was missing. In fact, pretty much everyone was ascribing fantastical powers to the little stone, powers that simply had to be imaginary, surely?

What had happened as he'd emerged from the caverns? The package he'd carried would have looked to an observer to have contained the crystal. Feydor had shown up at just the right moment to grab it, so he must have been such an observer. Somehow. That what he'd stolen from William was just shards of broken glass, while Matilda had been holding the actual crystal, was a delicious irony, worthy of the Grecan legends.

Why were the pieces of glass lying so close to where the crystal should have been? Someone must have tossed a glass vessel down a shaft at the surface and it had fallen a long way down into the cavern where it had shattered.

After Feydor had made his snatch, and when Queen Nannua had decided she'd been tricked by them, she'd ordered Jasper and himself to be executed, and Helena and the others sent into forced labour. Helena must have had no choice but to embrace her magic, to use it to save them all. Maybe in revealing herself, Helena had pushed Matilda over the edge. Instead of returning the crystal, she'd bolted like a smacked colt. Helena had then done what any decent mother would do. She'd tried to follow and make amends with her daughter. At least she'd taken the time to rescue them from the Janasà.

How had Matilda come to have the crystal in the first place? He recalled something he'd read in Ottavia's library, how a capricious spirit, whatever that meant, had taken it from the caves and lost it. That it could have ended up in the possession of a young woman in Anglonia was crazy, but just about credible. That the young woman had travelled alongside a man who, however unwittingly, was on a quest for this same crystal was an altogether different thing. How was such an epic happenstance possible?

His logical mind tried to find a reasonable explanation. *Could* it just be a simple confluence of events? The only simple thing about that was how ridiculous it was. No, he couldn't see it.

What other possibilities did that leave? A god-like being orchestrating events? Destiny? How would you tell the difference between the will of a god and destiny? They amounted to the same thing: what you did was decided by forces beyond your control and mere mortals like himself and Matilda had to make the best of it. Epictightus, the Stoic, would have loved it. But just supposing some external force had brought William and Matilda into the same place at the same time, there was still the big question of *why*.

Then another odd idea came to him. What if the *crystal* had made all this happen? Six months ago, he'd have rejected this out of hand, but now… now, having had to accept that reason couldn't explain everything, could he make a further leap into the unknown and also believe the crystal had the power to influence folk to do its bidding?

With his mind reeling at that thought like a child's spinning top, he picked himself up and made for the tavern.

It took well into the evening for him to explain everything to the others. Along the way, Jasper had filled in some of the missing details. Feydor, for whatever reason, had been double crossing everyone and had set in motion two quests for the same crystal. Jasper was convinced he'd been helping Mary and the twins and was therefore responsible for Morwena's death. That Jasper's own mother was no longer reachable made him suspect that Feydor or Mary or both had killed the woman. Mary and Imelda were cousins who'd always nursed a deep hatred for each other, and Feydor had a particular axe to grind in that Imelda had castrated him as a boy. Between them, she and Feydor would have had plenty of motives. In contrast, it was clear that Jasper worshipped the old witch and wasn't going to take her death lightly.

The tricky part of the conversation was William's theory about the crystal having a will of its own and using it to put William, Matilda, and everyone else on the same path. "It smells fishy as a cockle bed to me." Ridkin raised a finger. "First off, if it has its own powers, how did it get stolen away from under the noses of the cat? Second, how come Matilda didn't follow through and return it to the cavern?"

"The only way I can explain these things," said William, "is that the crystal can influence but not control us. Something happened to Matilda that made her choose to keep it for herself and that might have been to do with the ultimate discovery of Helena's secret. Of course, it could have been something else entirely."

"Where do you think Matilda is now?" asked Jasper.

"I don't know," said William. "Ridkin, you know her better than anyone. Did she really give you no hint about what was going on in her head?"

"None. I thought we was close. I thought she was my friend. Why would she hide all that from me?"

William put his good hand to Ridkin's shoulder, expecting it to be brushed away. How were you supposed to be reassuring without being intrusive? "I'm sorry," he said.

Regarding Ridkin, though, there was one thing about events underground that William couldn't make sense of. "Why did they line you up with Helena and Matilda, and not with Jasper and me? Could they not see you were male?"

The others went quiet.

"Ridkin," said Jasper. "Do you want to tell him, or shall I?"

"Tell me what?" asked an exasperated William.

There was a short silence, and then Ridkin spoke up. "My real name is Rondine. I'm a woman, Will. Female."

"Don't be ridiculous. You can't fool me so easily now, you know."

"No, straight up. I was born a girl."

"Wait… What?" He shook his head. "Nah, you're winding me up. A woman with… actual breasts?" He started to mime said breasts, then thought better of it.

"Those, yes. And all the other bits. Do I have to show you?"

"NO! Please don't!" his gaze slid from one face to the next, looking for inspiration. Ger smiled encouragingly. "It's just… a bit of a surprise. That's all."

"Does it change anything? Do you see me different now, like?"

William pondered that question. And decided it really didn't matter. "I don't see why I should. But… but why go to such lengths? Was it to hide from Travis and his crew?"

"Travis and the thousands like him, yeah. At first. Life is so much simpler if folk think you have a piece of skin hanging between your legs. A man has so many more choices. Mine, other than to marry, was to make a living on my back or run off to a convent. I'd make a bad mother, a terrible whore, and a worse nun. So that's how it started."

"And now?" William asked.

"Now? You know, it's become who I am. I'm comfortable as Ridkin. Rondine is inside me, a part of me, but that's all she is. Perhaps I'm the only woman who's ever felt this way. Don't matter. This is who I am, and I won't go back now."

"Actually." said William. "I could list off a dozen or so women from history who've done something of the sort[77]…"

~~~

Mary Grieve hobbled over to the shutter of her room and looked down at the town, castle, and sweeping river far below. After taking possession of Imelda's amulet from Stackpole's leering creep of a hard-man, she'd escaped here as the best place she could think of to hide in plain sight. From here she could plan her next moves undisturbed.

The deal she'd struck with Stackpole had worked out well. She'd told him in great detail how to neutralise Feydor and bring her the amulet. Sure, the priest hated magic as a sin against the gods, but he was a pragmatist. He'd seen the value of the arrangement and executed it to perfection. As for her promise to leave for Emeraldia, why ever would she do that? It'd taken her moments to work out how Stackpole had charmed the ebony box in which he'd placed the amulet, a charm that he must have thought would force her into exile. It was weak, tepid magic, the kind that a mere novice dabbler might have conjured up, and she'd brushed it aside in a moment. Pathetic!
~~~

Well, now she had the little black stone and everyone in the kingdom would soon know of her power. She'd start by erasing the priesthood and go from there.

Except it wasn't working out. She'd been unable to draw anything at all from it and she'd tried everything. Incantations, sacrifices, curses. Nothing worked.

Added to that, she felt exhausted. She collapsed back onto her cot, gathered her knees to her chest, and howled. This should be her moment of joy. She had everything she'd wanted. Well, not everything. She didn't have that Nurragù crystal thing, and she'd lost contact with Fraser and Irvine. Not that she worried too much about them. They often slipped out of sight, sometimes for months at a time. If they'd got the crystal for her, she'd have heard about it by now, so instead they must be lying low or enjoying themselves in some fleshpot or other. Bless their little black hearts.

Mite jumped up beside her and purred. She barely had the strength to reach up and stroke him.

The point was, Imelda was gone and nobody else could rival her in all of Anglonia. And right about now, the priesthood would be executing Feydor, and good riddance. So why did she feel so empty? Why hadn't Imelda's death filled her with unbounded joy? Instead, she ached in every muscle and joint of her body, and cold sweat ran down her face in rivulets. Sol's teeth. What was wrong with her?

~~~

Feydor the Fool padded across his cell floor, his feet waving in the air. As he went, a guard lobbed quail's eggs, which he caught with his mouth. Walking on his hands was good training in concentration, especially given his significant bulk.

"Do that back-flip thing again," said one of his guards. "Derrick hasn't seen it yet."

Feydor obliged, performing a series of flips from one side of the cell to the other.
~~~

"Stone the crows," said the guard, Derrick. "Never seen nothing like that."

There was a knock on the door. "Someone to see Mr Foolson." Keys tinkled, and the door clicked open. The guard called Jones entered Feydor's cell with a visitor.

"Hello Feydor," said the new arrival, "how have you been keeping?"

"Oh, mustn't grumble, Mr Travis," replied Feydor. "Although the décor could be better." He swept his hand around theatrically to point at the drab grey of the stone walls.

"Lovely jubbly. It's Walt. Call me Walt," said Travis. "Sorry for your situation."

"Do you have it with you, Walt?" asked Feydor.

"Straight to the point, eh Feydor? 'Course I've got it." Travis rummaged in the pockets of his cloak and pulled out a linen wrapped package, which Feydor grabbed in both hands.

"Thank the Stars!" said Feydor as he unwrapped the little butterfly brooch he'd given Travis for safe keeping. He nodded to Jones, who handed Travis a bag of coins.

"I can't accept it, Feydor. You've been a gent to me and my old mum. This one's on the house."

"Please yourself."

"Right, I'll be off. There's money to be made out there, what with food shortages and all." He clapped Feydor on the back. "Good luck with the execution! Looks like they're almost ready for you."

Feydor pinned the brooch onto his rough smock and felt a small surge of power flow from it. Sol's teeth, he was smart. Only *he* could have foreseen something like this and stored away a little magic for a rainy day.

He ushered the guards out of his cell. When the lock clicked shut, he smiled and tested his magic. A pair of squabbling ravens appeared from nowhere and flew around the room before vanishing again. Excellent. That conniving bitch Mary would never keep him down for long. Thinking of Mary, right about now, she'd be suffering the consequences of her actions. As yet another precaution, he'd poisoned his mother's amulet against her by fashioning an anti-charm, using the strand of her hair he'd collected after her disappearance. The more Mary tried to use the amulet, the sicker she would get. With his magic back, he'd track her down soon enough and recover it.

They'd scheduled his execution for that afternoon at four of the clock, and he expected Stackpole to preside over it in person. This was his chance for a huge show trial, a statement about his intent to rid the kingdom of magic and start a campaign to restore morality to all corners of Anglonian society. How insufferable! Feydor gripped the brooch. It would be a show trial alright, but not in the way the priest intended it.

Now where had Filthy gone? Not far away, he was sure. The little furball was pretty smart, too smart for Pyke to capture and burn him, at least. Filthy had an uncanny sense for human emotions and must have seen which way things were about to go.

His cell door opened up again and two guards stood there, ready with his chains. "Mr Ballache will see you now, Mr Foolson. If that's alright with you?"

"Oh, we mustn't keep my friend Arthur waiting. Lead on."

They showed him into Ballache's little dungeon and shackled him to the bench. "Afternoon Arthur," said Feydor. "How's it going?"

"Fine thank you, Mr Foolson. And yourself?"

"Tickety-boo, thank you. Call me Feydor, please. What shall we pretend to do today? The rack, hot irons?"

Blind Harry had been a fantastic asset to him during the last few days. The beggar had done all the things Feydor had asked of him, and more. This included procuring little luxuries and acting as Feydor's paymaster, settling all the bribes needed to ensure Feydor had a comfortable time. Thanks to such back-handers, Ballache now had new lodgings in a leafy part of the capital that his good lady wife loved. Gone were the days he and his family would need to skulk on the edge of town, shunned by popular society[78]. No, once the execution was done, he'd achieve his dream of showing wealthy tourists around the city.

He unshackled Feydor. "Let's do the rack today. If you'd care to lie down over here, please..."

Feydor obliged him and began screaming. "No please, don't do that... Agh!!! I beg you."

Ten minutes later, Ballache called for the guards, who returned to escort him to his cell.

"See you this afternoon, Arthur," said Feydor. "By the way, how do they plan to do it? Evisceration then beheading?"

"Pretty much. And they want me to burn your entrails[79] while you watch as well."

"How lovely! Well, just do your job and it will all go swimmingly."

It didn't matter. Feydor had zero intention of sticking around for the spectacle of his own gruesome execution.

~~~

The monkey known as Filthy had watched in fascination as the day unfolded. Many humans had just gathered below him. They now filled the little space outside the big building where they were keeping Red Top. They gave off smells of *unhappiness* and Filthy had the sense that they didn't want to be there. Surrounding them were more humans, these ones carrying pointy sticks.

A human was making throat noises while standing on something that Filthy might have called a *platform*, had he had a word for it. The other humans were all facing this human and making their own throat noises that sounded like what a monkey might think of as *laughing*[80].

The human he thought of as Red Top was led out of the *big building* and up onto the *platform*. There were big humans on either side of Red Top and on his arms and legs were long metal dangling things. Filthy had worn such things when he'd first been taken from his home. Filthy felt the familiar *empathy* for Red Top.

Standing near to Red Top was the nasty human with all the hair on his face. This was the one Filthy had bitten for trying to hurt Red Top. He felt something akin to *hatred* toward this human. Today, Hairy Face was *shouting* at Red Top while banging a heavy stick on the *platform*. Hairy Face was making a lot of noise about it. Every time he made a noise, the many
~~~

humans facing him made long, low-pitched throat noises. A good word for it might have been *booing*, but Filthy couldn't know that.

As Hairy Face's throat noises became louder, and the big stick banged even harder, Red Top lifted his arms. Filthy sensed what he understood to be *magic* coming from Red Top, however nothing else happened. Red Top tried again, and still nothing changed. Filthy sensed another emotion from Red Top that he interpreted as *fear*. Red Top had fear and a lot of it. The humans near Red Top cut away his clothes to reveal his strange hairless body covering, something a talking monkey would have called *skin*. They held a long metal object to Red Top's middle and Hairy Face made more throat noises. Red Top's fear hit a new level as he tried again to lift his arms.

Filthy felt the shape of his own sharp metal object, something he'd lifted from one of the humans earlier in the day. If he'd had a word for the thing, it would have been a *dagger*. He felt *comforted* to have this with him. He knew what to do.

Filthy swung down and executed a perfect dive at Hairy Face's head, plunging the *dagger* deep into one of his seeing holes. Hairy Face shrieked, made even more throat noises, and fell to his knees. He made another long throat noise, then collapsed onto his face. The many humans watching made huge throat noises and banged their hands together. They gave off smells of *happiness*. Filthy understood from this that they'd *wanted* him to kill Hairy Face.

The big humans released Red Top from his restraints and Red Top performed some impressive leaps, even at one point spinning upside down. The humans made even more *happy* throat noises.

Filthy felt good.

~~~

William awoke in a monk's cell in pitch darkness to a familiar scent. Helena? He'd dreamt of her more than once on the long journey home.

"Will, wake up."

"Is that you?" he asked.

"Yes. It's me."
~~~

She clicked her fingers, and a light hung in the air above them. She looked older, worried. "What's happening?" was the best he could think of at that moment. "What about Matilda?"

"That's where I've been, William. Trying to find her."

"She has the crystal, right?"

"She has the crystal, and she's a fast learner. For all my own power, I can't reach her. But I won't give up. She needs me."

"Are you alright?" he asked. "I thought you'd given up on me."

"Never. I feel better for seeing you. Hold me. Rock me to sleep."

She laid down on his cot and moved against him. There was quite a lot of rocking before they actually fell asleep.

During the night, William awoke from a dream and felt Helena's warmth beside him. He kissed her head. He thought of the day they'd met and Matilda's prophecy came back to him. Before his adventures, he'd never have given it any credit. Now, though, he wasn't so sure. What was it she'd said? He'd experience darkness before prevailing? She'd got that right enough. And there'd been something about making an important choice. Spot on. As for loving someone far away, he'd assumed at the time she'd meant his distance from Verity. Now it seemed Matilda had referred unwittingly to her own mother. Life was full of surprises.

As morning dawned and light fought skirmishes with the dust in the Gallian monastery room, William heard the bustle of monks preparing for their day and his three companions next door yawning off their slumbers. There was no Helena next to him, but she'd left a scrap of linen that smelt of her. He held it to his nose, breathed it deep into his lungs, then stuffed it down into his tunic. It didn't matter how long it took her to return to him again. He'd wait.

# ✦ Twenty ✦

William and his three companions reached Trotbury a little over five months after he and Ridkin had first met Helena and Matilda there. He'd not seen Helena since that night in Gallia, but had complete faith that she'd show up again at some point.

As they entered Ludnam, the four split into twos, with William and Ridkin bound for Eastminster palace and Jasper and Ger for a district known as Olde Ludnam Without. *Without what?*

"This is us," said Jasper. "Take care, Bookman. It pains me to say it, but you're not so effing bad after all. Goodbye Ridkin."

"There's one thing you might do for me," said William.

Jasper raised an eyebrow. "Go on."

"It's my guess your mother has or had a book just like the one I left behind in Nuorrù. Could you get it for me, please? You'll recognise it from all the coded sections."

"No promises, but I'll try. What do you want it for?"

"I still have questions to answer. Maybe I'll find the answers there. Maybe not. It's a precious thing, either way."

They all embraced. "So long now," said Jasper with a salute.

Feydor's role had expanded to cover all aspects of entertainment at court, and there was even talk of him receiving a knighthood from King John for his services. However, he was also taking a keen interest in the work of the Chief Inquisitor, something that allowed him to look out for signs of his mother's cousin Mary. Alas, so far there'd been no confirmed sightings, but he lived in hope.

"Mr Foolson, if it pleases you, there are two gentlemen at the main gate who say they have unfinished business with you." The page bowed low.

"Not now. I'm busy."

The man coughed. Boglets. Why was the pillock still there?

"They are most insistent."

"How tiresome," said Feydor, putting down his eyeglass. "Do these men have names?"

The page looked down at the tablet in his hand. "Uh, William of Coxwell and Ridkin Fairchild."

Feydor sat forward, interested. "Well, well. The great questing knight has returned. I wonder why."

"Master Foolson?"

"Have them brought here and let First Minister Crumbwell know as well. He will want to join us."

The page escorted William and Ridkin through the palace grounds and navigated the labyrinth of corridors and chambers that led to Feydor's working rooms. Off to his right, William caught the sound of a familiar thundering voice. From what William could make out, King John Scratchface was berating some young messenger. He smiled to himself, relieved to not be back in those shoes. From an adjoining passageway, they bumped into someone they recognised.

"Ant?" said Ridkin in surprise.

"You will address me by my title, Sir Anthony Ackroyd. Who, pray, are you?" He waved his palps around in front of him.

"It's me, Sir Ant. You remember me. Ridkin. And this is Sir William."

"I'm sorry?"

"Sir William of Coxwell? You sent us with a message to Ludnam."

"What? That was months ago. Last I heard, you'd gone to Italica. Why are you here?"

"We've come to meet the jester."

"Ah. Good luck with that. You must excuse me. I have things to attend to."

He backed off and scuttled away in the other direction, his antennae directed at some papers he was carrying.

"Sir William," said Feydor, on admitting William to his chambers.

"We know what you did. Everything."

"Everything? How nice for you." His voice turned to pure menace, his eyes narrowed into slits. "What do you expect to gain from coming here? Whatever you think I've done, you have no influence here. Do you not realise I could have you flogged and executed?"

The jester was correct, of course. The ridiculous man was unassailable, and William lacked the stomach for the improbable kind of legal battle that would change that in any way.

He held his distorted hand up to Feydor. "This is your doing. Along with at least three attempts on my life and the pointless death of many people, your sister included."

Feydor flinched at that last one. "If you say so. What of it?"

"You are untouchable, I know that. I just wanted to see your face when I accused you."

"And now you've seen it. If I were you, I'd get out while you still can."

First Minister Thomas Crumbwell entered the room. "Sir William of Coxwell, as I live and breathe."

William got straight to it. "I've brought the King his water. And I claim my reward."

Both men looked puzzled. "Water? What water?" asked Feydor.

"The King's aphrodisiac water. Do neither of you remember sending me on a fool's errand for it?"

"Oh, *that* water," said Crumbwell, looking less interested already. "Did you find any?"

"Well, yes and no."

Crumbwell raised an eyebrow. "Stop speaking riddles or be gone with you."

"We found the spring under the citadel of Nuorrù, but it doesn't produce an aphrodisiac."

The official feigned disappointment, shaking his head. "Oh dear. What a pity."

"The water *is* powerful, however, against warts. I wondered, I mean *we* wondered, whether King John could have a use for a cure for warts. I'm sure he'd be delighted with the results."

Feydor and Crumbwell looked at each other. Crumbwell sniggered. "You appear to have wasted your journey. King John has no warts that I am aware of."

"But what about his contract?" said Ridkin, pointing at William

"Contract?"

"This contract." William produced a roll of paper, somewhat the worse for having been immersed in the sea and stuffed down his britches for five months. He pointed to Crumbwell's signature next to his own.

Crumbwell smiled an oily, self-satisfied smile. "Did you not read the document, Sir William?"

"I did."

"Read it again. You will notice that the contract is void unless you produce the required aphrodisiac water. It says nothing about warts. We owe you nothing, and I will bid you a good day." He left the room, tutting as he went.

"There's a lesson for you," said Feydor. "Never trust a lawyer." He turned to the page. "These gentlemen were just leaving. Be sure they find the exit."

~~~

Once outside, Ridkin asked William, "What are we going to do now? And why are you smiling?"

"I expected that reaction, but I thought I'd at least try to do the right thing."

He scratched at his now full beard, gratified it was no longer the apology for facial hair that it had been five and a half months earlier. "Who might pay good money for an impossible curative for warts?"

"Um. Apothecaries?"

"I'm thinking of another group. Who would pay proper good *gold* coin for it? Think about it."
~~~

"Dunno. I give up."

"An alchemist. All we have to do is find one with bad warts and demonstrate the water. They'll be fighting over it."

Ridkin snorted. "Sounds like tosh to me. Why would alchemists have more warts than anyone else?"

"Let's just give it a go. What have we got to lose? We've scarcely any money left and no jobs."

Brimstone Gardens was where the alchemists lived and worked. Such was the risk of fire that each building stood several paces from the next, and the entire street, twenty paces from any other. They spent the afternoon knocking on doors and meeting a variety of men dressed in long, heavy leather aprons. After being sent away a dozen times, they hit gold, so to speak. At the thirteenth door, a plain but pleasant young woman answered.

"Hi, I'm Sir William Coxwell. Does anyone on the premises suffer from warts?"

The woman smiled. "That's neither the best nor the worst courtship offer I've heard."

"Um…"

She laughed, "Since you ask, yes, come in."

She showed them into a parlour and called out, "Father, gentlemen to see you. One of them says he's a sir something or other."

William could have hugged the old man that shuffled through from the back room. Except he didn't want to catch a disease. The man's face was a mess of burns, lumps... and warts. "Well?" he asked.

"Let me handle this, Will," said Ridkin. "It's like this, sir. Supposing we had in our possession a curative that could provide some relief for you?"

"Relief? Relief for what?" asked the man.

"Relief for…" Ridkin looked around at William and the man's daughter, his expression one of confusion.

William produced the Janasà flask, ready to dab some water onto the old man's face.

His eyes lit up. "Is that what I think it is? Of Janasà origin?"

"It is," said William, puzzled.

"Their glass has the most wonderful properties. Can I buy the container from you?"

They emerged onto the street carrying thirty pieces of gold. Ridkin had negotiated an extraordinary sum, handed the vessel over, and had watched fascinated as the old alchemist tipped its contents out of the window.

William and Ridkin burst into tears of laughter. "Did you see his face?" asked Ridkin.

"What face? I couldn't see one for the warts." They both collapsed into giggles again.

"What now Will?"

"You take half of this and find your family. I'll take the rest and head for Ebury. I'm going to buy out Verity's indemnity."

"You don't mean…"

"No. I can't marry her. I love Helena. When you've tasted ambrosia, you don't want rose water, do you?"

"Whatever ambrosia is. But…"

"Yes?"

"I'm coming with you. Don't go thinking I like you, mind, or anything soppy like that, but someone has to keep you out of trouble."

They shook hands, then embraced where they stood in the street with passers-by having to step around them.

~~~

Feydor slunk back to his rooms after a lengthy session with King John, whose stamina, while commendable, was also, in Feydor's view, deplorable. Where did the man get his energy from? He hummed a merry galliard, his mood light and optimistic, thanks to a sighting of a witchy looking woman in Northnimbia that sounded promising. He'd get that amulet back from her, one way or another.

He slumped into his favourite chair.

"Good afternoon, brother," said an icy voice from the other end of the room.
~~~

"Boglets, who's that?" He knew full well who it was. He'd been expecting this visit to come sooner or later.

Jasper sat toying with a hunting knife. "I've just been to the Castle and Ball."

"Find much?" asked Feydor.

"Nothing. Which is the whole effing point. Did you have anything to do with Morwena's death and mother's disappearance?"

He'd changed his mind a dozen times about how to play this conversation. There was no easy option. He caught sight of Filthy moving crab-like in stealth mode across the wall above and behind Jasper and went for the scapegoat approach. "It was Mary. It was all her doing. I was but a victim in her designs."

"Liar, liar, britches on fire. Here's the interesting thing. Somebody fed her information. Somebody told her where William would be and set us up for an ambush. And Mary couldn't have taken mother on without somebody's help. I think I might be looking at that somebody."

Filthy was getting closer. He had a dagger clenched between his teeth.

"I don't know what you mean," said Feydor, attempting his best look of injured innocence.

The monkey tensed for attack. This was about to get interesting.

THE END

# Preview of Witch Hunt, the second novel in the Fool's Journey series

Alberto climbed the stairs and entered the Abbott's study, taking care to adjust his appearance and compose himself.

"Come in, my son," said the old man beckoning, his once clear, baritone voice now weak and wavering. Hunched over his desk, he looked but a shadow of the man Alberto had always known. The young monk stood and waited, surprised at the disarray he found. *An ordered life is an ordered soul*, the Abbott had always preached. But today, his desk swarmed with unruly papers, documents, and open books that appeared as though scrambling over themselves like weeds in search of virgin soil to infest. However, at the centre of the chaos, in a clearing of its own, sat a book. The man tapped its cover, staring unfocused into the near distance. Seeming to gather his thoughts, he cleared his throat and spoke, his voice now more level and precise. "Alberto, I believe you to be the most diligent among our order. I have a task of the utmost importance that I no longer trust myself to perform." He fixed Alberto with a steady gaze. "And I confess, it carries some amount of danger. Nevertheless, it has to be done. I can depend on you, can I not?"

Alberto cringed. "But… I'm just…" He looked imploringly at the older man, who gazed back, an eyebrow raised in expectation. Alberto swallowed. "I am surely unworthy, Reverend Father. Some of the others are more…" he groped for the right word. "Robust?"

"Do you not trust my judgment, Alberto?"

"Of course I do, Reverend Father. Always."

"Hmm. You know, I see something of myself as a younger man in you. I observe an inner strength that perhaps you yourself cannot see. You *are* the right man for the task." The Abbott sighed again, looking down at the book. "I'm sorry. The truth is, we are about to be visited by… by evil, and I fear I won't see the end of this day."

"That can't be so, Reverend Father. You have many years in your bones, yet."

The Abbott lifted his head to look at Alberto. Was that a tear in his eye? "Alas not. The truth is I have failed, my son. I committed the sin of pride, and I must now pay the price. The fate of so many now rests in your care."

Alberto blinked and frowned. "Reverend Father?"

The Abbott peered down at the book before him, then picked it up. It was a thick volume, bound with what appeared to be faded animal skin. He held it in one hand and brushed the cover with the other, a light frown of something like regret written on his face. "I didn't destroy this abomination while I had the chance." He turned his gaze back to Alberto. "Now you must burn it in the hottest fire you can find and scatter the ashes. If you fail, they will get their hands on it, and I can barely imagine the harm that will result."

"*They*, Reverend Father?"

The old man's answer came out as little more than a whisper. "The witches." He slowly stood to embrace Alberto. One unshaven cheek, then the other scraped against his own. The man smelt unwashed, a sin against the purity of the Sun God.

Shouts came from outside. Alberto rushed to the open shutters and peered down at a dozen or more soldiers, some with dogs, gathered below. "Open up in the name of Duke Cosimo. Open up, I say!"

"So soon?" said the Abbott, his eyes widening in alarm. "Quick. Leave this place, my son. Use the old tunnel. Fair thee well and may Sol light your path."

Moments later, someone smashed through the ancient outer doors and more shouting came from the hall below. "Where is the Booke of Tales? Yield it now and no-one need die."

Alberto took the book. "You can depend on me, Reverend Father! Until we meet again." He stashed it under his cassock and scurried down the back stairs leading toward the dormitory block. The shouts of soldiers and of his brothers came from the direction of the main hall. A man screamed.

"Where is it? Hand it over."

"Please, gentlemen, we have a library full of fine books. Let me show you." That was the voice of his friend Francis, the librarian. He winced at the dull thud that followed, hoping against hope the big, amiable man was alright. Hurrying through the larger of the dormitories, he arrived in the tiny prayer room at the back and brushed aside a layer of rushes to expose a trap door. It would lead him to the tunnel that ran below the building and out toward the river, where he hoped he'd find the boat hidden close to the water.

The trap yielded easily enough, but not without the iron hinges whining at the unfamiliar movement. Damp, stale air plumed out. His fear of confinement made him recoil, but there was no option but to descend. Easing himself backwards into the opening, he took the first few rungs, hoping the woodworm riddled timber would sustain his bulk. Five steps down, he reached to pull the trap closed, but it slipped from his grip and slammed into place with a deafening *thwack*. The darkness closed in tight around him. Curse his clumsiness!

When his soles at last touched rough earth, he turned and pushed ahead as fast as he dared, groping his way forward, with one hand running along a wall. Frightened of stumbling, he lifted his feet high with each step; it would look comical if anyone could see it. Rounding a corner, his feet sloshed through water that reeked of stagnation. Cloying spider webs snatched at his face, and a sandaled foot caught on a root. He tumbled forward, gashing his knee and grazing his palms. As he dragged himself upright, someone heavy and awkward landed some distance behind. A man fired off a curse at the Moons and Stars before calling up for a torch. Alberto stumbled on.

A hundred paces further, the tunnel ended with a rough timbered grate jammed in place through which narrow shafts of sunlight picked out motes of dust. He pushed hard against it. Nothing budged, other than a sprinkling of loose dirt that fell from the roof. He turned his shoulder and leaned his full weight into it, his feet groping for leverage. The pounding footsteps of several panting men echoed closer. He *had* to get through. He cried out, pushing his knees to the limit, the wood resisting until at last it groaned and, with a loud crack, gave way. Staggering out-of-control and falling backwards into dazzling daylight, his head thudded against something hard. He sat up, dazed. He'd collided with an upturned boat. Ramming the grating closed, he dragged over a section of rotting tree trunk, wedging it in place as best he could. It might buy him the time he needed.

The river ran as expected a few yards away. Perfect. The boat slid over the grass as he yanked it to the water's edge, brushing off a coating of twigs and leaves. A little effort righted it, and a long pole fell to the ground. He took it, placing it on the flat bottom of the boat along with the book, then bent to lower the boat into the water, stepped in, and picked up the pole. He'd seen men doing this before, so it couldn't be all that hard, could it? Standing at the blunt end, he used the pole to push the pointy end out into the flow, keeping his weight low to maintain balance. It worked. So far, so good.

He leaned into a punt, but the pole tangled in the reed bed, twisted, and, despite his frantic efforts, tore itself from his grip as though it were a live snake. It made an agonising, almost mocking, slide past his flailing finger ends, splashing just out of reach in the shallows. Curse the Sun, Moons, and Stars above. Why had he been born so useless? Now he'd have to sit and drift downstream, praying to whatever gods remained who still gave a damn about his fate.

It hadn't rained in months, and the river had no particular reason that day to rush anywhere, certainly not on his account. The breezeless, humid air pressed in around him, making him sweat all the more. His fists bunched. How dare the birds chirp and squawk as though nothing were happening? He looked back to see the first man bursting from the tunnel. More joined him. His sense of panic rose a notch. He thrust his cupped palms into the water and frantically shovelled them backwards. It made no difference. *Come on!*

Something made him raise the book and stare at the odd cover. By Sol's teeth, how could this ghastly thing be so important? It felt like skin to the touch. Disgusted, he dropped it, and watched it fall open at a painting of a leering tree demon. The monster pointed an accusing twig-like finger at him, as though he'd already failed. Horrified, Alberto kicked it away, and vowed that if Lord Sola saved him now, he'd dedicate his life anew to simple worship and abstinence.

The boat snagged on a low branch near the far bank and stuck fast in a tangle of twigs. Behind him, men and hounds began wading out to reach him. He froze, his hands shaking, seeming to belong to someone else. An arrow whizzed over his head, jolting him into action. He couldn't give up without at least trying. Jumping where it ran shallowest, he sploshed to the bank, the book held aloft. Staggering onto dry ground, he scanned for a break in the trees. There! He sprinted for it, one arm flailing behind, the other clutching the book tight to his chest.

How ill-suited was he for flight? He lumbered along, cursing his sinful gluttony, with his wet and heavy wool cassock slapping against his shins. In no time at all, his breath came in gasping heaves, and his thighs begged for relief. His aching body begged him to stop, to take the easy way out, and hand over the book, but he just couldn't. There had to be a way out of this.

But wait, weren't there caves somewhere hereabouts? That was the answer. He spurred himself on. Ah. But could he find them? Unlikely. *Think man, think!* A few dozen staggering, laboured steps further on, and too exhausted to lift his dragging feet, he staggered forward. His toes caught in his ridiculous habit, and he rolled over. He wasted time and strength in righting himself. Come on! He *had* to escape.

The baying hounds sounded closer. A distant bell tolled. And just as he lost all hope, his exhaustion mounting, he found his prayers at last answered. Lord Sola had not forsaken him. Where his path intersected another, a tall, bearded, fair-haired man ambled along on an old white nag, deep in reverie and oblivious to the drama unfolding around him. Alberto recognised him at once as the mild-mannered Anglonian knight and scribe, a thoughtful man. Could he trust him? Did he have a choice? He reached up and, with intense relief, pressed the book into startled hands.

"Sir William, please, I beg you. Take this accursed thing and burn it in the hottest fire. Scatter the ashes. There are men behind ready to kill for it. Some brothers may have already died. Let their deaths and mine not be in vain."

"W-What?" stammered the man, juggling the book between his hands like a hot turnip.

Alberto was off and running again. "Go! Keep it from *them,*" he called over his shoulder. "The witches. And may Sol light your path."

Re-energised by his sense of relief, he ran up the track, shouting to draw the pursuers on, and leaving the Anglonian to escape. He hoped this William would complete the Abbott's instructions and destroy the book. Alberto had heard it said he was a decent man.

---

[1] The mythology in this book is loosely based on the Sardinian tales of the Janas, sometimes pronounced yanas or yanasa. Depending on the region of Sardinia, these can be tiny or as big as a goblin. In Sardo, the Unesco recognised Sardinian language, words that end with a are feminine and those that end u are masculine. I have added accents to the end of most of the names for no particular reason other than I like the percussive sound it gives the words.
[2] Ebury castle is based on the actual medieval castle at Ludlow in England.
[3] If this were really based in Medieval England, the cook and pretty much everyone else working directly for a lord would be male. Women were largely confined to working in the laundry (sorry!), although this began to change after the Black Death wiped out half the population and willing workers became more in demand.
[4] Medieval castles had holes in the walls called garderobes which functioned as toilets. The waste would either run down the walls into the mote or down a shaft where it was collected by so-called gong farmers. The smell can only be imagined. Sometimes a castle was whitewashed to protect the stone from weathering and the brown stains on that from the waste must have looked lovely.
[5] Contrary to what most people think, almost nobody in the Middle-Ages doubted that the earth was a sphere.
[6] I grew up near the villages of Little Coxwell and Great Coxwell in modern Oxfordshire. Strangely, even as a teenager, I never noticed the name Coxwell might have a possible alternative spelling and meaning.
[7] Gong farmers had the enviable position of clearing the castle and its moat of toilet waste.
[8] Syphilis and Gonorrhoea as well as any number of milder infections were common in the later Middle Ages at all levels of society. These diseases were collectively known as The Pox.
[9] Mubble fubbles: The OED actually defines this word as "A state of depression or melancholy; despondency, low spirits" and dates back to the 1500s. I've altered its use in this novel to mean something like "darn it" or "damnations".
[10] Ginnel is still part of modern northern dialect and means alleyway.
[11] The wandering womb was a real doctrine widely believed since antiquity. A woman's womb was held to be responsible for her many ills. For example, a severe headache might indicate the womb trying to climb through her neck to

attack her brain. It was further believed that, without regular "massage", a womb could cause disturbances of the mind. You couldn't make it up.

[12] Irrespective of gender, Verity's class as an indentured serf or villain wouldn't normally be taught to read unless they were high class or part of a religious order. In fact it was illegal to teach peasants to read, except under special circumstances.

[13]Serfs during much of the Middle Ages across most of Europe were tied to the land owned by a local lord who could place many restrictions on what a man and his family could do. This included the power to choose who the peasant's widow or daughters must marry. It was possible for villains to buy their freedom to become freemen, through a Charter of Manumission, although this would have likely required a 3rd party to make the payment since the lord owned everything the peasant had. Hence Verity is asking for the money to buy this freedom. In England, after the black death of 1349, many aspects of serfdom went into decline, and it became more common for tied peasants to up and move to a town to find paid employment. The main exception to this was the monastic estates that operated a more draconian bureaucratic policy.

[14] The kitchens tended to be in a separate building from the main keep to avoid the risk of fire spreading. As chimneys became a thing, they stopped separating them out.

[15] Court records from the time are horrifyingly full of instances of clerics taking advantage of the young women in their employ and getting them pregnant. The records tell of the punishments handed out to the women concerned, but we must assume, or perhaps at least hope, that the men concerned were held to account behind closed doors.

[16] Tallow catch is a phrase from Shakespeare that he applies to Falstaff, a portly gentleman much like Feydor. Tallow is the rendered fat from beef or lamb.

[17] The monkey's name Filthy Mote is a reference to a Star Wars character called Salacious B Crumb, a monkey jester in the court of Jabba the Hutt. It was quite common for jesters to have a monkey as a pet.

[18] The jester was often the only person at court who could safely mock or gainsay the king. Indeed, the jester's hat or coxcomb was intended to imitate the crown of a king. Although many of them were "natural fools" that is to say simpletons kept at court for charity or, unfortunately, mockery, it was not unknown for them to be highly articulate and intelligent. The examples I cite of jesters that Feydor reveres are based on actual historical figures (although I changed the names.) Note that noble women as well as men often kept fools for entertainment and such jesters could be female. A good jester was very well paid and had a status not unlike modern day celebrities.

[19] The idea of Feydor's room being decorated with phalluses isn't entirely silly. Penises, and indeed, vulvas, can be found on the walls of churches dating back to medieval times – check out "penis tree" in Google. Then again, don't. Better instead to lookup Eleanor Janega's videos on medieval sex.

[20] The groom of the stool was an actual role at court in the late medieval and Tudor periods. It involved helping the king to poo, checking his output, consulting medics about what it meant and so on. The position was filled by high nobles and highly coveted, giving as it did, closer access to the King than any other courtier could attain. You can't make this stuff up.

[21] The tapered shoes of men of high status came into fashion late in the 15th century. These shoes were called "crakows" or "poulaines" and the length of the tips became so exaggerated that King Edward VI passed a law limiting their length to two inches. I refrained from referencing cod pieces in the book because I think, as comedic devices go, it is somewhat overdone.

[22] Don Creosote is based on Don Quixote which was actually published somewhat later than the medieval period in 1605. I take a few liberties with timing in this book.

[23] The process of tanning, or softening of leather, was done using human waste. Urine, for example, would be left to ferment for up to six weeks before being used. The job of a gong farmer was to collect this waste from ditches around habitations and bring it to the tanneries. It's hard to imagine how bad this must have smelt.

[24] If you visit Hampden Court, you can see Henry VIII's Chamber of Easement.

[25] Jane Fool was the name of Anne Boleyn's personal jester, and, like the Jane I describe, was a natural fool – someone who'd possibly suffered a head injury at some point and had been adopted as a fool by someone wealthy. It was common for queens to have their own jesters and other entertainers as part of their entourages.

[26] The normal path to knighthood required a boy from a noble family to become apprentice in another household, learn the various skills, become a squire to a knight and then finally after many years to be knighted. A King did, however, have the authority to bestow knighthood for services rendered.

[27] Paper was invented in the far east well over a thousand years before the medieval period, but only gradually spread through Europe from the 11th century. The first English paper mill was established in Hertford in 1490. It therefore existed, but would not have been common during the period in which the story is roughly set.

[28] A letter of passage was a normal requirement for anyone travelling between countries and was somewhat akin to a passport.

[29] Pen and ink = stink in cockney rhyming slang

[30] It wasn't unusual to punish children as adults. There are court records of animals being tried and punished for crimes. And there was even a dead pope who was exhumed, tried, and beheaded. In any case, the concept of childhood is a relatively modern one.

[31] It's a myth that people had bad teeth in the Middle Ages. Today, refined sugars and soft processed food mean that a child's teeth are unlikely to form evenly and be free from caries.

[32] Brass is a northern expression for money. Lower value coins used to be cast with this metal.

[33] They didn't generally use plates. Trenchers were a thick type of bread that you ate along with whatever was spread on top.

[34] Witch hunts were not actually a thing until very late in the Middle Ages. In general, the church tried to guide people away from a belief in magic, but considered it largely harmless. Witch hunts started early in the Tudor period and became more common in the 16th and 17th centuries.

[35] The cockney rhyming slang expression To take a butcher's means to take a look. Rhyming slang only appeared in English in the 19th Century, but I include several such phrases in the book to represent London dialect.

[36] Mum's the word - Modern London slang for I won't tell anyone.
[37] The reference to The Ludnam Bridge is obviously London Bridge. During the Middle Ages, there was only one bridge across the Thames, known as The London Bridge. It had houses, shops and even, at one point, a church on it, and was almost impassible with traders and traffic. In fact, in general, the whole city was heavily congested. Some things never change. Other bridges across the river only appeared in the 16th and 17th centuries. People mostly used little row boats called wherries (pronounced werris) as a kind of taxi across the river Thames.
[38] Mary's cat is called Mite which was a common name for cats in the Middle Ages. Well bred imported cats were an expensive status symbol in Medieval Europe.
[39] Go to siege is an actual medieval expression for emptying the bowel.
[40] The Big Black Cow is the name I give to the ship that William and the others take for Gallia. I got the name from a Steely Dan song of the same name.
[41] Captain Dogwash I got from Captain Pugwash, a children's animation show from the 1960s. There is a long standing urban myth that the names of the crew of the ship The Black Pig were all suggestive - Seaman Staines, Master Bates, and so on. This has been fully refuted by the makers.
[42] The Via Frangipani is actually based on the Via Cartigena, which was an important section of the main pilgrim route from France through to Rome.
[43] It's hard for someone from an English-speaking country to understand the variations in dialect in Italy. In one small town in Sardinia, I discovered that you could tell whether someone grew up at the top of a hill or the bottom based on tiny differences in dialect. Dialects in Sardinia are especially distinctive based on region, with the ancient Etruscan based Sardo being the official Unesco recognised language, but many provinces having their own Latin-based dialect. It's not unusual even today for someone from, say Alghero on the East coast of Sardinia, to be unable to understand someone from Oristano near the West coast, except through standard Italian or English.
[44] Every region of Italy has its own take on Italian food with vastly different recipes for what is essentially the same dish. Heated arguments can ignite over whether to make risotto with butter or olive oil.
[45] I call out in this chapter the bureaucracy of Italica. In reality, this is a relatively modern phenomenon that comes partly from a public job creation frenzy that existed when the country flirted with communism, and partly from attempts to make it hard for the mafia and corruption to operate. Either way, it renders the population miserable.
[46] Uranus wasn't identified until 1690. Bear with me on this one.
[47] It was common during the Middle Ages for nobles to offer hospitality to travellers almost as a moral duty and a way of earning credit in the final judgement. I'm taking this very Christian tradition and assuming it applies in my world.
[48] The ridiculous belief that lustful women were the source of all evil predated Christianity, being first written about in ancient Greece. The church in Europe was only too happy to conflate such ideas with story of Eve's "fall", however.
[49] Modern Italy is horrible for taxes and fines. Every tiny infraction of a regulation requires the culprit pay a fine.

[50] There is plenty of evidence for eunuchs providing sexual services going on at different points in history. They were used to pleasure wealthy men in some eastern harem cultures while women got in on the act in 16th and 17th century Europe when castration might be done to preserve a certain quality of singing voice. As regards the story, according to my research, eunuchs, if castrated after early childhood, can 'perform' sex. I have found records of bored noble women starved of attention, who might avail themselves of a eunuch without the risk of difficult to explain pregnancies arising. To my knowledge, there is no evidence for this in the medieval period.

[51] The medieval church had a curious attitude to sex that conflicted directly with generally held beliefs. Sex was something that should only be done with the direct intention to create children, and the bare minimum of pleasure should be experienced. The widely held belief however was that only by orgasming could a woman conceive. (This latter idea meant women could have an especially hard time proving rape; if a child resulted from the act, the woman must have enjoyed it, therefore it wasn't rape!! ☹) In reality, the written record suggests medieval folk were having a lot of sex of a variety not dissimilar to modern peoples.

[52] The pressing torture involved placing a rock on the ground and laying the victim over it facing up. Then they would place a board over the chest and heavy weights onto the board. Then they would leave them for hours like that. Sometimes multiple ribs would break, puncturing a lung and eventually killing. This is the origin of the expressions such as I'll have to press you for an answer, a pressing engagement, and so on.

[53] I once heard a Yorkshireman say I'm from Yorkshire. We don't do excitement.

[54] Most medieval towns had a name like this. Shite Brook would literally be a channel through which effluent was conducted away from a town. Later periods would rename them to less offensive versions, like shire brook, although there is still a stream called Shit Brook in existence in Much Wenlock in the UK. They were pretty direct in what they called things, including their red light districts.

[55] The wealthy had the means to communicate long distance at speed via relays of horseback messengers.

[56] The Colosseum in Rome was originally named the Flavian Amphitheatre, making reference to the Flavian dynasty during which it was constructed. The modern day name is believed to relate to the colossal statue of the Emperor Nero that he had erected in front of it.

[57] In the medieval period, many buildings still had marble facades. The marble was taken off them in the 16th century by the catholic church and used to decorate the Vatican.

[58] A simulation of a full naval battle supposedly took place in the colosseum, although whether actual water filled the floor of the arena is very much up for debate. It would certainly have been before extensive underground passageways were added as a kind of backstage area.

[59] Rome was built on and around seven hills, the most famous of which were the Palatine and Aventine. Ovaltine, however, is a malted beverage available in the UK.

[60] This is essentially a description of the Klementium national library in Prague.
[61] I based the idea of the priesthood controlling (and profiting from) prostitution on the historically documented Bishop of Winchester in Southwark, London. In 1161, the bishop was granted many powers, including that he could licence (and profit from) prostitutes, which became known as Winchester Geese. To be bitten by a Winchester Goose meant to catch a venereal disease.
[62] In later periods, it became quite a thing for touring couples to visit the Colosseum at night. I don't know whether it happened in medieval times, but why not?
[63] The Romans used concrete long before it became common in much more recent times. William probably wouldn't know what it was. There are still apartment blocks to be found in Rome that were built and occupied 1800 years or more ago. Some of them are in pretty good condition, although, as far as I know, they are preserved monuments and not in use today.
[64] These are the words to John Dowland's In Darkness Let Me Dwell although the words are based on a poem by John Caprario. There is an excellent version by Sting and Edin Karamazov which is worth checking out. It's deliciously dark and perfectly captures my idea of how Imelda would have felt after losing her daughter. I'm messing with the centuries here in that Dowland was a contemporary of Shakespeare and both lived somewhat after the late medieval period on which the book is very loosely based.
[65] Bleeding pretty much was first (and second) aid in the Middle Ages
[66] Malaria was endemic to much of southern Europe in the Middle Ages, including Sardinia and was thought to be due to the bad airs from swamps. Treatments could include herbs, bloodletting, and even trepanning (drilling holes in the skull).
[67] The Nuraghe are thousands of stone structures on the island of Sardinia that date back to neolithic times. Nothing is known of the culture that built them, although they did leave a rich record of artefacts.
[68] Cork trees can grow with lesions in their bark that look like human wounds. Google it.
[69] The lunar valley in Galluria in northern Sardinia is a spectacular area to visit. Overall, the description of the island I have given is based on an early 20th century account by a traveller who visited much of the island. It was a discouraging mix of jungle and swamp. The dense coverage of trees has mostly disappeared since those times and the island has become arid and poorer for it.
[70] One prevalent myth on the island of Sardinia is that there are two chests (sometimes two boots), one of which contains treasure, and the other contains either a swarm of flies or a single huge fly, the size of a boar. A traveller when confronted by these two options must select one - if they pick incorrectly, the island will be destroyed by the fly/flies - the Musca Macedda – literally butcher fly/flies. The idea of the crystal is entirely my own invention.
[71] The myrtle is an important plant on the island of Sardinia, where they make a liqueur from its berries. It's almost impossible to avoid being given some when you visit the island.

[72] The spiral motif has shown up in the art of many neolithic European societies. It must have had widespread significance.
[73] This is an actual cheese found in Sardinia today called casu marzu. Technically illegal, almost everyone there knows someone who can get hold of some for you. If you are brave enough.
[74] I couldn't resist this joke. The original is "He's not the messiah, he's just a very naughty boy." From the Life of Brian.
[75] The eternal enigma cited here is an actual example of a Buddhist Koan, an unanswerable question designed by a master to enlighten a student, such as what is the sound of a single hand clapping?
[76] The OED defined a rantallion as someone whose scrotum is longer than his penis.
[77] There's plenty of evidence for women assuming male identity during the Middle Ages, and this was even celebrated in literature. Check out the 13th century Roman de Silence in which a woman assumes male identity in order to inherit her father's lands. My favourite documented example is St Marinas the Monk who was born female, but was accused of having fathered a child with a local woman. Rather than demonstrate her true sexuality, Marinas chose to leave his order and raise the child as the apparent father. Once the child was old enough, he returned to the order. Check out https://en.wikipedia.org/wiki/Marina_the_Monk.
[78] Torturers and executioners were well paid, but they and their families were shunned as being bad luck. They typically lived at the edge of town and folk gave them a wide berth.
[79] They eviscerated and burned the entrails of traitors while forcing them to watch. I couldn't make this up.
[80] Recent evidence has come to light that travelling minstrels were often very much like modern standup comedians. I'm imagining here that such a minstrel is being used as a warmup act for the main event.

## A Brief Thank You From the Author

Thank you so much for investing a slice of your precious time in reading my novel. It means a lot to me when people do that rather than A MILLION other things they could be doing. Please be sure to sign p to my newsletter at http://www.stevegrantauthor.com for updates on all things foolish. If you have just a few more minutes to spare, I'd seriously love to hear from you directly via any of the following links:

Website: http://www.stevegrantauthor.com
Email: info@stevegrantauthor.com
Instagram/Threads: @stevegrantauthor
Facebook: https://www.facebook.com/StephenGrantAuthor

Please let me know what you liked, didn't like, and what you'd love to see in future episodes of the series. Or anything that comes to mind – just write!

And thank you again!

*Steve*

Published in Great Britain in 2023 by Feydor Publishing



Cataloguing in Publication Data is available from the British Library

# Acknowledgements

I would like to thank my many Italian friends for having persuaded me to embark on this project. In particular, Gio, Giulia, Massimo, Carlotta, Ugo and Alessandro.
I must also thank my ever-patient lady wife for having tolerated my indulgence for the 18 months it has taken to write this. Without her, I wouldn't be who I am today.
Special thanks to the amazing writing coaches who helped me at different stages of my journey, Max Gorlov and Benn Brown.
Cover Art was done by Faith Grant and the cover layout by Gio Quarantini.
Internal formatting Steve Grant and Gio Quarantini.
Line editing and sense checking was by Jordan Ashley Editing

My historical sources are too innumerable to list in full, but I have to give a particular shout out to the following:
*Medieval Horizons: Why the Middle Ages Matter* - Ian Mortimer
*The Time Traveller's Guide to Medieval England: A Handbook for Visitors to the Fourteenth Century* - Ian Mortimer
*The Once and Future Sex: Going Medieval on Women's Roles in Society* - Eleanor Janega
*A Travel Guide to the Middle Ages: The World Through Medieval Eyes* - Anthony Bale
*The Very Secret Sex Lives of Medieval Women: An Inside Look at Women & Sex in Medieval Times* - Rosaline Gilbert

# About the Author

Steve Grant is a retired IT professional living in the county of Berkshire in the UK with varying numbers of children, grandchildren and dogs. He is married to an extraordinary, if shrinking, woman and is blessed in too many ways to count. They share a keen interest in all things Italian, having visited the country frequently and having spent countless holidays in the town of Castelsardo in Sardinia.

His preferred genre for reading is crime, particularly the work of Ian Rankin, Donna Leon, Peter Robinson, Andrea Camileri, and Federico Maria Rivalta.

These days he walks dogs, writes novels and teaches English.

It has been said of Steve, much like William, that he likes people, at least in theory.

Steve can be reached via the following links:

Website: http://www.stevegrantauthor.com
Email: info@stevegrantauthor.com
Instagram: @stevegrantauthor
Facebook: https://www.facebook.com/StephenGrantAuthor

# The Genesis of False Tidings

I started this novel late in 2021 after having travelled through Italy from Bolzano in the north to Rome in the centre and then across the Med to Sardinia. My official purpose in making the trip was to collect our effects from our recently sold apartment in the town of Castelsardo on the north coast of Sardinia. My personal purpose, the one that excited me most, was to visit as many of my Italian friends as possible. These were friends that I'd made entirely during the lockdowns of 2020 and 2021, and it was they who had encouraged me to think about taking up writing in my tender old age, having enjoyed the accounts and silly stories that I'd been writing in Italian. So you heard it here, you can blame a bunch of Italians for this nonsense.

This period of intermittent quarantines was a strange time for all of us. Those of us fortunate enough to be living in the countryside, and without having been directly touched by the virus pandemic through family loss, or being key workers constrained to work long hours perhaps directly confronting the sick and dying, had the joy of empty roads in which to walk, run or cycle. I was one of these fortunates and was supremely grateful for that.

One of the most striking aspects of the pandemic was the torrent of fake news that got spouted by politicians and conspiracy theorists. I got to thinking that the medieval equivalent of fake news would be false tidings. Thus, my novel shows many instances of strong leaders messing up the lives of their citizens for cruel and selfish motives. History is littered with instances of this and it's not a modern phenomenon, even if today it gets disseminated at a much more frightening speed.

Anyway, during my journey through Italy, I imagined myself as an English pilgrim or questing knight making the journey. Given that there was no country called *Italy* hundreds of years ago, I have invented *Italica*, which represents the various ducal and papal states of the time, and I've also come up with a political system and tried to explain how it affects the people living there. I've had a little fun with a couple of things that drive me mad about Italy: the bureaucracy that pervades everyday life, and the crazy number of different dialects that people still speak. There's no other way to deal with these things than by using humour.

I can't call this a historical novel in the sense that many great authors manage to wrap fascinating fictions around known historical events, it's more *inspired by history*. The astute reader may want to point out inconsistencies with the timing of different customs, legal practices, technological innovations and much else. Send me an email if you think I need to fix any inaccuracies.

Finally, I've mixed a bit of fantasy into the story for the way it provides opportunities to take liberties with a plot line, literally magicking away obstacles or inventing interesting ones.

Above all, though, I've just had fun.

Steve Grant, August 2023

# Cast

William Grey - Protagonist. Feeble Ex Monk.
Feydor Foolson - Court jester to King Inglebert
Helena Jarvis - Fellow traveller, looking for missing husband in Trusca.
Matilda Jarvis - Daughter to Helena
Ridkin Fairchild - Stable Boy & Sancho Panza figure
Imelda Foolson - Black Witch, Mother to Feydor
Mary Grieve - Albian witch, cousin and fierce rival to Imelda.
Filthy B. Mote - Feydor's Monkey
Jasper Foolson - Brother to Feydor
Morwena Foolson - Sister to Feydor
Anthony Ackroyd - Chief Clerk and chamberlain to John Scratchface
Aileen Spey - Head of housekeeping at Ebury castle
Abbott Strange - The man that kicks William out of the monastery in Coxwell
Alfredo Foolson - Feydor's father.
Antoine de Longuedongue - Gallian ambassador
Aunt Agata - Feydor's dead witch aunt
Ballache - William's torturer in Ludnam
Big Ger McMighty - One of Jasper's Men
Bisgattù - Two headed feline
Blind Harry - Beggar that Feydor passes in the street.
Bonnie Prince Albert - Albian prince.
Brother Anselm - William's tutor at the monastery.
Brother Bool - Logician and tutor to William at the monastery.
Captain Dogwash - Captain of the ship that sinks with William and friends on it. based on UK children's program from 1970s – Captain Pugwash
Carter - Member of Prince Albert's Household
Don Creosote - Don Quixote
Duke Cosimo - Italican nobleman

Edmond Rowbotham - Miller's son
Edwin Porritt - Page that Feydor knows.
Epictightus & Epicurious - Stoic philosophers
Fraser & Irvine Grieve - Twin sons of Mary the witch
Gallenio - Ancient writer of dubious medical texts
Giobbo - Helena's guide in Trusca
Great Granny Prentice - Matilda's maternal grandmother
Ignatius Stackpole - Lord High Priest
Jacopo di Matteo - One of Jasper's men
Johannes Klarson - One of Jasper's men.
King Inglebert - Anglonian Monarch
Laddà - Elite fighting gnome and hand to Queen Nannua
Lady Charlotte of Biston - Consort to Scratchface
Lina & Rasa - Queen Ruthenia's Ladies in Waiting
Lord John Scratchface - Earl of Ebury. William's employer in Ebury castle
Ludovico - Son of Duke Cosimo
Mallo - William's guide in Sardonica
Margaret Downey - woman falsely accused of witchcraft.
Ottavia Medici - Widow and owner of a Truscan villa
Quaggià - Janasà that attacks the camp.
Queen Nannua - Queen of the Janasa
Queen Ruthenia - Queen to King Inglebert
Ralph Jarvis - Helena's estranged husband living in Trusca.
Richard Armitage - Will's rival as suitor for Verity
Richard Pyke - Lord High Priest Stackpole's factotum and thug
Rodnye Randall - The Landlord at the Castle and Ball Tavern
Roger Latimer - Anglonian nobleman.
Sargent Pollock - Member of palace guard
Silas Grieve - Brother to the witch Mary Grieve
Sir Morris - Groom that administers the palace.
Sir Thomas Crumbwell - King Inglebert's First Minister at court in Ebury
Teo - Guy who William befriends while in captivity.
The Ninfiné - Wood nymphs of Italica
Tomothy Small - One of Jasper's men

Verity Bull - William's childhood sweetheart
Walter Travis - Ludnam gangland leader.
Wymond The Weird - One of Jasper's Men

## Key to Place Names

Albia - Scotland
Anglonia - England
Bell End - This isn't based on any particular town or district, but it means, in British slang, the glans of a penis. There are actually several towns called Bell End in England.
Billygate - Billingsgate where there's a modern fish market that dates back to the 16th century.
Blackchapel - Whitechapel
Bordax - Bordeaux
Caligulari - This is the Sardinian capital city, Cagliari (Worth a visit)
Camptown - Camden
Civitax - Civitavecchia the main port town of Rome
Coven Garden - Obviously where witches would meet, it's based on Covent Garden, London or Convent Garden as it would have been originally known.
Coxwell - The name was already amusing so I didn't change it
Cymria - Wales
Eastminster Palace - Westminster Palace where today the British parliament sits, but in Norman times, this was a sumptuous palace.
Ebury - York. Eborica was the Roman name for York.
Effing Forest - Epping Forest
Flavianid Amphitheater - The Colosseum
Frasciatti - Frascati
Gallia - France
Ianua - The Roman name for the port of Genua

Italica - Italy
Lombaro - Lombardy
Ludnam - London. A mythical King called Ludd was supposed to have named the city and there is still a part of London called Ludd Gate.
Luthenia - Country where Queen Ruthenia comes from. Based on Lithuania.
Mediola - The Roman name for Milan
Ninfia - Ninfa where today there is a fabulous medieval ruin and garden.
Nuorrù - This is the Sardinian city of Nuoro
Oakford - Ashford in Kent
Port Bellows market - Portobello market
Sardonica - This is a mashup of Sardinia and Corsica, two neighbouring Mediterranean islands with something of a similar vibe about them.
Senapia - This is Dijon. The names comes from the Italian for mustard, which is senape
South Ark - Southwark, a district of modern London but a separate Kent village before
Standingbourne - Sittingbourne in Kent
Trotbury - Canterbury in Kent, namesake of the Canterbury tales
Trusca - Based on a tribe that inhabited much of Italy from Tuscany to Lazio before and during the early Roman empire called the Etruscans.

# Days of the week

Lunaday
Runaday
Wigglesday
Turdsday
Fritterday
Sableday
Soladay

# Months of the year

Janrye
Febrye
Marche
Avrilio
Maggio
Junio
Julio
Augero
Septimo
Ottimo
Novimo
Decimo

Printed in Great Britain
by Amazon

58022045R00199